Graves Gate

Graves Gate

Dennis Burges

CARROLL & GRAF PUBLISHERS
NEW YORK

GRAVES GATE

Carroll & Graf Publishers
An Imprint of Avalon Publishing Group Inc.
161 William St., 16th Floor
New York, NY 10038

First Carroll & Graf edition 2003

Library of Congress Cataloging-in-Publication Data is available.

ISBN: 0-7867-1202-3

Interior design by
Printed in the United States of America
Distributed by Publishers Group West

For Jená.
She always writes
the best lines.

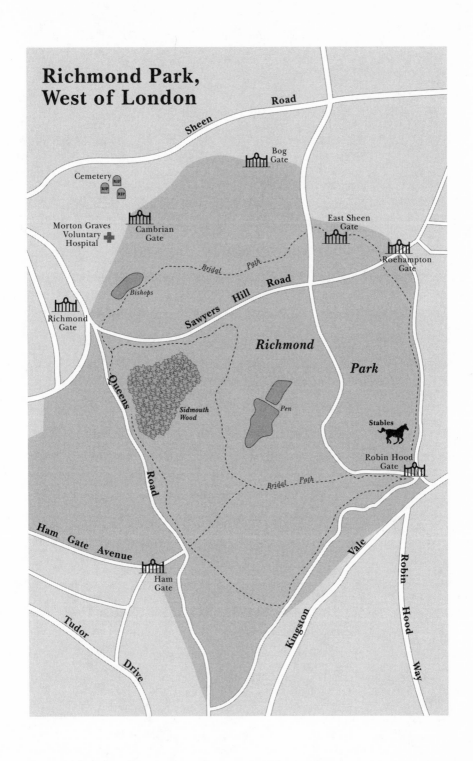

Richmond Park,
West of London

Sheen Road

Bog Gate

Cemetery

Morton Graves
Voluntary
Hospital

Cambrian
Gate

East Sheen
Gate

Roehampton
Gate

Bridal Path

Bishops

Sawyers Hill Road

Richmond
Gate

Richmond

Park

Queens

Sidmouth Wood

Pen

Stables

Robin Hood
Gate

Bridal Path

Road

Ham Gate Avenue

Ham
Gate

Kingston Vale

Robin Hood Way

Tudor Drive

Part One

The only conceivable escape for him lay in silencing my tongue.
—"The Adventure of the Final Problem"

LONDON, JANUARY 19, 1922, 10:00 P.M.

FEELING A PUNCH THAT left me breathless, I flew backward as I watched the curious sight of my own feet flying into the air. Between them was an image—a swirl of blond hair with a scarf falling away from it. In the image was a large pistol flying lazily from the woman's small hand and her oversized coat flapping as she, too, flew backward, spinning away from me. Then I was staring up into the London night sky, thinking that there was something very familiar about her. I was sure that I didn't know her, but I had seen her recently somewhere.

Then I actually heard the shot, or my brain finally registered it. I had been shot before, but it had been a few years, and I had forgotten some of the details. My ears were ringing so loudly that all other sensations were forgotten and the pain was yet to come. I remembered from my days in France that the pain would soon follow. So I lay there on the street, looking up at the black sky, and reminisced about France. It was peaceful and nostalgic for a while, and then I started to drift off to sleep.

I would have made it to deep sleep, too, but for all of Adrianna's noise. She was screaming for help and simultaneously screaming at me.

3

"Charles! Open your eyes, Charles! Look at me, Charlie!" I was dimly aware that she was shaking me, but I could barely feel it. I vaguely remembered that I wasn't supposed to be here with Adrianna Wallace and that her husband didn't know where she was. I tried to think why that should be important, but I couldn't concentrate. I wanted to concentrate on Adrianna. It seemed that there were things I should say to her. Maybe I should try to touch her.

Finally I did open my eyes, and hers were three inches in front of them. I would have turned my face away, but I couldn't seem to move my head. Then I tried to move assorted limbs and realized that nothing much was working. I thought that Adrianna was tearing my shirt open, but I couldn't be sure because I couldn't turn my face downward to look. Mixed with the ringing in my ears was the sound of cloth ripping, and then red and white cloth being waved about. I was practically certain that she shouldn't be tearing my shirt off— not here.

"Oh, Charlie! Jesus! They've got you this time," she said through clenched teeth, but she didn't really seem to be talking to me. "Give me your apron!" she said loudly. I thought that was odd because I didn't have an apron. "Has someone got a car?"

I could see a leg in trousers beside my head, and when I focused upward, there stood the waiter from Lancers. "They're calling for an ambulance now, miss," he said to Adrianna.

"A car!" she shouted at the waiter. "Forget the ambulance! Run! Get someone with a car! Is there a taxi in sight? He'll be dead before you can get an ambulance here!"

"I don't think we should move him, miss," said the waiter politely.

"Are you a doctor?" she shouted.

"No, mum."

"Well, I *am* a qualified nurse! Just get someone out here who has a car. Royal Hospital, Chelsea, isn't a half mile away. We could *carry* him there faster than we could get an ambulance." The waiter had handed his apron to Adrianna, and she seemed to be stuffing it right into my stomach. The waiter's leg disappeared from beside my face, but Adrianna's face appeared again, very close to mine. "Can you hear me, Charlie?" she asked in a normal conversational tone.

"Yes," I said. "How bad is it?" Everybody always asked that in the war. I had asked it myself when I was shot in France. I felt that it was the normal thing to ask—the kind of question she would be used to in the circumstances.

"Charlie, if we don't get you into surgery very fast . . ." she said softly while she was stuffing more apron into my stomach. She sounded very calm. Then she moved so that I couldn't see her anymore, and I heard her talk to someone else. "Help me roll him over. I've got to see his back."

"Maybe we shouldn't, miss. Moving him could make him worse," said a man's voice. I thought about that myself and concluded that I certainly didn't want anything to make me worse.

"Maybe," Adrianna said calmly, "but if the bullet came out the back and I don't pack the wound, he'll die right here, right now. How much worse than *that* are we going to make it?" That possibility sounded even more discouraging to me.

My view changed to the wall as they turned me over. I heard a woman's voice say, "That's Adrianna Wallace." I could feel someone pulling my coat up and then hear my shirt tearing again. Then someone was stuffing something into my back.

Adrianna's face was down in front of mine again when another person said, "That's Adrianna Wallace. Aren't you Mrs. Wallace?"

Another voice agreed. "That *is* Adrianna Wallace, but that's not Frederick. Who is . . . oh, my! Look at the blood."

Adrianna was silent for a moment as she looked into my face with a pained expression. Then she looked up. "Yes," she answered.

"Where *is* my husband, Frederick? He was right here." She looked into my face again and then appeared to be trying to peer through the crowd. "Freddy!" she shouted. "Where did he go? Did he chase the gunman?"

"I didn't see him, Mrs. Wallace," answered another voice. "He may have done. There was no one out here but you and this man when we heard the shot and came out."

Leaning over me again, she muttered loudly enough to be heard by anyone in the small crowd, "Just like Frederick to do that. He'll probably be shot next," she said as she pulled on my eyelid and stared into my eye.

"Liza Anatole," I whispered. "That was Liza Anatole."

But Adrianna was looking away again, and I wasn't sure that she had heard me. I thought about trying to speak louder. I tried saying the name again, but I couldn't hear well enough to know if I'd done any better. Then came the sound of a tire coming to a halt a few feet away behind my head, and I went to sleep and drifted back to an evening at a posh London party six nights earlier.

1

For strange effects and extraordinary combinations we must go to life itself,
which is always far more daring than any effort of the imagination.
—"The Red-Headed League"

ONE WEEK EARLIER.

THE REVERED STORYTELLER HAD never lacked intelligence when I'd talked to him before, but his library was cluttered with things that I thought only a naive fool could take seriously. Obviously used as a personal office, it was cluttered with open books, boxes with galley proofs in them, numerous photographs scattered here and there on tabletops. I didn't take the liberty of reading any of his papers, but I did study some of the photos. They were smoky images of people's faces, young girls staring at miniature winged figures, some shots of nothing recognizable at all. These, I knew, were usually explained as pictures of the dead who were present as smoke, as clouds, as voices in darkened rooms. All of these photos were printed on the highest-quality paper and with the utmost care. It was obvious that he had spared no expense in their processing. I sank into a nice leather chair by a wall of books to make a skeptical study of one of the smokier images while I listened to the sounds of the lively party in the adjoining room.

The invitation that brought me to his London apartment on this Friday night had seemed like a godsend for a rising American journalist. I was outclassed by at least half of the people at the elegant but glittering soiree, and that's exactly the way I liked it. I knew I couldn't advance socially or professionally by hanging around London with people like me. On the other hand, my host had recently developed a knack for getting himself into embarrassing controversies, so it was with mixed feelings that I waited for the private conversation he had requested in a handwritten postscript on my engraved invitation.

When Arthur Conan Doyle entered a few minutes later by a door that led to a different part of the large apartment, I felt embarrassed to be sitting there with one of his enlarged photos in my hands. It was too late to hide it, but he didn't seem to notice, or to mind if he did. Though I hadn't seen him in three years, he was exactly as I remembered him—a large, smiling man with neat gray hair and mustache. A powerful build added to the image of a man who might have been a gentleman farmer. His hands were large and freckled. It seemed that powerful arms filled the sleeves of his tuxedo.

"Charles, good of you to come. It's been a long time." He came directly toward me and extended a strong hand.

"I'm flattered to have been invited, Sir Arthur."

"Sorry about the short notice," he said. "The fact is, Charles, I need your help—and I need it rather quickly." He turned abruptly toward his desk and moved some papers aside, as if looking for something he had misplaced. "I hate to sound melodramatic, but it may well be a life-and-death matter." Actually, his voice didn't sound at all melodramatic, merely factual. There was a professional concern in his voice that I had heard a thousand times from experienced officers during the war. Then I realized that had been the voice of a doctor speaking to a fellow practitioner, and I remembered that the famous author was, in fact, a medical doctor.

Fortunately he did not see me as I glanced involuntarily at the silly photos behind him on the table. Life and death? "I can hardly imagine being able to help you," I said slowly. "I'm not exactly the best-placed newspaperman in London." The remark was not nearly modest enough. I was an outsider in London even after several years—still just an American.

"It's not a newspaperman that I need," he said, making direct eye contact and riveting my attention. The calm seriousness in his gaze made me forget all about the silly photographs on his desk.

"I'm afraid that's all I am," I answered. "The war's over—you don't need me as a German interrogator, do you?"

"You know how to investigate, Charles, and you have a keen mind. At least my son said you had one during the war. You would seem to be singularly able to help in this situation." He apparently found whatever he was looking for on the desk and turned back to face me without picking it up. "You're not too well known or too recognizable, yet your press credentials will be very helpful." He paused then, as if he wanted to elaborate on the point, but changed direction instead. "You are in no way a fool, and you know a great deal about being discreet."

This itemization of my qualifications seemed out of place. I wasn't looking for a job with the man, yet it sounded almost as if he had been verifying my background.

"You seem sure of all that," I said, "but we've only met a few times. I'll help, of course, in whatever you need . . . whatever I can do," I added with a certain hesitancy. I knew that he was involved in some pretty crazy business, and I didn't actually mean that I was willing to do *anything* he wanted me to do. I liked and respected the man, and normally it would have been an honor to be associated with an author of his stature, but there were limits to what I was willing to take on. I had my own career to consider, and it almost seemed that he had abandoned any concern for his reputation in the past few years.

"I've done a good deal of checking to see whether you could do what I need, Baker. One way or another, I can discover what I need to know about almost anything in England." He sat down in the chair next to the one I had been using and gestured for me to sit again. There, leaning forward in his chair, my host reminded me very much of a photo I'd seen as a boy, one of Teddy Roosevelt posing at the controls of a steam shovel in Panama. He had the same rotund, powerful build, the same intensity. Even at past sixty, his large frame seemed forceful. He was clearly agitated about something.

"You really are a detective, then?" I smiled, taking my chair.

"You mean like my man Holmes?" He seemed to wince as he named his most popular, but far from his own favorite, character. "Not at all. People like to tell things to famous people, especially famous writers. I've been involved in government for years. I'm a knight of the realm; at least that's what they call me. So if I want to know something, I usually can think of someone to call, and I usually get an answer." He paused for a long moment and considered his glass before continuing.

I could think of nothing in my career—or in my life, for that matter—that would possibly be of interest to this man. I was a well-paid reporter and analyst for Associated Press, but there were many better reporters who would gladly help him. He had used the word *investigate,* but I really wasn't an investigator. I was an economics reporter who did background research. "And you wanted to know more about me?" I asked. "I'm pretty much an open book, Sir Arthur."

"Quite. I knew from talking with you during the war that you were a solid young man. My son Kingsley thought highly of you and spoke of you many times." He paused and stared at something on his desk before continuing. "I know from what you write these days that you are intelligent." He counted these observations on his upheld fingers as he spoke, "I know from some of what you have decided *not* to write that you can show proper restraint." He paused again for a long sip of his drink.

"I try to be sensitive to my situation." I wondered what he wanted to get me into that would require my supposed intelligence and restraint. I wondered, too, just how much I was willing to get into for the privilege of working with this man. Would I go to a séance for him? Would I photograph fairies in the garden?

"It required some checking in New York to find out if you have the skills that are needed. Your intelligence service for the Crown is some evidence of that, but I needed to know if you could do a certain kind of . . . research."

"People always think that an intelligence officer never quits. They like to romanticize, but I assure you it wasn't worth the cost of the telegrams," I said. "I'm just a reporter." This was not precisely true. I had on rare occasions done a little covert work for Washington since the war, but nothing of importance—mostly just passing along information I thought the embassy would like to know.

"I discovered, for instance, that you spent much of last summer working inside Germany on the final American armistice agreement. Associated Press confirms that." He gazed directly at my eyes. "Do you deny it?"

"Everyone thinks that an American who stays here after the war must be a spy for Washington, but it's just the stuff of romantic fiction. I'm just a reporter looking for the news." It wasn't the first time I'd had to make similar disclaimers. Because of my unusual background, I was often the subject of speculation—why was I *really* still in England? "They sent me in last summer because I speak fluent German. Is it an investigator you need?" I asked.

He looked me in the eyes and nodded. "Exactly so! I need a good sleuth, and one who will be willing to forget the whole incident afterward." He had lowered his voice, almost as if we were not alone in the room. It seemed for a moment that he was reevaluating whether to continue.

"I take it this is a personal matter?" I lowered my voice, too, but I couldn't see why we were talking so quietly.

"Personal, professional, and spiritual, actually, and extremely confidential. Moreover, it's damned peculiar. Can I ask you to read something?" He turned back to his desk and picked up a folded piece of paper. "You're not going to believe this," he said.

Before I could take it from him, an elegantly groomed middle-aged woman in a beautifully cut evening dress walked into the library from the adjacent party, and he retracted the piece of paper in his hand as she spoke.

"Really, Arthur! We have thirty guests here. You can't monopolize this young man when there are so many ladies in the salon who've seen him arrive." She walked across the room and extended her hand toward me. "I don't believe that Arthur has introduced us." I rose and took her hand.

Conan Doyle stood and spoke as his wife and I shook hands. "This is Charles Baker, dear. He's an American journalist I met in France. He was a friend of Kingsley's. He's with Associated Press here in London now." He turned to me. "Lady Jean Conan Doyle is my better half, Charles." As he said this, he dropped the folded scrap of paper into an open drawer, nodding toward me to signal that the paper was private. "I'm afraid that Jean's right, my boy," he added. "After all, you were invited to a party, not a meeting."

"Certainly. I'm very much looking forward to it."

Lady Jean looked at me with a smile. "Do you know everyone here, Charles?"

"I've just arrived, Lady Jean, but I saw several friends. I'll join them. Please, don't let me keep you."

We made our way out of the cluttered library. Just as we closed the door behind us, he leaned toward me briefly. "Please, Charles. It's very important. Can you rejoin me in the library in a couple of hours?"

I nodded as he turned back to his wife and they swept into the crowd. I was left on my own to mingle with the other guests. After some conversation with a few friends, I encountered Frederick Wallace and his wife, Adrianna. She was in a black sheath that caught and held my attention. The dress was slit high on her left leg, and she stood with her weight shifted to her right. Her left foot was pointed outward and raised onto her toes at the moment so that much of the left leg was exposed all the way to above her lace-topped silk stocking. It was a stimulating sight.

I'd met Adrianna Wallace a few weeks earlier, and we had become pretty good friends. In fact, I'd had lunch with her only two days before. I knew a little bit about her and had been making it a point recently to learn more. She was twenty-nine, I knew, though she looked somewhat younger. She might almost have passed for twenty, except for a certain seriousness of expression. I'd learned that her distinguished husband, to whom she had been married for three years, was fifty-four. He also looked younger than his years.

He stood now in his tuxedo as if he were in military uniform— ramrod straight. Except for a somewhat pronounced limp when he walked, he seemed every bit the naval commander he once had been. Only a little gray peppered his shaggy hair and rather massive mustache.

Wallace was a hardworking barrister from a very good family and a notable member of Parliament. I had not realized, though, that the couple would be at this gathering. When Freddy cloistered himself with some other lawyers in a corner, Adrianna and I found a pair of over-stuffed chairs near the fireplace and sat down with our glasses of wine.

"Well, tonight I'm moving up a point or so on the social scale for Americans in London," I said cheerfully. I felt the need to gloat a little and felt safe enough with Adrianna to do it.

"You can't really know that, can you, Charles?" She looked at my smug expression. "Do you really mean that?" she asked with interest.

"I know it." I leaned back in my comfortable chair and took a sip of my wine, but mainly I was drinking in the beauty of the moment—being at a party at Sir Arthur's, not to mention gazing at Adrianna Wallace.

"You really think there's some sort of social-acceptance scale for Americans in London on which you can place yourself?" she asked with an amused smile.

"Six and a half." I smiled and raised my glass, waiting for the inevitable question.

"Out of?"

"Ten," I explained. "An exchange student would be a one. The American ambassador's a ten."

"And you're a six and a half?" she asked.

"I am," I said brightly, "and I'm about to move up to at least a firm seven."

"Amazing, Charles. And how is this improvement in rank manifested, may I ask?"

"In this case, my dear, by invitation." I extracted an envelope from an inner pocket of my jacket and extended it toward the young socialite. If anyone could appreciate the importance of its content, she could.

She removed and opened the invitation and gave a clear nod of approval. "Sir Arthur Conan Doyle . . . London home . . . Friday evening. Oh! And a P.S., no less. 'It's very important . . . get some private moments . . . Charles. Please come.'" She looked up at me as if she actually might be impressed. "Addresses you as Charles. Are you sure a seven is enough of a jump, Charlie? Just a half-point move for this?"

"I don't like to presume." I sat back with a self-satisfied smile. Actually, I felt I had to take stock of such things regularly. My good social standing here was the result of a long climb, and I had worked hard to get this far. If it were true that most Englishmen would recognize within seconds that I was American, it also was true by now that most Americans probably would think I was British. My accent had changed a great deal, and my posture and bearing were no longer that of a casual westerner.

"You are aware that this is rather a last-minute invitation?" she asked, clearly teasing me. "Freddy and I have been invited to this party for weeks. That makes you sort of an afterthought."

"Does *your* invitation have a handwritten postscript?" I asked as I just brushed her forearm for emphasis.

"No. You've got me there, Charles." She glanced at my fingertips, and I promptly withdrew them, silently berating myself for my boldness. I almost expected to see smoke rising from her forearm.

"I'll stand by my appraisal of the importance of this invitation," I said. "Not only is this a genuine engraved invitation to the home of a peer of the realm, but also Mr. Frederick Wallace, M.P., and his charming wife are here. That's a distinctly better class than attends most parties to which I'm invited." I tried not to think about what was certainly going to be an uncomfortable conversation that I now knew awaited me in the library. That's what this invitation really meant, I realized. Perhaps I was not moving up socially. Rather, I might be a workman whose services were needed, and the invitation was the pretext for my presence, nothing more.

Adrianna Wallace leaned over the table. "Well, Conan Doyle is a bit out of the social center at the moment, but this is, nevertheless, impressive. Explain to me how Charles Baker got to be a six and a half in the first place," she said. "How do you know you aren't starting out as an American four?"

"I thought you would want to know," I said as I, too, leaned forward, which brought us awkwardly close. I imagined I could feel warmth radiating from her face to mine. "First, I was born here and my mother was British. I figure that's worth a plus one above my basic score."

She raised an eyebrow. "You have a basic score? How do you know your own basic score?"

"It is a five because I'm an adult with a good job, not a student or a tourist. Add another point because I was in the war as a British soldier, not American forces," I answered with the self-assurance of an expert. I had lowered my voice because our faces were now fewer than eight inches apart. I thought it pleasant that neither of us saw fit to pull back a little. At that precise moment I was more interested in whether I was moving to a higher scale with Adrianna Wallace than with London society.

"So already you're a seven. Five and two sum to seven in England, Charlie," she said, apparently loving this new social-scoring game. She seemed delighted that I had invented it for her amusement.

"That's before subtractions," I explained soberly.

"There are subtractions? I'm very disappointed to hear that, Charles. A lady doesn't like to think that her friends have subtractions." Her flirtation bordered on the blatant.

She pointed at her now empty glass; I quickly caught the eye of a servant who silently refilled it with a flourish as she sat back in the chair and looked at me appraisingly. I continued my explanation. "Raised in the States, public college education, German father. That's one half subtracted for each of the first two—a full minus one for the father. I'm back to a five."

"And how do you regain a point and a half?" she asked before leaning over to pick up her glass. "Do you keep a chart, Charles?"

"All in the head," I answered. "I get a point for always writing nice things about England in my columns. And I get a half point for keeping good company."

"If everything were known about the company you keep, you might well lose two or three points," she said with a wink. "By the way, you're uncanny. You've guessed our whole scoring system without a flaw. It usually takes people of breeding half their childhood to learn it."

"High praise, milady. And when I think of my own misspent youth . . ."

". . . chasing cows in the cactus forests of Arizona, wasn't it? So how do you think you came to rate a personal invitation from Sir Arthur?"

"The invitation itself was unexpected, but I've met him before—three times, actually." I paused for a sip of wine to build the proper suspense. I distinctly felt Adrianna's shoe brush my leg. It seemed to linger there, actually. "By the way," I asked, "is he called Conan? Kingsley Doyle always used that middle name, too."

"It's not a middle name, Charles. His full surname is like a hyphenated name, Conan-Doyle, only without the hyphen. Two notable names," she explained. "You ask me to believe that a lowly six-and-a-half-point American like you has met Arthur Conan Doyle three times?"

Nodding, I raised three fingers. "The first was in 1916 in a hospital tent at Armentières. He was there as press attaché for the War Office and had already been to another front in Flanders with his brother Innes. Besides being a patient myself at the mobile surgery, I was a friend of his son Kingsley." With that I folded one finger down.

"You must have made an exceptionally good impression to be invited to this get-together after all these years," Adrianna said. I may have imagined it, but I thought there might be something slightly sexy in her tone.

"I did make a good impression, actually, and quite by accident. I asked him about his article 'England in the Next War'—the predictions about the importance of submarines. As it turns out, that was exactly the right thing to do. People always ask him about Sherlock Holmes, you see, and it turns out he hates being asked about his detective fiction. Just luck for me. I was going to ask him about one of his detective stories, but hadn't gotten to it yet."

"You said you'd met him three times?" she prompted as she reached out and touched my two fingers that had not yet been counted.

"After Kingsley's death I saw him again, briefly, in early October 1918 at the rift in the Hindenburg Line, after Haig pushed his right flank through the Germans. Doyle—I guess I should say Conan Doyle—was there as a guest of the Australians at their front, and I was up there to help interrogate some German prisoners—"

"Interrogate, Charles? Adrianna interrupted. "How do you mean? How does one go about interrogating a prisoner?" Her voice held a hint of disapproval. No doubt she envisioned beatings or torture.

"Talk with them in German—ask them to discuss their situation. I tried to gather information about the relative strength and positioning of their units by talking with them, even sharing information with them about our conditions. I could learn a lot over time."

"Oh, sorry I interrupted. You were telling me about another meeting with Arthur?"

"Yes, that second time I saw him things turned bad for a bit, and we were all pinned down. There he was in a trench not twenty feet from me. He recognized me, and we got to talking. He invited me to come around to visit him sometime after the rotten business was finally over." I folded a second finger, leaving only the index raised toward the ceiling.

The young Mrs. Wallace grinned and shook her head in disapproval. "And you did? You're not supposed to take those things literally, Charlie. You Americans! What would the world be like if every casual acquaintance just came on over to your flat every time you were being polite and said to drop around sometime?"

"Well, I know that!" I said defensively, my index finger wilting back into my fist, "but I was stuck out there near his summer home near Crowborough once in 1919, and so I took a chance and dropped around at Wendlesham. We had a nice visit, actually. I wanted to give my condolences about Kingsley's death anyway."

Adrianna's smile disappeared. "That was such a blow. When Kingsley was sent home, everyone here prayed he'd recover, but I'm told there was never much hope." Her tone had lowered and gone flat, a sadness that I had heard in her every time any reference was made to the war.

This was the first I'd heard about her knowing Kingsley, and I wanted to know more. He and I had been good friends at the front in Belgium, but I hadn't been with him in the Somme Valley when he'd been hit. My mind went back to what I knew about the Somme, where the British casualties on the first day numbered sixty thousand. Twenty-one thousand died, most within a single hour of battle. I had calculated once for an article that of all the Britons who died in the entire war, more than 3 percent of them were killed in that one hour at that one place.

"Did you see him when he . . . came home?" I asked.

"No," she answered quietly, "I wasn't in England at the time. I was in France. Verdun, the whole time. I was a nurse, a VAD, Charles."

She paused and squinted into the fire. I tried to remember what I knew about the Voluntary Aid Detachments. They had been an extension of the Territorial Army. If my researcher's memory served me, their numbers grew from about forty thousand women in 1914 to nearly double that by the end of the war. Any VAD at Verdun would have lived through unimaginable carnage. I had spent much of the war along the Moselle River, near Charmes, and I knew a lot about the front at Verdun.

She looked back up at me with what seemed to be a conscious effort. "So continue," she said. "You went to see Conan Doyle down in Crowborough to talk about Kingsley?"

"Neither of us had mentioned Kingsley's death at all when we met that last time in France. I just wanted to give my condolences, so I stopped by the house when I had the chance."

"You haven't seen Arthur since then?" she asked with an attempt at more cheer in her voice.

"I haven't thought much about him since that visit. I've never written about him or discussed him with anyone," I said.

"Wouldn't an interview with him be something of a prize, Charles?"

"Not for me. The only press interest in him now is in bashing him for his Spiritualist nonsense. I don't want any part of it."

"The bashing or the Spiritualism?" she asked.

"Neither," I said flatly.

"It must be hard to be a reporter when a friend makes the news in a negative way." Her eyes widened suddenly. "You wouldn't put a friend in the news, would you, Charles?"

"Oh, maybe a woman, if her husband were important," I teased. "In Sir Arthur's case, though, any story would be way off my beat. I don't think I could go after him, anyway. No matter how good the scoop was, he'd still be Kingsley's father."

"And you'd still be Kingsley's friend. Still, a lot of journalists are disparaging him now," she said. "I can't say he's not bringing it on himself, though. Since he got involved in the business about the fairies, he's been a positive laughingstock." She was referring to his piece in *The Strand*. The 1920 Christmas issue a full year earlier had been dominated by his embarrassingly naive and foolish article about two Yorkshire girls who had photographed fairies in their garden. The article was illustrated with photos that shouldn't have been taken seriously by any child, much less a respected adult writer.

We were joined just then by Harry Carstairs, a *Times* theater critic we both knew.

"What plays should I go see downtown this season, Harry?" I asked him as an invitation into our conversation. As he sat down, my real attention returned to wondering what was waiting for me in the library.

"Don't go see anything until spring, Charles. Then I'll be sure to let you know where to go. Any chance you can get to Paris next Friday? There's something *there* worth seeing."

"My French isn't that good, I'm afraid," I said honestly. "I'd lose track of the dialogue."

"It's not a play, dear boy. It's a ballet. Honegger's *Skating Rink* opens in a week, and I've got two tickets that I can't use. If you have a friend and can get away . . ." He looked at Adrianna, who returned his gaze and ignored his possible innuendo. Then he turned back to me.

I smiled. "Don't hold them for me, Harry, but thanks for the offer."

"I want a tip from *you* now, Charles. I want to know something about Italy." He lowered his voice. "My father's about to get into some venture there, and I'm afraid he's going to lose his shirt in the turmoil. Tell me the truth, Charles. I know you AP men get the inside information."

"What turmoil is that, Harry?" I asked. I knew a good deal about trouble the Fascists had been causing in Milan the previous year, but that appeared to have calmed down. At one point I had almost been dispatched to Italy to check things out, but it had proven unnecessary.

"You know. I mean this Mussolini character and his *Fascisti* in Milan. That's brutal business, Charles."

"It was brutal enough last summer, that's for sure," I agreed.

"The *squadrists* are dangerous enough right now. If they grow much more, it won't be safe to earn a profit in Italy. Pulling businessmen's teeth! Clubbing shopowners in the streets! I've told Father to just stay clear of Italy." Carstairs waited for corroboration, and his tone showed that he was clearly serious.

"Most of that was over by the end of the year," I said to calm him. "I hear from our correspondent that the party platform is much more responsible now. Besides, in the last elections the Fascists got only thirty-five representatives into the Chamber of Deputies." I patted Harry reassuringly on the arm, glad to be able to lend my knowledge of European politics to something practical for a friend. "I think you can pretty much forget about Mussolini and his band of thugs."

About halfway through my little speech to Harry, Adrianna excused herself with a nod and pursed lips that *might* have been a teasing kiss. She rejoined her husband at a group nearby and made the whole group look better. Carstairs moved over to the chair she'd vacated, and we exchanged gossip about the news industry for what must have been another hour. I didn't have my mind on the conversation most of the time, but it wasn't one of those conversation that anyone cares about. We were both just killing time and drinking someone else's wine. Finally the party started to break up. I got up and shook a few more hands as people started to drift out. I was beginning to feel pretty conspicuous as someone who doesn't know when to leave when a maid came over and hurriedly ushered me back into the library.

2

It is a capital mistake to theorize before one has all the evidence.

It biases the judgment.

—A Study in Scarlet

DURING THE WAIT FOR my host to finish up with his guests, I roamed around the library and resumed looking at the photographs that were scattered on practically every surface in the room. Some of these were the crazy ones I'd seen in *Strand* magazine.

Conan Doyle had been making a complete fool of himself with this sort of thing in recent years. That was not only the popular view, it also was my view. He had toured Australia with his Spiritualist message in 1921, and a lot of articles had come across the AP wire about it. Actually, he'd been pretty well received on some of that tour. At least the Australians were polite in their news reports.

Because I had known his son, and because the old man had been kind to me in France, I wanted to like him. I was flattered that he'd invited me here for the party and that he seemed to value my services. But I was about as far from a Spiritualist as you could get. This room brought back unpleasant memories of thin explanations and senseless rituals. It was beginning to disturb me. I'd been raised, until the death of my parents, with little attention to religion. Then my adoptive parents had done their best to make me take Catholicism seriously. I guess I had for a while, but the Great War had dashed the last vestige of religion right out of me.

My host entered the library about five minutes after I did and walked straight to his desk without speaking. He removed the scrap of newsprint that he'd dropped in a drawer when his wife had interrupted us earlier. With an expression both somber and guarded, he unfolded the piece of paper and handed it to me without comment. I nodded and began to read what turned out to be a handwritten note, scratched rather crudely in what appeared to be brown ink, in the white space on a half-page advertisement from Monday's *Times* of London. "January 9, 1922" appeared at the top of the paper.

> Dear old friend, from Montrose,
>
> I need your <u>immediate</u> help, and I offer something to you in return that no other person on earth can offer—absolute proof of communication with the dead. You know what this would mean for you.
>
> This fact will reveal to you who I am:
>
> Your father's third sketchbook from the Montrose asylum contained a drawing of a reclining nude woman across the bottom of a page. On the reverse was writing that made you so angry that you tore it away. Later, in my office, you discarded the drawing. Only you and I were present. Now, Arthur, you know who wrote this note.
>
> I will prove what I have promised, but first you must use your influence to do a simple thing for me, and do it quickly! A condemned woman named Helen Wickham, who is due to hang soon, is now held at Holloway Prison. You must take any one of the following three people to meet with her as soon as you can. I ask nothing more.

At this point the writing ended on this side of the paper. I turned it over and found that it continued on the reverse with a list of three names: Mary Hopson, Robert Stanton, and Liza Anatole. An address was provided for each.

Conan Doyle reached out for the paper, and I handed it to him. "What do you make of that so far?" he asked with a grim expression, dropping the partial sheet of newspaper back on his desk.

"Do you think that was written in blood?" I asked, referring to the peculiar brown color of the ink.

"Perhaps, but that isn't the interesting part. What do you think of the promise he makes?"

The question opened the very area I didn't want to get into, but I didn't want to antagonize my gracious friend. Everyone knew that the famous novelist was spending virtually all of his time now promoting Spiritualism. I really didn't want to get him started on the topic of "communication with the dead," and I certainly didn't want him to ask my own views on the subject. "Do you know the person who wrote it?" I replied instead of answering him.

"I did, quite well, many years ago. It must be Dr. Bernard Gussmann. He was the principal psychiatrist caring for my father in an asylum in Scotland—not something that I want known, of course." He turned partially away from me with a strange, shy expression.

"And you're sure this is from him?"

"The description of the sketchbook is accurate." He paused for a moment. "What he doesn't say there is that I was outraged at the remarks about British treatment of the Irish that my father had made on the reverse side of the drawing. I ripped the whole of the bottom of the page out of the book," he continued without looking at me.

"Others might have seen the drawing before that," I cautioned.

"My father had just written his comments that very morning. Dr. Gussmann took me to my father's room while Father was out on a supervised walk with other patients. Gussmann wanted me to see the drawing of the young woman and to discuss something about that, but I cut him off short and tore the page after reading the other side. I took the scrap with me to his office and dropped it in the dustbin."

"But who else might have seen that piece of the drawing after that?" I asked with growing interest.

"It would have meant nothing to anyone else who might have seen it, a scrap among wastepaper," he answered forcefully. "It could not have meant anything except to my father, and he's been dead since 1893. I remember the event, and I've double-checked the sketchbook. I still have it. The missing portion was just as he describes it—a strip torn off about the bottom fifth of the page."

"I admit it sounds like good authentication so far," I agreed. "It certainly sounds like this letter must have come from the doctor. When was the last time you saw Gussmann? That page of the *Times* is from this Monday," I said as I gestured toward the paper that Conan Doyle had replaced on the desk.

He turned his face back toward me. "Dr. Gussmann has been *dead* for years, Charles! I knew that he was dead, but I had to check the details when I got the note on Tuesday. Gussmann died here in London in 1909 and was buried here. If he were alive now, he'd be at least ninety years old."

Surely he didn't expect me to believe that a dead man had penned this note. "So who sent the letter?" I asked.

"One question is who sent it, Charles; the other is who delivered it. And before you ask, no, it was not delivered by a wizened old man. Two people on my staff saw the delivery as they looked up through the basement window. It was hand-delivered and left under the door-knocker at the entrance. One said it was delivered by a man—because of the shoes she saw—and the other said it was by a woman because whoever delivered it was wearing a black dress."

I was stunned to silence for a long moment. It was impossible, certainly, that what I had just read was actually a note from a dead man, but I knew it wouldn't seem impossible to him. Then I offered a guess. "This *is* Friday the thirteenth. In my country, that's supposed to be a spooky day—bad luck and all that. Could this be an elaborate joke?"

He shook his head slowly to indicate that he didn't think so. "As I said, I didn't receive it today. Today just happens to be the day of this party. You must be more superstitious than your reputation would indicate, my boy," he said with a chuckle.

"No, of course not, but there's got to be some reasonable explanation." I certainly was not superstitious, but more than anything I wanted to avoid any discussion of my own views about Spiritualism or superstition or fairies or. . . . "When did you last see him—Gussmann?"

"In '92, shortly before Father's death. That was at the asylum in Scotland. Apparently Gussmann moved to London a few years after that. He was in practice here at a large clinic, Morton Graves Voluntary Hospital, in West London, Richmond-upon-Thames, actually. He died there."

"Did you like him—trust him?" I asked as I rose from my chair, which suddenly had become too confining. I took a few steps and turned back to face Conan Doyle.

"He was a good enough chap when I knew him, and my inquiries this week indicate that he was highly regarded by his colleagues here. A hypnotist friend of mine thought well of his medical articles on the subject. I can't say that I liked the man. He had an arrogance that one sees in older doctors sometimes. He didn't really have any regard for patients as people—or so it seemed to me.

"But did you trust him personally?" I couldn't believe that I was actually standing there discussing a letter from a dead doctor as if I believed it plausible.

"Yes, I trusted him. You see, I was rather the family member in charge regarding Father after he went into resident care. I approved the bills for payment from a trust fund that my older sister had left for Dad's care. I was the only one who went out to visit him. I talked to Gussmann at some length on every visit for years. I had to trust his discretion many times." He rose and put his hands in his pockets, then removed his hands and shifted his weight nervously. "Actually, I went with him in '89 to see Professor Milo de Meyer in Southsea. Ever hear of him?"

"De Meyer? No."

"He lectured on 'mesmeric force' to a group of doctors. The demonstration of his hypnotic techniques was disappointing, to say the least. I took de Meyer to be more of a vaudevillian than a doctor."

I again paced a few feet away from the desk and turned back to face him. I didn't want to discuss mesmerism with him. "And the sketchbook—the whole book? Who has seen it besides Gussmann?"

"Virtually no one, ever. I have it locked in my library desk in the country house. In the Montrose asylum, Gussmann used to show the sketchbooks to me from time to time when he could get them away from Father. Dr. Gussmann had a theory that the books might have given us useful insights into Father's mental state. I've never shown any of the sketchbooks to any of the family. We don't talk much about Father, certainly not about those last years."

"One doesn't," I replied without knowing what else to say.

"Quite. It can make people worry needlessly about themselves, for one thing. Heredity and all that."

"But you've kept the books?" I asked.

"Sentimental, I suppose. Besides, he was really a creative artist. Ahead of his time, maybe. He did some damned fine buildings for Public Works in Edinburgh, I can tell you.

"No one else could know of this particular incident? No one was present when you tore the page?"

"No. Gussmann might have described it to someone else, I suppose, but they couldn't have seen the drawing. There's the problem, you see. You know what I'm working on now—everyone knows. This letter could lead to a real breakthrough for me if it's not a hoax."

There it was. I knew he was going to get to this; he couldn't wait to drag me into some sort of Spiritualist investigation that would waste my time and hurt my reputation. "But it could—certainly might—be a hoax." I looked for some change in Conan Doyle's expression. The authenticity of Spiritualism was a critical professional issue for him just then. He was committed to it, but he was more aware than anyone that his belief had seriously damaged *his* reputation.

"Good possibility it is a fraud," he agreed. "I've been humiliated pretty thoroughly a couple of times." He paused to read my response, but I gave him none. "That's why I need you. You can investigate this without anyone knowing that I'm even responding to this note. Depending on what you find, I can proceed or not. Even then, I don't have to be identified with it until it proves out, one way or the other. I checked on the woman—she hangs in a week. In that sense, it truly is a life-and-death matter."

"You think you could accomplish what the note asks?" I gestured toward the paper in his hand. "Could you get someone in to visit a condemned woman in Holloway Prison?"

"Certainly, and, as this note may imply, few men could. Getting in to see a condemned prisoner isn't easy for anyone. Getting some stranger who isn't part of the legal system in there will take someone with considerable influence."

I thought about what he was asking me to do—take a stranger into the maximum-security section of a prison to visit with a condemned murderer. Certainly I would be safe enough. Presumably no one would know about it, and it would be a favor for a man of considerable influence. "And you want me to do this?"

"I want you to come out to Windlesham tomorrow. I want to show you the sketchbook and tell you what I've found out so far. We can talk at length, and you can help me make some decisions." He put his hand on my shoulder. "One of the things I heard consistently during my inquiries about you, Charles, was that you are a thorough skeptic when it comes to such matters as these. Believe me, I want a skeptic for this," he added with apparent sincerity.

Under other circumstances, I surely would have been among those making fun of my famous middle-aged friend. I was certain, personally, that Spiritualists fell into only two categories: crooks and fools. On this matter, I counted Conan Doyle among the latter. Worse, it occurred to me that maybe the father's need for an asylum was catching up with the son. Moreover, I was not in the investigation business, not this kind of investigation. I didn't like to be near jails— or gallows.

"Sure," I said, "I'll take the early train to Crowborough." As soon as the words were out of my mouth, I wondered how I could have said them. Just as quickly, I realized that there was no way I could refuse this request.

We shook hands again, and he said he'd pick me up at the station because he intended to motor out to Windlesham very early in the morning. When I left the library, there was no one in the salon but two servants who were cleaning up. I let myself out and faced the prospect of a bracing walk back to my rooms, a distance of about a mile. I had left my own car at my lodgings and arrived earlier by taxi, thinking I'd catch a ride home with someone. Now it was too late to do that.

As it turned out, though, I walked fewer than a hundred feet before I heard a car driving up behind me. As it pulled slowly alongside me, I turned to see who drove it.

3

Women are naturally secretive, and they like to do their own secreting.

—"A Scandal in Bohemia"

"YOU'RE GOING TO FREEZE, Mr. Baker," said a voice from within the car. I immediately recognized it as belonging to Brian Donleavy, a clerk in Whitehall and a good friend who had been at the party.

I stooped over to peer into the car and saw that Tom Courtland was with him. I had spoken with them briefly at the party. We met regularly for a pint at Lancers, a late-night pub near my rooms in Pimlico. Part of my job was to have the right clerks as friends, but these two were friends from the war, fellow survivors. I never pumped them for information. As a result, I often got information from them even though they knew I was an American reporter. I couldn't guess why they would still be in the neighborhood so long after the party had ended. Before I could ask, Brian suggested a last drink at Lancers. Since he had a car, and the pub was only a few hundred feet from my lodgings, I was happy to agree.

Lancers was in a modern building but decorated to look like something out of the early Renaissance. A starched lace collar would not have been out of place in the dark-paneled room. There were even a few pieces of genuine armor displayed on the walls, along with portraits that looked more Dutch than English. The place was nearly empty at this late hour, and my friends had no difficulty finding a table well toward the back of the room. It seemed clear that they wanted to talk confidentially, but only trivial chatter was exchanged until we were secure in a booth with our pints, and the waitress was out of earshot.

Brian Donleavy leaned across the table toward me with a bit of a leer on his face. "We've heard your name bandied about some this week, Charles."

"'Bandied about?'" I repeated with a grin. Donleavy was a joker of the first rank, and I felt that I was about to be treated to some sort of roasting.

"Right thoroughly bandied, I'd say," Tom added.

"Not 'praised to the rafters' nor 'mentioned in high places' then?" I joked back at them. I was nervous, though. Even if they were just teasing me, I didn't like to think of my name taking a beating in any circles they might encounter.

"No," Donleavy said, "'bandied about' is what I said and what I meant."

"Bandied good and proper," Courtland chimed in. Then both men started to laugh.

This was ominous, but I couldn't show any concern. I had to just let the joke play out. "So, what have you heard?" I asked. "Is it that I'm a German spy or a Yank spy?"

Brian Donleavy stopped laughing and lowered his voice. "A bit more serious, actually, Charles. Bit more personal, too—"

"Word is you've been having it on with a lady beyond your station, old chap," Courtland cut in. He was smiling, but his eyes looked somehow serious. Courtland was a sensible young man with a good position. If he was concerned, I knew better than to take this lightly. And I could see that beyond his outward good humor he was concerned.

If people had taken notice of my attention to Adrianna Wallace and were gossiping about it, it could mean all kinds of trouble.

"'Word is'?" I probed. "This is actually being talked around by people?"

Donleavy made a forward gesture toward me with his pint of bitters. "A few say that a certain Mrs. W, by which I mean a person married to a gentleman whose name starts with a W, has been seen rather too often with a certain Yank reporter. Eyebrows are raised when this is said, Charles."

"When it's bandied about," Tom Courtland said with a laugh and looked at me for a reaction.

I hoped that I was giving no reaction, but I couldn't be sure I wasn't blushing. "I can figure out that I'm the Yank reporter, but which of the many women I meet and talk to is supposed to be the mysterious Mrs. W?" My tone of voice had gone up an octave.

My two friends looked at each other in embarrassed silence for a moment. My professed ignorance hadn't fooled either of them for a minute. "Well, enough of this foolishness. Bad taste of us to have teased you, Charles. Just joking," Courtland said. That made things even worse. I could tell that he thought he'd embarrassed me by bringing something out that I really did want to hide.

"Of course. Sorry, old man," Donleavy added, leaning back in his chair.

I raised my pint in a salute with a look of good cheer that I did not feel. "No offense taken." I paused for a moment and then added, "Still, it wouldn't do to have people getting wrong ideas. I should probably make it clearer what kind of business I'm on when I'm interviewing a married woman of quality, right?" I thought I had my voice pretty well back under control.

Tom and Brian exchanged a quick glance. "You didn't help things any tonight at the party, either, old chap," Courtland said. "Pretty chummy."

Donleavy's face took on a distinctly serious cast. "Quite right, Charles, quite right," he said. Then he added, "Listen, nothing all that nasty has been said so far. Lot of childishness—wishful thinking from jealous, frustrated gossips. Bored bureaucrats can be the worst, Charles."

"Do you think this talk is being taken seriously by anyone, Tom? . . . Brian?" I asked quietly. "The very last thing I want is to cause embarrassment to a friend." I was feeling pretty guilty about flirting with Adrianna Wallace and even more guilty about most of the fantasies I'd had about her recently.

"It'll die down. We've both come in on your side a couple of times. I doubt any more will be said," Donleavy answered, but somehow I didn't believe he meant it.

Courtland tapped my sleeve with his glass. "It does *need* to die down, though, Charles. Careers involved—that sort of thing." He paused and then added, "Yours, among others."

I simply nodded with what I hoped was a look of gratitude rather than mortification, and nothing more was said on the topic. After another round of stout and a hearty pile of chips, it had faded into the background. Still, though, I was preoccupied by my own stupidity. How could I have been so careless? I thought I had hidden any possible infatuation I might have been feeling—almost from myself and certainly from everyone else. Clearly I had not. As bright and well connected as Adrianna was, she surely would hear of any such talk that was circulating. She would hate me for exposing her to the "jealous, frustrated gossips" who would, no doubt, delight in criticizing someone like her.

Finally I broke away from my friends and started walking home. I declined their offer of a ride, saying that the distance was too short. Actually, I wanted the night air to help me think.

I arrived at The Captains, my residence hotel, shortly after midnight. For the entire walk home, I tried to figure out how I was going to make a withdrawal from this business with Conan Doyle. Some pretty good excuses were starting to come to mind as I entered the lobby. I might have gotten the excuses perfected within an hour or so if I'd been left alone to think, but I could tell as soon as I stepped into the lobby that I wasn't to be left alone.

I recognized her perfume before I saw her because I'd been very aware of her fragrance at the party. Then I just followed the scent over to her. Adrianna Wallace was reading a back issue of *The Strand* in a comfortable chair off to the right side of the entry doors. Her fur coat was draped across her shoulders, and a small valise rested on the floor next to her.

"You're earlier than I thought you'd be, Charles," she said.

"You're presenter than I thought you'd be."

"Do they say words like 'presenter' out in Arizona?" she asked as she stood and turned her upturned face toward me.

I walked over and gave her a light, socially acceptable greeting kiss on the cheek. "Where's Freddy, Adrianna?" I asked as I looked around the lobby. I saw no husband, but I also saw, with some relief, that there was no one else in the lobby either. I whispered, "No, in Arizona they say, 'Where the hell's your husband, ma'am?'"

"Oh." She stood and slipped her fur off and tossed it onto the chair. "Then they're not very sophisticated. We'd never say that here." Then she turned her back to me and gestured toward the elevator as she reached for the valise. "Freddy has gone quietly out of town for the rest of the weekend with a friend. He would be pleased if I would stay quietly out of sight until Monday morning. I could stay home as usual—probably I should—but I could stay out of sight here just as well." There was unmistakable anger in her voice.

"Oh, I don't think you could do that, Mrs. Wallace," I said only slightly louder than a whisper. "This is not the sort of place you'd want to risk spending the weekend, no matter how angry you may be. Pimlico's not exactly out of the way."

"Pick up my coat, Charles, and let's get out of this all-too-public lobby, then."

"Really, Adrianna," I said as I picked up her fur. "I'll get some coffee into you, but then you've got to leave. You can't afford the kind of gossip that this would cause."

"Are you under the impression that I am drunk, Charles?" Adrianna said sharply, and suddenly I was sure she was not.

We walked swiftly to the elevator, which was resting at the lobby level. I was relieved that we were quickly out of sight of any others who might come in. "What about Freddy?" I asked. "What would he say if he knew you were here while he was away? Where did he go at this time of night, anyway?"

"He's with Rodney, and they've got work with them. Officially, it's a working retreat at Freddy's hunting lodge. Freddy knows what he's doing—he's no schoolboy. He's never been close to a scandal."

That answer struck me as odd because it wasn't Freddy who was likely to be in a scandal over this. And it certainly didn't explain why Adrianna was at my lodgings, but I had my mind full at the moment just trying to figure out what might be going on. In a few minutes I had managed to get her to my door and get us inside without encountering anyone. I had already learned that Adrianna Wallace liked to present herself as very modern and independent, but this went beyond all boundaries. No woman who wished to maintain any reputation could behave like this—visiting a man at his lodgings, much less in the middle of the night.

Once we were in my rooms, I thought that Adrianna might regret having removed her fur. The modern gas fire had been down while I was gone, and the temperature was in the low fifties. I draped the fur around her and guided her to my favorite lounging chair. "I have to go out to East Sussex tomorrow morning," I said as she curled up and rested her head on the well-padded armrest. She looked very comfortable, really, as if she were familiar with the chair and my rooms, which she certainly was not. To my knowledge, she had never been in my hotel, much less in my rooms. But no one would have believed that, looking at her now.

"Or we could go out to East Sussex and stay quietly out of sight," she continued in response to my statement.

"You can't go out there with me," I said in a voice that was almost a shout. I was thinking about my very recent conversation with Courtland and Donleavy. What would they say about my reputation if they could see me now? It all seemed pretty unfair since Adrianna and I were not having an affair, and I wasn't reaping whatever benefits I might have enjoyed as compensation for the damage to my reputation.

"We can go on the same train, I suppose," she continued as if she hadn't heard me at all, "but we can't be seen as being together, not that near London, anyway. Are you going out to Conan Doyle's?" Adrianna snuggled deeper into the chair. "That's in East Sussex—Crowborough?"

"I don't know that I'm supposed to say where I'm going, and you certainly can't go with me," I said with all the gravity I could muster. I couldn't tell if she was teasing me, but I couldn't afford to humor her if she were serious. Spending the weekend with a married woman, especially the wife of an M.P., was a dangerous business.

"I don't know that I'm supposed to be like this in your rooms either," she said reasonably, "but here we are. Is this a secret government meeting, then?" Clearly she had no intention of taking this conversation seriously. Whatever she had in mind, though, she intended to stay in control of the situation.

"I'm going out to see someone for a little while, that's all. Want a drink?" Immediately I regretted asking that particular reflex question. If she wasn't drunk—and I was pretty sure that she wasn't—I didn't want to help get her there.

"I'll fix the drinks while you change into something more comfortable," she said as she climbed out of the chair and started toward the brandy tray. On her way past me she raked a fingernail across my chest.

"I'm certainly *not* going to change into something more comfortable! I *am* comfortable," I said.

"I'm surprised you're not cold!" she shouted from the other room. By the time she returned with my brandy and glasses, I had turned up the fire some. It was decidedly chilly in the room, and I thought about putting on a lounging robe instead of my dinner jacket, but I didn't know how Adrianna might interpret that.

Her thinking was far ahead of mine. "It's cold in here, Charles. Get something to put on. Do you have a robe? What do you have for guests? Have you got two robes, by any chance? I can't sleep in my coat, and I'm not getting into a cold bed in this gown. This gown cost me ten pounds, and it's new."

It occurred to me that I could have taken her out to a decent lunch many times for the price of that gown. Odd equations like that jumped out at me all the time. It was because my job required me to do currency-exchange calculations. I'd gotten in the habit of translating currency amounts into numbers of lunches or loaves of bread or cans of beef. It was a way of keeping money real in my mind. That dress would likely have bought more than a thousand loaves of a good-quality bread. I couldn't help working that out in my mind as well. "You're not going to need a robe, Adrianna, and you're not getting into bed. I don't have a guest room, in the first place, and. . . ."

She didn't appear to be listening as she sipped her brandy and stared off into the distance. As to what she might see in that unfocused distance, I could not guess.

I returned to the gas grate in the fireplace and turned the flame all the way up.

"Haven't you got pajamas, warm ones?" she asked. "Surely you have."

I remembered that I'd been given new pajamas for Christmas and hadn't yet worn them. "Yes, I have some very nice ones."

"You want me to wear the pajamas, or do you have a robe, Charles? Hurry up and decide. I want to get out of this dress."

It was clear to me then that Adrianna had no intention of being sent out into the night. I would just have to make the best of it and figure out how to sort everything out. Most importantly, I would have to figure out how she was going to get out of there tomorrow without getting our names "bandied about" yet again. I'll admit that I also wondered if I could get by without making love to her. I even fantasized that this might be why she was here. I removed my new pajamas from their drawer and took them to her. "I'm going to go into my bedroom and change, Adrianna. You may wear these," I said with a note of resignation. "My lavatory is through the little kitchen; you may have noticed it. You may change in there."

She stood, dropped her fur onto the chair, and turned away from me. "There are three buttons at the top, Charles. Be a dear, won't you?"

"Can't you . . . ?"

"No, I cannot, Charlie. They're not easy to reach. I had help with dressing, but there's no one to help but you now. Someone really ought to invent something better than buttons for the backs of dresses, don't you think? Do be helpful, Charles."

I obliged her request and unbuttoned the three buttons. Apparently the shoulders of the gown were spring-loaded in some way because no sooner had I unbuttoned her than she shrugged her shoulders out of the dress, clutching its front to her chest. She was wearing an undergarment, but I didn't see how that would mitigate anything at the trial that was surely forthcoming. YANK JOURNALIST NAMED AS ADULTERER. I was sure I would be reading that soon. Or perhaps I would be able to read YANK FOUND IN POOL OF BLOOD. M.P. IMPLICATED.

"Later I want to hear what you're going to do in East Sussex," she said as she picked up the pajamas and headed toward my lavatory.

"I'm not going to tell you what I'm going to do in Crowborough. Do you have your car?" I asked as she left the room. "Can you drive home tomorrow?" There was no answer. I went to my bedroom, changed into pajamas and robe, and returned in a few minutes.

She was standing next to the fire grate, shivering in my new pajamas. "I know that you're not going to tell me anything, Charlie, but let me tell *you* something."

"What's that?" I asked as I nudged her over to get some of the fire's heat for myself.

She surprised me by reaching out and taking hold of my shoulders. She turned me to face her and looked directly into my eyes. "Conan Doyle is not a fool, in spite of what they're saying about him. That's one thing. And another is that he's still quite a force to be reckoned with in some quarters in government. He could end your career, whatever it is, just like that," she said with a quick snap of her fingers. "So don't you get any ideas about some kind of exposé on him. I mean it." Her tone had a certain head-nurse quality about it. She could do that impression pretty well, and our conversation earlier on had told me where she'd learned it.

"I promise I won't underestimate him," I said.

"See that you don't. Freddy watched his debate with Joseph McCabe last March in Queen's Hall. Did you happen to see it?"

"Are you joking? It was sold out, and the scalpers were impossible."

"Well, Arthur was brilliant, Freddy says. It was a *tour de force* for the Spiritualists. Freddy says he never wants to debate with him, and Freddy is no slouch when it comes to debate."

"I know," I said, "and I'd rather not debate your whereabouts with him. So what's going on here, Mrs. Wallace? As you have chosen to come here, I won't pretend that I'm not glad to see you." I put my arm around her shoulders in a brotherly way and turned her back to face the fire. "Just what, though, is going on?"

"I don't want to talk about it just now. Tomorrow, maybe. I'll tell you about it in Crowborough when we take the train," she said as she leaned against me. "Tonight, just give me a place to sleep." She looked down and lowered her voice. "One that isn't home alone." After a pause she added, "Be a gent, Charlie. Take the chair, give me the bed."

I resigned myself to two facts: first, she would be spending the night in my rooms whether or not I agreed; second, she would not be left behind when I went down to Crowborough. "So the train it is, then," I said. "God help us when this gets out, Adrianna."

She was silent for half a minute. "Separate trains, on second thought. I'll come out later and meet you in a little pub in an inn that's across from the station if I remember right, about five o'clock." Then she added, "Let's stay over."

I hardly knew how to respond to that suggestion. "Shall I get two rooms?" I asked, figuring that if she could come up to my rooms and get into my pajamas, I could ask maybe one bold question.

"Yes, two rooms, Charlie, not that it would matter. If we're found in the same hotel in the countryside in January, it's as good as finding us in the same bed." She turned to face me and said softly, "It's fine, Charlie. No one's out there this time of year—no one who wants to be seen, anyway. We'll keep our heads down, and we'll have two rooms, and I'll tell you all about it tomorrow evening. I need a friend—one who isn't tangled up in my family and Freddy's position. I need some fresh air." And with that, she walked into my bedroom and closed the door.

4

Depend upon it, there is nothing so unnatural as the commonplace.

—"A Case of Identity"

I **LOOKED AROUND THE** impressive library in the massive country home, Wendlesham, at about eleven on Saturday morning and waited for my host to return with tea. There were no servants in evidence at the house, and Conan Doyle had insisted that we have a cup of tea before beginning. I was glad for that hospitality after my train ride and drive out to the house. This library was not like the one in London; there was no clutter. In fact, this didn't appear to be a library in which anyone worked at all. Many of the books were in leatherbound sets, and all were arranged neatly on their solid, well-crafted shelves. The room was comfortably furnished with a definite tilt toward the lavish. A very nice fire was going in the fireplace when we arrived. I assumed that he must have built that up himself before driving down to Crowborough to pick me up at the station.

Resting on the otherwise cleared top of a large desk in the room was an open sketchbook. I walked to it and looked it over without touching it. It was opened to a pair of numbered pages with sketches and penciled printing covering them. The bottom of the right-hand page, number twenty-five, was torn away—about the bottom fifth of the page, all the way across. That page contained a large drawing of a brown predatory bird in flight, talons extended as if about to strike prey. The portion torn away had taken only a small piece of the bird's wingtip. I had just shifted my attention to the left-hand page when the door opened behind me and Conan Doyle walked in with a tray.

"So you've seen the sketches?"

"I just started looking at these pages. This is the book mentioned in the letter?"

"Yes, that's it. That is the page. Under that bird was a young woman in the nude. She reclined across the left half of the bottom of the page, more or less in mirror of the dressed woman on top of the bird. Her face resembled that of the girl on the center of the facing page—short, dark hair. The reason I tore the page was to remove writing on the reverse page. Take a look, Charles."

I turned the torn leaf and saw additional sketching and a page of printing. The ink sketch was of two uniformed policemen, each with a hatchet in one hand and a crying baby in the other. In the background was a kneeling woman, a look of alarm on her face and both arms extended skyward, perhaps in supplication. There also was a small group of other people in the background. Under the sketch was the centered title, "The Olprert Evictions." Under that was a reference to the *Dundee Advertiser* of April 18, 1889. I didn't examine the writing closely enough to decipher what it said.

"There's a passable sketch of Dr. Gussmann's likeness upper left on page twenty," Conan Doyle said as he tended to the teapot, filling it from a kettle full of steaming water. I turned to that page and saw a caricature of a handsome man with a groomed medium-length beard and a slightly receding hairline.

He continued, "Among my father's excesses was a rabid alignment with the Irish cause—the family originated there, though I grew up in Scotland. Father could be quite embarrassing about Irish issues. His brothers wouldn't even stay in the room with him when he got started. His remarks could border on the treasonous at times, and

I was rather more rigid in the other direction than I would be today. Just as unreasonable, in my own way. I regret to say that neither of us showed much restraint in our remarks at those times."

He brought a cup to me and pointed to the wording on the top of the torn page. The note could be made out to be first a reference to an arrest of "inmates, including two babies of 4 and 6 months old." Following that was a reference to the Austrians in Hungary. The remainder was missing, torn from the page long ago.

"This made you angry enough to tear the rest off?" I asked when I had read the page.

He nodded. "It was related to an argument we'd had a few weeks earlier. I'd been rather overbearing during that argument and had made some personal insults, I'm afraid. This was Father's way of getting back at me, or so I felt at the time. Silly way for grown men to act. Especially so for me—I was a man of science, medical doctor and all that. Acted like a mental patient myself, I guess." Conan Doyle paused for a moment and then continued. "Poor old Dad. Nothing else to do but draw sketches and be mad at England—and argue with me. I could have done better by him."

There was nothing for me to say to that so I shifted the subject. "You've kept this sketchbook, then, all this time."

"Yes. I was ashamed when I realized what I'd done—torn his private sketchbook. I wasn't even supposed to be looking at it, you know. And then it had this nice drawing on the other side. I felt embarrassed and sheepish. I remember that old Dr. Gussmann was looking daggers at me, you can imagine. I put the scrap in my pocket and took it away with me. A bit later I tossed it into the dustbin beside his desk. There was no use in trying to repair the page. That sketch was done in the spring of 1889. I have kept all of his sketchbooks. There are several of them. "

"Gussmann would have remembered this incident, then?"

"Clearly he did."

"Or he told someone about it—someone who remembered it."

"That's a possibility, surely, but it seems unlikely. In the course of dealing with one patient and his family, this was just a momentary problem. He'd have to explain something to Father—or not explain anything to him. Whatever he decided to do, it would have been enough to make it memorable for him, but it would not have been a subject for talk around the hospital. Good God, man, far more bizarre things happened in that asylum every hour!" He had explained this while staring down the whole time at the sketchbook with one hand resting on the scrap of page that remained. Finally, he turned away from the desk and walked to the fireplace a few feet away.

I returned to my questions about Dr. Gussmann. "Why do you suppose he would still remember it, if he were—is—still alive?"

"Because I became famous—was already somewhat famous then. That sounds immodest, but it's simply true. So Gussmann remembered it. And as agitated as I was by the whole incident, he could assume I would remember it if he prodded me with a few details."

"You said last night that Dr. Gussmann would now be quite old, if he were alive. Tell me more about him and the hospital, starting from the very beginning," I asked.

Doyle gestured for me to be seated in front of the desk. He sat down in the oak swivel chair behind the desk and collected his thoughts for a moment, then began. "My dad, Charles Altamont Doyle, was confined in the Montrose Royal Lunatic Asylum in the spring of 1885, under a detention order." He paused here and clearly had to compose himself before he could continue. "He was there until early in ninety-two. Then he moved to Edinburgh Royal Infirmary; then, to the Crighton Royal Institution at Dumfries in the spring of that same year. He died there in October 1893." He went silent again and sipped tea for a full minute.

That much silent time between two acquaintances in a conversation can seem unbearable, and I was trying to find something to say when he began again. "Dr. Gussmann was the primary physician on Father's case from early in '86 until Dad left Montrose, a period of six years. He and I got to know each other well."

I knew that he had risked exposure by the Victorian scandal-mongers by visiting his father in the asylum. "You were taking a bit of a chance with your reputation by then, weren't you?"

"I can't say the risks didn't cross my mind plenty of times," he answered, "but those doctors are very sensitive to confidentiality. In their profession they have to be. Anyway, that's how I came to know Gussmann."

"Did you ever see him after your father left Montrose?" I continued.

"Never. He sent me a letter of condolence when Father died, so he had followed the case for more than a year and a half. Maybe he just saw the obituary. I wrote a brief thank-you note in reply and never heard from him again"—Sir Arthur looked directly at me—"until . . ."

"Until now, possibly," I continued. "What was his age?"

"Let me see. In 1892 I would have been thirty-three. That's the last time I saw him, the day Father moved out of Sunnyside—"

"Sunnyside? You haven't mentioned Sunnyside," I interrupted.

"Sorry. That's the name of the building he was in at the Montrose Royal Lunatic Asylum. You can see why we preferred to call it Sunnyside. At any rate, I would have taken Dr. Gussmann to be about the age I am now—early sixties. I'm fairly good at ages, and I was then, too—my medical training. If I'm right, he'd be at least ninety now. But he's dead."

"Let's deal first with that," I said. "How sure are you that he *is* dead?"

"In the first place, I vaguely remembered reading his obituary in the *Times* several years before the war. I noticed it because I recognized his name, but also because it said he was a resident at a hospital here in London. I remember that I was surprised that he was in London, rather than Scotland, and that he was still practicing medicine. The obituary did not give his age, but it did mention his early career in Scotland and his long years of distinguished service here. Had to be the same fellow, you see. I thought then that he'd be nearly eighty. That's why it stuck in my mind."

"Do you recall mentioning that to anyone at the time?" I asked. It seemed more likely to me that the answer to this puzzle would be found among Sir Arthur's acquaintances than among the dead.

"Could have, but I don't know anyone who knew Gussmann, and, as I said, I don't talk about this—family matter. I doubt I would have mentioned it to anyone."

"Did you send a note or flowers or anything?"

"I hadn't seen the man in nearly twenty years. No, I didn't. Now that you mention it, though, I suppose I should have done." He shifted his considerable weight in the swivel chair at his desk. It gave out a metallic groan. "When I got the letter this past Tuesday, I immediately made some calls and determined that Dr. Gussmann, the same Dr. Gussmann I had known, had indeed died at the hospital in the spring of 1909. He was buried in a little cemetery right there near the grounds." With that, he opened a desk drawer and extracted the letter he had shown me the night before. "This was left under the striker of the doorknocker out at the street door in London. It was folded up inside a regular postal envelope with just my name on it. If Gussmann wrote this letter, he wrote it from beyond that grave out in Richmond." There was almost an expression of satisfaction on his face as he dropped the letter onto the desk.

I was faced now with a topic I didn't want to discuss, but there seemed no choice. "You have written for publication, more than once, that you have communicated with your father since his death—"

"And I have!" the older man cut in.

"Exactly. And many thousands of people have read that. A confidence trickster of some kind would know that getting something connected somehow to your father might touch a chord in you. A determined and clever confidence man would dig out a few names from your father's life. We don't know who might have seen that sketchbook in the three years your father was at Montrose—Sunnyside—after it was drawn."

"That's true, but only Gussmann would know about the circumstances of the page getting torn. Even Father wouldn't have known—couldn't have told anyone. Only Father and Dr. Gussmann ever saw the drawing of the young woman on the other side. I accidentally tore out the entire drawing of her." He leaned toward the sketchbook and pointed.

"Think about the possibility that someone wants to secure your help to free this Wickham woman," I said. "You've been very influential in freeing condemned prisoners in the past."

"Like the Oscar Slater case back in 1910?"

"Yes, that's one I've read about. Note that it was after Gussmann's death. If someone got an idea about this case by reading about that one, it's not likely to be him—or do ghosts read?" I said, hoping to cast some doubt on his letter from a dead man.

"It's true that the Slater case came after Gussmann's death, but those on the other side often demonstrate that they keep apprised of what's going on in the temporal world. In fact, letters from the dead often make reference to current events. I could show you several pieces taken down by my wife."

It took great concentration to keep my breathing even and my face calm but interested. Debating the investigative habits of the dead with Conan Doyle would be both unpleasant and unproductive.

I stirred my tea quietly for a moment before asking, "Didn't you also go to great lengths in some other case to try to save a condemned man on grounds of insanity?"

"Roger Casement, yes."

"And when was that?" I asked.

Conan Doyle thought for a moment and then answered, "During 1916."

"So anyone might assume that you could be drawn into this case because of possible injustice," I said. "But the evidence that you might do so occurs after Gussmann's death."

"I was involved in other such cases long before Gussmann died. Whether anyone is trying to draw me into the Wickham case remains to be seen, Charles. What is in evidence here, so far, is that the letter comes from someone who knows what only Dr. Gussmann and I ever knew."

"Dr. Gussmann *could* have shared the whole story with someone, in detail, at any time for twenty years after the event," I persisted. "It seems unlikely, I admit, but that's all it would take, Sir Arthur. If he did that, and if the wrong person heard the story, this could be another . . . a trick," I added gently.

"You needn't be embarrassed, Charles. Everyone knows I've been tricked before. Why do you think you're sitting here at my request? If this is what it purports to be, it's amazing! But if it's not, I don't plan to be identified with it in any way. I can get you in to see this Wickham woman with one of the requested guests. No one will ever know I arranged it."

"Whoever sent that letter will know you did it," I answered. "If this is fraudulent, that person will know you're on the hook."

"No. If this is fraudulent, and it certainly could be, they won't be able to hook me. You'll be investigating every aspect of this at a distance from me. Outwardly, I'll be ignoring whatever happens as if I have no knowledge of any of it. Believe me, Charles, Dr. Gussmann's ghost will have to walk up and shake my hand in my home before I'll acknowledge this in any way. I'm no fool, my boy, in spite of what you may have heard." His look held a challenge for a moment, and then he turned away.

"I have a good friend who says that you're no fool, Sir Arthur. I think plenty of people know that."

"Plenty of people are not so sure anymore, too. Maybe something will come of this that will help them see. I wouldn't be involved in Spiritualism myself if I hadn't seen unexplainable things with my own eyes." He studied my face for a moment. "You don't have to think so, Charles. I'm not asking you to become a Spiritualist. I'm asking you to be an intelligence officer—an investigator."

I remained silent while I thought for a moment. In the first place, I had not been an intelligence officer for more than three years. Second, I was sure that he underestimated my aversion to Spiritualism. I was not a believer in anything. In fact, I was an evangelist for not believing in anything.

"To be fair, Sir Arthur, I've got to say that I'm very unlikely to become a Spiritualist. I'm not an intelligence officer anymore either. I will help you sort this out, though. I'm damned curious for one thing, and I'd love to stop one of these frauds."

"Considering what I'm writing about these days," Conan Doyle said firmly, "I might be one of those frauds you'd like to stop. Am I right?" He made direct eye contact and waited for my answer.

I hated to admit, even to myself, that I was that narrow-minded. "Well, you're certainly no fraud, Sir Arthur. I'll admit that you present an intellectual quandary for me. I know you, and know enough about you, to believe that you're no fool. On the other hand, you are committed to a belief that makes me uncomfortable—one that makes me more uncomfortable than most beliefs. All of them make me somewhat uncomfortable. I'm willing to deal with that discomfort and try to sort this out with you—I'm happy to do so." I found that I was forming this position as I spoke it. I hoped that I wouldn't regret it.

After a moment he replied, "When it became clear to the rest of the family that I wasn't practicing Catholicism, when I admitted it and announced my own agnosticism, I learned what it was like to become alone, an alien in the Scottish society I valued. Spiritual discomfort is what motivates spiritual discovery, I think. At least I know that scientific discomfort is what motivates scientific discovery. So look at this as scientific discomfort, Charles. Find out what's really going on! Be willing to discover a ghost if that's what you find." His eyes were sparkling now. He was clearly excited by the challenge ahead.

"I'll admit that the preliminary evidence opens the way for a ghost, Sir Arthur, but I'm going to work hard to find something else. We may even find that Gussmann is still alive."

"Fair enough," he said. "Let's look at the rest of the problem."

I made a list of the names and addresses on the reverse of the letter while Conan Doyle filled me in on what he had learned so far. He had gathered a little information on each of the three names through some discreet police inquiries made as a favor to him. He had prepared a partial page of neatly penned notes about each one and a more complete set of notes about the condemned prisoner, Helen Wickham.

"Researching the condemned woman, Helen Wickham, was easy. She committed a brutal murder that drew considerable press attention last year. Wickham was a piecework seamstress who worked at her home near the river in St. Margarets—"

"You say she's a murderess. Was she some kind of madwoman?" I interrupted. "Sneak out and do people in at night?"

"Another Jack the Ripper, you mean? No, she was quiet, but well liked, and has never been in any other trouble. Except for a few illnesses, she has never missed keeping a decent production schedule. Apparently she was trained to do production sewing while she was a patient in Morton Graves."

"Morton Graves?" I asked. "Isn't that the same asylum you mentioned for Dr. Gussmann?"

"Just so, my boy. Intriguing, isn't it? This woman was released in 1914, after Dr. Gussmann's death, by the way." He paused to sip his tea. "Since then, as I said, she's been a steady worker."

"Model citizen," I said.

"Then, one fine day in 1921, she committed a brutal murder—a lady victim. It seems that the victim came to Wickham's flat specifically to confront her about a love affair with the victim's husband. In fact, the lady did confront Miss Wickham in the street in front of the flat in full view of several witnesses."

He went on to tell me the entire story of the woman's arrest and conviction. He concluded with the fact that she would hang on the coming Friday.

"Not much time for us to take action," I said.

"No, but in spite of that, I'm not going to do anything without some further investigation. The short timetable might be part of a ruse to persuade me to act precipitously. I want you to check out these three other people. In the meantime, I'll make preliminary inquiries about getting you in to meet Helen Wickham." His voice was clear and purposeful. He had no intention of being made a fool in this case.

"I can start making contact tomorrow afternoon," I said. "Sunday is a good day to find people at home."

"Good. I think we can meet the minimum requirement—get one of these three people to visit Wickham at Holloway," he added. "That's all that the letter demands of me. We can investigate the details after that is arranged."

I picked up the list of names and information about each. "I'll see if I can reach this Mary Hopson first—may as well start at the top of the list," I said. "If no problem presents itself, we'll go with her."

He nodded in agreement. "Have you thought about how you'll persuade her?"

"I'll probably start by offering her some of your money," I said with a smile.

"There will be expenses like that, Charles," he said as he reached for an envelope on his desk. "I've put fifty pounds in here to get started. Let me know if anything comes up that requires more. For things like you mentioned—paying for cooperation or information— give out whatever is required."

"There's also the matter of keeping in touch with one another. Just who should know that I'm working with you?"

"No one, if possible. Use your own judgment, but my objective here is to stay totally removed from this until we know what's going on. I haven't told anyone but you about this letter, not even my wife. I'll give you my home number. Call me there—just leave a message for me to call you."

I understood that he really meant to stay at arm's length, and that gave me a problem with Adrianna. She wasn't likely to stop prying into this now that she was meeting me down here later. I wondered how I got myself into these things. Certainly it was through no fault of my own. I was not a Spiritualist, I was not a philanderer, and I was not a detective. In fact, I didn't seem a likely candidate for this predicament at all.

"There's something you have to know," I said. "Adrianna Wallace already knows that you and I are working on some project together.

She gathered that from our closed-door sessions last night and my evasive answers when she asked me about it."

He considered that for a moment. "This may seem an indelicate question, Charles, and I don't mean it to be. Are you saying that you and Adrianna Wallace had a conversation *after* you and I talked late last night?" The surprise in his voice was justified. I had been the last of his guests to leave his party, and Adrianna had left much earlier with her husband.

"Well, yes," I answered. "Actually I met with some friends after your party. I was out quite late." I hoped that I had sidestepped the real question on his mind with that answer.

"But Adrianna is the only one who pressed you about working with me?"

"Yes."

"So you talked with her alone at that hour of the night." He paused. "Forgive me again, Charles, but will you be seeing quite a bit of Mrs. Wallace while you're working on this?"

A sort of chill came over me. Was it possible that our names were being "bandied about" even in his circles? "Probably," I answered. "She and I are good friends and see each other quite a bit. It would be awkward to change my patterns—might draw suspicion as to what I was doing. Adrianna is curious. Frankly, with her pressing me for information, I'll probably need to tell her something about what we're doing—at least something she'll believe."

He was silent again for a minute, then said, "Frederick Wallace and Adrianna have been friends of mine for many years. If you trust her discretion, and I gather that you do, you must tell her whatever you feel is necessary. Please impress on her that I wish to remain completely uninvolved in this as far as anyone is to know."

"I'll try to withhold whatever information I can from her as well."

"Well, I don't want you to tell any deliberate lies to your close friends—to her or Frederick. Avoid discussing it if you can."

"I'll try."

"I hate to ask this, but you aren't about to receive any notoriety yourself, are you, Charles? Any publicity would undo what I'm trying to accomplish."

"You mean notoriety about me and Adrianna Wallace?"

"I . . . well . . . I do mean that. It had never occurred to me until a few minutes ago." He avoided looking directly at me. "*You* brought it up, Charles."

"Actually, I have just heard from a friend that there *is* some gossip about us. It's unfounded, but I suppose it's going around. Adrianna and I have been seeing a lot of each other—but all out in the open."

Sir Arthur spoke slowly and distinctly, considering his words carefully. "There's the age difference with her husband. You're much closer to her age. If you've been out till late hours with her, as you say, even with others, people will talk. It can get pretty unpleasant, my boy, no matter how innocent. I know at firsthand, believe me—very unpleasant, that sort of speculation."

"Well, I hope it won't come to that. I'd hate to break off a good friendship."

"Or break up a marriage," he said, staring me in the eye. "When do you expect to see her again?"

"I'm not sure," I lied. "Quite soon, I expect."

He just nodded and suggested that it was time to take me back to the station. On the ride back into town, we reviewed what we knew and what I would be doing next. It was after four o'clock, in time for the evening train to London, when I stepped out of his car at the Crowborough station. When he had driven away, I bought a ticket for the Sunday late-morning train, and walked with some sense of guilt to the inn where I expected Adrianna to meet me soon.

It occurred to me that on Friday afternoon I would have described my life as pretty ordinary. Twenty-four hours later I was on the edge of a scandal with a well-known married socialite, I was working covertly for one of the most famous men in the country, and I was hunting a ghost. Each of those three things seemed utterly unlike me.

5

I have seen too much not to know that the impression of a woman may be more valuable than the conclusion of an analytical reasoner.
—"The Man with the Twisted Lip"

I TOOK ONE ROOM at the inn, a single, and went into the pub to wait for Mrs. Adrianna Wallace, who should not, if she were in her right mind, be showing up. I was fully aware, also, that if I were in my right mind, I would not be waiting here for her. The pub, which was part of the inn, was a more authentic version of what Lancers tried to duplicate in Pimlico. The paneling had been on a very long time, and the noblemen who once wore them might well have nailed the bits of armor on the wall there. I studied the room's charm while I wondered if Adrianna would arrive on schedule. I hadn't waited very long when she did arrive.

"I like this place," she said as she walked up to my table and sat down. She was wearing a conservative wool suit under her open fur coat. "It suits you, Charles."

"What do you mean?" I asked.

"The pub shows its age a little more than you do. Of course, it's old and you're not. It's a bit scarred, like you. It smells masculine but clean. Do we have rooms? I have bags at the station. Do you?" Adrianna spoke in a rapid stream of words. She was clearly cold.

"I do have a room, a single, and I have to leave early tomorrow. Sorry. And I don't have bags, just a toothbrush in my pocket." I rose and held her chair as she sat down. I squeezed her shoulders and felt that her fur coat was surprisingly cold to the touch, considering the short walk from the station. "Why don't we eat dinner, and I'll put you on a train back to London?"

"Conan Doyle wants Sherlock Holmes to start early tomorrow, huh?"

"Who said anything about Conan Doyle?"

"I have a confession, Charles. I didn't come in on the last train. I saw him drive you up to the station." Adrianna shuddered and took my wine for herself. "And I already have a room, also a single. I registered in my maiden name, but that won't make any difference if anyone sees us here."

"And yet you waited until now to come into the pub?" I reoccupied my seat opposite her.

"This is the time I said I'd come here. Also, I wanted to watch the street for a while and see what might happen."

"I can't talk to you about this thing I'm working on, Adrianna. Let's just have a nice dinner and talk about something else." I smiled, but tried to sound firm. I opened a menu and began to scan its short list of offerings.

"It's fish and chips here, isn't it?" she asked.

"Best in England, it says here," I answered.

"Is this a government thing?" Adrianna asked. "Because if it's a government thing, mine or yours, I wouldn't think of prying. Well, if it were a *British* government thing, I might have to go back on that because of Freddy. Freddy *is* British government, now, isn't he? I'm the wife of British government. In a way, British government is my husband, wouldn't you say?" Adrianna's was still speaking rapidly and still shivering from the cold.

I waved my hand for service, signaled for two more glasses of the wine I had been having, and stared at Adrianna in silence. The silence didn't last long.

"But if it's American government stuff, then I'm right off it, naturally. Unless *you* are American government, as some say you are. Well, then I'm right on top of it, so to speak." She gave my leg a slight kick under the table and grinned at me for response, but got nothing but a subdued smile.

"Of course," she continued, "it might not be government business at all. In which event it would be just mean of you not to talk to me about it. Petty and mean, really. If it's not a government secret, then it's just a matter of your choice not to tell me, not national security. I did hold officer's rank in His Majesty's service—did you know that?"

I gave her a look that was intended to convey that I did not intend to tell her anything. I continued with an answer that I hoped would show her the same thing. "Yes, sir, best fish and chips in England. Right here in this pub. Did I tell you that?" I said after a pause, but I was pretty sure I wasn't going to succeed in changing the subject.

"Is Arthur staying out here for the weekend?" Adrianna asked while she slipped the fur coat off her shoulders. "His family is in London, you know."

I gave up. "I think he's going back to London Monday morning."

"Let's order dinner when the barman brings the wine. I'm starved," she said. "I don't want fish, though. Surely they have a shepherd's pie."

"No doubt," I answered, "but I'll have the fish—best in England would be hard to pass up."

The fish and chips were nearly as good as the menu promised. In the past three decades the dish had become a national obsession, and it was good everywhere. We made small talk about the food and the pub and Crowborough in general. Finally I ordered a bottle of brandy to take upstairs and we went up to our respective rooms, agreeing to meet a half hour later in Adrianna's room, where she had informed me that there was both a sitting area and a fireplace.

"And he really thinks he got this letter from a dead man?" Adrianna asked over her brandy. She was wearing a casual shift now and was sitting comfortably in a chair near the fire. I sat on the floor with my back leaning against the other chair.

"That's what he seems to think," I answered with a nod.

"What do you think?"

"I don't believe in ghosts, Adrianna."

"Somebody's putting one over on him," she agreed. "But how are they doing it? How did they get the information?" She leaned forward with her questions and looked into my eyes.

I found that rather than trying to figure out how I could get her out of this case, I was wondering how I could keep her in it. I wasn't sure that thought was in Conan Doyle's best interests, and I was certain it was not in hers or mine. Come to think of it, Freddy Wallace probably wouldn't have liked it much either. "We expect to find out," I said. I meant it, too. Somehow I would expose whoever was trying to prey on Sir Arthur's . . . eccentric beliefs.

"No. *You* expect to find out. *He* expects to find a ghost—maybe I should say a fairy."

"What?" I asked.

"*Coming of the Fairies* is the title of his next book," she announced with a laugh.

"What makes you think that?" The idea seemed too bizarre for me. This was a respected, intelligent gentleman she was talking about, after all.

"I know publishers, too, not just reporters, or whatever. His next book is *Coming of the Fairies*. It's due to come out in March. Just wait and see," she said with authority.

"Oh, God! What am I getting into? Is it about that incident in Yorkshire—the Wright girls with the camera? After he wrote that piece in *The Strand,* the tabloids savaged him. Has he lost his mind?"

I turned to look up at Adrianna. Then I struggled to my feet and moved closer to the fire.

"Some say, but not I," Adrianna answered, though she knew the question wasn't serious. "Did you read about the Yorkshire case, Charles?"

"I did. The Kodak film laboratories could find no tampering or double exposures," I answered. "That doesn't mean I believe any of it, but some level-headed people couldn't explain it away."

"Nor did that diminish the attacks any," Adrianna said. "The papers, including your Associated Press clients in America, crucified those girls, and Arthur along with them."

"I was no part of that, Adrianna, and to be fair, AP just reported the straight facts from London. The twist was put on at the other end," I said quietly. "I hated to see that happen to Sir Arthur, but I have to say that I think the photos are obvious fakes. The supposed fairies look like storybook cutouts that someone has pasted onto the negatives—even if Kodak says they aren't retouched. I don't see how anyone takes them seriously." In fact, no one did take them seriously. The photos of supposedly live fairies were clearly amateurish fabrications, and I couldn't see how a man of his intelligence could believe in them at all. With that thought in mind, I couldn't see how I was sitting here at this moment discussing the pursuit of a ghost.

"Did you ever meet Harry Houdini?" she asked.

The idea was preposterous. How would a man of my humble stature meet such a famous star? "Of course not," I answered. "What's Houdini got to do with it?"

"Harry and Arthur are friends—a lot of us have met him. Anyway, he thinks Conan Doyle is completely wrong about spirits and all the rest. They've had some heated arguments about it in public—quite distasteful."

I moved back over to my chair and folded myself back down to the floor in front of it. "I'm afraid I'm solidly behind Houdini on that topic. Sir Arthur's position is ridiculous."

"Yet Freddy says Arthur is one of the best minds in England—just batty about Spiritualism. Besides, in this case, there is the letter. Something really interesting is going on. What if this Dr. Gussmann isn't dead? That's possible, isn't it?"

Apparently she had read my mind. "That's one of the first things I'll look into. The Hopson woman first, then Gussmann's death, I think."

"Time is very short, so you'll have to get busy finding the people on the list first," she said. "The question of Dr. Gussmann's death is important, though. *I'll* start on that." Adrianna rose and began to pace slowly around the space in front of the fire, swinging her foot out on each turn, as if dancing.

"I guess we could get into an argument about whether you are going to get involved in this," I said.

"But there seems no point, does there?" she answered. "I do generally what I want to do, Charles."

"No point at all," I answered cheerfully. "This isn't my business; it's just confidential help for a friend. He's just as much your friend as mine, and I do need the help. I have a regular job, remember, and I can't spend unlimited time on this. At the moment, though, my curiosity makes it worth the effort."

"Curiosity? What about the execution of that poor woman in Holloway? Doesn't that enter into it for you?"

I was shocked to realize that I actually hadn't given that any thought at all. "It may be a terrible injustice—possibly one we can prevent, but probably not at this short notice."

Adrianna continued her slow dance back and forth in front of the fire. "I know a lot of people who stayed in nursing around

London, Charles, and quite a few doctors I know are in practice in the city. With luck, I may be able to get information on Dr. Gussmann more easily than either you or Arthur could."

"Discreetly," I warned. "Remember that we must keep Arthur out of this. What will you tell your friends?"

Adrianna slowed her pace for a couple of tours across the hearth rug. Then she sat down in silence for half a minute. "I know. I'll say that a cousin of mine—no, an uncle in New York, a doctor—wants me to look up an old friend from Scotland."

"Can you say that convincingly? Isn't your family tree pretty well known?" I had almost said "pedigree."

"I do have an uncle in America somewhere, though no one in the family has heard from him since before the war. I'll say that my uncle is very elderly and ill and wants to contact his old friend while he still can. I'll say they were best friends in medical school at Edinburgh and for years afterward." She paused and placed her index finger to her lips.

"Good. Try it out and let's see how it sounds," I said, encouraging her creativity.

Adrianna was up and pacing again. Since I had resumed my place on the floor, my legs were taking up most of the floor space near the fireplace so she had to walk around the bed while her next idea came to her. "Okay, here goes. They had a falling out, a serious row, over a woman, a nurse. They stopped speaking to each other years before Gussmann moved to London. No, *decades* before," she added, turning toward me quickly.

"Good enough. Fine. Let's keep it simple, huh?" I signaled a dampening downward motion with both hands.

"Do you want enthusiastic help from nurses, or not? I'm not going to ring up someone I haven't talked to in years and say, 'Hello, got a minute? Would you like to help me find out everything I can

about a doctor who's been dead a few years? Oh, no reason. It probably won't take up more than several hours of your time.' Honestly,
Charles, is that your way of getting information?" Adrianna glared
at me.

I could see that she was right. She would need an interesting
story. "Right. And so now your old uncle wants to mend the fences?"

She thought a moment longer. "No, it's because they own property together."

"Who owns property together?" I was getting lost.

"My uncle, Dr. Matheson of New York, and his old friend Dr.
Gussmann. Actually, they own quite a nice little tract of land near
Glasgow. They bought it as an investment together decades ago,"
Adrianna rushed on.

"And now?" I encouraged her.

"My uncle has just learned that it may have some real value now.
He'd forgotten about it over the years, but now there it is. They own
it jointly, you see. Uncle Matt—we call him Matt—wants to clear the
matter up. Estate matters can be so messy, worse when there are
courts of two countries involved. Don't you find that?" She resumed
her pacing.

"Well, it's up to the family here, then, to trace it down," I chimed
in, enjoying the game and seeing the purpose in it as well. If Adrianna was going to be able to gossip her way into information that
would be years old and probably forgotten, she would have to make
it juicy.

"Well, it *is* up to us, isn't it? Uncle Matt can't be coming over here
in his condition. I'm the only one in the family with enough time on
her hands to take on the task, so it falls to me. I'll start tomorrow."

"Carefully."

Adrianna rose and stepped over to my chair and leaned over,
extending her hand. "What do you see there on that finger, Charles?"

She paused and stood erect. "Would that ring there, taken with the fact that my husband is a member of Parliament, taken with the fact that I'm here in East Sussex on a Saturday night in the same hotel as you . . ." She halted for a moment. "Well, what would that suggest to you about my ability to be discreet?"

"Sorry."

"Damned right," she snapped, deliberately shocking me by using a word that was far beneath her station.

"For what it's worth, I think your story *will* work. I think it will get more information faster than either Conan Doyle or I could hope to do," I said, hoping that I sounded sufficiently contrite. "I really do think so. Do you have any idea how to contact these friends?"

"Some of them I talk to quite often. Some of the ones I don't see very often are still in regular contact with some I do see. When I think about it, I probably have a contact or two in every hospital of any size in London, including Morton Graves Voluntary. I even know a couple of doctors who were from Scotland. They probably went back there. Some of the girls will know." Adrianna downed the rest of the brandy.

"It's exciting, isn't it?" I offered.

"It is, Charles. Let's do something. Let's get coats on and go for a walk in the cold."

"Not yet," I said. "You promised me an explanation."

She tried silence with a quizzical expression for a few moments to see if she could pretend that she didn't know what I was talking about. I outwaited her.

"For last night," she said quietly.

"And for tonight," I said. "Your . . . our being here could cause some real problems for us both—certainly for Freddy as well. If I'm going to be involved, and obviously I am, I'd like to know what I'm involved in." I nodded toward the chair she'd been sitting in. She stared at it a moment before moving over to sink into the cushions.

"Freddy and I . . . our marriage . . ." She sat in silence without continuing and stroked her fingernail casually along the arm of the chair.

"Your marriage is in trouble?" I prompted.

"It's a marriage of convenience," she answered. "We *are* actually married, I mean, but not . . . we're not really . . ."

It occurred to me that Frederick Wallace might be impotent, but I didn't think he was old enough for that problem. There were other possibilities in what she said, but I didn't want to imply such things. "Freddy's age," I said. "Uh . . . problems."

She laughed, but with tears in her eyes. "Freddy's not lacking in vigor, Charlie. He's just not interested in me." She looked up at me and added, "In women."

"My God!" I said. "How long have you known?"

"Always. Calm down, Charles. We only married, both of us, to stop rumors from spreading."

I didn't know how to react to what she seemed to be trying to tell me about Frederick Wallace—and about herself. Finally I ventured a question: "You prefer women?"

She laughed again. "That wouldn't say much for you, Charlie, the way I've been flirting." She wiped her eyes with the back of her hand. "No, but I don't prefer men, either."

I sat silently, waiting for her to continue. After she went to her suitcase and retrieved a handkerchief, she returned to her chair and started again. "Freddy got by with being single for a long time, longer than most. He took a lot of women out, keeping none around for very long, right into his late thirties. Then pressure mounted. There was some unpleasant talk. He put up the front of being a busy barrister—no time for women. That wasn't too convincing, but it got him into his midforties. Then the war gave him a reprieve. He was a respected and decorated naval officer. No one had time for women until after the war. He didn't step down from the navy until 1919."

"Then what?" I asked.

"Then he had serious problems ahead," Adrianna answered. "He had decided to stand for Parliament, and some of the old rumors were starting up."

"So he asked you to cover for him," I said in disgust.

"No. I asked him to cover for me," she said, "and it was a good deal for both of us. I had figured Freddy out long before that. That's why I asked him."

"But if you don't prefer women . . . ?" I said, with no end for the sentence in mind.

"I prefer no one, Charles. No women, no men, and most certainly no children."

I reached for her hand as she struggled to maintain her composure, but she pulled away and went on.

"I once preferred handsome, frivolous young men. They died. When that happens in a rapid enough succession, something dies with them, I suppose. But mostly I didn't want children, or childbirth—none of it."

"I think I understand," I said.

"Well, London society certainly doesn't understand, Charlie. One is supposed to come home from France, marry a proper gentleman, and pop out four kids. It would have killed me—*I* would have killed me."

"So you talked to Freddy."

"Right. He got a visible young wife—twenty-five years younger than him. I got a wealthy man—as wealthy as I am—incentive enough on the face of it. We had a big wedding. Rumors about Freddy stopped. Men stopped asking me out. Friends stopped setting me up."

That story didn't seem to fit with her recent behavior, but she didn't have anything more to add so I asked, "What are you doing here, Adrianna? What were you doing coming to my room last night?"

"I don't know," she said, dabbing her eyes. "I spend a lot of weekend time alone, just being the visible wife. Sometimes I get lonely and depressed. My old girlfriends have their lives, husbands, and families. As the wealthy wife of an older M.P., I don't fit in with them anymore. I don't really belong with Freddy's crowd—I can't even vote for another year—women can't vote here until they're thirty. They see me as a pretty possession of Freddy's."

"I don't," I said. "I suppose I should."

"Exactly. Since I met you, I've had a friend. Do you know that you're the only single friend close to my age I've had since I got married? We've had so much fun, Charlie, just talking about things and roaming about. But I don't get to see you very much."

"Some say we see each other too much, Adrianna. It doesn't seem to *me* that I see you much at all—a couple of lunches a week, a tea now and then," I said.

"We've never even gone out to a concert or a motion picture or even a proper dinner. Who says we're seeing too much of each other?" she asked defiantly.

"I've been warned by good friends that people are talking," I answered. "You're a married woman. To hear them tell it, you're seen out with me more than you are with your husband."

She looked at me in silence for a moment. "I *am* out with you more than Freddy. Here I am with you now. This is the first Saturday night since before Christmas that I haven't been home alone."

"Have you asked Freddy to stay home more?" I asked.

"Well, that's not really too fair of me, since I married him so that I could be alone, but yes, I have. When he does stay in, we bore each other to tears, Charlie." She looked at me and shrugged her shoulders.

"Have you ever thought of divorce?"

Her long silence said that she had thought of it, but that's not how she answered. "Not really. It wouldn't be fair to Freddy. Since

Lloyd George is out of office, Freddy and his bunch are really getting things done. I wouldn't be surprised if he got a ministry position after the next elections. Besides, divorce is unheard of in both my family and his. It's not easy to get a divorce in England. What grounds would we give?"

"Well, the fact that he's—"

"Don't say it, Charles. Don't you say it. Freddy is a good friend, has been as long as I can remember. He hasn't done anything to me or gone back on any promise. And if I were single, a lot of things I don't want would just start up again. Every bloody friend would be offering me eligible young men." She looked over at me. "And you wouldn't be one of them, Charlie." She paused and then added, "I didn't mean that like it must have sounded."

I understood perfectly. "An American six and a half," I said.

"Too right, old man," she said softly. "You wouldn't be eligible if I were eligible, and no one would ever think otherwise. Much as I might want, sometimes . . . you don't understand the rules here, Charles."

I waited and considered whether to say anything more. Then I said, "England isn't the only place to live."

"Oh, God!" she said. "Don't *you* start. You think I want a house and kids in the colonies? I certainly do not!" She rose and came over to my chair and took my hands in hers.

"So what did you want last night? What do you want tonight?" I asked.

"Last night I wanted to be defiant. I wanted to take command of my situation and go out and spend my weekend with my friend. That's you, Charlie. Then I found out that you were doing something interesting in secret with Arthur. You can't guess how long it's been since I did anything really interesting. I just had to have a share in it—even more so now. Do you understand?"

"I do, and I like it, but we've got to think about what it looks like," I answered. "We could get in a lot of trouble, Adrianna—trouble for all three of us."

She released my hands and returned to her chair. "It does look like that, doesn't it? It feels a little like that, too, just now."

"Let's see. We're in a hotel room in Crowborough. My room is right next to yours, and your husband has no idea where we are."

"The rooms don't have an adjoining door," she joked. "That should be offered in testimony."

I felt like an adolescent with a bad crush. I could just imagine the foolish look on my face. "This isn't a laughing matter, Adrianna."

"Don't start any of that, Charles. It *is* a laughing matter. I *insist* that it is. Now let's figure out what to do about the doctor's ghost. Tell me about the Wickham woman."

Obediently, because I could think of nothing else to do in the strangest situation I'd ever found myself in, I began about the fight between the condemned woman and her boyfriend's wife. I told her how Helen Wickham had argued with the woman and killed her.

"Husband wasn't inside the shop, by any chance?" she asked.

"Not at all. Wickham was the picture of injured innocence. She protested in front of everyone that she had no idea what this lady was talking about. The two women then retreated from the stares around them by going into the flat. A few minutes later, Helen Wickham hurried back outside, locked her door, and ran away up the street. Witnesses said she had a nasty scratch on her face.

"What about the interested bystanders?" Adrianna asked. "Didn't they wonder what had happened to the other woman?"

"Indeed they did, but it simply didn't occur to anyone that serious harm could have come to her at Helen Wickham's hands," I answered. "Still, when Helen had not returned in more than two hours and the other woman still had not emerged from the flat, the landlady was summoned and she unlocked the place.

"And found a body, I'll bet."

I nodded and smiled. Then I wondered why I was smiling at a murder. "And found the well-dressed lady on the floor with an open pair of shears plunged into her upper abdomen. Autopsy revealed that the shears tore through her diaphragm and paralyzed her breathing. She must have died within a minute. Of course, her unborn child died with her."

"Unborn child? Very unfortunate, but it sounds like no more than a manslaughter to me, maybe even self-defense with a good barrister."

"Right. This was not the sort of killing that usually earns the death sentence, but there were further circumstances. Wickham was arrested a few hours later in a pub she frequented—one in which she had often been seen with the deceased's husband, by the way. She simply waltzed in as if nothing had happened and ordered a pint of her favorite stout. She was accosted by other patrons who knew her and who had heard about the incident on her street. At this, she again took the position that she didn't know what they were talking about and tried to leave. A brawl ensued while the bobbies were summoned."

"She'd obviously had a relapse," Adrianna offered in defense of the condemned woman.

"Given her behavior and her former status as a mental patient, a defense of insanity might have seemed a natural one, and indeed her barristers took that approach. Expert testimony by neurological examiners showed, however, that she was *faking* insanity."

"How does a common seamstress fake insanity?"

"Prosecution contended that her years in an asylum had taught her how to feign insanity at will. Things took a worse turn for her when there were unexpected innuendos made about her sexual conduct in the asylum itself—suggestions that she had been intimate with another inmate and perhaps a doctor." I paused and waited for a response.

"Was the doctor named during the trial?"

"Surely you don't mean—no, Adrianna, no names were mentioned, but the rumored misconduct was long after Gussmann's death."

"Oh. Well, I thought that perhaps our mysterious physician at the asylum had left himself open to that accusation. Anyway, what was supposed to be the motive for the murder? Love?"

"The prosecution's claim was that Wickham had murdered her lover's pregnant wife and then could think of no better defense than to feign insanity. The prosecutors charged that she had killed the woman in cold blood and then presented her act at the pub with the full intention of using insanity as her plea—"

Adrianna interrupted, "Nevertheless, the scene in the street was obviously the beginnings of a fight. Clearly it must have been a fight-or-flight situation."

"The circumstances of the killing itself don't seem to support pre-meditation, but the jury was swayed by the grisly nature of the death, the delicate condition of the female victim, and by the apparently callous nature of the killer after the crime," I said as I ticked off three fingers.

"Helen Wickham must have had a poor barrister. I can't imagine that she's about to hang for this," Adrianna said. "It's far from a convincing first-degree-murder case."

I consulted my notes. "There also was a matter of a thousand pounds, which were found locked away in Helen's flat—an impossible sum for a pieceworker with a sewing machine."

"From the lover? That's a bit much for her services, wouldn't you think?" Adrianna asked.

"The husband, as might be predicted, denied having ever given Helen money. Then he changed that to saying that he hadn't ever given her *a lot* of money. Prosecution made a convincing picture of her as a gold digger who had a good deal of money from unknown men and who was determined to have this man for her own."

"Was there testimony about other men?"

"A number of them, some of whom testified that the Wickham woman was unnaturally aggressive and perverted in her sexual conduct."

"A thousand pounds would be impossible to explain," Adrianna agreed, "even if there were a lot of men."

"Moreover, regular patrons of the pub where she was arrested testified that she'd had a long string of ardent boyfriends, both before and during her time with the victim's husband. Apparently her conduct was often pretty scandalous, even for the jaded crowd who frequented the pub."

"Scandalous how?" Adrianna asked with a bit too much enthusiasm.

"There was testimony that she was often quite brazen—allowing herself to be touched in scandalous ways, pretty much in plain view. Arresting police testified that she had tried to bribe them into releasing her, offering a very large sum."

"Surely she's not going to hang for attempted bribery. I still haven't heard any justification for the sentence," Adrianna said.

"Suspicions also were brought forward in testimony that she might have previously killed another rival woman. One such local patron of the bar *had* disappeared in the past—a woman rumored to have worked together with Wickham in entertaining men. The woman had been found brutalized and murdered. Wickham had been questioned at the time, but her alibi was solid. I gather that the Wickham trial was very entertaining, if you like that sort of thing."

"Didn't anyone speak in her behalf?" Adrianna asked.

"There *was* countertestimony from people she worked for. They said she was a perfect lady. These were people of some standing, and they were quite sincere in their belief that Helen Wickham was no strumpet—not in the daytime, when they knew her."

"I can see why there's been pressure against the hanging," Adrianna said. "But then, I don't agree with most hangings."

"In the end, though, the jury found her guilty of murder in the first degree, and the judge of the Central Criminal Court of the Old Bailey sentenced her to hang. She has less than one week to live now. Execution is slated for this coming Friday." I looked at Adrianna sadly. "It's very unusual for a British court to sentence a woman to hang, isn't it?"

Adrianna nodded. "Very. And in this case there is considerable pressure to commute the sentence. There even have been a couple of public protests, but so far the sentence has not been commuted."

We both stared into the fire for a long time then. My head felt crowded. My thoughts probably were with Helen Wickham, Dr. Gussmann's ghost, Harry Houdini, Sir Arthur, Frederick Wallace, and most of all, Adrianna. I was too tired to sort everyone out. Patting Adrianna gently on the shoulder, I murmured, "Sleep well," and left for the solitude of my own room.

6

It is of the highest importance in the art of detection to be able to recognise out

of a number of facts which are incidental and which are vital.

—"The Adventure of Silver Blaze"

LATE ON SUNDAY AFTERNOON, I lurked in the shadows facing toward the front door of Mary Hopson's dressmaking shop. I had determined before taking up my post that there was no rear door; in fact, there was no alleyway behind her shop, which was wedged between a greengrocer and a chemist. It was a simple two-story building on a narrow street in Richmond-upon-Thames and was clearly in need of maintenance. Most of the buildings on this street had sagged and shifted over time. Their tile roofs were crooked; their brick facings were misaligned. The street itself was narrow, crooked, and paved with old bricks.

The sign over her door, badly in need of repainting, read simply, "Mary Hopson, Prop." It did not reveal just what sort of business said Mary might be proprietor of. I assumed that her customers simply knew where she was and what she did. The exterior woodworks, too, were in need of paint, and the roof was clearly missing some tiles. It had been clear during my long, cold wait that she was there at home that Sunday afternoon because there was a steady stream of white smoke coming from her chimney. Obviously she used coal for heat, and from the scant amount of white smoke that climbed straight up from her stack, I could tell that she knew how to bank a good, clean fire.

With considerable effort, I turned my thoughts from the cozy fire in that shop to the section of the *Times* I held in front of me in what I hoped was an attitude of casual nonchalance. I read again about the death, at eighty-nine, of Dr. John Kirk Barry, an explorer companion of David Livingston's. I reviewed the sensational news that Michael Collins had just been named prime minister of the Irish Free State. I idly thought how pleased Conan Doyle's father would have been at this news, and then realized with a start that the poor old man's pro-Irish rant in a sketchbook somehow began the chain of events that had landed me on this chilly side street. Could there be some connection between the political events of that troubled island and this attempt to see Helen Wickham? It didn't seem likely, but then neither did a letter from a doctor long dead. I made a mental note to check for Irish sympathizers among the assorted players in this whole unlikely situation.

By the time the dressmaker finally emerged from her shop, I had been shivering behind the newspaper for nearly two hours. Just at four o'clock, she walked out, locked the door behind her, and started briskly away from the shop, moving southward toward Sheen Road. She wore a good wool coat against the brisk January weather. I fell in behind after she had made half a block of progress. There were very few people out on the streets, and I thought I would have to keep my distance if I had any chance of escaping notice.

It was soon apparent, though, that I needn't be so careful. Mary never looked back during her walk and never slowed her pace. She turned eastward on Sheen Road and marched along briskly to Kings Lane, where she again turned south. A hundred yards farther on, the lane narrowed to a gravel path, which ran along the border of a cemetery. More than a quarter mile farther south Mary Hopson walked through a gated entrance into a park. As I entered the same way, I noticed an iron sign that read "Bog Gate." Another hundred yards into the park, Hopson turned right onto the first crosspath she came to. Again she did not pause, nor did she look back. I took the risk of closing the distance a little in the park, but it was difficult to appear to be a casual stroller when I had to match her pace. I calculated that she had now walked at least half a mile in fewer than ten minutes.

After a further ten minutes of walking at her brisk pace, perhaps half a mile from where she entered the park, she stopped abruptly at a bench that was placed beside the path. She sat on it just as suddenly as she had stopped, and she sat upright, staring straight ahead. I skidded on a patch of gravel in my attempt to stop and turn away from her, but I might as well have been invisible, for all the attention she paid to her surroundings.

I paced quietly and as casually as possible to a nearby tree trunk, leaned against it, and extracted the folded newspaper from my greatcoat. Instantly, that seemed the most obvious of deceptions, and I turned back to the path and continued on toward her. She scarcely seemed to notice me as I walked past her bench and proceeded on as the path led me down a slight hill. It curved so that I was slightly behind her line of vision. When I had walked so far beyond her that I feared I would lose sight of her through the denuded winter shrubbery, I paused and leaned once more against a tree beside a large pond.

While I waited and watched, I did a mental review of what I knew about this woman. Mary Hopson was single, thirty-five years of age, and lived alone in Richmond-upon-Thames. She was an independent seamstress who had been living at the same address since 1915. There had never been a police report on her in her jurisdiction, and she was respected in the neighborhood. There had, however, been instances of arrest in London on charges of lewd conduct. It was noted that, considering the discrepancy in the reports, this may have been a different woman. The local bobby on the beat in her area had a nodding acquaintanceship with her and considered her a solid citizen. It was noted that her shop kept odd hours and often was closed during regular business days.

I was to stand there freezing in the last haze of twilight for twenty-five more minutes before Mary Hopson moved from her bench. In that whole time, she sat somewhat rigidly, looking straight ahead at the lawn on the other side of the fence. I assumed she was waiting for someone, but no one showed up. When she did move, it was to rise abruptly and walk directly back the way she'd come. Without slowing her pace or looking behind her, she simply retraced her steps all the way back to her shop. She unlocked the door and disappeared within as swiftly and deliberately as she had emerged for her walk. I was painfully aware that Mary was now inside her warm abode while I was still freezing at a nearby corner. I decided to find a place to thaw out before making my next move, and quickly found a warm pub nearby.

I thought for a few minutes about the fact that she'd waited so long in an uncomfortable place where nothing discernible had happened. It reminded me of standard rendezvous procedure in military intelligence work. An officer would often visit a certain spot on a regular schedule, regardless of weather or other inconveniences, knowing that his contact depended on his being at that spot at that time. Usually nothing happened, but when it did, it was important. I downed first a hot tea and then a pint of stout. I decided to approach the Hopson woman and braced myself for the cold walk back to her shop. Once there, I used the bell cord that hung beside her door and waited.

The woman who answered was neatly attired in a plain cotton dress covered in front by a simple lace-edged apron. A pincushion was tied to the left wrist, and its dozens of pins and needles stood upright as she folded her hands in front of her waist and smiled at me. Both her smile and her general appearance were attractive in a wholesome way. Her yellow hair was pinned neatly into a bun.

Standing about five and a half feet tall, she looked fit and strong. Her blue eyes were clear and direct as she spoke.

"Yes, sir, what may I do for you?" she said in an open and pleasant voice while looking over the gentleman who stood in front of her shop on this nonbusiness evening.

"Are you Mary Hopson, miss?"

"I am, and who are you, sir?" she asked as pleasantly as if I had been a new customer at midday on a Wednesday, rather than a stranger in the dark on a Sunday night.

"I am Captain Baker, Miss Hopson. Please forgive my intruding on your Sunday evening, but I've come here on an important inquiry. Could you spare a few minutes?"

"Would you be the policeman who's been making inquiries about me in the neighborhood? I've nothing to hide, you know."

I had to decide how far I should stretch the truth. In a way I was now involved in that same inquiry, and that inquiry had been made by the police. I decided to let her own assumptions do the lying. "I didn't make the interviews last week personally, Miss Hopson, but I am here on that business, yes. Our investigation is not into you or your business, miss, but your name has come up in a matter with which you could be of help. May I ask you a few questions directly?'

"Not while we stand here and freeze, you can't. Please come in, Captain. I can see you're cold. I was out for a walk earlier myself, and I know what it's like out tonight." She opened the door wide and gestured a welcome.

"Out for a walk on an evening like this? What could have possessed you to endure such a chill?" I asked cheerfully.

Hopson seemed perplexed, rather than amused, by the friendly question. She brought one hand up to her cheek and moved her head from side to side. "I don't know, really. I get a feeling . . . restless, very restless. Walking helps calm me down. I enjoy a brisk walk."

I found myself in a spacious workroom once I had walked past her. It was in a better state of repair than was the exterior of the building. The walls showed signs of relatively recent repainting. A large worktable was placed just inside the front window, where light would be best during the day. Spread across the table was a bolt of blue satin, and it was clear that she had been pinning a pattern to the material. A small coal-burning cookstove against the back wall was keeping the room comfortable. Two doors led to rooms at the rear of the shop. These were closed. Several bright electric lights were switched on in the room, and it appeared that she was prepared for an evening of work.

"So how has my name come up, exactly?" she asked when she had centered herself in the shop and stood facing me.

"This is an unusual case, Miss Hopson. Do you mind if I take a few notes while we talk?" I said as I removed a notepad from my coat and prepared to write. I did not normally take notes much unless my interview was to be a long one, but I somehow thought I looked more like a police detective with a notepad. "Did you ever know a woman named Helen Wickham?"

"Oh! Goodness! What can I have to do with poor Helen?" she asked. "I haven't seen her for years, and I barely knew her! I've got nothing to do with that terrible business that's been in the papers. Surely you know that!" She had brought both palms up to her chest, and the pincushion stood bristling toward me.

"Perhaps you'd like to sit down. No, you're not suspected of any involvement with Miss Wickham. It's just that we need your help in clarifying a few matters. Don't be alarmed. May we sit down by the stove?"

Mary led the way, and we sat at a small table nearer the warm stove. I laid my notepad on the table and continued without it. "You knew Helen Wickham?"

"In Morton Graves Voluntary, yes. I was a patient there for eight years," she said with a quieter voice and her face looking down at the floor. "I don't like to think about that time."

82

"It's all right, Miss Hopson. Did you know Helen for long?" My mind was racing. There *were* connections among Gussmann and Wickham and this woman. Morton Graves Voluntary Hospital was one link, but maybe there was more of a connection, and a more current one, than she was admitting.

"No. I probably saw her around the grounds most days, but I don't think I spoke with her more than a time or two. She left there quite a long time before I did, I think. I left in 1915—been here ever since." She looked up into my eyes. "I've got a good shop here. I've never had any trouble since I was discharged. They used to check up on me regular, Captain."

"There's no trouble about you, Miss Hopson. This is not about you. It's all right," I said gently. "Did you know Dr. Gussmann?"

She straightened her posture and continued to look directly at me, but a definite blush flooded her face and neck. "He was my doctor in Morton Graves at first—until he died, that is. There were rumors about him, but they were all lies. He always behaved very properly." She paused for a moment. "Then I had Dr. Green—then Dr. Townby until I left. Dr. Gussmann was very nice, but I don't remember much about him. He was very old."

"Do you remember when Dr. Gussmann died?"

"Surely. I was only there about two years when that happened— I was there for several years after that. He was very old and he just died. They buried him over here in East Sheen Cemetery, I think. What's Dr. Gussmann got to do with anything?" she asked with clear agitation. "I don't like to think about that!"

I was convinced that she was genuinely upset. I'd had years of practice at interviewing people, and I rarely misjudged them face-to-face. "Please answer a few more questions. I won't take long. Did Helen Wickham know Dr. Gussmann, do you think?"

"I'm pretty sure that he was her doctor until he died. I remember that Helen was Dr. Townby's patient later. That's where I met her. Dr.

Townby introduced us, and once or twice he had us talk to him in a group. I remember Helen as a nice woman, quiet. When I read about what she did—couldn't believe it, really." She turned her gaze back to the floor. "What's this got to do with me, Captain?"

"Nothing to do with you, Miss Hopson. Did you know Robert Stanton? That's another name that has come up."

Her eyes showed further alarm, and she remained silent for a moment. "I don't like to talk about any of this, Captain. Yes, I have met Mr. Stanton. He also was a patient of Dr. Townby's. I was with him—in . . . in some group sessions," Hopson answered quietly. "I didn't ever see him other than that."

"And Liza Anatole? Did you know her?"

Mary Hopson sat back and thought a while before answering. "That name doesn't sound familiar to me. I'm pretty sure I never met her, though I'm not so good with names, sometimes. Please, sir— what's all this got to do with me?"

I decided to attempt to get her cooperation in case arrangements could be made to see Wickham later in the week. "We don't know what it has to do with you, but Helen Wickham has asked if she could see you. It's a sort of last request, actually. Does that make any sense to you, Miss Hopson?"

She looked up in obvious alarm. "No! Honestly, Captain Baker, I never knew Helen as a friend! She was just a sad woman in the hospital—we all were. I had friends in there, people I visited with all the time, but Helen surely wasn't one of them. I have no idea why she would want to see me. Must I go to see her? Isn't she about . . . ?" She halted and looked away toward the wall behind the stove.

"Her sentence will be carried out, I believe, this coming week, Miss Hopson," I answered, "and no, you don't have to see her." I paused and considered her reaction. "But if it can be arranged, I'd *like* for you to come with me to see her. Just say hello to her and maybe talk for a short while. It seems to be a harmless enough request from her. We haven't yet discovered anything that would make us think we shouldn't try to do as she asks. Maybe she considered you to be a closer friend than you realize."

"Is this normal? I mean, I didn't know the police did things for . . . prisoners." She looked at me with a gaze that was questioning rather than suspicious.

"No, this isn't normal, but it's something we may want to do. Could I persuade you to help?" I was judging my voice and volume carefully. It reminded me of countless interrogations of young, frightened German prisoners during the war.

"I really don't like . . ." she halted.

"Of course, we would help to cover your expenses, certainly. I think I was told there would be a remuneration of ten pounds. And you might be a great comfort to the woman. We don't know why she made the request, but it might do her some real good."

The mention of such a large sum of money had clearly caught her attention. "Expenses? What expenses would I have?"

"It's just a stipend we give sometimes when we have to interrupt the business of someone who's helping us," I said pleasantly, sure now that she was going to help. "Can I count on you if you're needed?"

Hopson looked around her shop, her eyes no doubt taking in a dozen places where ten pounds could make further repair or add to inventory. At last she turned to me. "Is it safe?"

"What place could be safer, Miss Hopson? You'll be outside of her . . . room, and I'll be beside you."

"Oh, goodness. Poor Helen. I can't imagine!" But then her face showed that she *could* imagine. She had been confined herself—not in a cell, perhaps, but in a place more feared than prison. Those years were not forgotten, and her face showed the painful memory. She looked up at me and said, "I honestly don't think I would lose any earnings by going with you, Captain."

"The expense funds are set aside anyway. They have to give them to you or go through a lot of trouble with the budget. Now, I don't know for sure that we are going to grant Helen's request, but if we do, can I say you'll help?" I was sure I knew her answer already.

Mary Hopson did not take too long in her silent deliberations. "You can," she answered. "I'll go see Helen. I don't know why she'd want to see me, of all people, but if it might be a comfort to her. . . . Would you like a cup of tea, Captain Baker? I'm just about to make some."

"No, sadly, I have to be going. Thank you for the offer, though. I've taken enough of your evening as it is. I'll let myself out, and I'll be contacting you within a day or two." I stood and added, "But there's one more thing. As you said, this isn't the normal thing. Could you honor our request to say nothing of this to anyone for the time being?"

"I can do that," she answered. "For how long, do you think? This might make quite a story to tell my friends."

"Not forever, but we might need to keep this confidential for a while. It could be months. Can you do that?"

"I can keep a secret a lot longer than a few months, Captain Baker."

"May I call you, then, when I know, Miss Hopson?"

"I've got no phone, I'm afraid, Captain. You'll have to send word or come around. I'm almost always here."

I nodded my approval, turned, and let myself out of the shop into the dark January evening.

When I returned to my flat, there was a note under the door from Adrianna saying that she had waited for me as long as she dared. Freddy would be home by the time she could get there. She *had* managed to find out a few things but would be unable to talk to me until midmorning. She would be at her home until lunchtime.

I called Conan Doyle using the private number I had been given. After three rings, the phone was answered by a butler, who said that Sir Arthur was out. I left my name and asked for a return call. I was assured that the master of the house would get the message. Half an hour later my phone began to ring.

"Baker here."

"Do you have news, Charles?" Sir Arthur asked immediately.

"Yes. I met with Mary Hopson. She did know both Wickham and Gussmann, and she is willing to go with me to make the visit."

"Well done, my boy. That's a day's work! And I've made a few calls myself. A friend of mine will start tomorrow to try to arrange a time when you can go into Holloway Prison—completely unofficially and off the record. He expects confirmation by Tuesday, the latest, and will try for a visit at least by Wednesday."

"Amazing! Does he know the warden?"

"Quite the other end of things. The contact will be made at the guard level. If it can be done at all, it will be arranged by a very few warders. Some money will change hands. You will go in unobserved. I gather there will be a narrow window of time. There will be no witnesses and no records."

"I'm not unfamiliar with that method," I said. "It's like a few border crossings I made during the war."

"And a few since then, I'll wager."

"I cross borders with a simple passport now," I said. "If you want to go on believing the other sort of thing, I'm not going to argue the point. But it's just romanticizing on your part."

"Romanticizing is what we writers do best, Charles," he said with a laugh. "Well, anyway, it looks like we may be getting somewhere. What's your next move?" he asked.

"I'll follow up with the others on the list starting tomorrow. I may get more information on Mary Hopson. Also, I may be able to find out a few things about Gussmann and the hospital through some medical contacts of mine. The more we know before we go into the prison, the better." I thought it best not to tell him that the medical contacts were actually through Adrianna Wallace.

"Absolutely! Ring me again tomorrow night after nine. Call anytime that you have information."

"Good night, and good luck with the prison system."

I walked over and turned up the heat before removing my overcoat. Then I rummaged around in the kitchen and settled for bread and cheese with half a bottle of inexpensive burgundy. While I ate, I reviewed the little I knew.

I sketched out a little chart for myself, complete with circles and arrows. Hopson, first on the Gussmann list, said she knew Dr. Gussmann, Helen Wickham, and Robert Stanton, but not Liza Anatole. There was now a Dr. Townby, who knew all of these as well. It would be a good idea to check him out.

As for the letter and the sketchbook, they presented a real puzzle. A note from a dead doctor about the drawings of a dead lunatic—and about another lunatic who would soon be dead. Insanity, promiscuity, murder, and ghosts—what else was waiting to unfold?

7

Life is infinitely stranger than anything which the mind of man could invent.
—"A Case of Identity"

WHEN I ARRIVED AT the Associated Press office at nine o'clock on Monday morning, there was a level of chaos even beyond the usual. Word was out in Whitehall that votes in the U.S. Senate were again clearly lined up to defeat the proposal for the United States to join the League of Nations. On top of that, Germany seemed sure to default on its next reparations payment to France.

I busied myself with work on a packet of untranslated German press releases from Munich. Clippings from *Völkischer Beobachter* were the worst. The paper was owned and operated as a propaganda tool by a relatively new Bavarian political party, the Nationalsozialistische Deutsche Arbeiterpartei. This Nazi group (as they were called for convenience) had been growing rapidly in both numbers and in power since July. The faction controlled its own small private army, called the Sturmabteilungen. The clippings were hate propaganda, mostly against Jews.

I got to reviewing my notes about the German situation, and it was ten-thirty before I could get enough time to call Adrianna at home. I managed to get a phone in an empty office so I could talk privately, and I caught her just as she was preparing to go out.

"I can't talk long, Charlie, but we're making progress. I found out through the nurse's registry that I have an old friend working at Morton Graves Voluntary Hospital itself. I called her last night. She was at Morton Graves before the war and returned there afterward."

"Did she know Gussmann or any of the others?" I asked.

"All of them. She knew Dr. Gussmann before he died—he did die, by the way. She saw his body in his office when they found him. To hear her tell it, she didn't shed a tear. She said he was an arrogant bastard who treated staff like property and patients like lab rats. And she knew Helen Wickham—said she was a nice woman. There were rumors—very spicy ones—that Gussmann was having a bit too much fun with Wickham and other patients behind closed doors, but Ann wasn't sure she believed it."

"It hardly seems likely. The man would have been in his seventies," I said. "On the other hand, I imagine most men that age would like to at least be thought capable of such . . . indiscretions."

Adrianna ignored that remark and stuck to the subject. "That's not the worst of the suspicious events during Gussmann's time. There was a death associated with him."

"A death! What kind of death?"

"Apparently one patient was murdered there while Gussmann was with the hospital, a woman patient of his who was due to be discharged. She was sexually assaulted before she was killed."

"Was Dr. Gussmann implicated in any way?"

"No, he was in the hospital the night of the murder, but was asleep in his office. There were signs of a break-in. All of the patients, including the victim, were locked in their rooms and couldn't have done the murder unless someone let them out and then put them back in their room. No real suspects ever surfaced."

"But apparently it wasn't done by Gussmann," I said.

"Apparently," she agreed, before rushing on to the next name on her list. "My friend Ann knew Robert Stanton, too, but she says he couldn't have known Dr. Gussmann because Stanton came there after Gussmann died. She knew Mary Hopson and Liza Anatole. She says the Anatole woman couldn't have known Gussmann or Hopson—"

"That's strange. I sort of expected to hear that all three of the people on the list knew each other in some way," I interrupted, "and certainly that they all knew Gussmann."

"It's stranger than that, Charles. My friend says that Liza Anatole couldn't even have known Helen Wickham! Why would someone want to send Wickham a visitor who never knew her? Why would our girl Liza be on the list when she knew neither Gussmann nor Wickham?"

"Why indeed? Why *would* the list include someone who never knew Helen Wickham? That's very curious. How did you get all of that out of your friend, anyway? I thought your story was that you were tracking down Dr. Gussmann about some property dealings."

"And that led naturally to the topic of wills and how strange Dr. Gussmann's will was," Adrianna answered. "She said that the deed I'd told her I was looking for would probably belong now to either the hospital itself or Gussmann's private secretary or another doctor there, named Townby. His entire estate went to the three of them—"

"I've heard of Townby from Mary Hopson," I interrupted. "How would he come to own any of Gussmann's property?"

"I'm getting to that, Charles. I mentioned how strange it was that Helen Wickham, who I'd heard was Dr. Gussmann's patient, had become a murderess. That, in turn, led to a discussion of whether any of Dr. Gussmann's other patients were still there in the hospital— only two are—and she mentioned Mary Hopson while trying to remember Gussmann's patients. Then I said I thought I'd met a former patient of his, Liza Anatole."

"How would you have met her?"

"I'm getting to that. Anyway, she corrected me on that one and said Anatole couldn't have known Gussmann, so I tried Stanton on her and got corrected again because she said Robert Stanton never knew Gussmann either. She asked how I knew these people, and I said I was doing some social work from time to time and had met them."

"Oh, good story," I said.

"We talked for more than an hour, and most of it wasn't even related to the hospital. I just chatted and listened and wove these names and events in where I could."

"You're amazing, Adrianna," I said sincerely. I was pretty sure she could get any information out of anybody, given enough time. "Now, what about this Townby, and who are the Gussmann patients who are still in the hospital?"

"That's another strange thing. One of the Gussmann patients who is still a resident at Morton Graves was once a psychiatrist there himself. Can you beat that?"

"A psychiatrist? What's his name, Adrianna? Not Townby?" I asked as I opened a note pad.

"Yes, Dr. William Townby. It gets more weird still, Charlie. This Dr. Townby character wasn't just named in Gussmann's will, he was named *big* in Gussmann's will."

I was writing it all down. "Incredible! Dr. Townby knew Stanton and Wickham, too. He is a psychiatrist who knew Gussmann, and now he's a patient?"

"He *was* a psychiatrist; now he's just a patient. But my friend Ann says he's the sanest person out there. As I understand it, he was a patient of Gussmann's, then a psychiatrist at the same hospital a few years later. Now he's a patient there again."

"I've got to find out more about him. Who is the other Gussmann patient still in there?"

"A guy named Tommy Morrell. He's been in there forever. According to Ann, he's pretty much of a vegetable most of the time.

He's ambulatory and feeds himself, but that's about all. He mostly just sits or walks about the grounds. I can get in to see both of these men. The property-search story is doing fine. I expect to be able to go out there tomorrow or Wednesday."

"And where is Gussmann's private secretary now?" I asked. "Does she still work at the hospital?"

"My friend heard that the secretary died a couple of years ago. Her name was Alice. She retired after Gussmann died. A couple of years ago some of them heard that she was seriously ill and then that she had died. Cancer, she thought."

"I'd rather interview this Townby character myself—"

She started speaking before I finished, and I could almost hear her shaking her head. "But *your* uncle isn't the one who owned land with Gussmann, is he? Listen, Charlie, I've got to go. I'm going to a luncheon with Freddy. I'll be tied up all afternoon. Call me in the morning around ten." She was gone before I could answer.

I returned to my desk and tried to work on the piece about German economics, but it was no use. I couldn't keep my mind from drifting to Morton Graves Voluntary Hospital and all its strange inmates, past and present.

What kind of hospital is it where a mental patient becomes a doctor and then returns to the wards as a patient once again? Why are all four of the names in the Gussmann letter former patients from the same asylum?

One thing is certain: the letter to Conan Doyle wasn't from Gussmann. Not only is he dead, but two of the people mentioned in it never could have known him.

Was Dr. Gussmann a lecher who preyed on his female patients?

After a wasted half hour, I left my desk and the building. Ten minutes later I was in a reference library near the office, one I frequently used. There I began my search for more information about Morton Graves.

I learned that the term "voluntary," when applied to a hospital or clinic, meant that it was run by a charitable institution or was largely supported by voluntary contributions. There were several other types of hospitals. Royal hospitals were supported by the government. There also were municipal hospitals, church-supported hospitals, and university hospitals. A few were private-for-profit facilities, called proprietary hospitals, though these were uncommon in this country, whose Crown government had been supporting health facilities for centuries. All of those designations addressed only how the institutions were funded, not what services they performed. Sometimes mental wards were part of regular hospitals; sometimes they were separate institutions. They might be called asylums (though that seemed to be rare), clinics, institutes, or hospitals.

Morton Graves Voluntary Hospital was supported by charitable subscription. It enjoyed a sizable endowment fund made up of large contributions over the thirty years of its existence. It was a long-term residence for mental patients only—what would have been called an asylum in times past. It enjoyed a reputation as a research facility where innovative approaches were tried. One Dr. Bernard Gussmann (deceased) had been among its more famous neurological practitioners over the years.

Periodical reference lists revealed that Dr. Gussmann had published numerous articles between 1880 and 1900, including one in 1885 that argued with the famous Dr. Jean Charcot of Paris. Many of the articles were published in Edinburgh and London, but even more were published in Austria and had titles in German. Sigmund Freud's *Studien über Hysterie,* published in 1895, was said to owe much to Dr. Gussmann's earlier articles on therapeutic uses of hypnosis in neuropathy.

A newspaper article about Dr. Gussmann after his death paid tribute to his contributions to neurology in general and to Morton

Graves Voluntary Hospital in particular. He had bequeathed a large part of his estate to the hospital. Also mentioned was the remarkable fact that Gussmann had left much of his fortune to a patient at Morton Graves, one William Townby, who had since been released from the hospital. That had to be the Dr. Townby who was now again an inmate at Morton Graves.

By four-thirty I had left the library and was trekking back to my office in the twilight gloom. I had learned nothing about Dr. Gussmann that might shed light on the mysterious letter that the man, now dead for twelve years, had supposedly sent to Sir Arthur Conan Doyle a week ago. There had been one brief human-interest story about William Townby, written when he joined the medical staff at Morton Graves Voluntary in 1914. The chief interest in the piece was that the former mental patient, now a medical doctor specializing in neuropathy, had been a stellar pupil in medical school in Edinburgh. He was quoted as saying that he was delighted to be admitted to the staff of the very institution where he had been so effectively treated.

When I entered my office, there was a message waiting that asked me to see my supervising editor. That was often an unpleasant task, but I was the one who had requested the meeting. I was ahead on my regular columns, and I had accumulated some leave time. I wanted to ask him if I could be away for a week or so.

The meeting actually went quite smoothly. I was a specialist—both an economist and a linguist—part of an experiment that AP had taken up in an attempt to have people on site who *understood* the news. As a result, my boss usually couldn't see much real use for me, and he didn't object to my taking a vacation. We agreed on two weeks of leave.

By five o'clock I was home and dialing Conan Doyle. He answered the phone himself.

"This is Charles Baker."

"So you got my message," he said.

"No. I haven't received any message, but I've been out all afternoon. I have good news, though: I'm taking some time off so I can concentrate on your mysterious letter."

"Good. Arrangements are proceeding for a meeting with Wickham in the prison tomorrow, for one thing. Then there's the matter of looking into the other people in the letter. I think this could take your full attention this week at least."

"What are the arrangements for getting into Holloway tomorrow?"

"I'll know later this evening, but it looks like our only opportunity will be very early tomorrow morning. If so, will our Hopson woman be available, I wonder?"

"I'm not worried about that. Let me know as soon as you have word. I'll stay in all evening, but I may be on the phone from time to time. I'm gathering information about Morton Graves Voluntary Hospital on Chisholm Road. I hope we can answer many of our questions there," I said.

"I hope so, too. Who's your connection to the hospital?"

I pondered how to answer him. "Mrs. Wallace used to be in the VAD," I said. "She has a friend at Morton Graves." I waited for a response, but he was silent. "I think that her help is going to be very useful," I added.

Finally he replied, "Apparently you're quite confident that she should be trusted, Charles. I would not have brought her into this matter myself, but what's done is done." He was silent for ten seconds. "Not my place to say anything, my boy, but I fear that the two of you are being a bit careless, considering her standing in society. Anyway, I'm sure that you've impressed on her how I feel about my anonymity." He paused momentarily and then added, "I'll clear the line now; I'm waiting for word about Holloway. Good-bye, Charles. I'll call again soon, either way." He hung up.

I had just changed into comfortable old clothes and was heating water for tea when the phone rang again. The voice was Adrianna's. "Charlie, I've just got a few minutes before Freddy gets home. Listen, guess who has an appointment to talk to the chief of staff at Morton Graves."

"I *do?* Thanks, Adrianna, you're amazing."

"No, idiot. Why would *you* have an appointment to talk about *my* uncle's land held in common with Gussmann? *I,* on the other hand, *do* have an appointment for tomorrow. And they're very anxious to talk to me. Dr. Dodds, that's the man's name, hopes I'll be able to shed some light on questions about Gussmann. I don't know how I'm going to fake this, but then I haven't said that I knew Gussmann, only that my uncle did." Adrianna spoke this all in one breath and then paused for a gulp of air. "I need to know more about Gussmann fast, Charles."

"Well, I've got a few things for you that might help. Let me get my notes." I laid the receiver down on the table and walked to my desk. I returned to the phone just in time to hear a parting shout.

"Car coming in, Charlie. Too late!" The line went dead.

Tea, biscuits, and canned soup didn't go especially well with the last of the inexpensive wine, I discovered, but that was all I had on hand. I read the evening paper and found a brief insert on page three that said that Helen Wickham was to die on Friday. The article briefly recapped the circumstances of the case, but added nothing new to my knowledge. I had read every scrap of any possible interest in the paper before the phone rang again.

"Charles," Conan Doyle's voice began abruptly, "you can get in, but only briefly, and only at five o'clock tomorrow morning. Can you call the Hopson woman?"

"She has no phone. What time is it now?"

"Nearly nine," he answered. "I'll send my car around now. You'll have to go out there and see her, I'm afraid."

"I have a car of my own, Sir Arthur. Thanks for the offer. I'll go right over and talk to her."

"When you've confirmed things with her, please call me back here," he said.

"Right. I'll call when things are arranged."

The drive out to North Sheen to see Mary Hopson was successful. As I had suspected she would be, she was willing, if somewhat apprehensive, to undertake our adventure for the next morning. I arranged to pick her up at 4:30 A.M.

It was 11:00 P.M. before I could inform Sir Arthur that the arrangements had been made.

8

"Many men have been hanged on far slighter evidence," I remarked.
"So they have. And many men have been wrongfully hanged."
—"The Boscombe Valley Mystery"

VERY EARLY ON TUESDAY morning I parked my Morris Oxford at the curbside a block from Holloway Prison. Mary Hopson sat shivering in the passenger seat beside me. The little car was an open model, and even with the top up, it funneled major drafts through the interior. Having driven from West London in the coldest hour of the predawn morning, both of us were frozen.

I checked my pocket watch at 4:55 A.M. and turned to my reluctant companion.

"We just have time to walk to the door where they'll let us in, Mary. How are you feeling?" I asked the obviously frightened seamstress.

She looked up and down the street, peering into the darkness. "I'm all right, Captain Baker, but I still don't know if I should be doing this. Clearly no one knows I'm coming. Are you sure this is not going to cause trouble?"

"There'll be no trouble. It's just that this is the only way to try to meet Helen's request without attracting the press. I explained that to you. We can't have the public thinking we're softhearted, now, can we?" I attempted a chuckle, but I was too cold and worried myself to bring it off. After all, it seemed unlikely to me that Mary Hopson's trepidation was any more than an act. Her name had been at the top of the list of those who were supposed to be brought here. I was fairly certain that she had a better idea of why we were here than I did. Nevertheless, I continued my pretense.

She placed her gloved hand firmly on the door handle. "Let's go, then. I don't want to be any longer than I have to." She opened the door of the fabric-topped car and stepped out onto the street. I scrambled out my side of the car and moved quickly around to her, offering my arm and hoping that I seemed gallant rather than suspicious.

A few moments later I was rapping on a steel door that faced directly onto a service street just off Parkhurst Road. A uniformed warder with a distinct look of worry opened it immediately. He nodded without a word and led us straight to a set of poorly lighted iron stairs and upward to another steel door two stories above. There he opened the door with one of the many keys he carried and led us into a dimly lit hallway. He signaled for us to wait and walked away down the narrow corridor, never looking back.

Fifteen seconds later, a third steel doorway opened ten feet away, and an arm emerged, waving us to enter. That led us into a well-lighted, wide hallway, where a female warder faced us.

"You sure you want to do this, Baker?" she asked in a whisper. "It's not a good time for Helen."

"Is there another time?" I questioned in a muffled reply.

"No. This is the last time you could see her," the guard whispered, "but it won't do no good, sir. She's in a state, I tell you."

"What kind of state?"

"Well, she's asleep just now, finally, but she ain't right in the head. Didn't they tell you?"

Mary Hopson's eyes went wide, and she stepped away from me. "What do you mean?" she demanded aloud, her voice clearly showing alarm.

"Quiet, miss!" the guard whispered. "We ain't supposed to be here, you understand. There's other cells opening onto this hall down the other end. You mustn't speak out so." She turned to me and continued to whisper. "Helen went off her nut yesterday afternoon, sir. The strain finally got to her, I guess, but she's been so calm like since she was brought here. Now she's raving mad. It won't do no good to wake her and try to talk to her."

Mary stood in obvious horror and stared at me without making a sound.

"We've got to see her!" I whispered. "Has anyone told her we were coming?"

"Yes, and that's another odd thing, sir. Recently she's been *expecting* to get a visitor, even though none are allowed," the warder answered. "But when I tried to calm her down last night by telling her you was coming, it was like it meant nothing to her. She's in a terrible despair, and nothing's getting through to her."

"She'll calm down when she sees us," I whispered. "As you say, she's been expecting this visit." I tried to sound like I knew what I was talking about.

The female guard looked skeptically at me. "She never said it was a man and a woman, but she never said it wasn't. You're sure you want to see her?"

I answered without looking again at Mary Hopson, "Yes, wake her. As you say, it's now or never. She's been expecting us." I took Mary gently by the arm and led her behind the guard.

The uniformed woman walked to a steel door with a small window in it and selected a key. "Operates from the outside only, mate. I have to let you out from out here. You hold the door open here while I go in and wake her. Then I'll wait out here."

Centered within the room she had opened was a cage of steel bars. The distance from the bars to the outer concrete walls was about eight feet all around the inner cell. This cage itself was approximately eight feet square. Inside it was a built-in steel bunk, a toilet, steel shelving, and a steel bench bolted in front of a steel shelf, which passed through the bars to accommodate a food tray.

"I'll be waiting, but only for fifteen minutes, understand?" the guard said before entering the room.

"Thank you. That should be plenty of time," I whispered as I held the spring-loaded door open.

The warder walked to the edge of the inner cell closest to the bunk, reached in through the bars, and gently shook Helen Wickham. "Helen," she said in a slightly lowered voice. "Helen, wake up. You've got your visitors."

Wickham opened her eyes and lay still for a moment. Then she seemed to realize where she was and swung her feet abruptly to the floor and stood. "Still in jail," she said softly, turning to the jailer. "Still you," she said.

"Still me, Helen, but you've got your visitors now," the warder said as she walked back to the door where Mary Hopson and I waited. She walked out and gestured for us to enter. "You can talk normal in there, sir. No one will hear you out here. Fifteen minutes. I'll be right out here." As we entered, she closed the steel door behind us and peered in through the thick glass pane, which was centered five feet off the floor.

Helen Wickham stood silently and stared first at me, then for a longer time at Mary Hopson, who stood well back from the inner cell and close to the outer door. Hopson's face showed a clear compassion, and a tear spilled out onto her cheek. I stood still, my back against an outer wall, and observed without comment. I was stunned by the attractiveness of the woman prisoner. Even disheveled by sleep in her loose-fitting prison garb, it was clear that she was a beauty. *In a minute I'll know what's going on. Whatever our letter writer was trying to do, this is where it will happen.*

"Do I know you?" Wickham asked, looking back and forth at the two of us.

Finally Mary answered, "I'm Mary Hopson, Helen. Do you remember me? You wanted to see me."

Wickham stood in silence and studied the woman a few feet away from her. At last she nodded, blushed, and looked away. "With Dr. Townby. I knew you in Morton Graves. Is that right?"

"Yes," she answered softly, "with Dr. Townby. You wanted to see me, Helen." She nodded in my direction and I saw that she, too, was blushing. "That's what *they* told me."

Wickham narrowed her eyes. "Why am I in here? This is a prison cell, I think, not a confinement room at Morton Graves." She turned toward me. "Who are you?"

"I just brought Mary here to see you."

"Why? Where *is* 'here'?" Her question, though ridiculous, seemed oddly honest.

When I made no reply, Mary started to answer, but checked herself. "*Did* you want to see me, Helen?" she asked.

The prisoner stared at her for a moment before answering. "I don't think so. I can't be sure. I can't remember anything. They won't tell me anything. I shouted and shouted at them, but they still won't tell me anything. One of them told me this wasn't a courtroom—said it wouldn't do no good carrying on in here. I don't know what she meant." Helen said this while moving her eyes back and forth, looking first at one of us, then at the other. "The jailer said last night that this was January of 1922. Is that the truth?"

I was fascinated by what I was hearing. Here was a murderess who would hang within a week. Yet she seemed to want me to believe that she wasn't sure where she was. Neither Mary nor I made a sound.

"It's because of that lady at my flat, isn't it?" Helen Wickham asked in a whisper. "She died, didn't she?"

"Yes, Helen," Mary answered. "Don't you remember?" Then she

turned to me, "She doesn't remember, Captain. They can't do this! It's not right—this can't be legal! She doesn't *know*, I tell you."

"Do what?" Wickham spoke aloud. "They can't do what?"

I maintained my silence and watched.

Mary turned back to face the prisoner, her head lowered and her eyes filled with tears. "How do you feel, Helen? Are you well? Are you sick?"

"They're going to hang me," she stated rather than asked. "It's because of that lady who came to my flat. Do I have solicitors? Do I have a barrister? Have I been tried, Mary?"

Again Mary Hopson turned away from Wickham and faced me. "You can't let them do this, Captain Baker. You see how she is. This isn't legal! It isn't bloody legal! You see how she is?"

I stood rigidly but silently and returned her gaze. Whatever their game might be, I had no intention of playing it with them.

Mary Hopson stepped closer to me and raised a clenched fist. "Well, by God, *I* see how she is! And I *bloody* well won't keep quiet about it! Damn me if I do! You can't hang this woman, Captain— she's insa——" She lowered her voice to a faint whisper, "She's not well! You know! It's against the law, and you bloody well know it's against the law!"

Helen Wickham had begun to shake violently and sat back down on her bunk. Then she pulled her feet up under her and turned her face into the pillow.

Mary turned toward the prisoner. "I won't let them do it, Helen. So help me, I'll tell the newspapers while there's still time." She whirled around to face me, but when she saw my impassive stare, she straightened and froze, as if another idea had suddenly occurred to her. Her face changed from rage to fear.

I didn't speak. *This is what I was meant to see, then. Somehow they plan to pull off the insanity plea, even now. Somehow they're in this together, these two and several more. Somehow they knew they could get someone in here to witness this—someone respectable. No, of course they thought they'd get Conan Doyle himself. Who are these people? Surely they know that it's too late. What are they trying to do?*

Then Mary Hopson spoke again, and her words didn't seem to fit the scenario that I had just constructed in my mind. "What will happen to *me* now, Captain? Now that I've seen this and . . . ?" Her face gave every appearance of genuine fear. "Can I leave here now?"

I still said nothing. *Nothing has happened here. What have I failed to see? I came expecting to see something that would explain . . . but nothing.* I carefully examined the room and the cell. Hopson and Wickham had never been closer than six feet apart. I had commanded an unobstructed view of the space between them and had heard every word. *Do they just want me—or Conan Doyle—as a witness?* I turned and walked to the door and rapped on it once.

The guard outside held her key up to the window, and I nodded. In a few seconds we stood in the outer corridor. Mary Hopson kept her head down and was silent.

"Are we through, then?" whispered the jailer.

"Yes," I answered, "we're leaving now." I turned to face Mary Hopson. "Unless there's something else you wanted to say . . . do?"

She stared at me with a puzzled expression. "You're the one who knows what we're doing, Captain, not me. I'm more than ready to go."

The jailer nodded and said, "Wait here a minute. I've got to get my partner to take you back down." She walked quickly away from us and down the long corridor.

"What's going to happen to me now, Captain?" Mary asked in a whisper.

I still refrained from an answer. I didn't have one, in the first place, and it seemed more likely that she had an answer than that I did.

"I'm not going to say anything to anyone, Captain, honest to God," she continued with a little voice in her whisper. Her eyes were anxiously riveted on my face.

She's very good at this. I'm going to find, when I investigate this—and I will—that she's an actress, not a seamstress. Time is short—I'll be called before this day is out. We can expect to be called by barristers making a last appeal for Helen Wickham's life. Maybe the call will be from the tabloids. Maybe both.

By the time the guard returned to let us through the door to the staircase, Mary was weeping openly. Her sobs echoed through the stairwell as we descended the two flights to the street door. The second guard looked unhappily at me as he let us through to the street. As Mary Hopson stepped through the doorway and started toward the car, the guard put his hand on my sleeve.

"Hold on," he said. "Let me offer you a word, gov'nor. Don't be taken in by that bit up there. It ain't like it seems."

"How's that?" I asked, stepping back into the building with him.

"This is just her latest act, gov'nor. She's got a lot of 'em, see? And we've seen 'em all."

"Such as what?" I asked. "What one is this?"

"This here's her insanity-plea act; you can see that plain. Somethin' like the one she done in court, I guess. But she's got others. If you's to go up there, just you, mind, without the lady, you'd likely see another of 'em." He winked at me and touched his finger to his cheek just under his eye.

"What do you mean?"

"You're a man o' th' world, gov'nor, man who can pay his way in here this mornin'. You know what I mean. She's got some acts that're pretty common, I can tell you, and she'll try 'em on anybody."

"On guards, you mean."

"On guards, man or woman, on a vicar, even on a priest."

I showed real interest. "You don't say? You mean . . . well, what could she do in that cell, man?"

"I know she used to slip her knickers off from under her shift and hide 'em under the mattress when clergy was comin'. Find ways t' let it show, you know. That guard up there used to spy her doin' that through the door—when company was comin', you might say. Scared that little priest near out of his skin, they say. And she tried leanin' up against any man who ever worked in there. Talkin' low-like. Even tried it on a matron of the guards," he said with a wink. "Damme if I don't think she had that one pegged right. But don't you be fooled none, gov'nor. This here last couple of days is just one more try. I don't know who you are or what you're up to, but she'll make a fool of you soon enough if you'll let her. Just a word to the wise. You done me a good turn with that bit in the envelope. I'm just tryin' to return th' favor."

"And I hear what you're saying. Thanks," I replied. "Didn't seem to do her any good—no one has come to break her out of here."

"No, that's all she got was sympathy, I guess, 'specially from the young priest. He took to spendin' a lot o' time wi' Wickham here lately."

"I'd like to talk to him. What's his name?"

"Father Kelly, young bloke from the local parish."

"Do you think he's doing her any good?"

"Thought so until yesterday. It was just after he left she got like she is now—wild-like. I guess he ain't helpin' her so much after all."

I nodded and stepped back out into the cold, feeling guilty that I'd kept Mary waiting outside.

Neither Mary nor I spoke during the long miles back to West London, and eventually she stopped sobbing. When we had come to a stop at the curb in front of her tiny shop, still in the freezing, predawn gloom, she opened her door and got out without looking at me. She stood facing her little storefront, her left hand resting on the door of the Morris. Slowly she turned and leaned over to peer at me under the flimsy canvas roof. She was weeping again, silently this time, and her pale eyes were huge in her anxious, gray face. She spoke in a desperate whisper that was clear as a church bell.

"Please, for God's sake, tell them, Captain. I won't say nothing. Nothing!"

I handed Mary Hopson a folded ten-pound note, nodded as if agreeing to her request, and drove away.

I wondered what was going on and who these people were. How did they find out about that sketchbook of Doyle's? How many hours would it be before the hue and cry to release Helen Wickham began? What made her so important to someone that they would set all this into motion?

9

"I would call your attention to the curious incident of the dog in the night-time."

"The dog did nothing in the night-time."

"That is the curious incident."

—"The Adventure of Silver Blaze"

I WAS AWAKENED LATER that day by a knocking at my door. I had to get up and walk into the sitting room to answer. I was afraid it would be a newspaper reporter, but it was Conan Doyle who stood at the door.

"What happened, Charles?" he asked as he entered the room. His tweed suit made quite a contrast with my bathrobe-over-underwear ensemble.

"You mean at the prison?" I asked, thinking that the tabloids might have accosted him already.

"Of course, at the prison! What else could I mean?" he asked impatiently.

I took a deep breath, settled into the creaking window chair in front of the desk, and thought about my answer. No shortcuts—he needed to know all. "Maybe nothing yet. And nothing much happened at the prison, either. Have a seat," I said as I gestured toward my best chair. I described every word and every detail of what had taken place at His Majesty's Prison, Holloway. Then I explained what I guessed was the purpose of it.

He listened without comment, and when I finished, he still did not speak. After a moment of silence I continued, "I don't understand. Last

Tuesday you got a letter saying that it was imperative that this visit be made. One week later, the actual visit seems meaningless."

"Astounding, Charles!" He paused, clearly running the whole scenario through his mind. "And you think that's what it was, a ploy to get me to work for a stay of execution?"

"That's all I can think of so far," I answered. "I wish I could be more helpful, but this makes no more sense to me now than when it began."

"And they'll try to drag me into it even though I wasn't involved directly," he said angrily.

"A person of your stature would be just the publicity edge they might need if that's what they're after," I agreed.

"A person of my notoriety, you mean, but thanks for not saying so. You think they'll go to the papers—do it that way—or will solicitors call?"

"No telling. Honestly, though, if you could have seen the two of them this morning, you'd have been amazed. They were really convincing. Wickham pretended to realize just now that she was in prison. Hopson seemed shocked and surprised, full of moral indignation. As a crowning touch, she pretended to be afraid that the authorities were going to do something to *her.*"

"This doesn't explain anything to me, really, Charles. How were they able to get that information about my father, and why this elaborate, and risky, way of getting me involved? What if I hadn't gone for it?"

I thought before I made the next remark but decided it needed to be said. "Forgive me, Sir Arthur, but you *did* go for it. It's probably a good bet that they could get you involved if they could promise you a ghost. It's more like a sure thing. If anything could bring you into a controversy, it would be this. Besides, it isn't the first time you've come to the aid of a convicted murderer, and used the press to do it."

"But they didn't try to elicit my support, Charles. They might have tried that first, I would think. They just drew me in!"

"Exactly," I said. "They found a way to make us come to them, and it worked. At least we came to them—I'm not sure that anything else worked, though. What do you want to do now?"

Conan Doyle was silent for a moment before he answered cautiously, "I see nothing we can do but wait and see how they proceed. We're certainly not going to go to anyone with this ourselves. Do you think we can deny involvement in all this?"

"When they come, they'll have all the proof lined up that I was there. They no doubt have enough circumstantial evidence to convince the public that it would have to be you who sent me. That's the only way they could use you, and apparently it's you they mean to use."

Quietly, and without much conviction in his voice, he muttered, "The possibility remains that the letter is actually from Dr. Gussmann." I said nothing, so he went on, "Well, whatever his—their—next move is, it's got to be soon, though. Helen Wickham hangs on Friday."

"I'm surprised we haven't heard anything already, but the evening editions aren't out yet," I said. "Look, Sir Arthur, if, by some miracle, this actually was engineered by Gussmann, something went wrong."

"If, on the other hand, this is more of a publicity move, as you think it is, the papers are their most likely avenue, don't you think?" he asked.

"Mary Hopson is the one who mentioned the papers. I think I'd bring out the barristers if I were doing this because it's not lawful to hang an insane prisoner. She mentioned that, too, so I can't guess what they'll do. They're damned clever, though. We've got to give them that."

"Bloody invasion of privacy! Had to get into my private library—Dad's sketchbooks—to do this." He was almost shouting. Then he spoke more quietly, "Clever, though, as you say. Cost me about a hundred pounds so far, and I didn't have the slightest idea what I was even looking into. I'll get them back in the end, you can bet."

I looked at the clock. "It's past two, Sir Arthur. Early editions will be out anytime. We may know something soon. Call me if you hear anything. I'll be in, except to go out for the papers."

"About the sketchbook," he persisted, "we still haven't answered anything. They couldn't have just *seen* the sketchbook! The scrap they described wasn't even with the sketchbook. Only Gussmann ever saw that fragment. Even if someone secretly got hold of that sketchbook . . ."

"You're still expecting that ghost, Sir Arthur."

There was a pause while he apparently decided to react to this, and then he chuckled softly. "And you didn't see one at Holloway?" He laughed. "Are you sure, my boy?"

"No. What I saw was . . . I don't know."

Sir Arthur seemed to turn this over in his mind before looking at me piercingly and asking me the same question I'd been asking myself since leaving the prison: "In that case, Charles, who exactly are we talking about? If this is a conspiracy to release a murderess, who is behind it?"

I shook my head. Having thought about it for much of the morning, I was no closer to an answer. "Perhaps the tabloids will soon tell us."

Since there was nothing further we could do at the moment, Conan Doyle took his leave, promising to call as soon as there were developments.

After our conversation, I tried to imagine what might happen next. I conjured up images of being hounded by reporters like myself. I wondered if any of them would drag Adrianna into this. I hoped that no one had found out about our weekend together. It would be the cruelest of ironies to get crucified in the tabloids for a tryst I had never even been able to have.

But there was not a word in the early editions, and by seven o'clock it was clear that whatever plot there was to stay the execution of Helen Wickham, it wasn't going to make the Tuesday evening papers. At eight I went out for dinner at Lancers. When I returned three-quarters of an hour later with a fresh bottle of brandy, Adrianna was in the lobby, sitting by the fire.

She rose as I entered. "You didn't call. I said to call me around ten, and you didn't."

All I could do was slap my palm to my forehead and shrug my shoulders. "I was asleep."

"It's been a big day for me, Charlie. How about you?"

"Nothing much, really. What happened to you? Come on up and tell me about it," I said as I turned toward the lift.

She matched her stride to mine. "Don't hold out on me, Charlie. I know you weren't at your office all day. Where were you?"

"I'm going to tell you, Adrianna, but you go first. Nothing exciting happened to me. I want to hear your news."

"Wait until I get settled down with a brandy," she said. We continued in silence until we were in my rooms and I had turned up the gas flame in the small grate. She sat down, slipped off her shoes and tucked her trim feet under her. Looking greatly pleased with herself, she started her tale.

"Well, Dr. Dodds, chief of staff, was certainly interested in me. Or rather, he was certainly interested in anything to do with the finances of Dr. Gussmann. He told me quite frankly that there had been irregularities involving Gussmann's estate and that the hospital had an interest in finding out more about his former holdings. He had researched their files, and no record of any land in Scotland was among their papers. Of course, I knew that."

I handed Adrianna her drink and then walked over and opened a desk drawer. I took out a spare key to my rooms and delivered it to her. "It probably would be better if you had this instead of sitting down in the lobby. Fewer people will see you." She took the key without comment. Then I sat down in the chair facing hers and asked, "What's your impression of Dodds?"

"He's an arrogant doctor, but there's nothing secretive about him. He said that at one time Gussmann had willed his entire fortune to the hospital. Then he had changed his will and left the hospital a small endowment, with the remainder going to his patient William Townby and a small sum to his personal secretary. The hospital didn't know about the change until Gussmann died. It was so unusual that they thought for a while of contesting the later will, but their solicitors advised them against it. Apparently the will was solidly legal."

"Did he tell you anything about Townby?"

"I said that maybe somehow the papers about our Scottish land had gone to Townby or to Alice Tupper, Gussmann's private secretary. I asked how I could contact them. Dodds came right out and told me that Townby was currently a patient there in the hospital. He said they *might* agree to my seeing Townby with one of their doctors present. There was the strong implication that he thought something was crooked about Townby—that he'd engineered the inheritance somehow. I tried to charm a little more out of Dodds, but he said he really couldn't discuss a patient."

"And the secretary?"

"He said he'd heard Alice Tupper was dead. He thought that was two or three years ago. I don't think he actually knew her, certainly not very well."

"So where do things stand now? Will he see you again?" I asked.

"I told him I was expecting the arrival this week of one of my uncle's solicitors, lawyers from the United States, and that I'd call and make an appointment to visit again. He seemed pleased enough at that. You'll be the lawyer. Think you can handle it, Charlie?"

"If he'll be expecting a hick from the States, I can be that," I answered. "I really want to get to Townby. He might be behind all this. Obviously, he at least knew Gussmann well. We're sure he knows Wickham and Hopson and some of the others. He may know all of them."

"I was only able to visit briefly with my friend Ann, and I couldn't think of any way to get her to say more about any of the patients. She wanted to know more about my uncle and the land in Scotland." Adrianna leaned forward in her chair. "I've waited long enough now. What happened? Did you get in at Holloway?"

I told her the entire story, including the fact that no call had yet been made to either Conan Doyle or myself and that the newspapers were silent concerning Wickham.

Adrianna listened intently and then replied, "I don't think you'll hear anything like that. I think something else was supposed to happen, and it just hasn't." She sat back with an air of confidence.

"Something like what?" I asked. "I'm ready for any theory just now."

"I don't know. Something to do with Arthur? Surely they—whoever *they* are—might have been expecting him to go there himself. You didn't notice a ghost lurking about, did you?"

"Very funny. You can bet I looked for one. For that matter, there probably are plenty of them there. But nothing happened. The two women, Hopson and Wickham, scarcely even looked at each other, but they knew each other well; that was obvious. We were in the room with Wickham for a little over seven minutes, that's all. The only theory I have come up with is that I—actually Conan Doyle—was supposed to see a convincing scene in which it would be clear that an insane woman is about to hang. He would have to do something about that if he saw it."

"I don't think so. Something else was supposed to happen and it didn't, that's what I think. Whoever tried to send Sir Arthur there was expecting something else to happen. Maybe you took the wrong person from the list. Maybe you weren't supposed to be able to get Mary Hopson."

"Wait for the morning papers," I answered. "You'll see—there'll be a new appeal for Helen Wickham."

"I wish I could wait *here* for the morning papers, Charlie, but I've got to go soon. Freddy had to go out. He asked that I be home by ten." Unfolding her elegant legs, she put her feet on the floor.

I pulled Adrianna gently up out of her chair and squeezed her shoulders. I wished things could be different, but there was no reason to say anything. Adrianna Wallace had married Frederick Wallace, member of Parliament, three years too early for me. They both had their reasons, and the arrangement had been a good one for them so far. Now it was too late. Even if she'd been willing to renege on her deal with Freddy, divorce was nearly impossible. The whole situation ran through my mind that clearly and logically.

Adrianna said it all one more time: "Things aren't so bad, Charlie. We cooperate pretty well. Freddy lives up to his end of the bargain, and I live up to mine. Maybe you and I met a little late, but things could be a lot worse for us."

"At least we met," I said. "Maybe we're meant to find a way to make it better."

Adrianna looked at me as if I were a child in need of correction. "Hasn't life taught you anything? We're *meant*? Nothing out there *means* anything for us, Captain Baker. We might mean to do one thing or another ourselves, but let's not lay the responsibility out there in the universe."

Two minutes later, she was gone.

As I prepared for bed, I wondered if I agreed with her. I had never interpreted my life as a string of chance happenings in a neutral universe. It had been more pleasing to me to think in terms of choices and consequences. While I thought it was true that we made most choices on the basis of too little information, they were still choices. I especially wanted to think that Adrianna and I still had choices in front of us and that if we made the right ones, we'd get what we wanted. I had to admit to myself, though, that to choose correctly, I had to know what I wanted—and what she wanted. About *that*, I was not so sure.

10

"I have usually found that there was method in his madness."

"Some folk might say there was madness in his method."

—"The Adventure of the Reigate Squire"

I SEARCHED THE WEDNESDAY morning editions looking for some mention of Helen Wickham and any plea for commutation based on her insanity. At worst, of course, there could also have been mention of Conan Doyle or of me or Adrianna. Instead, I read that Irish author Liam O'Flaherty and a group of dissidents had occupied the Rotunda in Dublin. Police felt that the situation was under control.

There was mention of a vigil that was to be held by a group that opposed capital punishment, but nothing related to the conditions of this execution in particular. So far, at least, the game didn't involve breaking that kind of story to the newspapers. No reporters or solicitors had called me, and as far as I knew, none had called Sir Arthur. Whatever the writer of the mysterious letter had hoped to accomplish with his list of names, whatever the visit to Helen Wickham had been meant to do, nothing had happened yet.

At ten o'clock it began to rain while I was driving the Morris westward on Upper Richmond Road toward the river, and I had to slow to a crawl. The window glass was totally obscured by rain, and every cart and car on the street had come to a near halt. The fit of the fabric top admitted not only wind, but some rain as well.

I tried to figure out what was happening. Was Mary Hopson supposed to see something I couldn't see? Hear something I didn't understand? Was Helen Wickham? Was the jail matron involved? I crept forward, never getting above first gear for half an hour.

If Robert Stanton was in his boat shop on Hardwick Road in Ham this morning, I intended to meet him. I wasn't sure what I hoped to accomplish there, but since my trip to Holloway Prison with Mary Hopson had proven useless, I wanted at least to meet the other two people whose names had appeared in the letter. His had been the second name, and Liza Anatole's had been the third.

I drove to the side of the road and reviewed my notes. Robert Stanton was about forty, a boat builder who lived and worked in a small shop in Ham near the Thames. He built small sailboats and dinghies, and worked without employees. As was the case with Mary Hopson, Sir Arthur had learned that the local constable knew Robert Stanton. It was noted that he frequently closed up his shop and went on vacation for days at a time with a simple notice in the window. He had once been held on suspicion of interfering with teenage girls in Richmond Park. No coherent testimony could be obtained, and he had been released pending further investigation. Nothing had ever come of the case, nor had there been further incidents of that nature. He had twice been arrested and held on charges of disorderly conduct in taverns.

Perhaps if I'd chosen one of the other two names for my first contact, things would have been different at the meeting with Helen Wickham. There was no possibility that I could now take Robert Stanton to the death-row cell, but I hoped that further events would unfold that might shed more light on the whole mystery. It could do no harm at least to be able to recognize Robert Stanton and Liza Anatole on sight. If they were involved in this game, whatever it was, I wanted to have the advantage of recognizing them, too.

The rain eased just as I finally managed to turn south on Petersham Road. Two miles farther on, I turned right onto the Common and passed St. Michael's Convent as I again headed west toward the Thames. I pulled to the curb and consulted my map, then continued straight across Ham Street. A few blocks and a few turns later, I sat looking through light drizzle at Stanton's Boats, a small shop just off the corner of Riverside Drive and Hardwick Road.

I had decided to present myself to Stanton as a customer who wanted a boat built, so I walked up to the shop prepared to begin in that vein. The shop door was closed and locked, however, and a sign hung in the window saying that the proprietor was out. I noted that the sign was a professionally printed one intended for regular use, rather than some hasty scrawl on a piece of paper. It was printed on heavy card stock and had a neatly punched hole in its center top. Moreover, a small brad had been driven into the inside frame of a windowpane just above the sign so it could be placed in the window easily. No doubt this proprietor frequently went out during business hours. As to what those business hours might be, there was no clue to be found. Unlike so many businesses that informed the public as to their normal hours of commerce, Stanton's Boats apparently wished to remain somewhat mysterious in that regard.

"You looking for Bob?" asked a boy who suddenly appeared behind me.

I spun around, startled by the unexpected and somewhat loud voice, and saw a youth in his early teens standing curbside with a push broom balanced over his shoulder. In spite of the light, continuing rain, the lad wore only his work clothes and a wool cap. "Yes, I'm hoping to get Mr. Stanton to work on a boat for me," I answered. "I seem to have missed him, though. Any idea when he'll open up?"

"Barely missed him," the young man said. "He headed round to Lock Road just as the rain was letting up—maybe five minutes ago. I seen him inside the shop." The youth shrugged in the direction of a large hardware store on the opposite side of Riverside Drive. "Could be he's heading to Ham Gate. He often walks over there. Surprised you didn't see him when you drove down. I saw you come in that way. I noticed the car, see. My dad used to have a little Oxford like that."

I remembered that there had been a pedestrian walking in the rain near St. Michael's. The tall man in a dark coat had been huddled under a good umbrella and was walking eastward. "I wouldn't know Bob," I said. "We've never met. Did he have an umbrella?"

"It was raining harder then. He's got his umbrella; do you think he's daft as me? He was wearing a good watch coat, too. Ham Gate's more'n a mile from here. If he's going there, you'll catch him easy. Even in that car, you'd catch him easy." The boy suddenly swung the broom down from his shoulder, stepped over to the doorway of the boat shop, and leaned the handle against the wall. "Hey, you let me drive you the way he went, and I'll point Bob out to you if he's along the street. I'll walk back."

I thought about how badly I'd wanted to drive cars when I was younger—and cars were much more rare. I couldn't see how it could hurt to let the lad drive the Morris a little. Maybe he'd prove to be a good source of information about Stanton. "I'm not sure I want to bother him on his walk," I said, "but maybe you could just point him out to me. You can drive over, and I'll bring you back here. What about your boss?" I gestured toward the store up the street.

The boy seemed to weigh that question in his mind for a moment. "Dad's always telling me to be helpful to everyone—good for business. I'll tell him you asked me to show you where to find Ham Gate."

A minute later we were driving eastward. The Morris Oxford had reached the midpoint of Ham Common before we saw the pedestrian I had noticed earlier.

"That's Bob there ahead," the boy said. "You want me to introduce you?"

"No, thanks for the offer, but I really don't want to disturb him on his walk. Turn around when you can and take me back. I can catch Mr. Stanton at his shop later."

"Whatever you say. I can turn right on Church Road up here in a minute. It'll turn right around and go back to Upper Ham—Petersham Road."

We drove past Stanton with his large black umbrella folded under the arm of his sturdy watch coat and turned right a hundred yards beyond him, as the boy had suggested.

Within ten minutes I was alone in the car again and heading east toward Ham Gate. When I parked the car at Parkgate House, just outside the gate I could see Stanton walking into the park fifty yards ahead. Shortly after I was through the gate myself, I could see that he was turning north. On an impulse, I stepped up my pace and began to close the distance between us. When I had come to within twenty yards of my target, I called out, "Hey there, Mr. Stanton!"

The man ahead of me stopped and turned. He was not only taller than I was by several inches, he was also solidly built. He seemed to study me as he spoke in return, "Do I know yer, sir?"

I was nearly beside him when I replied, "No, Mr. Stanton. I was just by your shop, and a young man was good enough to suggest I might find you here in the park. I wanted to talk to you about building a boat." I was a little breathless as I continued, "I'm sorry to intrude on your walk, but I didn't know when I might be able to catch you again." I extended my hand. "Charles Baker."

Stanton shook my hand briefly. "Build yer a boat, did yer say?"

"Yes, just a small one."

"Sorry, mate," Stanton said as we continued to walk, "I don't build no custom boats. I don't take no orders for boats, Mr. Baker."

"I'm sorry. I was told you *were* a builder of small boats, Mr. Stanton," I continued. "You were recommended to me by a friend."

"Well, yer friend was right and he uz wrong," Stanton answered. "I do build small boats for sale. Got one finished now, matter of fact, finished her yesterday, but I don't take no orders to build. I never take on custom work, neither. I just build boats that are popular-like, easy to sell. When I'm through 'th one, I put a price on her, put a sign in the window, and I starts another. My boats all sell just the same, and I'm spared from folks wanting their bloody boats done by such-and-such a time—or done in such-and-such a way." He paused and looked at me. "I've just finished a dinghy, though. Haven't even put out the sign. I don't take reservations, neither—same reason—so this one ain't spoke for if yer want her."

"A dinghy," I answered. "Bit smaller than I was thinking of, but maybe. When could I see her?"

"I'll be out walking for a while. Can't say. Maybe yer could find me in around two-thirty or three if nothing takes my fancy and keeps me out. Tell yer what, though, I won't put that sign in the window till you catch me in or until Friday anyway. That way, if I get held up by something and don't get to see yer this afternoon, yer'll still get first look at her." He stopped and extended his hand. The signal was clearly that he didn't plan to share any more of his walk with this potential buyer who had intruded on him already. "Who did yer say recommended me, Mr. Baker?"

I watched Stanton's eyes carefully as I answered, "Actually, it was Sir Arthur Conan Doyle who gave me your name, but he had it from a friend."

"That's mighty odd. 'Course I've heard of him, but I'd be surprised if I know any of his kind. Do yer know who it was told him about my boats?"

I had seen nothing unusual in Stanton's reaction so far. "I think it may have been Mary Hopson or Liza Anatole," I answered slowly, watching carefully.

There seemed to be a moment when Stanton showed some recognition of the names, but after a pause he answered, "Nope, I don't think I know neither of them. Somethin' sounded familiar about the names, but I don't think I know them."

"I'll hope to see you later, then, Mr. Stanton, to consider that dinghy."

Stanton turned away to continue his walk northward. "I'll hold her till Friday, Mr. Baker," he said over his shoulder.

I turned back toward Ham Gate and began to stroll at a leisurely pace. I considered trying to follow Stanton unobserved, but the risk of discovery was too high. That decision made, I walked somewhat more briskly to the car and drove away in search of a pub where I might have a good meal and a pint or two before trying to catch Stanton at his shop later in the afternoon. I didn't know what might be accomplished by pretending to be interested in the dinghy, but at least I'd get to see the inside of the shop.

It was right at noon when I selected a likely pub where there was room to park. The place was fairly busy with noontime trade, but I was able to get a table at a window and spread my map in the light. After some struggle with the index, I discovered that Liza Anatole's address was not far from there. If I continued a couple of miles south and then turned back to the northeast, I would enter Kingston-upon-Thames. Before I'd get to Wimbledon, I would pass Kingston University. It appeared that her address might be on the university grounds, but I couldn't be sure with my map. After a moment's calculation, I decided not to try to fit her into my plans before trying to see Stanton again. The beef sandwich was especially good, and I ordered another wrapped for take-away. The two generous pints of ale were even better, and time passed pleasantly for me as I waited to see Robert Stanton at the boat shop. Roaming around the outer boroughs and drinking pints sure beat working at my AP desk. I wondered what kind of job change I might make so that every day was like this.

At quarter to three I again drove to the curb in front of the boat shop and could see immediately that "The Proprietor Is Out" still hung in the front window, but the door was ajar, and the shop lights were on. When I entered the shop, Robert Stanton was counting money at a table well back from the front of the shop. A small iron safe stood open a few feet away from him. I guessed, before Stanton turned to place his body between me and the safe, that what I had seen was at least a hundred pounds.

"I will be right with you, sir. I've got to finish this up," Stanton said. He put something in his coat pocket and walked to the safe with a small box. This he locked inside the safe and turned toward me. "What can I do for you, sir?"

"I came to look at the dinghy," I answered, moving several feet closer to Stanton.

"Dinghy?" Stanton looked carefully at me and then turned around and looked toward the rear of the shop. A freshly painted boat was turned keel-up on support stands about twenty feet away. The dinghy's hull was a gleaming white, and her gunwale was a bright green. No other boat was in sight. He turned back toward me. "You mean this little boat, dinghy? It is not yet finished." The craftsman was smiling pleasantly and looking directly at me. "Come back in a few days—Monday—and it might be finished."

It seemed that Stanton didn't remember our conversation of about three hours earlier, yet that talk had taken place at close range and in good light. I took a second to evaluate the illumination in the shop now and concluded that I should be perfectly recognizable in this light. "When we spoke earlier, you said I could be the first to look at the dinghy, Mr. Stanton. I expected to have the first opportunity to buy it this afternoon."

Stanton looked puzzled at first, then his face relaxed into a rather theatrical smile. "I, er, yes. That was earlier, but I had to go out after that, and I was unable to finish it, the boat, after all. I am sorry, I really could not show it to you until Monday, Mr. ah . . ."

"Charles—"

"Oh, yes, Mr. Charles, is it?" Stanton interrupted before I could finish introducing myself. "When I told you earlier you could see it today, I expected to finish it, but I could not. I had to go out on an errand. I cannot show it to you now. I am sorry."

"But this morning—"

"I don't show a boat until it is quite finished to my satisfaction. I know you will understand, Mr. Charles, and I *will* give you the first opportunity to buy it. I will put a note on it saying, 'Hold for Mr. Charles.' Unfortunately, I must go out again now. The little boat, it will be finished by Monday." Stanton took my sleeve and began to lead me toward the door.

I was disoriented for a moment. Stanton should have been expecting me. When we had talked in the park before noon, the man had seemed standoffish about his boat business, but nothing weird like this. Then I remembered that Stanton was a former mental patient in Morton Graves Voluntary Hospital. I had no idea what his mental condition was or how it was manifest. Perhaps he had little or no memory or had multiple personalities. That could explain the peculiar way he ran his business and his inability to remember the names of his customers. We were nearly at the door when I spoke again. "Did you remember Miss Hopson or Miss Anatole, Robert?"

Stanton's hand dropped from my arm. "What did you say?" His eyes narrowed as he looked at me. "What did you say, Mr. Charles?" he repeated.

"When I mentioned earlier that you may have been recommended by Mary Hopson or Liza Anatole, you couldn't remember them. I just wondered if you had recalled them since we spoke."

Stanton said nothing for just a bit too long before he replied, "No, I do not recall them—as I said earlier, I do not remember those names. Where did you say you had met them, Mr. Charles?" I was more aware than before of Stanton's size and power. He seemed cautious now, perhaps angry. There was an intensity about him that had not been there until this moment. I felt his sudden interest as almost a vibration.

"I haven't met them," I said. Suddenly I felt I should be very cautious—that I had overstepped by mentioning the others on the list. "They were mentioned to me as people who might have been the ones who said you build good boats. A man in a pub near here, over by Ham Common, was telling me you were a good man to come to for a boat. I was asking around about boats. When I asked him who could recommend your work, he mentioned this Mary and Liza. He said it might have been one of them who had said you build good boats. It's not important, really." I kept my eyes on Stanton's face. For the first time since this whole business had begun, I was seeing the kind of reaction I was looking for. There was no question about it: the names had obtained a strong reaction. Stanton was clearly agitated and thinking fast.

"No, this is very interesting, Mr. Charles. As it happens, I have not ever sold any boats to any women, not with those names or any other names. I wonder why a man would say that. Over here by Ham Common, on Upper Ham Road?" He looked straight into my eyes. "Did this man know me himself?"

I looked down at Stanton's large, calloused hands. I was not sure, but they appeared to be tensed. "No, I don't think he knew you. I wouldn't worry about it, Mr. Stanton. No doubt it's good to be recommended around the neighborhood. I should think that would be good for business." I tried to remember things I had heard about the insane. This man wasn't acting at all like he had earlier.

Stanton took a step back and continued to study my face before he answered, "Certainly it is good to be recommended, but there are some women not far from here . . . Well, when people are saying one's name around, one has to be concerned about what *kind* of woman is talking. Pardon me, Mr. Charles, may I ask what it is that you do? You are an American, are you not?"

"Yes, a lawyer, actually. I live in London now. Not everyone can tell I'm an American."

"No, you are wrong, Mr. Charles. I think everyone can tell. And you want a boat. Why?" Stanton's piercing gaze never left me for a moment.

Multiple personalities. There's some theory about this. That's what it is about Stanton. He's not quite the same man he was earlier. This side of him seems more dangerous and smarter. "Oh, I . . . just with the river here, I might like to have a boat. I got to asking around, and your name came up."

"At that pub on Upper Ham Road?" he asked skeptically.

"Yes."

Stanton continued to gaze directly into my eyes. He even leaned forward and tilted his face downward into more direct alignment with my own, as if studying, memorizing, my face. "Well, I will hold the boat for you, Mr. Charles," he said at last. "It will be ready on Monday, but I really have to bid you good day now. I mustn't be late for an appointment." Stanton stepped forward as I backed out of the shop. Then he closed the door and locked it from inside.

I could hardly stand there peering through the windows, so I walked to the Morris and drove away. *He knew those names, and they rang an alarm for him. This will get things rolling. Now he is wondering if*

I know what they are all doing. Maybe he even thinks I do know what they are doing. Keep a sharp eye behind you, Charlie boy.

As I opened the door to my flat at four-thirty, I knew from the aroma of onion and garlic that Adrianna had been in my kitchen. That was only partly correct; she was still in the tiny kitchen area and was being none too quiet about it. Drawers were rattling, cupboard doors were banging, a skillet was scraping across the hob. She did not hear me approach behind her and was startled to see my hand reach out to capture a morsel from the skillet that held all her attention.

"Oh, Charles! You're lucky I wasn't still chopping things up when you did that. You'd have a knife in your arm for sure."

"Sorry. How is it that you have the chance to be here cooking? Home by seven, the latest, is pretty much the house rule, isn't it?"

"Permission asked and granted. Freddy said he'd meet me at the Savoy at ten for drinks. We'll go home from there. He's spending the early evening in his office. He says hi, Charles."

"Hi to him. What's cooking?"

"I think it's going to be a pasta sauce. I'm following a recipe from the *Times*. It's supposed to be authentic Italian. I'm pretty sure I can boil the pasta all right; the rest is more of a gamble. I've got good news: I called Dr. Dodds and told him my family's American lawyer had arrived. We have an appointment for tomorrow at ten to meet him and then meet the mysterious Dr. Townby. How was the trip out to scout Stanton's neighborhood?" She paused in her stirring and pointed me toward two cans of tomatoes that were on the drainboard. "Open those, please."

I took up the task while I answered, "I met him, actually—talked to him twice. We're finally on to something now. I dropped the names of Mary Hopson and Liza Anatole, and it got to him. At first he was able to cover pretty well, but later he was so rattled that he couldn't remember my name. I surprised him in the middle of counting out quite a sum of cash, too. He's up to something, but I haven't any idea what it is. First chance I get I'm going to follow him until I find out what."

"What's he like?" Adrianna asked as she gestured impatiently for the tomato cans. "Does he act crazy or anything?"

"Yes, actually, but he's not stupid. He's a big man, strong-looking. Seems like he can talk different dialects. At least he can sound like an uneducated laborer and then sound more refined and polished. He got confused, though, and mixed them on me. He could be a dangerous guy. Just a feeling I had."

"A strong feeling?"

"Definitely. He was upset and cautious, but there was something else, too. I wouldn't want him around behind me in the dark."

"And you're not planning on letting him get there," Adrianna said more as an instruction than as a question.

"No. We've got him wondering if we're a step ahead of him now. I plan to keep it that way. After we go to Morton Graves tomorrow, I want to spend some time behind *his* back, though. He knows what's going on, I think, and he's not the only one."

"And you didn't see a ghost? Charlie, I don't think you're finding what Sir Arthur wants you to find. Are you sure you're trying?"

"I look for ghosts everywhere I go, Adrianna."

11

There is nothing more deceptive than an obvious fact.

—"The Boscombe Valley Mystery"

WHILE WE WAITED OUTSIDE Dr. Dodds's office in Morton Graves Voluntary Hospital, Adrianna scanned the Thursday morning paper she had found in the lobby. "Listen, Charles, we'd better all sell our cars. Once people read this, the price of petrol will jump again."

"What's that?" I asked.

"The United States Geological Survey has published its conclusion that the American oil supply will be completely exhausted in twenty years."

"Really?" I asked. "By 1942? How would they know something like that?"

"Remember that you read it in Thursday's *Times,* Charles. You've been scooped. Is that the word?" She lowered her voice, "Oops! I forgot. You're supposed to be a barrister."

"Lawyer," I said. I looked as much like an attorney as I could, which meant that my best suit was freshly pressed. It was a London-tailored suit, but I figured that a U.S. lawyer might have a suit made in London. I also hoped that the British hospital administrator might not notice the difference. Adrianna and I sat waiting for Dr. Dodds in the outer office of the administrative suite at Morton Graves Voluntary Hospital until he came out of his own office to meet us.

"Mrs. Wallace," he said as he nodded at Adrianna and extended his hand, "as I said before, your newspaper photos do not do you justice. I'm so pleased to see you again." He turned toward me, "And Mr. Baker, so glad to meet you. I'm Douglas Dodds, chief of staff, for what that's worth. Won't you come in?"

The three of us entered his inner office and settled into very comfortable surroundings considering that this front building of the institution tried to give every impression of being five hundred years old. The early conversation reestablished the story that Adrianna had told earlier: I was a family attorney from New York and was here seeking to clear up a property matter that involved the deceased Dr. Gussmann.

"I understand from Mrs. Wallace that you have a patient who was also once a doctor here, and that he may be somehow involved in Dr. Gussmann's estate. I admit I'm a little confused about that, Dr. Dodds." I said. "Could you explain that to me?"

"It's certainly confusing enough, even for us here, Mr. Baker. Let me start with the situation as it was more than twenty years ago. Dr. Gussmann was quite a successful neurologist in Scotland—quite well known. He specialized in cases of serious depression and was very effective in administering hypnotherapy for such patients. We invited him to join us straightaway when he applied to work here, even though he must have been nearly seventy at that time. Though I didn't often agree with his methods, I don't hesitate to say that he was one of the most brilliant neurologists I've ever known, right to the last. He died here—well, he collapsed here—in 1909." Dodds began to pack a pipe.

I glanced at Adrianna, who kept her eyes on the doctor's face with a pleasant, mildly interested expression on her own. She looked for all the world like a dutiful niece acting on behalf of family interests. I turned my attention back to Dodds. "You disliked the man personally, I gather."

"I don't believe I said that, but there's no harm in my admitting it after all these years. No, I didn't like Gussmann. He treated his peers as if we were students. He treated staff rudely, to say the least. He managed to combine arrogance about his money with arrogance about being educated and accomplished. Worse than that, now that I'm being frank about it, he had an unprofessional attitude toward the patients. To him, mental patients were somehow defective human beings and therefore beneath normal medical ethics. He didn't make much of a secret of that feeling. Mental patients were just good subjects for experimentation as far as he was concerned."

"He mistreated them?" I asked.

"He certainly wanted to. He frequently argued for permission to use electric shock—we don't do that here. He stressed patients into crying fits. There were rumors that he physically mistreated some, but no charges were made openly."

He shook his head as he continued, "That's why the bequest was such a shock. One of his patients was William Townby, a young fellow who had come to us in a state of nervous collapse in 1907. Appeared to have a remarkable recovery. Apparently Gussmann felt very close to the young man for reasons that escape me. Anyway, when Dr. Gussmann died, it was discovered that he'd left the lion's share of his estate to this patient."

"A large sum?" I asked.

"A bit more than forty thousand pounds, all told. Dr. Gussmann's wealth had accumulated over time. I don't mind admitting it was a shock to me and to everyone else at the hospital. Prior to this, Gussmann had made no secret that he was without heirs and would be leaving most of his estate to Morton Graves, you see. Instead, he specified ten thousand for the hospital, a very generous sum, granted. There also was a nice sum to his private secretary. She retired and lived on it until she died, I think. He left that in cash and securities, with the entire remainder of his holdings to Townby."

"Remarkable," I replied. "I would think that you, the hospital, might have challenged the will. Was Dr. Gussmann himself of sound mind, you think?"

"Sorry to say I think he *was* of sound mind. That's not to say we didn't give thought to a challenge. We thought we might find signs of mental instability in his written work, but what we could find of it was lucid."

"Do you mean that some of his work was missing?" Adrianna asked.

"Quite a lot of it was missing. He was gathering material for a book—had been for years—but no important notes or manuscript have ever turned up. We might have pushed one little point on sanity, but we'd have looked like a bunch of greedy psychiatrists to most people. He'd made this new will months before his death, though we didn't know about it until afterward. It was all in order. In the end our solicitors advised against a challenge. Ten thousand for the hospital was very generous. The income off of that supports a senior position here. We shouldn't complain."

"You said you had one point you might have pushed regarding Gussmann's sanity?" I asked.

The chief of staff looked embarrassed and turned briefly toward Adrianna, who had continued to sit silently and demurely through the discussion so far. He puffed his pipe nervously. "Well . . . delicate matter. Not something to talk about, really. Just say he had a condition that could have given some grounds to question his sanity and let it rest there."

"Do you mean syphilis, Dr. Dodds?" Adrianna said quite directly. "I'm an experienced nurse. You needn't hold back anything on my account. My family does have an interest in Dr. Gussmann's estate, and we'd like to know anything that may have any bearing."

Dodds was clearly surprised by Adrianna's directness and lowered his pipe. "He was syphilitic, yes. And there were rumors—unsubstantiated—of behaviors that could have been unstable. We might have requested an autopsy to examine the corpse for evidence of brain damage, but, honestly, there had been no real indications of that in his behavior. Not the sort of thing we wanted brought up, anyway. Could have done more damage to the hospital than the money could do good, don't you see."

"A hospital can hardly claim that one of its psychiatric doctors is a demented syphilitic, do you mean?" Adrianna said without rancor. "Yes, we can see that. So Gussmann's bequest to William Townby was left unchallenged. What happened then?"

"After that, things were even more remarkable than the discovery of the will had been. Townby was fully recovered; that was no surprise. But straightaway he announced that he was going up to Edinburgh to read in medicine! Claimed to have been inspired by Gussmann. Townby had a degree in engineering—not a good one, but a degree. He certainly had the funds to go to school if that's what he wanted. So away he went."

"Was most of his bequest in cash?" I asked.

"Much of it was, but he owned a nice home here in Richmond-upon-Thames and some rental property as well. Over the course of his time at Edinburgh, he sold all that off—sold it well, too. Converted everything to cash and bearer bonds and the like. I know because he asked for my recommendation for land agents and securities brokers. I recommended Willoughby and Martin, Limited, men from my club." He paused a moment. "Well, they kept me informed, you know. I felt I had a right to know what was happening to the estate. Anyway, Townby read medicine like a genius. Stood for his degree and did some specialty internships in neurology. Gussmann had died in 1909, and by early in 1913 Townby was at our door looking for a position in the very institution where he had been a psychiatric patient."

"And you took him on," I said. "Was there no resistance to that? I mean his being a former patient."

"Certainly there was opposition, but it was unspoken. Frankly, Mr. Baker, some of us felt that he had forty thousand pounds of the hospital's money. It was not out of the question that some of it might come back our way. In truth, some of it did. The new young doctor offered to fund a five-thousand-pound research grant here if he was accepted. This is a voluntary hospital, Mr. Baker. Do you know what that means?"

"I presume it means that the staff are largely volunteers," I said, even though I knew that was not correct.

"No, it means that the sources of *funding* are voluntary. For instance, we are named after Morton Graves, the philanthropist who funded our first major endowment. Staff here is salaried rather well. Our support, though, comes from endowments, grants, charity drives, and the like. Gussmann had been extremely generous to us, and here was his primary benefactor offering a sizable additional allotment of that same inheritance. He turned out to be a fine doctor, for the most part."

"'For the most part'?" I repeated. "But not entirely a fine doctor, do you mean?"

"We had our differences of opinion—rather strong ones. He was much like Gussmann in his attitude toward patients. His treatment methods could be rough. He wanted to do electric shock—believed in aversion therapy. He could be quite cruel, by my standards. All in all, though, he was an effective psychiatrist."

"Obviously that didn't last," Adrianna said. "He's a patient again now, isn't that what you told me?"

"It is. One day in 1915, he suddenly fell apart again." Dr. Dodds lifted his pipe again and puffed on it until aromatic clouds of smoke all but hid his face. "He was giving a lecture, young Townby was, on invitation from resident staff over at Priory Hospital. I was in attendance myself. In midsentence—mind you, in midsentence—he halted his lecture and stared blankly ahead for what seemed like an eternity. It was probably about twenty or thirty seconds. Then he continued his talk by referring to his notes on the podium, but only for a minute or so. Abruptly, he cut it short. He apologized briefly by saying he was suddenly quite ill. Then he left the dais and walked straight out. Now Priory is better than two miles from here, but he trotted here on foot directly. Less than half an hour after he walked out of that lecture, he was in the wards here. He made some rounds—that is, talked to several of his patients, I'm told. Then he collapsed in a hallway. He's been a patient here ever since."

"That's an amazing story, Dr. Dodds," I said. "And he had returned to his former state of . . . insanity?"

"Not the same as his original breakdown, no. At first he was worse than I had ever seen him. He was suffering from total amnesia and disorientation. After some time, though, he was really quite normal, except that he had lost nearly six years of his life. He has never regained those in the least. He claims he has no memory of being a medical doctor, no memory of medical school, and no memory of receiving the money. Because of the missing money, we've devised some rather elaborate psychological traps to try to catch him lying, but they've all failed. I believe he really has no memory of those years."

"Where is the money? Does he manage that himself?" I asked. "We will want to know what he can tell us about the land, you see."

"There is no money," Dr. Dodds said quietly. "His bank account held fewer than a thousand pounds at the time of his collapse—quite a lot of money, granted, but a small fraction of his worth. The property had been sold, as I said. Whatever securities he had, and there should have been a lot of them, were—are, to this day—missing. He was salaried here and lived within his means as far as anyone could tell. Considering the earnings on the funds, there should still have been in excess of forty thousand deposited somewhere in 1915. We have taken it upon ourselves, with our private funds, to investigate his life in Edinburgh. His expenditures were modest—spent rather too much on the . . . ladies of the evening, but nothing serious. Excuse my frankness, Mrs. Wallace, but I gather you don't want me to mince words. It is my belief that the fortune is intact somewhere. Assuming that he left most of it in the securities he purchased in 1910 and 1911, purchased through men I know personally, the fortune might well have increased substantially."

I let out a near-whistle of exhaled breath. "That would pay three or four times a professional salary and never touch principal. And it's gone?" I studied the face of the chief of staff and saw there the answer to why the now-recovered William Townby was still confined in Morton Graves. "Is Townby dangerous to himself or anyone else now, Dr. Dodds?"

He looked down for a moment and seemed to be trying to arrange an expression of genuineness. "We think he might be," he said at last.

"And any decision to release him would be up to your staff, am I right?" I asked.

"That particular case is in my hands. Two other senior staff members and I regularly review Townby's case. So far we think he should remain here—"

Adrianna broke in, "Has it been put to him in just that way, Dr. Dodds? Does he know that he could cooperate about all the missing money and probably leave here?" She did not bother to disguise the judgment in her voice. I caught her eye and lifted an eyebrow. She gave a somewhat conciliatory smile and continued, "Forgive me, I'm sure you know what treatment is best for him."

"You are not a nurse in a mental hospital, Mrs. Wallace, am I right?"

"Actually, I am an experienced nurse, Dr. Dodds, but I am not currently working. I was never a nurse in a mental facility, you are right."

"Allow me to admit frankly that we want to know where that money is. Under the circumstances, Morton Graves Voluntary Hospital would certainly be entitled to recover substantial costs if we have been defrauded in some way. That is the confirmed opinion of our solicitors. But that is not why William Townby is still here. He is still here because he is mentally ill and because there are documented discrepancies in his story. Such a man may or may not be dangerous to himself or others. In our judgment there is some risk. Townby is safe here. His living conditions are well above the average."

"Above the average for an asylum, you mean?" Adrianna asked.

The man winced visibly, but focused his eyes steadily on Adrianna's. "He is not being victimized, Mrs. Wallace, he is being treated. As to the matter of the land which was jointly owned by a member of your family and Dr. Gussmann, I have been working in your behalf these past couple of days. No one who was involved in Dr. Gussmann's property can remember any such deed. Two of his investment counselors are deceased, however. I strongly doubt that Mr. Townby will be able, or perhaps I should say willing, to shed any light on the matter. Certainly, though, I would not presume to keep a person of your stature from pursuing every possible avenue of information. Is the property thought to be very valuable?"

Adrianna nodded an affirmative while she formed an answer. "Inquiries are being made up at Glasgow. My uncle is of the opinion that the land may have enough value to make it worth pursuing the matter," she answered convincingly. I knew she was loving the charade.

"May we talk to Townby now, Dr. Dodds?" I asked.

Dr. Dodds looked at each of us in turn, as if he were evaluating the various positives and negatives that might weigh in the balance. Finally he answered, "Of course, Mr. Baker. We're only too glad to assist you in any way we can. I hope our mysterious William Townby can shed some light on your missing document."

12

ON THE WAY TO Townby's room, I assured Dr. Dodds that I would share any information I got from the interview, but asked to talk to Townby alone. Dodds actually agreed readily, saying that a new interviewer had at least some chance of getting new information. Clearly, though, he didn't believe anyone would ever get any new information from William Townby.

As we walked along, it seemed that we were being followed by a patient who held back but made every turn we did as we walked through the corridors and crossed through a garden. Finally I asked Dodds about it: "Is that patient stalking us, or is it my imagination?"

"It's not your imagination. He probably thinks he's being very stealthy. That's Tommy Morrell—he's harmless."

"He doesn't look harmless to me," Adrianna said. "He looks like a predator after his prey."

"He seems a bit more sprightly than usual today. You must realize that two well-dressed visitors are something of an oddity around here," Dodds observed as we reached Townby's wing.

After polite introductions, Dr. Dodds left Townby alone with Adrianna and me. We sat in a comfortable, sparsely furnished sunroom with a nice wall of glass looking out northward over the grounds.

Townby had been reading in his room when we arrived, and he brought the mystery novel with him to the sunroom. In spite of his confinement, he appeared fit and healthy. He was neatly groomed and presented a pleasant smile. He was dressed in comfortable but well-tailored slacks and a good wool shirt. Quality leather slippers and thick socks added to the image of a country gentleman at home in his own conservatory.

"Such distinguished visitors for a man who never has any," he said enthusiastically. "Mrs. Wallace, I recognized you at a glance. I do get the newspapers. I have been here, off and on, for fifteen years, Mr. Baker, and I have never had a single visitor. Now I have two hand-some ones at once. It's astounding! You haven't found a clue to my money, have you?" He looked amused and pleased at his own wit.

"Is it true that you have money, Dr. Townby?" Adrianna asked with a smile. "We've just been hearing from Dr. Dodds that you have none."

"Oh, apparently I have lots of it. It's just that none of us has the slightest idea where I put it. And please don't call me Dr. Townby. My parents called me Will; most people around here call me Townby. I think one ought to be qualified—currently qualified, I mean—to be called 'doctor.' So you do want to talk about the money, then." He sounded a little tired at the thought.

"Can you keep a secret, Will?" Adrianna asked, leaning forward and putting her hand on his.

He glanced down at her neatly gloved hand and then gazed up into her face. His eyes then slid over to me before he smiled back at Adrianna.

"It might be fun to have a secret to keep—one that I actually know something about."

Giving his hand a reassuring pat, Adrianna straightened and looked over her shoulder, as if to be sure she wouldn't be overheard.

"We don't care at all about the money. We want to talk to you about an old friend," she said in a low murmur. "We're here to talk about Dr. Gussmann."

There was no visible response to the name. "One and the same thing, isn't it, Gussmann and the money?" Townby asked reasonably. "I don't think I've heard a single thing about old Bernard himself for several years. No, Dr. Gussmann has simply become Gussmann's money around here." He seemed momentarily saddened by the thought. "Unless you mean the missing journals. Is that what you're after?"

"Not us," I answered. "We want to know about Dr. Gussmann the doctor. Can you remember him, Will?"

Townby sat up straighter and looked me in the eye. He took his time and made sure he had our attention. "We'd better get something clear to begin with. I have an excellent memory, I'm not insane in the least, and I'm not depressed. I don't have blackouts or behave strangely. Everyone here, especially the doctors, knows all that. You'll do better talking to me if you know it too, Mr. Baker."

I nodded quietly, holding his gaze. "Call me Charles, please, and please accept my apologies. I phrased my question badly. I don't doubt what you've said. It's pretty clear to Adrianna and me that you're not being held here because of your mental health."

"Too right!" he said.

"What I should have asked is *what*—not *whether*—you can tell us about Gussmann's methods. We aren't concerned with the missing money or the medical notes. We didn't even know about them until a couple of days ago, and we have no stake in them. We need to know more about Dr. Gussmann for an entirely different reason."

"A reason that you are going to tell me, or that you aren't going to tell me?" he asked with open curiosity.

"A reason we probably aren't going to tell anybody, Will,"

Adrianna broke in. "That's a secret that doesn't belong to us, but to a friend of ours."

Townby turned and looked out over the winter grounds in front of the window. After a few seconds he looked back at us. "Do you think there's any way you can help me leave here, Charles?"

I shouldn't have been surprised at the bluntness of the question, but I was. I sputtered rather incoherently, "I doubt it, really, but as we come to understand the situation, who knows? We're not without influence. Actually, the idea hasn't entered our minds until now. We came here expecting a mental patient who might be able to give us some help with our Gussmann questions. Instead, we find what I take to be a perfectly sane prisoner." The word hung in the air between us.

"It's a very nice jail, though," Townby said pleasantly, and he let the matter drop for the present as he turned his attention to the reason for our visit. "Well, I'll help if I can. I knew Dr. Gussmann about as well as any of his patients, I guess. The legacy would make you think I knew him better—a close friendship or something—but that wasn't the case."

"But he left you all that money," Adrianna said.

"I honestly have no idea why he did it. Frankly, I didn't like him much. He's been dead since 1909, nearly thirteen years. For the first six of those years, I remember nothing at all. For the past seven, I've been right here worrying about other things, so I'm not too sure I'll remember many specific details about how Gussmann worked. I never knew him well."

"Fair enough," Adrianna said, "and until today we knew nothing of your situation, or what appears to be your situation. But now I do know. I'm a nurse and, as you know, my husband is an influential man. If it turns out that you are being treated unfairly, I'll try to do something. I promise. Now Charlie here, he can't help you. He's not influential, in the first place, and he's not in a position to get involved for other reasons. But my help and your information are two different things, Will. I'll help you, if you are what you seem to be, regardless of what you tell us."

Townby seemed to accept this, but he made no reply. Adrianna glanced at me and then plunged right in, asking, "Now tell me, was Gussmann going batty toward the end, do you think?"

I winced at her directness, but Townby just looked thoughtfully out at the frozen landscape.

"Some say he was always crazy. There are rumors among staff that he took liberties with women patients. There were even nutty rumors among patients that he had killed a woman here. But if he was crazy, I couldn't tell it—"

"Killed a woman?" I interrupted. "What is that rumor, exactly?"

"Oh, it's just crazy talk—plenty of that around here. A woman named Clare Thomas was due for discharge to her family. Most of her team of doctors agreed that she was ready to leave, but Gussmann didn't think so. That's the rumor. Anyway, the night before her release she was murdered right in her room. She was raped, apparently, and strangled to death."

"Why did anyone suspect Dr. Gussmann?" Adrianna asked.

"Well, she was one of the patients with whom he was rumored to be having sexual relations. The whispered rumor was that he couldn't afford to have her out, where she might tell."

"Is there any possible truth in that?" I asked.

"No. He was too old and feeble to have overcome and strangled a healthy young woman. Besides, he was seen sleeping at his desk at about the time the murder must have taken place. The rumors were just because the patients didn't like him. He was feared by most of them."

"Was there any reason for that?" Adrianna asked. "What was it like to be his patient?"

"It's hard to remember much about his sessions with me. He used hypnosis, you know. We had some conversation each session; usually it was pretty depressing—that part. Then he'd put me into a trance, I guess. So all I can tell you about the sessions is that we'd talk about my life before coming to Morton Graves, or we'd talk about a book I was reading. Then he'd put me out. I didn't like it, but he usually could put me under."

"Do you remember how he did that?" I asked. "Did he use anything? You know, like those conjurers do for entertainment?"

"I know what you mean from reading about them, but I've never seen one. No, he didn't wave anything in front of me. He'd just get in front of me and get my attention; then he'd ask me if I was feeling okay, or something like that. Then we'd talk. I'd feel my attention drifting. Disoriented. That's about it."

"What did you talk about?" I asked.

Townby hesitated a moment. "Usually some of the unpleasant parts of my life. Sometimes the depressing parts of whatever book he had me reading at the time. His own life had been remarkably like my own, I think. He was able to empathize with me because he'd lived through similar things. I found myself having some very vivid fantasies about something pleasant. I remember that I couldn't distinguish between my real surroundings and the surreal memories."

"What about afterward?" Adrianna asked. "How did you feel?"

"Usually pretty good. Drowsy for long periods. My depression would be gone for a long time. Toward the end, I was rarely depressed anyway, but I had to go to the sessions and I didn't feel very different afterward. Sometimes a bit tired and confused. Sometimes I'd be confused about where I was. It would seem to me that I had gone to his office, but I'd wake up in a dayroom or in my own room."

Townby shook his head, as if confused even by the memory of it. Then he continued, "Shortly before his death he told me that I was perfectly fine and that he would be releasing me one day soon. Actually, I think that's the last conversation I remember having with anyone before my long blank period."

"You mean that you don't remember talking to anyone else after you left his office?" Adrianna asked. "How soon after that did Gussmann die?"

"We were talking in his office and then I lost consciousness; I guess he put me into a trance. I know from others that he died several days after that session—within a week, I think—but he was fine the last time I saw him. I was out for a very long time. When I woke up, I was on the floor in a hallway near one of the common rooms. Several patients were standing around, and a nurse was trying to help me."

"How long were you unconscious, Will?" Adrianna asked. "Several hours?"

"Six years, or so I'm told. Sometime later, weeks after I became conscious, I came to understand that it was 1915. Dr. Gussmann had been dead for years. Everything that I know about those six years is strictly hearsay as far as I'm concerned. Lots of people have told me different parts of the story—patients as well as staff. I know the story quite well, actually. But in spite of all the details I know, it's all just a story I've learned, a totally unreal fable. I call it the legend of Dr. Townby." He looked at Adrianna.

She squeezed his hand. "During the war, Will, I knew many boys, young men, who couldn't remember long periods of time, days. A few of them never recovered any memory of those days. Sometimes they couldn't remember much of anything that had happened to them since they had left England, a period of months. We didn't keep them in mental wards long. We just sent them home. My guess would be that some of them still don't remember much, but they're out there working and having lives."

Townby looked at Adrianna hopefully but said nothing. He probably was thinking about the life he'd like to have, and I hated to intrude, but our time was growing short.

"Do you remember Mary Hopson?" I asked quietly.

"I do. She was a beauty. Came here about the time I did. She was a patient of Gussmann's, too. I don't think I ever talked to her much—just out on the grounds a few times. I know more about her from stories than from my own memory."

"Stories?" I asked.

"Part of the legend of my Dr. Townby life. She was a patient of mine, too, as the story goes. It's been hinted to me that I was behind closed doors with her a bit more than propriety would allow." He lowered his voice. "Actually, I've had fantasies about that."

"Do you remember Alice Tupper, Will?" Adrianna asked.

"Gussmann's very private secretary? Yes, I remember her, too. She was kind to me when I was a patient of his. I blanked out not long before she retired, and by the time I was back to my old self, she had been gone from here for years. She used to come back once in a while to visit some of the staff, but I heard that she was dying quite a while ago—cancer or something."

"What about Helen Wickham?" I continued. "Do you remember her?"

"Only in the legend. She came to Morton Graves less than a year before Gussmann died. The story is that she was one of my patients, too. People hint that she may have been more than a patient to me, too. She was released before I woke up in 1915. Most of the time she was here was during my six-year gap. Sorry." He shrugged somewhat helplessly.

"And Liza Anatole?" I continued.

"Now, her I remember well. She's a beautiful girl. Came here when she was just a teenager, seventeen or so. She was seventeen because her age matched the year. She told me that once. She was born early in January in 1900. Her father and her brother died in the war within days of each other. She cracked up, tried suicide—deadly serious attempt from what I heard. I talked to her lots of times once she was better. She left a couple of years ago."

"She couldn't have known Mary Hopson or Helen Wickham, then—"

"If I may interrupt, Mr. Baker," Townby said, "you said you wanted to know about Gussmann, but these names have nothing to do with him. Well, Mary does, I guess, and Helen knew him for a while, but Liza never knew Dr. Gussmann."

"That's part of our problem," Adrianna interjected. "Someone has alleged a connection between Gussmann and all these names—and one other. Part of our problem is to figure out what the connection may be. The other name is Robert Stanton."

Townby sat back deeper into his chair and shrugged his shoulders again. "Another part of the legend. His name has come up in discussions about my patients. I have no recollection of him at all. He left here before 1915. Are these people in danger or anything? Are they alive? Can't you tell me something more about what it is you're doing?"

I answered, "They are all alive. You must know about Helen Wickham, though. She won't be alive for long. The rest all live and work here in West London. As far as we know, they're in no danger."

"Are you people trying to help Helen Wickham? Is that what this is a part of? I've read about the demonstrations over hanging a woman, of course. And she tried an insanity plea at first." He looked quizzically at each of us. "You've got my curiosity up more than I've got yours, I'll wager. What's going on?"

I reflected for a moment on the notion that this interview itself was somehow an attempt to save Helen Wickham. That seemed highly unlikely, though, and any collusion on Will's part seemed even more far-fetched—in spite of Dodds's suspicions. "No, we feel sorry for Helen, but we don't know her, and we don't know how to help her. Her name was just connected to Gussmann's in this thing we're investigating."

"Investigating! Dr. Dodds said you were a solicitor, a lawyer. What kind of investigation? Gussmann's been dead for more than twelve years, Charles. Except for Mary and Helen, none of these people knew him. Was my name mentioned in this thing, whatever it is?"

"No, Will," Adrianna answered, "and that seems odd. Your name came up when we were looking for connections among these people. So far, actually, you're the only link that ties to all of them—you and this hospital. Maybe there's one other link: Tommy Morrell."

Townby sat upright. "That's right! Tommy Morrell is the only patient here now, besides me, who ever knew Dr. Gussmann. Tommy's an odd duck, my dear. He's been here forever. He could have known all of these people. Have you talked to him?"

"No, we haven't, yet," I answered.

"Well, good luck. Odds are against your actually conversing with him, but I don't think it's impossible."

"What do you mean?" Adrianna asked. "Isn't he well?"

"If you mean physically, yes, he seems quite healthy," Townby said, smiling, "but mentally he's often not at home, or that's what he wants us to think. I'm not sure which."

"Go on, Will," Adrianna probed.

"Well, Tommy never talks to anybody, I mean never! But some times are different than others. Sometimes Tommy, I don't know, he simply can't talk, can't even focus his eyes, it seems. Other times he's more like a fox watching the hounds run by his hiding place."

"We saw him today. I assume he was in his fox-and-hounds phase," I said.

"Sometimes I'd swear that he is sitting out there on the grounds thinking up the solutions to all the puzzles of the universe. Sometimes he eats like a gentleman, sometimes like an animal. Most of the time he walks as if he has some deformity, but once in a while I see him walking quite normally. I've even seen him reading. My hunch is that he wants to look a lot more insane than he is. Though sometimes he's crazy, no doubt about that."

"Was he a patient of Gussmann's?" I asked.

"Yes. Dr. Gussmann treated him regularly."

"Hypnosis?" Adrianna asked.

"I presume, since that was Gussmann's primary method of treatment. Mine, too, they tell me."

"You are a hypnotist!" I said.

Smiling, Townby made a large sweeping gesture, bowed deeply in his chair, and said, "Part of the legend."

13

The lowest and vilest alleys of London do not present a more dreadful record of
sin than does the smiling and beautiful countryside.
—"The Adventure of the Copper Beeches"

ADRIANNA AND I ATE a quick lunch near the hospital; then I put her
on the train for London. I wanted to stay in Richmond for the afternoon to see what I could learn of the third name on the list in the
letter, Liza Anatole.

Adrianna wanted to find out anything she could about any of the
investment bankers whose names we'd learned at Morton Graves.
She was sure that she and Freddy had no social engagements that
would interfere, so we agreed that she would slip out and meet me
near my place at Lancers at eight.

I drove west to Kingston University and took a slow drive through
it to familiarize myself with the place. The address I had for the Anatole woman was on a street called Coombe Park in Kingston-upon-
Thames, and I expected that to be a street name on the university
grounds. It turned out not to be so. The street was just adjacent to the
college and became a circle drive bordering on the Coombe Hill Golf
Course. Her address, as it turned out, was that of an imposing manor
that backed the course itself.

I parked down the street and reread my notes on Liza Anatole.
She was in her early twenties and lived with her sister and brother-in-
law. Doyle had discovered that the local constable did not know her,

but college students at Kingston University did. She had a reputation there as a rather wild participant at parties on occasion. There was one very disturbing police report in her past. Two children—a brother and sister age eleven and thirteen—had disappeared and never been found. Reliable witnesses had seen the children in the presence of the Anatole girl walking near the river.

Miss Anatole had "blacked out" during what had apparently been an abduction, which may have taken place while she walked with the children. Liza was badly bruised herself, and it was assumed that some trauma had occurred there that had driven the already unstable young woman into amnesia. She could not remember having been with the children at all. The abductors were never apprehended, no ransom was ever demanded, and the children were never seen again.

I put away my notes and took another slow drive around the circular street in my Morris, which was about as out of place here as a fishmonger's cart. I continued a hundred yards beyond the house and out of sight of it around the loop and paused to contemplate my next move. I did not come up with any new ideas, so after several minutes I started up again and continued hastily around the circle back to where it became one road leading out to Kingston Vale. At that three-way junction I nearly collided with a young woman riding a bicycle. I managed to come to a sliding halt, which killed the engine and just avoided striking her. If she hadn't been doing some skillful braking and swerving herself, she'd have been seriously injured. As it was, she didn't even take a spill. With hardly a backward glance, she continued out toward the main road. The young woman, in gray trousers and thick sweater, was a blonde. I took a chance that she might be Liza Anatole and decided to follow her.

By the time I got the car started again, she was making a right turn onto Kingston Vale. I decided to employ the surveillance trick of following by leading. It was reasonable to speculate, I thought, that she would be headed up the road to Kingston University, where the rest of her family was on the faculty. I drove out onto Kingston Vale and passed her. She didn't appear to take any notice of me. I turned into the university and parked along the lane a mere hundred feet from the entrance. In my car mirror I could see the entrance behind me and would be able to see her turn in. Then it would be a simple matter to follow on foot once I knew where she was going.

But she didn't enter the university grounds at all. She went sailing past the entrance at a good clip and continued up Kingston Vale. This meant I had to get the Morris started again, turn it around in the narrow lane, and head back out to the main road. There I stopped and watched her ride away. When she was nearly out of sight, I began to follow. My plan was to pass her and drive on until she was just a speck in the distance behind me. Then I would find a place to park and wait for her to pass by me again. I arrived at Robin Hood Gate and pulled into the parking area at the stables there. I got out of the car and strolled over near a post where I could lean against the fence and look back down Kingston Vale. And here she came, but she didn't ride past the stables. Instead, she turned into the park at Robin Hood Gate, just as I had, and continued speedily up the park lane. Where it was intersected by a crosslane, some hundred yards farther on, she went straight.

Now what was I going to do? I couldn't drive the Morris into the park because there was a closed gate and a pretty clear sign in front of me proclaiming that no private motorcars were to proceed into the park. At the rate she was riding, she'd be out of sight in two or three minutes. I spun around and walked through the entrance to the stables. A few feet farther on was a groom who had just removed the saddle from the horse in front of him.

"May I rent a horse?" I asked him.

He looked me over without an immediate answer. In my business suit and street shoes, I'm sure I violated the dress code. "We do let some of our own horses by the hour, sir, but none are ready, just now. Perhaps if you inquire inside—"

"What about that horse you're holding?" I asked. "I prefer to ride bareback."

"This mare's just come in from a ride, sir, but she's had an easy time of it. Ask inside, and they might send her right back out." He regarded me with obvious amusement.

I stepped forward and extended a pound note toward him. "Couldn't you arrange that for me? I'm in rather a hurry. I've just seen a young lady I want to catch up with right away."

He looked at the note as if it were a jewel. I wondered if he saw the hundred loaves of bread it represented, my economist counters clicking away.

"Arrange it for me, and there'll be no need for change," I said, reaching for the reins. "I'll have her back within the hour."

He released the reins and winked at me. "I'll be working back through that gate by your car, sir. You just bring her back there to me." He looked me over again. "You'll likely ruin them trousers, sir. It won't take me a minute to throw the saddle back on her. You'll be glad you took the time."

I nodded, and he replaced the saddle in record time. Nevertheless, by the time I was headed up the lane, the bicyclist was long out of sight. I rode up the lane at a gallop. In the next half mile I passed a small sign that said Martin's Pond on my left and arrived at a smaller path veering left off of the one I was on. Here I had to stop and look for bicycle tracks. Unfortunately, there were several. I decided that the freshest-looking ones continued up the lane I was on. A farther hundred yards on, another path went off to the left, and it appeared to me that the freshest bicycle tracks went in that direction. I followed them for at least another half mile before I saw her up ahead.

I reined the mare to a walk and kept the young woman just in sight ahead of me. She was a full two miles from Robin Hood Gate when she turned onto an even smaller lane, one that lacked the gravel surface she had been riding on. This one was all mud. A short distance along that path, she stopped, parked the bicycle against a tree, and continued on foot. Still she kept a brisk pace.

With the great height advantage that being on the horse gave me, I was able to stay far behind her. About five minutes after she left the bicycle, she turned sharply right onto another riding path and walked almost due north. Five minutes later she left the path altogether and skirted the edge of a pond until she intersected yet another path and continued in more or less the same direction she had been going.

As I came upon the pond myself, I realized that I had been here before. I had come in on foot from the north that time, but I had stood looking over this very pond. Had I not been on the horse, I might have recognized it earlier. I had watched Mary Hopson from just about this same spot on the previous Sunday evening. I could now see the person whom I presumed to be Liza Anatole approaching the very same bench where Mary Hopson had sat during that cold twilight.

I turned the mare around and walked her back up the rise beyond the pond to put more distance between us while I waited. In doing so, I lost sight of the woman for perhaps three minutes. When I turned the horse back toward my quarry and shifted my gaze to see what she was doing, she was already nearly back at the north edge of the pond and was striding straight toward me.

Remain calm. She probably won't recognize me from when I almost ran her over. It's a nice afternoon; people are all over the park. She'll walk right past me. Maybe I'll even speak to her if I can just think of a reason why I'd be here. No, not now. I'll ride on down past her and past the pond and then circle back to where she left the bike. Good plan.

But it didn't go exactly that way. I started the mare down the path toward the young woman who was striding so purposefully toward us. I tried to appear not to be paying any attention to the girl and was looking out across the pond when she suddenly stopped and stared directly at my face. There was still a distance of perhaps thirty feet between us, and I was watching her with my peripheral vision, but felt that she was clearly shocked to see me. She must have been paying attention, after all, back on Coombe Park when I nearly hit her with the Morris. Without making eye contact, I turned the mare away from her gaze and rode along the south edge of the pond and up to a bridle path along its east side.

Again watching her with my side vision while I tried to appear not to notice her, I saw the young woman begin to trot southward back toward where she had abandoned the bicycle. I continued to walk the mare northward until she was out of sight. I knew where she was going, and I knew that she was about half a mile away from the bicycle. I had the advantage of the horse as well, so I was sure that I would not lose track of the woman.

I continued northward until I intersected another bridle path that veered eastward. Half a mile farther on, I turned southward on another path. Yet another half mile brought me to Queen's Ride, according to a sign, and I turned eastward again. I was riding parallel to the path I'd ridden most of the way across the park so I was retracing my steps, more or less, but on a different path. At first I could see the other path a hundred yards off to my right as it tended gradually more toward the south than Queen's Ride. There was no sign of the girl on the bicycle, and I couldn't calculate with any certainty whether she should be ahead of me or behind. Then Queen's Ride entered a thick forest, and I lost all sight of the other path.

I urged the mare to a gallop all the way to the east end of Queen's Ride and turned southward along the road to Robin Hood Gate. At this pace I knew I'd be back at the gate well ahead of the blond woman. I'd have time to return the mare and get the Morris out of sight. When I reached the intersection with the path she'd be on, I reined in and looked back westward toward where she would be. I could just make out that there was a bicyclist coming down a gentle slope perhaps half a mile away. I wished I could walk the mare back to the stables to cool her down some, but there wasn't time.

I rode to the small gate that the groom had indicated and dismounted. No sooner had I done so than he was at my side and took the reins.

"She's a bit lathered up, sir. You should walk 'em off when you're coming in," he said as I turned toward him.

"I know. Sorry. I hope it'll be all right. I've forgotten an appointment, and I've got to be going."

"Didn't work out with the young lady, then?" he said with a smile. He looked back toward the entrance to the stable yard and then led the mare through the gate beside us. "No harm done, sir. I'll walk her around a bit. You can be on your way." With that he closed the gate between us, and I realized that he wanted me away from there before his employers had any idea that I'd rented the horse.

I got the car started and drove out onto Kingston Vale, heading back toward the university. A short distance down the road on my left, I turned into Robin Hood Lane and parked, knowing that I would soon see Liza Anatole riding along Kingston Vale. Two hours later, though, at about five o'clock, I gave up the wait. I had a good view of a long stretch of the highway, and she had never returned from the park, at least not by way of Kingston Vale.

So what had happened? Was this blond woman Liza Anatole after all? The look she gave me in the park had certainly seemed more malevolent than our simple traffic incident warranted.

Finally, why had she never come back out of the park through Robin Hood Gate?

Why was her name on the list anyway? What could she possibly have to do with Dr. Gussmann, Helen Wickham, Mary Hopson, Robert Stanton, and Conan Doyle?

14

There's plenty of thread, no doubt, but I can't get the end of it into my hand.

—"The Man with the Twisted Lip"

IT TOOK ME AN hour to wind my way back to The Captains and squeeze the Morris into its tiny spot in the alleyway. I decided that a relaxing bath was just the place to unwind and collect my thoughts, and by six-fifteen I was drawing the hot water and starting on a brandy.

While the bath was trickling in, I called Conan Doyle and got right through to him. I told him that Adrianna and I were meeting at Lancers at eight, and he promptly said that he would join us there to get caught up on developments.

"Do you think that would be wise now, Sir Arthur?" I asked. It began to look as if he couldn't resist more direct involvement in spite of the risk.

"Just trying to observe the proprieties, my boy," he said a trifle too heartily. "A chance meeting of three friends in a popular pub would be much wiser than a married socialite's rendezvous with a young man-about-town."

I could hardly argue with that.

He continued, "If you'll delay your arrival by a few minutes, I can genuinely surprise Adrianna. Then we can invite you to join us when you get there."

"Sir Arthur," I said, "have you done this sort of thing before?"

He chuckled, "Only on paper, Charles. But I do have something of a flair for it."

I hung up with the assurance that I would wander into Lancers no earlier than eight-fifteen, and went in to my bath to think through everything I'd learned.

I was unfamiliar with the westernmost reaches of London and had never been to Richmond-upon-Thames until the previous Sunday. It had not been until I was driving home this evening that I was fully aware that every place my investigation had taken me so far this week was very near Richmond Park, though the locations were miles apart. Mary Hopson's North Sheen shop was half a mile, more or less, north of Bog Gate, which I now realized was a northern entrance to the park. Robert Stanton's boat emporium was in Ham, on the park's western side. His place was about a mile and a half west of Ham Gate.

Though I hadn't put it together until now, Morton Graves Voluntary Hospital, with its address in Richmond, also had to be somewhere very near the park. I had driven there from the north, taking Queens Road southward off of Sheen Road. Remembering the drive as best I could, I realized that I must have been nearly to the park when I turned onto Chisholm Road. Finally, there was Liza Anatole's home in Kingston-upon-Thames. The girl I assumed was Anatole had ridden her bicycle a little more than a mile to Robin Hood Gate and entered Richmond Park from the south.

Soaking in the tub with my second brandy, I put more facts together. I had followed Mary Hopson more or less along the north edge of the park, heading westerly about half a mile from Bog Gate. This afternoon, I had followed a woman whom I presumed was Liza Anatole for roughly three miles across the park from Robin Hood Gate. We had traveled northwest and had ended up at the very same spot to which I'd followed Mary Hopson on Sunday.

When I had followed Robert Stanton yesterday morning, he, too, had walked to Richmond Park, entering it through Ham Gate and turning northward. He might have been going toward the same general area, at least, as Mary and Liza. Morton Graves Voluntary Hospital must be near the north edge of the park and couldn't be very far from where Hopson and Anatole ended their respective walks. I needed a map for this, and I knew that I had one in my desk in the other room. For the moment, I remained in the bath to think, making a mental note to look at the map later.

Where had Helen Wickham lived before she committed murder and got herself thrown into Holloway? St. Margarets? I made another mental note to find out where that was. Then I remembered that Helen Wickham was due to hang tomorrow. That seemed wrong to me, somehow. I was not so sure that the prisoner I'd met was insane; but from the account of the case, I was not sure she was guilty of premeditated murder in the first place. In the end, though, as with so many things in life, there was absolutely nothing I could do about that apparent injustice.

Who was Gussmann's private secretary? Alice Tupper. And where was she now? Was she dead? I made another mental note. *That* was too many mental notes for the amount of brandy I'd already sipped. I realized that I'd better get out of the bath and get a notepad. I got out quickly, squished across the tile floor, dashed into my sitting room to retrieve pad and pencil, and hurried back into the bath. The water seemed to have cooled down twenty degrees. My dash had chilled me, and the bath was no longer satisfying. I got back out and dressed hastily, still tracing an expanding web of connections among all the people in the case.

My map of Greater London confirmed my earlier mental image. Richmond Park was an enormous old royal park to the west, near Wimbledon. Within the past few days I had become familiar with several of its entrances: Bog Gate on its north edge, Ham Gate on its west side, and Robin Hood Gate on its south. I could see that Morton Graves Voluntary Hospital was directly adjacent to the park's north edge. My guess was that the bench where Mary Hopson had waited probably faced the hospital grounds. The girl I thought was Liza Anatole had gone to exactly the same place and was returning to her bicycle when she encountered me that afternoon.

The time spent with my map and notes made it easy to delay my appearance at Lancers, as Sir Arthur had suggested. When I arrived, fashionably late, Adrianna and Arthur Conan Doyle waved at me from a booth near the back. My favorite stout ale also was waiting for me when I sat down. I wondered which of them knew to order that. My money was on Adrianna.

"You first," she said as I took my first sip. "Tell us what you found out from Liza Anatole."

I described my afternoon in detail and provided them with my list of questions to be answered.

"I can answer one question," she said immediately. "Morton Graves is right on the park. You have to be blind to miss that."

"I've figured that out," I said.

"Did you notice the lawns beyond the south fences?" she asked. "That's Richmond Park right there. It must be a million acres or so. It's huge, Charles, and it's been there forever. It's got deer and everything."

"A million acres?"

"Well, what would you say? You're the one who went out there and played cowboy all afternoon."

When I thought about it for a moment, I realized that the park had to be about two miles east to west and well more than that north to south. I didn't know its overall shape, but I guessed that it might be close to four or five square miles in size. I pulled my notepad over and did a few calculations. "It's probably more than two thousand acres."

"Now you're showing off," Conan Doyle said. "I imagine that you cowboys ride around measuring acreage all the time. That wasn't part of my education." He chuckled softly.

"Actually I did do some of that as a kid. Not very useful here, usually."

Adrianna said, "Well, I found out a few things myself this afternoon. I telephoned around and found out that one of the partners at Willoughby and Martin, Limited, is an old friend of my Uncle William. The old boy agreed to give me tea at four o'clock."

"Is there anyone in London you don't know, or who doesn't know you?" I asked her.

"Too many people know me, that's for sure. I think one of them followed me here tonight, as a matter of fact."

Sir Arthur and I looked around the room. "Who? Which one followed you, Adrianna?" Arthur asked.

"He's not in here, but I'm pretty sure he was following me. I walked from our house to the nearest train station and came straight in to Victoria. I walked directly here from there. Anyway, I noticed this little man—like Toulouse-Lautrec in a watch coat and a sailor's hat, that was the impression he made on me—walking along, half a block behind me. I didn't notice, but he must've caught the same coach into Victoria Station, because I noticed him again as I walked along St. George's Drive. Could have been coincidence, I know, but it was dark, and I didn't like it. I lost sight of him after I turned onto Clarendon. It was spooky."

"No doubt it was Dr. Gussmann's ghost," I said, with a wink at Conan Doyle. "Or maybe an investigator hired by your husband to find out how you occupy your time." I was joking—but not entirely.

"He'd have no need, Charles. I tell him where I'm going. We've no secrets from each other. Well, not many."

Conan Doyle raised an eyebrow and asked, "So who would follow you?"

"I don't know. Photographers do sometimes when Freddy and I are out at some gala event. I suppose some reporter might be looking for a scandal to print."

"Someone trying to get something on Freddy? Would a reporter know exactly where you live?" I asked.

Adrianna rolled her eyes. "Anyone who reads the papers would know exactly where we live, Charles. Not only do they throw our address into articles, but also the grounds are on garden tours in the springtime." After another quick glance aroung the crowded room, she leaned forward and lowered her voice. "Anyway, I found out more about the money trail, or in this case the end of the trail."

"There's no trail?"

"There's a good trail, but it comes to an end, and the money is not sitting there at the end of the trail," she said as she raised her hand and signaled for the waiter. "Do you want to eat?"

"Yes, and I want to hear about the money."

"Dr. Dodds is right. Townby has to have it," she said.

"He sure had me fooled," I said.

"Me, too, but he's got to have it somewhere."

We were interrupted by the waiter, who addressed Adrianna as "Mrs. Wallace" and Conan Doyle as "Sir Arthur." She gave me a see-what-I-mean look. We ordered our supper before she was able to resume. "Townby systematically and steadily converted all property and securities to cash, some of it gold. Because the partners at Willoughby and Martin were curious and suspicious, they asked around and found out that the one thing he was buying was what are called bearer bonds when he could get them."

"Dodds mentioned that, too," I said.

"I've heard the term," Conan Doyle said, "but I'm not entirely clear on what it means."

"Bearer bonds are interest-bearing notes that are redeemable by 'the bearer,' instead of having an owner of record," I explained.

"Anyone who's got them can redeem them?"

"Or trade them—buy them and sell them," Adrianna answered. "They are a way of investing at interest without providing a trail of ownership."

"So the trail ends," I said.

Adrianna continued, "The trail ends whenever you get everything converted to cash and bearer securities. Townby sold every piece of real estate, so there were no deeds. He sold every share of stock and every bond that had a registered owner. He started this while he was up in Edinburgh at medical school. He did a little every month or so. He finished up the whole conversion during his first year back in London."

"Was there any guess as to the total pile of cash that should be at the end of the trail?" Conan Doyle asked.

"They're pretty sure that it was well over thirty thousand by the beginning of 1914, but he had managed to acquire quite a few bearer bonds at high interest, and a good bit of it was in gold. War inflation pushed the gold up quite a lot. Wherever it is, it's enough to live the life of a rich man and never touch the principal," she answered.

I couldn't believe that the Will Townby I'd met this morning was that good an actor. After all, he'd *told* us that apparently it was he who had spirited the money away. He had encouraged us to find it. "What about you, Adrianna, do you think he knows where it is?"

She waited quite a while before replying. "No. I don't think that William Townby, in his current state, knows where it is. But the evidence is overwhelming that some other William Townby, the personality he was in 1914, knows where it is."

"That multiple-personality stuff is pretty theoretical, isn't it?" I asked.

"A lot of neurologists and a lot of students of psychical behavior are starting to say that there's something to it," Conan Doyle answered.

"And a lot of Spiritualists," I countered.

"Them, too. But just because someone believes something you don't, doesn't make it wrong," Adrianna added. "And it doesn't make everything *else* they believe wrong, either." She nodded vigorously in Arthur's direction.

He reached over and patted her hand in a fatherly way and said, "Very true, my dear. Thank you."

Our food arrived, and we ate in silence for nearly five minutes. Then Adrianna began again. "What's it got to do with the letter, gentlemen? You know they're going to hang Helen Wickham tomorrow, and we haven't made any connection that could help her."

"Maybe helping her has nothing to do with it," I offered.

"Then why make me send someone to see her?" Arthur asked.

"I don't know. Maybe she knows where the money is. At any rate, I think Adrianna was right before. I don't think that whatever was supposed to happen did happen."

"It's all connected to Morton Graves somehow," Adrianna said.

"And Dr. Gussmann," Conan Doyle said.

"No," she countered. "Remember that Liza Anatole couldn't have known Dr. Gussmann or Mary Hopson."

"That's true, and you said she couldn't have known Helen Wickham, either. Yet Liza was on the list of those we could take to see Helen," I added.

"Remember that Robert Stanton never knew Dr. Gussmann either," she said.

"But William Townby knew them all, one way or another!" Conan Doyle said. "And he's cashed in all his chips."

"But the letter was from Gussmann," Adrianna added, shaking her head in confusion.

"Not really. Townby would have inherited plenty of Gussmann's stuff. He could have learned a lot about the man," I said.

"So paint me a picture, Charles. Give me something to argue against. What do you think could be going on?"

After a few minutes of silence and ale, I began. "Theory number one. Townby is trapped as a patient in Morton Graves. He somehow gains the confidence of Dr. Gussmann and manages to inherit the bulk of the estate. He decides to enter the same profession as Gussmann—maybe because there's something at Morton Graves that he needs and hasn't found yet. For reasons of his own, he wants everything in cash. Then the pressure builds up in him and he has a nervous collapse. The hospital sees its chance and commits him. They want their money, and they're not letting him go until they get it."

"So where does Helen Wickham come in?" Adrianna asked.

"Helen Wickham knows something that Townby needs, but now she's going to die. Somehow he persuades three different people he knows to go get the information from her. Any one of them can do it, but he needs a way to get them in. Sir Arthur, here, is the way. Townby knows enough about Arthur's father, from old Gussmann notes or something, to trick Arthur into helping. But whatever is supposed to happen at Holloway doesn't happen. Townby has dropped everything for now, and we're stumbling around out here at the dead end." I waited for a response. It took a minute, but I got one.

"Sliced Swiss cheese, Charles. It's really thin, and it has a lot of holes in it." Adrianna absently fiddled with the saltshaker on the table before she continued. "First, Townby wouldn't bother to go through becoming a doctor when he was already rich. He even paid Morton Graves to take him on. Second, if he knew where the money was, he'd hire a good barrister like Freddy and be out of there in a wink." She paused for a sip of wine. "How am I doing so far?"

"Those are good," I admitted. "Actually, those are very good."

"I've got a better one," Conan Doyle said.

"Let me have it," I said.

"It's about the end of the trail, Charlie, your trails through the park."

I nodded. "They all go to Morton Graves. I can see that. Townby's room probably looks right at that bench in the park."

Adrianna pursed her lips and shook her head slowly from side to side. Her expression said that I was a sad case. "Townby's wing and its fenced garden are on the north side of the hospital. Richmond Park is on its south. What do you make of that?"

"That Sir Arthur contacted the wrong sleuth," I said, smiling at Conan Doyle.

"But he's got me in the bargain, hasn't he?"

Conan Doyle looked at her fondly. "A fortunate bonus, to be sure, but I'm not certain there's anything left for you to investigate. Unless someone sends me another note, I think I'm out of ideas. Helen Wickham is about to die, that's a certainty."

Adrianna said, "I don't know about you, Charlie, but I couldn't stop this investigation now, even if Sir Arthur is through with this thing." She turned toward Conan Doyle. "You've still got that letter from what seems to be a ghost." She finished her wine. "Can you drive me home, Charlie?"

Conan Doyle looked toward the front of the pub. "If you *were* followed here, Adrianna, I think I'd better leave by the rear exit. I'm still trying to avoid direct connection with this. Someone may be making too many connections."

"Though we, unfortunately, are not," I said weakly as Conan Doyle left the table.

I paid the bill, and Adrianna and I walked out into the January night air through the front door. We slowly strolled along the quiet street toward my parking space near The Captains Hotel.

"I don't think he'll get anywhere with his ghost theory," I said. "I'm thinking more and more that Dr. Gussmann is still alive."

"You'd rather believe that a sick eighty-year-old man faked his own death and is still running around London a dozen years later," Adrianna grumbled. "Honestly, Charles, I'd sooner go along with Sir Arthur and that bunch. Gussmann's dead and buried. The people we're looking at are very much alive."

"I don't see how these people could have known about old man Doyle's sketchbook, Adrianna, and I don't see what possible purpose they could have in sending us to see Helen Wickham. Two of the people on the list never even met her."

"Just because we can't see their reasons, Charlie, doesn't mean they don't have reasons. Don't forget that there's a lot of money unaccounted for. I'm betting on live people taking real action, and not so they can save the Wickham woman—she'll hang in a few more hours." She stated the sad, but obvious, truth.

We had walked only for a couple of hundred feet when we passed the recessed doorway of a closed shop. A small blond woman, wearing a sailor's watch coat several sizes too large for her, was sitting in the recess with a woolen scarf tied around her head. A sailor's cap rested on her knees. Her hair was flowing out underneath the scarf as she looked up at me. I nodded slightly at her as a polite gesture and walked past.

Then it occurred to me that there was something very familiar about her. I paused and turned back to see if I knew her, and my mind shifted into a sort of slow motion as I recognized several things at once. First, the woman was the one I'd followed in Richmond Park that afternoon. Second, she was stepping out onto the walk.

"Charles Baker?" she said clearly. Opening the front of her coat and withdrawing a large automatic pistol, she brought it awkwardly up to point toward us, grasping the heavy gun in both hands, as if she could barely lift it. Nevertheless, her gaze was steady and deliberate.

I shoved Adrianna, who was still moving forward, pushing her forcefully toward the wall a few feet away. As Adrianna lost her footing and fell to the side, I saw the woman bring the pistol to bear on me.

Part Two

15

We can't command our love, but we can our actions.
—"The Adventure of the Noble Bachelor"

THEN, AS I'VE SAID before, Adrianna saved my life on the street.

When I woke in Royal Hospital, I half expected to again see my feet floating at eye level with Liza Anatole's visage between them. Instead, I saw a nurse in a white uniform. It wasn't entirely white because there was quite a bit of blood on the front of it. She was putting a screen mask over my face at the time.

I awoke again in what seemed like only a few moments. The person I saw then was an orderly. His face was upside down, and the ceiling was moving along over his head. I was aware of a lot of pain in my stomach; in fact, it was all around the middle of my body. "He's awake," the man said to someone. Then he was wrong, because I wasn't awake anymore.

Finally, I saw Adrianna's face leaning over me, and her husband's face was right beside it. She was smiling; he wasn't. "Can you hear me, Baker?" he asked.

I could hear him. I could hear him quite clearly. I just couldn't talk at first. I think I moved my lips a little because Adrianna said, "Don't try, Charles. You can talk later. You're going to be all right."

I felt that I had to talk if I could. "Liza Anatole," I said hoarsely.

"Who does he think you are, Adrianna?" Frederick asked.

"Liza Anatole shot me," I said to Adrianna. "Didn't you see her?"

"I didn't see anyone, Charles. You shoved me down, and I heard the gun and stayed down until I heard footsteps running away. When I looked up, there was only you, lying wounded in the street."

Frederick Wallace leaned over close to my face. "Look, old man, people are under the impression that I was there, too, outside the pub. We were all there together, you see?"

Then I remembered Adrianna's little charade on the street. "You chased the gunman," I whispered.

Adrianna laughed at that. "You are going to be all right, Charlie. Good memory. Listen; there will be a lot of questions when word gets out that you're alive. There are reporters in the lobby. Arthur will be coming in if we can get rid of the newspapermen. The police have questioned us already—me when I got here with you, Freddy later. They even went to see Conan Doyle because he was with us in Lancers."

"I understand," I said, my head clearing fast. I thought about how serious this could be for Adrianna and Freddy. The gossip columns could make two pages out of this without even trying. "What did you tell them?"

"Pretty much the truth," Adrianna answered. "We had just left Lancers, where I had been expecting to meet Freddy, when you were shot. I didn't see the assailant. I didn't think you did either."

"Freddy," I said, "you've got to tell the police that I said it was Liza Anatole who shot me. Her address is in my notepad in my car—first page."

"I'll take care of it, old boy. I'll tell them you recognized her."

"Where did you tell them you were when I was shot?" I asked him.

"You were all waiting to meet me," Wallace answered. "When I was late, you left without me. I showed up and met you on the street just before the attack. I gave chase, but lost the assailant after a few blocks. Too young for me. Say, how big is this Anatole woman? I rather gave the impression that the assailant was a man of at least average build."

"She's very small," I said, "but she was wearing a big coat."

"I told you!" Adrianna said sharply to her husband. "I said it had to be the woman we passed in the doorway." She turned to me, "How are you feeling, Charlie?"

"Like I've been kicked in the belly. Where—"

"The bullet went right through your stomach, Charlie, nicked a vertebra, and went right on out the back. You're a mess, but you're alive, and you'll be okay. They've got all the best here: the latest arsenicals for all the germs I stuffed into you on the street, mor-phine—you're wanting some of that now, I'll bet." She looked pained herself. "Too soon after surgery, I'm afraid. The surgeon on duty spent two years on abdomens at the front. You couldn't have picked a better time to get shot in the stomach."

"Will I walk? I can't move my legs; in fact, I can't move anything much." I wiggled my fingers and then lifted my left arm up to within my view. It was a relief to be able to do that.

"Too soon to tell, but they don't think there was any actual spinal damage. You won't eat much for a while, though. Your stomach is a little smaller and has a lot of stitches in it. You lost some blood; you're going to be weak." I could see tears welling in her reddened eyes and remembered that she hadn't shed any tears when I was on the street and she was working on me.

"It's my ticket home, I guess." That's what they said in the war when they got shot bad enough to go home, but not bad enough to die. "When will I be out of here?"

"Too soon to tell, Charlie. You've only been out of surgery for a couple of hours. I don't think it's one o'clock yet," she answered.

"Ten past two," Freddy said. "There's still a long night ahead. You get some sleep if you can, old man."

"He'll sleep after they give him this morphine," Adrianna said as a nurse showed up with a hypodermic syringe.

I woke to see Conan Doyle sitting beside my bed. I was able to see him because I could move my head quite easily. Sunlight was streaming in through a window. Sir Arthur was reading a newspaper. I looked around enough to realize that I was in a small room with no other patients in it. There were trays of instruments and supplies on a table along one wall.

"What time is it?" I asked.

He snapped his paper down. "My boy! You're awake!" he said. Then he pulled a watch from his vest pocket and opened it. "Three-fifteen, Charles, Friday."

"Friday the twentieth?"

"Of January 1922, Charles. You haven't been sleeping long."

Suddenly I remembered the significance that Friday held for us this week. "The execution?" I asked. "Did anyone stop it?"

The old man looked down sadly. "Sorry, Charles. She was . . . it was just before noon. I'm sorry to say nothing changed there. But you seem to have stirred something up, Charles—shot by Liza Anatole!"

"I think it was Liza," I said. "I've never actually met her—confirmed it was she—but the woman who shot me is the same one I followed from her address yesterday."

"Oh, it was she, all right. She's in custody now," he said cheerfully. "She was picked up this morning, wandering along the towing path on the Thames in Kingston. Nearly frozen to death, they say." He showed a clear satisfaction in that statement.

"Did she give any reason why she shot me?"

"She swears she didn't—hasn't been out of the area, she says. She says she went for a bicycle ride in Richmond Park yesterday. Parked her bicycle and went for a walk. Then she had one of her 'little spells' and woke up on the Thames in the middle of the night. Her sister and brother-in-law had put out the police to find her after sundown yesterday and, of course, there was the London police looking for her by sunup this morning because of what Freddy told them. Kingston force picked her up on the missing-persons first. She was already home when London's 'wanted for questioning' got called over to Kingston. So London went over and nabbed her."

"Did she have the gun?"

"Oh, no. The gun never left the scene of the shooting. It was lying right there on the walk. The constable picked that up last night. It's a mighty big pistol for such a little woman—a model 1911 Colt .45, American military issue. Loaded with full-jacket military bullets—cut through you pretty cleanly, I gather."

"Is it her brother-in-law's pistol?" I asked.

He shook his head. "He says not. Says he's never owned a gun. Wife and housekeeper confirm that. Nevertheless, the girl is now in custody in London on the strength of your report. No one else has identified her, not even Adrianna. You're sure, Charles?"

"There's no mistake. The woman I followed from Liza Anatole's address is the woman who shot me in London last night." I found myself doing a mental replay of the face of the woman between my flying feet.

"Any idea how she followed you into London, Charles? Where did you last see her?"

"In Richmond Park, riding her bicycle. I presumed she was headed back through Robin Hood Gate toward her home." I paused my speech to rest for a moment. Conan Doyle sat back patiently. "I waited for her along the route, but she never came past me. She might have noticed me where I was parked and stayed out of sight, I imagine, but she never could have followed me all the way back to London on her bicycle."

"Certainly not, yet there she was, waiting for you outside your favorite pub. You'd never met her, you say? Did she know who you were?"

"I can't see how she could have known who I was. But there is something funny there. When we were in the park, she got a good look at me. She stopped dead in her tracks—seemed to recognize me. It was quite unmistakable—I seemed to frighten her. She took off on the double toward where she'd parked her bicycle."

"But she never went home," he reflected, "and when she was found, she didn't have her bicycle. It's still missing. How on earth did she follow you?"

I thought for a moment, and then the obvious answer struck me. "I don't think she did follow me. She couldn't have. I think from what was said last night that she followed Adrianna to the pub from the Wallace home, which means, obviously, that she knew to connect Adrianna Wallace with me." I rested again and thought for a minute. "And *that* information had to come from Morton Graves! That's the only place the two of us have been together while I've been working on this."

"And Morton Graves Voluntary Hospital is on the edge of Richmond Park, where you followed the Anatole girl yesterday! Did she have time to get that much information?"

"No. Not then, not unless she picked up a message somehow."

"She may not have been headed home at all when you last saw her."

"You said she was freezing when they picked her up. Didn't she have a coat?"

"No. She was reported to be wearing wool trousers and a thick sweater. Fine for the afternoon ride, I suppose, but not the thing for an overnight walk in January."

"When she shot me, she was wearing a man's coat—a sailor's watch coat, and gloves, and a wool scarf," I said. "She could have weathered any storm. If I'm right, she left the park and somehow came up to London to find Adrianna. She would have had several hours to do that. Then she could simply follow Adrianna until the next time the two of us met, which happened to be right away."

He hesitated and paced a few steps back and forth before he continued. "Charles, this will be a question you won't like, I know, but here it is anyway. Don't you think that this Townby fellow that Adrianna told me about could be a medium? You know, talking to Dr. Gussmann?"

"You know that I have to believe that there's a more down-to-earth explanation, Sir Arthur, but Townby does seem central in all this. Adrianna doesn't think he's the cause, though. I can tell you that if you met him, you wouldn't suspect him either."

"There's quite a lot of money involved in his and Gussmann's story. What the hell does any of it have to do with me?" Sir Arthur asked, shaking his head.

I tried to think through the question. "Apparently nothing. The names you were given in the letter all lead to Morton Graves. But none of them mean anything to you, and neither does Morton Graves Voluntary Hospital. No one there mentioned you when we talked to them." I paused for a few extra breaths. "Whatever Gussmann, or whoever it was, wanted to accomplish by sending you that note, it hasn't done anything."

"On the contrary! It got you shot, my boy. You started following the people on that list and asking questions at the hospital where Gussmann worked. Shortly thereafter, one of those three people shot you. She found you, waited for you, and shot you in cold blood," he said firmly. "It *has* got something to do with me. The note was sent to me. Whoever spotted you surely knows I sent you. That somebody will just as surely see to it that I'm killed—and that Adrianna Wallace is, too." He paused and leaned over toward me for emphasis. "And that someone has got to be Dr. Bernard Gussmann!"

"But he's dead, Sir Arthur. There seems to be no denying that."

"Just so! Hence my question about the possibility of a medium. I think that's our best avenue of investigation now."

"Perhaps," I said without conviction, "but I certainly can't be of any help there."

"No"—he smiled at me—"not since you survived. You might have been *very* useful if you'd died, though." He patted my arm and chuckled. "I'm going to leave you to your rest now, Charles. I may look in on you again, but I'm likely to stay out of sight for a while. Glad to see you looking so well, my boy." And with that, he left.

I lay there and thought over what he'd just said about the danger to him and Adrianna. It was true that Conan Doyle's involvement was revealed by the mere fact that I'd done what the note asked, and that I'd followed up on all three names. It was just as certain that Adrianna was vulnerable. She'd clearly worked with me on this. If my death served the purpose of this group—and now I was certain there was a group behind all this—then Arthur's and Adrianna's deaths might as well. I was drifting back toward sleep when Frederick Wallace appeared at the side of my bed. He seemed to materialize there while I blinked my eyes.

"Charles, I've got to talk to you. Are you awake enough to talk?" he asked.

I said that I was, and I even managed to pull myself somewhat more upright in the bed. "What do you want to talk about, Mr. Wallace?"

"I think, in the circumstances, that you can call me Freddy, Charles. That's what Adrianna calls me all the time. I'm sure that's how she refers to me around you."

"Freddy, then. What can I do for you?"

"This is awkward, Charles. I know that Adrianna has revealed certain things to you. I know that you've become . . . close these past few weeks." He paused and looked at me as if he were expecting some answer.

"It's not like you might imagine it, Freddy," I said.

"Quite . . . No, I know that, Charles. Adrianna has told me that it isn't, and I believe her. It's just that . . . well, it might at some time *become* like that. You know what I mean. Adrianna is a healthy young woman, Charles. You're—"

"Definitely not a healthy man at the moment, Freddy," I interrupted, "but I get the idea of what you're saying. Go on." I had the very uncomfortable feeling that Adrianna's husband was about to ask me a question I didn't want to answer.

"Do you think that's unlikely, or likely, Charles? I have to ask." There was a politeness—even, maybe, a genuine curiosity—in the question that I wouldn't have expected. Then again, I'd never been in this situation. Maybe this was the way it was done.

"I think it's rather unlikely, Freddy. Adrianna says so, and I certainly haven't said or done anything to change that," I said. "We're good friends. I guess I give her something harmless to do when you're . . . out of the house. She seems committed . . . to the arrangement you have. From my standpoint, she's a married woman. I've never been involved with a married woman and was always determined that I never would be."

"And now?"

"And now here's Adrianna, your wife. And as far as I can tell, she's a married woman who plans to stay married. I think she loves you, Freddy." I didn't add that the love seemed to be something like that of a daughter for her father.

He smiled at that. "I'm sure she does, Charles, but I think she may grow to love you, too. And I think you may grow to love her. Any man would."

I shrugged and looked away as my eyes suddenly filled with tears. Damned morphine, brings one's feeling so close to the surface. Freddy simply stood beside me, no sign of impatience or awkwardness now as he waited quietly until I was able to speak. "You want to know what I would do about that—and what she would do about it."

He took his time before answering. "It's best to talk about it beforehand, don't you think? In our case, Adrianna's and mine, we talked it all over before we were married."

"And you think it would be better if you and I talked it over before your wife has an extramarital affair with me," I said, a little too loudly. "Well, I do, too. If there's ever going to be an affair, and I don't think there is, we will certainly talk it over." I could hardly say the words and would have been entirely incoherent with embarrassment if it hadn't been for Freddy's compassionate face and soothing voice.

"I know this isn't easy for you to discuss, Charles, but I want us to be friends. If Adrianna is going to have you as a close friend, you're going to be involved in some ways, whether you like it or not, in her unusual marriage. I want you to know that I'm a fair man. I wouldn't expect Adrianna to hold to our original plan if things have changed for her, but I would expect warning. I would expect to be able to work things out in whatever way might be best for everyone."

"No need for a scandal," I said, trying not to sound sarcastic.

"We've always wanted to avoid scandal, Charles, but not just that. It was always the idea, also, to allow *both* of us to live our lives as we wanted to, not just me. Adrianna wanted an unusual life of her own, one that is no more tolerated than mine is. I know she has told you that."

"Yes."

"Well, I've seen twenty-five years more of life than she has, and I know that things change. I know what she doesn't know about herself."

I took a deep breath, trying to feel as reasonable and sensitive as Adrianna's husband sounded. "And what is that, Freddy?"

"I know that she's healing, Charles. I know that she is still getting over that surgical station at the front at Verdun. I know she is coming back to life. And when she does, she's very likely to find out that she's *normal,* and that the sanctuary she thought she wanted in 1918 isn't going to be what she wants for the long run." He turned away from me and took a few steps before turning back to face me. "I won't stand in the way of that, but I've got to know it in plenty of time to do what's best. Not only for me, but for Adrianna as well."

"I understand," I said. "A divorce is very hard to get—should she ever want one, I mean." I hoped that I didn't sound like I wanted that to happen.

Sighing, he walked back to the chair beside the bed. "Without compelling cause, Charles, it's nearly impossible to get. And a divorce for cause is always damaging for everyone. Obviously, Adrianna could bring charges against me easily, but it would literally ruin me and cast her in a very bad light as well. By a different arrangement, I could be allowed to bring charges, false ones, against her, but not without destroying her reputation in the bargain. We're both of old families. More reputations than our own hang in the balance. Perhaps you could say that we should have thought of this possibility three years ago. But we didn't. We're very close old friends, and we thought we had hit upon a solution to our respective problems."

"Then up jumps the devil." I attempted to smile, but the morphine kept me closer to sleep than to levity.

He answered with a smile of his own. "No devil has jumped up. Adrianna is just changing—changing for the better, I'm sure—but we're in rather a box now. We might be, anyway, at some point. That's why I'm talking to you now. Even if you aren't a reason for her changing, you're going to see it. As her good friend, keep in mind what I've said. If she does want to make other arrangements, it won't be simple, but it won't be impossible."

Before I could reply to what he had said, there was a warning tap at the door, and Adrianna walked into the room. Her face was wary as she looked at the two of us, but her tone was cheerful as she asked, "What's going on in here, boys? I thought you'd wait for me in the lobby, Freddy. I'm running a little late." She leaned over and kissed Freddy on the top of his head.

"Just getting our stories straight, love," Freddy said. He stood and smiled at her fondly. "It's the curse of the devious, you know."

She reached up to rest her hand on his cheek, looking into his eyes for a moment before answering lightly, "And has there ever been a less likely band of conspirators?"

They both laughed.

16

There is nothing more unaesthetic than a policeman.

—The Sign of Four

I WAS AWAKENED NEARLY twenty-four hours later, on Saturday afternoon, by pain as much as by Freddy's nudging of my shoulder. I felt like I'd eaten the worst meal of my life. The sensation of heartburn was overwhelming, and Freddy's shaking me, even though he was gentle, just made it worse.

"I'm awake, I'm awake," I said to make him stop. Then I opened my eyes just as he stepped back and Adrianna's face came into focus.

"I made him shake you, Charles. You can't sleep all day, though you very nearly have done. I've got things to tell you. Are you listening?"

I struggled to sit up, and Freddy moved back over to me and helped. After some rearranging of pillows and some gentle lifting, he managed to get me more or less upright at the head of the bed. "There you go, old boy," he said. "They say you'll be up and moving around soon."

"I hope not," I said. "I'd just as soon stay here." I really was quite disoriented. It seemed to me that I had been speaking to Freddy and Adrianna just a few moments earlier, but then I noticed that both of them were dressed differently than when I had seen them last. I realized that some time had elapsed.

Adrianna broke in with her best lady-of-the-manor tone. Her chin was high, and she was quite literally looking down her nose at me. "You can stay here as long as you like, Charles. I think I'm doing quite well without you. Shall I presume that you don't want to hear about Alice Tupper? I wouldn't want to burden you with the wealth of information she provided."

"Who is Alice Tupper?" I asked dully. The name rang a bell, albeit faintly.

"Dr. Gussmann's very private secretary. Remember?"

"Now you sound like Sir Arthur, Adrianna, talking to ghosts—everyone says she's been dead for years."

"Well," she said tartly, a smug smile on her face, "I asked her about that and she quoted your compatriot Mark Twain: 'Rumors of my death are greatly exaggerated.' She's alive, Charles, but not for long, I fear. I found out yesterday that she is living right here in London."

"And now, today, you've talked to her already?"

"Already? It's three o'clock in the afternoon, Charles. I talked to her practically all morning. She's in a rest home, a geriatric nursing facility, just a few miles north of here. She's not well at all, Charlie, but she's lucid enough."

"Did she confirm that Gussmann is dead?" I asked. My first concern, even in my fog, was to find out who had written the letter. "Could she absolutely confirm that?"

"She discovered him, Charles. He wasn't dead at the time, but in a coma. He died several days later—right here at Chelsea, as a matter of fact. She saw his body, though, in his casket at the funeral parlor. She mentioned that they had done a nice job—looked like he was alive."

"So she *thinks* he was dead."

"She didn't say whether she had tried to pinch him, Charlie. Honestly! He was dead! That's why they put people in caskets: their doctors say they're dead." She glared at me in exasperation. Standing behind her, Freddy suppressed a smile.

"All right, all right. What was she like?"

"Small, fragile, but very opinionated. And still very striking. My guess is that they were on intimate terms, but there's an edge to her voice when she talks about him. It was probably a complicated relationship they had—maybe even a difficult one."

"No question in my mind," Freddy added. "I went along with Adrianna this morning. I'd say the Tupper woman was remembering very mixed feelings while she talked to us." He sounded as pleased as Adrianna did about the results of their investigative excursion.

"How much could she remember?" I asked.

"Everything, Charlie, anything. There's nothing wrong with her mind. She's cagey, though. There are things she doesn't want to say—"

Freddy interrupted, "It was an odd mix of being delighted to have visitors—wanting to talk—on the one hand, and being careful and evasive on the other. She didn't mind talking about Gussmann as a man, but Gussmann the researcher—especially Gussmann the hypnotist—was off-limits. Wouldn't you say, Adrianna?"

"Exactly. She did let something slip, though, when I tried to inquire about his missing journal. She said something about it being his and for his eyes only. What was it she said, Freddy?"

"She said, 'No one was ever allowed to see his personal journal. It was for his eyes only, and I made sure it stayed that way.'"

"That's it. She emphasized the word *I*. '*I* made sure it stayed that way.'"

"Do you think she burned it or something?" I asked.

"Sounded like that to me," Freddy answered. "And the thing about hypnosis—"

"Whenever I mentioned hypnosis," Adrianna cut in, "she got very upset. 'Bernard was no conjurer,' she said. 'He was a neurologist.' That's what she said."

I stared for a moment at the two of them. They really did seem comfortable together, and I could see some sense in the marriage arrangement that had seemed so unorthodox to me. I was not happy with Freddy's direct involvement in the investigation, but that was my own damn fault for getting shot in the company of his wife. I sighed and focused again on what they'd told me.

After a moment I said, "I really wanted to see if he had ever written about the incident with Conan Doyle and his father in his own records. There has to be some way that someone got that information. You know—the scene that produced the scrap of paper—the one that was torn out of the sketchbook." I realized that if Gussmann's notes were unavailable, we would just have to find the answers some other way. "Did you talk about money with her at all?"

Adrianna nodded. "Yes. She tells pretty much the same story as Dodds and Townby. She said the bequest for her was unexpected. Apparently it was added at the same time as Townby's. It would have been enough for her to live modestly for the rest of her life, but medical bills have eaten it all up by now. She went through some up-to-the-minute treatments. Very modern stuff." Adrianna paused a moment before continuing sadly, "She's a charity case now."

"Dr. Dodds thought she was already dead, I gathered. What *is* wrong with her?"

"Cancer. Abdominal tumors. She had an operation two years ago that prolonged things until now—a resection of the colon, a new procedure—but now there are new tumors. Some are in the chest, and those are inoperable. They can't do anything. I spoke with her doctor this morning. He thinks she may have a few more months at the very most."

Freddy added, "She's in a lot of pain, and they're using heavy opiates on her much of the time now. It's a shame. Her doctor says she's not yet fifty, but she looks much older."

"She would have been in her thirties when Gussmann died," I said.

"And in her late twenties, perhaps, when Dr. Gussmann joined the staff at Morton Graves," Adrianna added. "She said she remembered when he joined the hospital. 'Such a distinguished man,' she said."

"He would have been in his sixties at least," Freddy said. "Like Adrianna, I suspect that theirs was more than a doctor–secretary relationship. And there *was* definitely something about his journal that she didn't want to discuss."

"Do you think we can get her to tell us more about what was in it?" I asked. "Could the opiates help us there?"

Freddy piped in, "Oh! Remember, Adrianna? She *couldn't* know what it said. She made a point of saying that his private journal was always written in German and that she didn't know any German. It was when she was talking about his private journal being for his eyes only. She said he was so secretive that he always kept his private notes in German so even she couldn't read them."

"German?" I said. "I can handle that if we can find the journals."

"Tell him about the jealousy, Adrianna," Freddy said. "That was really interesting."

"Oh, yes, Charles. When we mentioned Helen Wickham and Mary Hopson to see what she could tell us about the connection, she got livid. Made some very nasty cuts at both of them. Freddy and I agreed later that it was pure jealousy."

"She imagined them as younger rivals, I guess," I said.

"Maybe they *were* younger rivals," Freddy countered.

"But he was in his seventies by then, Freddy," I said.

"I know a few prominent men in their seventies here in London who are chasing young women, probably as we speak. Anyway, she was clearly jealous of them—and still furious at him, I thought," Freddy answered.

"I agree," Adrianna added.

"Did you question her about any of the others?" I asked.

"She wouldn't have known them, except Townby. We talked about him. She said he was easily cured of depression. She liked him. She was surprised that Dr. Gussmann didn't have him released. By the time Townby returned from Scotland, she had retired with her bequest. She never knew him as a doctor. I asked if she'd ever seen him after his return, and she said no. In fact, she says she hasn't returned to Morton Graves very often since she retired. I gathered that Gussmann was really her only connection to the place."

"The blackout periods, Adrianna. Don't forget the blackouts," Freddy said. "This was great, Charles." He was clearly relishing his part in telling this story.

"Yes, I saved the most interesting bit for last, Charlie. She said that she used to have blackouts when she worked for 'Bernard,' but that he cured her."

"Blackouts like some of the patients?" I struggled to sit straighter, and Freddy stepped over to help me again. "Go on!"

"It was when she was praising Dr. Gussmann as a great doctor. She said he was wonderful at helping patients who were severely depressed and patients who were disoriented. She said that many of his patients suffered from brief blackout periods, times when they couldn't remember where they'd been. Some of them had spoken to her about it. Then, she said, she began to have these blackouts herself. Sometimes periods of her day would disappear. All of a sudden, it would be half an hour later than it should be. A couple of times she came to consciousness in a different part of the hospital than she had been in. She said she became terrified about this and went to Dr. Gussmann for help. He told her he would treat her and she would be cured. And that's what he did."

"How did he treat her?"

Freddy answered, "She said he merely talked to her and told her that the blackouts would go away, and they did. She never blacked out again after she talked to him about her fears. She says that was a couple of years before his death." He walked to the doorway and opened the door. "I'm going to call for some tea," he said.

"Cured by hypnosis, do you think?" I asked Adrianna.

"Or maybe the blackouts were caused by hypnosis and he stopped putting her under," Adrianna answered. "Another thing I was able to do was bring Conan Doyle's name into the discussion. There was a copy of *The Strand* at her bedside, and I asked if she'd ever read any of Sir Arthur's stories and articles in it. She's an enthusiastic fan, to hear her tell it. She thinks his Spiritualist work is great, too. I couldn't detect any reaction that was out of the ordinary. When I asked her if Dr. Gussmann had been a fan of detective stories, she said she had no idea."

"So it doesn't look like she's involved in whatever is going on, then," I said.

"What do we do next, Charles?"

"I lie in bed next," I said. "How much longer, do you think?"

"As far as actually lying around goes, not long, I think. They'll have you walking a little by tomorrow, probably. As far as staying in Royal Hospital goes, that could be a week."

"Too long," I protested.

"Maybe less."

We were distracted by the sound of talking at the doorway. Freddy's voice and that of another man were in a muffled conversation. Adrianna stepped aside as she turned to see what was going on, and, looking past her through the open door, I saw Freddy Wallace, head down, a look of concern on his face, talking to a shorter man whom I did not recognize. Wallace looked and noticed that both Adrianna and I were staring at them. He nodded at us and stepped out of sight into the hallway. Adrianna leaned over close to my ear.

"Police," she whispered, "chief inspector. I've talked to him already. Remember about Freddy being with us."

"Outside as we left."

"You remember. Good. Sometimes on opiates . . . you know."

The man walked into the room and stood just inside the door. "Good afternoon, Mrs. Wallace, it's good to see you again. Mr. Baker, may I have a few moments of your time, sir?"

"My husband and I were just leaving, Chief Inspector," Adrianna said. "We'll see you later, Charles. Get well." She patted my arm and left the room with a nod to the policeman as she walked past him.

The chief inspector walked over closer to my bedside and extended his hand. "I'm Chief Inspector Willis, Mr. Baker, Homicide Division. I have a few questions about Thursday night's incident." After we shook hands, Willis moved to the foot of my bed and lifted my chart up so he could read it. "Opiates for pain and arsenicals for infection." He replaced the chart and again moved up closer to me, smiling with what I recognized as a stock about-to-start-the-interrogation smile. I had used pretty much the same smile countless times for starting my interrogations of German prisoners. "Are you feeling well enough to talk, Mr. Baker? I have a few questions, but I can come back another time if you aren't feeling up to it."

"I'm fine, Chief Inspector Willis. I'm about halfway between medications just now—clearheaded and not in too much pain. How can I help you?"

He withdrew a notebook from his inside coat pocket and a pencil from his outer pocket, turned through a few pages, and began.

"Charles Baker, employed by Associated Press, London office, American, currently you are on holiday." He looked up at me for confirmation. "Is all that correct, Mr. Baker?"

"Yes, that's right."

"Spending your holiday right here in London, then?"

"So far. I may do some traveling. I haven't decided yet."

"What have you been doing with your holiday so far, Mr. Baker, if you don't mind my asking?" He had already made some notes in his pad, even though I didn't think I'd said anything noteworthy.

"I've done a bit of driving in the country, explored a few places near London that I've never seen. Nothing, really, just resting."

He made notes as he spoke again. "And how long have we known this Liza Anatole girl then, Mr. Baker?" he asked casually, looking down as he wrote.

"Pardon me?"

"I have it here that you related to Mr. Frederick Wallace, during the early hours of Friday morning, that it was one Liza Anatole, Coombe Park, Kingston-upon-Thames, who is the person who shot you. Later that day we were able to take Miss Anatole into custody on investigation of attempted homicide." He looked up from his notes and smiled again. "Is that the name you gave Mr. Wallace, sir?"

I could see a problem of real proportions looming ahead in our conversation. How would a reporter for Associated Press come to know Miss Anatole from West London? Why would she shoot me? Who was I working for in this matter? I realized that we were about to have a discussion I really hadn't prepared for. "Yes, that's the name," I answered finally.

"And so how long have you been acquainted with Miss Anatole, sir? You recognized her at the time she shot you. Isn't that what you told Mr. Wallace?"

"Actually, I've never met her, Chief Inspector. I merely knew what she looked like."

"And why would that be, Mr. Baker? How would you know what she looked like?"

"She was part of an investigation once," I answered, thinking that this wasn't going well at all.

"A news story, Mr. Baker?"

"It might have become a news story, but it didn't. I've never met her."

He took more notes in silence, turned to a fresh page, and looked back up at me. Now he was not smiling. "Miss Anatole also says that she does not know you, Mr. Baker, and her brother-in-law insists that he doesn't know you—has never seen you. Is that correct?"

"I don't know her or her family. I simply knew what she looked like and where she lived," I answered.

"And what was the nature of this investigation that never became news, Mr. Baker?"

"I'm not at liberty to say. It was confidential." Now I tried the smile.

Chief Inspector Willis lowered his pencil and pad and stared directly at me. "Mr. Baker," he said after a long silence, "let me explain some things to you. I am a chief inspector of police. I am a senior officer investigating an attempted homicide. Normally I do not investigate homicides that were not completed"—he paused again—"but this case involves a member of Parliament; at least he says he was there. We use only senior personnel in such a case. Attempted murder is a serious matter, and now it is a police matter."

"I quite understand that this is a serious matter," I said.

"Sometimes we wish we could keep things in our private lives— well, private. But this is no longer a private matter, if that's what it ever was, Mr. Baker. This is now an official police investigation, and

I am the investigating officer. My reputation is involved now, not just Miss Anatole's or yours or others." He paused to tap his pencil against his notebook. "So now I want answers to my official police inquiry, Mr. Baker. Withholding of information in a serious criminal case is itself a crime, and journalists are not immune from prosecution."

So now I had Sir Arthur on the one side and Scotland Yard on the other. I lay in the middle with a hole in my stomach. "I understand, Chief Inspector. The case involved a letter that had been sent to a prominent citizen. I was attempting to find out who had sent the letter. Miss Anatole's name came up in my investigation, so I endeavored to find out who she was. That's how I knew what she looked like and where she lived."

He was taking notes as I spoke. When I had finished and enough time had elapsed that he was sure I was not going to say more, he asked, "This letter. Was it blackmail?"

"No. The letter was not of a criminal nature."

He looked up from his notes. I met his gaze directly, and after a very uncomfortable few moments, he glanced back down. "Let me move on to some other questions. We will return to your knowledge of Miss Anatole later." He turned back to earlier pages in his notepad. "You own an automobile, Morris Oxford model. Is that correct?"

"Yes."

"A woman who lives on Coombe Park in Kingston made a complaint call to her local constabulary early on Thursday afternoon to report that a man who did not belong in the neighborhood was repeatedly driving slowly around the circle. Once, he had stopped opposite her home and parked for several minutes without exiting the car. It was a Morris Oxford. The constable told her to call back if the car continued to drive the area. The woman never called back, and the matter, though duly noted in the log, would have been forgotten except for a missing-person report on the same street that same evening. Was that you in the car, Mr. Baker?"

I definitely didn't like the turn that this conversation was taking, but it didn't seem the time to try to evade the question. "Yes. I went out there to check the address that I had for Liza Anatole."

"I see. So this other investigation you mentioned—the one that involved a letter—this is a *current* investigation, isn't it? And did you meet with Miss Anatole on Thursday, Mr. Baker?"

"No, I didn't meet her. I saw her—I confirmed what she looked like."

"And did she see you?"

"I think she may have, but she wouldn't know who I was. As I said, we'd never met."

Chief Inspector Willis seemed to consider saying something and then stopped short of speaking. He turned back through his pages but didn't seem to be reading them. It was a ploy I'd used myself in interviews when I just wanted time to think. Finally, he lowered his notepad and looked up at me. "Sometimes we have cases in which a young woman is keeping company secretly with someone she is not supposed to be seeing." He looked at me for a response but got none. "In such a case, there are unaccountable periods of time in the young woman's life—unexplained absences. Sometimes we have cases in which a woman discovers, somehow, that her lover is romantically involved with another woman. In such cases, it is not uncommon for the outraged woman to attack, even to kill, her lover or her rival or both of them. Do you see how these types of cases would come to mind for me now, Mr. Baker?"

I could certainly see what he thought, and I had to disabuse him of any such notions. "Easily, but in this case, I do not know the Anatole girl, much less have an affair going with her. That should be simple enough to check," I said, though I wasn't at all sure how I could prove that I wasn't having a secret affair. "Moreover, I'm not seeing anyone else, no one at all. The shooting was not a crime of passion, Chief Inspector."

"There is another curious thing here," Willis said, actually consulting his notes this time. "You and Mrs. Wallace met with Frederick Wallace on the street just before the shooting. Is that correct?"

I gave an uncomfortable affirmative.

"So all three of you would have seen the assailant, at least briefly. You saw her clearly enough to identify her positively—and, I believe, correctly. Yet the Wallaces were unable to do so. In fact, they both thought she was a man. On the other hand, their initial descriptions of that man differ significantly. Then there is the fact that no one else can corroborate the presence of Mr. Wallace at all. While many people affirm that you and the well-known Mrs. Wallace were in the pub together for some time." He paused and made a show of consulting his notes. "And Sir Arthur Conan Doyle was with you both, is that correct?"

"Sir Arthur was actually waiting for Freddy with Adrianna, and I joined them at the pub," I answered.

"You and Mrs. Wallace left together. No one ever saw Mr. Wallace. Even though several patrons of the pub heard the gunshot and came out onto the street pretty quickly, none of them saw Frederick Wallace. How do you explain that?"

"Did anyone see Liza Anatole?"

"No."

"Precisely!" I said. "None of them saw Liza because she had already run around the corner or up an alley. For the same reason, they didn't see Freddy. He had already run in pursuit."

"That's odd, too, isn't it? You were still sprawled on the pavement having just been shot. Witnesses say that Adrianna Wallace was herself still down on the sidewalk, yet Frederick Wallace had immediately run away from the scene, apparently without taking a few seconds to check on the condition of either of you."

"He is a courageous military man. It was instinctive to pursue the enemy," I said.

Willis consulted his notes again. "Not only was he a courageous officer, Mr. Baker, but he was badly wounded in the leg and walks with a slight limp to this day. It seems curious again. You can see my problem. The accounts that I am given seem improbable, while more plausible explanations are denied all around."

"On the contrary, Chief Inspector, it seems to me that you do not wish to accept the very consistent explanations given not only by three well-known London citizens in addition to myself, but by the assailant herself," I retorted, trying to bluff my way into advantage.

"On the contrary, to borrow your phrase, Mr. Baker, Miss Anatole does *not* confirm that she shot you. She says that she's never heard of you or met you; that's true. But she says she wasn't in London, and as far as we know she had no way of getting here," he said. "Don't misunderstand me. I tend to believe that she's the one who shot you. She had plenty of time to do it, and she cannot account for her whereabouts. But one thing I'm still looking for is motive."

"Believe me, so am I. Have you charged Liza Anatole with my shooting?" I asked.

"Not yet. In fact, we may not be able to hold her much longer. Her brother-in-law is insisting that she be released to his care. His position is that she has done nothing. Though this is a rather long blackout spell for her, it is not particularly unusual. According to him she is not dangerous, and we have no grounds for holding her."

"Obviously she *is* dangerous," I said, "and I'm the one who'd be in danger if you let her go."

"I believe you're right, Mr. Baker, even though there is no real evidence you are right. You are really the only witness who says it was she, and you are unwilling to explain that adequately." He paused as if waiting for a reply that did not come. Finally, he continued. "Nevertheless, some instinct tells me that she is the one who shot you. I'll do what I can, but I expect her to be released as soon as her family's solicitors can get into a courtroom. That would be Monday. When we feel that we're going to be forced to release a prisoner, we usually do so before it's a matter for the court." He shrugged his shoulders. "I expect to be ordered to release her Sunday evening at the latest."

I realized that he was right. Given the lack of evidence and the apparent lack of motive—in fact, no connection between her and me—I had to expect her to be out soon. The inspector folded up his notepad and slipped it back into his pocket. He was through with me for now. I wondered if Liza Anatole was through with me.

"Get some rest," he said with a pat on my arm. "We'll talk again." Before he reached the door, he turned again to face me and then walked back to my bedside. "I really feel I have to warn you, Mr. Baker. The Anatole girl *is* dangerous. She has been involved in the past in a disturbing case of the worst sort, and she's not been cleared of the implication of guilt in it. If you have any involvement with her, sir, I urge you to tell us about it. You think about that." At that, he turned away and left me.

17

When you have eliminated the impossible, whatever remains, however improbable, must be the truth.

—The Sign of Four

SUNDAY WAS NOT A day of rest. It started early, with a nurse who made me get out of bed and sit in a chair. She said that this was so she could change the bedding, but it was obviously a form of torture. A little later another nurse made me get up again and walk to a toilet. So far, no one had given me a shot of morphine, and I was definitely ready for one. After that, I endured a succession of people changing bandages, sponging me off a little, changing my gown, and making me drink tepid water. Still no morphine.

At noon I was brought half a cup of warm milk. I explained that I didn't drink warm milk, but to no avail. My own preferences were obviously not to be taken into account at all during my recovery. My pain level was bearable, and I knew from experience that it was best that I not use opiates unless it was necessary. No one seemed to be offering me any, anyway.

I was walked to the water closet—the bathroom—again after my small liquid lunch. While I was being aided in my small steps back toward my room, I saw Robert Stanton, the confused boatbuilder, thirty feet away. He was standing at my doorway, peering in through the glass. I stopped dead, nearly causing myself to fall over.

The nurse held me upright and looked into my face. "Pain?" she asked. "Are you all right, sir?"

I turned as rapidly as I could so I had my back toward Stanton. "Take me back," I said in a whisper. "I want to go back to the lavatory, please."

Her face showed a questioning concern. "You can't need that, Mr. Baker, you've got nothing in you. I'd better get you back to bed and get a doctor."

"No!" I whispered sharply. "Just get me back to the W.C., now."

She decided not to argue this time, and we started our shuffle away from Stanton. I wondered if he had a gun and whether he'd dare to use one in such a public place. "Is it time for visitors?" I asked the nurse, still whispering.

"Not until three, Mr. Baker, those are the rules, though we've rather been ignoring them with you. Now that you're getting better, we'll be treating you like everybody else."

"I just wondered, because there was a man at my door just now. I didn't recognize him, and I don't feel like seeing any visitors."

The nurse turned her head and looked behind us. "He's leaving," she said. "Going on down the corridor. Maybe he's looking for some other patient. It's all private rooms on this wing—people come and go more freely." She looked back again. "He's gone down the stairway now." She looked into my eyes as I stopped walking again. "Was that why you wanted to turn around, Mr. Baker? You didn't want to be seen by that man?"

"I was shot by a stranger a few nights ago. I guess I'm afraid of unfamiliar faces just now. Can anyone just come up here?"

She considered what I had said for a moment. "I see what you mean. Normally, yes, people come and go without too many questions on a private wing. Police cases aren't usually on this floor." She paused for another nervous glance toward my room. Leaning close to my ear, she spoke very softly. "We heard that the woman who shot you was in custody. Isn't that so?"

"We don't know why she shot me or who else might try," I answered. "Could you take me back to my room, please, and get me the matron?"

"I can take you back to your room, but there is no matron here on a Sunday."

"Of course. Who would be in charge around the hospital today?" I asked as we shuffled along. "Is there a sister on this ward?"

"To tell the truth, there's not too much authority around the regular wings on a Sunday. If you've got enough authority, you don't work on Sunday," she said with a little air of complaint in her voice. "What is it that you want, Mr. Baker? Maybe I can figure out who can help."

"I want to change my room, and I don't want very many people to know about it," I said.

She looked startled. "You think someone might try to shoot you again, right here in hospital?"

"I really do, yes. What security is there? Is there a constable in the hospital? Anyone like that?"

She was showing real concern as we reached my room. "No. Unless the police bring someone in, there aren't any police in the hospital. Should I call the police?"

I really didn't want to have to explain Robert Stanton to the police if I could avoid it. "Isn't there some way I can change rooms? I think I'd feel safe then. We can call the police if we see any more strangers. I don't want to seem silly to Scotland Yard."

She paused and considered the question, running a mental map of the floor through her mind. "There is an empty room, three doors down. Mrs. Thomas was discharged yesterday. I'm not supposed . . . well, you'd have to speak up for me if we get caught moving you.

There's another nurse on this wing, and a few others come and go on other duties. I don't think Penny would approve. I'll have to just do it on my own."

"I'd be very grateful," I said. "Just walk me over to that room right now, if you will. We can talk about it later."

She started shuffling me along as she answered. "I'll bring in your chart in a few minutes."

"No," I said, "just leave it, and leave my bed mussed up, as if I'll be right back."

"Good idea!" she said with obvious excitement. "And I can go you one better. I'll get some gauze and wrap your face—just one layer. I'll put a chart with some other name on it on your bed. I don't think anyone will find you then, but I'll keep an eye out. I'm on duty until six." She was a born coconspirator.

We entered the new room, and she got me into bed. She left momentarily and returned with a wide roll of gauze, which she tossed to me. "I've got to help another patient, Mr. Baker. I'll be back soon, but you'll have to wrap your own head." She hurried out of the room.

I made a rather clumsy, thin bandage around my whole head and face with the short length of gauze she had provided. I felt much safer than I had a few minutes earlier, but there still seemed to be danger everywhere. My stomach was killing me, I realized, and I really wanted some morphine. On the other hand, I could hardly afford to be asleep, or even groggy, until I was sure I was safe. Perhaps fifteen minutes passed before the nurse returned. It seemed like an hour. She came in with a penciled sign in her hand.

"I'm looking for sticking plaster," she said as she walked to the bedside stand and opened a small drawer. "Here. Just a minute." She walked to the door, stuck the card directly onto the window glass, and closed it. "It says you're a burn patient and not to enter," she explained. "There's lots of danger of infection with burn patients.

Unless they have a good reason for coming in here, other nurses will stay out."

"You're a lifesaver," I said.

"I hope not. I hope that this is all for nothing, Mr. Baker," she said firmly. "I've been thinking, and I don't much fancy the idea of people with guns wanting to come into my wing, so I'd just as soon be wasting my time with all this." She came to my bedside and laughed. "I'll have to change that mess. You don't look like a burn patient— you look more like a feather boa's been thrown over your face. You wouldn't likely fool anyone, and you certainly wouldn't fool a nurse." She removed my bandage and replaced it with a fresh one from a new roll of gauze she had brought with her. Then as an afterthought she wrapped my right arm with the discarded piece of gauze. She stepped back to admire her handiwork and decided to wrap the other arm as well. "Can't even tell for sure if you're a man or a woman now," she said when she had finished. "I checked to see if the log down at the nurse's station still says that Mrs. Thomas is in here, and it does. I explained our disguise to the other nurses, and they agreed it was a good idea."

"There are some people I'll want to see if they come to visit today," I said.

"Mrs. Wallace, I'll bet."

"Frederick Wallace and his wife, yes—or either one of them, naturally. Also a gentleman named Conan Doyle," I said, somewhat uneasy about her assumption that Adrianna was at the top of my list. Did we give off vibrations?

"Oh, yes, Sir Arthur was here yesterday. It was a thrill for me, I can tell you. I bet I've read every one of his stories. Sherlock Holmes—I feel a bit like Dr. Watson myself today, what with all this disguising of my patient. Except you're a reporter, they say, not a detective, but that's something like a detective, isn't it?"

"It feels like it is today, Dr. Watson," I said. "Say, the pain is getting pretty bad. What does my chart say about morphine?"

"We can give you an injection if it gets bad. I'll get it for you."

"Just a small shot. Can you do that?"

"I can give you less, just not more. Do you want to stay awake?" she asked.

"Yes, and be able to talk."

"We'll start with a little," she said as she turned to leave the room.

In ten minutes my pain was down just enough to function, and I was calmer. I doubted if anyone could find me. The nurse had left my eyes and nostrils uncovered, and my fingers were exposed. Other than that, as long as I stayed under the sheets, I was a mummy. The faces of a couple of nurses appeared briefly at the little window in my door, but neither one entered. A few minutes before three I got out of bed on my own and shuffled about for a couple of minutes as an experiment. I passed the test. The pain was no worse, and I felt more steady than I had earlier.

Just past three o'clock, Sir Arthur entered the room and closed the door behind him. "A young nurse named Millie pulled me aside and told me where you were, Charles. What has happened? My God! What has happened to your face?"

"Nothing," I answered. "It's a disguise. I saw Robert Stanton roaming around trying to find me. Luckily, I wasn't in my room, and I don't think he saw me. I persuaded Millie to hide me, and she's done a good job."

"Robert Stanton, you say?" he said as he walked to my bedside and lowered his voice. "That can't be good. If one person on Gussmann's list tried to kill you, we've got to expect that the others may, too. Bad luck that you've got to stay in hospital, old boy. I'd rather get you out of sight behind something more substantial than gauze bandages."

"This will have to do for now. What about you, Sir Arthur? I think you must be in the same danger. Whoever is behind this must realize that my investigation was prompted by the letter to you. And we know they have Adrianna Wallace tied into it."

"You mean *you* have her tied into it, Charles," he said with a disapproving glance. "Actually, she's proved quite useful, she and Frederick. He told me in detail about finding the secretary, Alice Tupper. That should be an important avenue for us."

"Absolutely. I'm anxious to talk with her"—I gestured at my helpless condition—"when I can."

"I'd like to go along when you do," he said.

"Aren't you afraid of being recognized?"

He waved his arm dismissively. "I don't think it likely that this woman is involved, after what Fredrick told me, and I don't think we'll attract much attention by visiting a woman in a care facility."

I sighed. As much as he professed to dislike the sleuth he'd created, Sir Arthur was clearly driven by a dogged curiosity that would put Holmes to shame. It seemed that keeping Conan Doyle's name out of this tangled situation would probably prove impossible because—as I could see now—he just could not resist a mystery of this sort.

Rubbing his hands with glee, he sounded like one of Scotland Yard's finest as he said, "Let us review what we know." Confirming my suspicion that he intended to wade right in, he continued, "There are several people involved with that letter, and Bernard Gussmann is tied to all of them. He wrote the letter, or caused it to be written."

"By a medium, you mean? I'd rather consider the possibility that he wrote it himself," I said.

"You mean you think he's alive?"

"Not exactly. I mean that I want to be *sure* he's dead. There's a remote possibility that he somehow faked death. He was a hypnotist, and I don't know what he was capable of doing."

"Weren't there people at his funeral? Surely we can confirm with doctors who were in attendance at his death."

"I'm not sure I'd be convinced," I countered. Perhaps he somehow hypnotized the other doctors into believing that he was dead when he wasn't."

"Well then, what would convince you that he's dead?"

"His body—let's dig him up," I said, as if it were the simplest thing on earth.

Conan Doyle raised his bushy eyebrows. "I really doubt I could get permission for that, Charles, especially with my reputation these days. I shudder to think what people would say about such a request from me." He was right. Asking to dig up a long-buried body would shred what remained of his tattered reputation.

"Let's just dig him up anyway. I'd rather that there be no way for anyone to know in advance that we're going to do it."

"You mean exhume him illegally? What do you hope to learn, Charles? What can Gussmann's corpse tell us?"

"Honestly, Sir Arthur, I hope his corpse is not in the casket. A live Gussmann who faked his own death is a lot easier for me to track down than a ghost would be. I can imagine ways—all of them fantastic—that he might have used drugs and hypnosis to fake his death. If that's what happened—however unlikely it might be—it is more plausible for me than a letter from the dead."

He smiled in reply and patted my arm. "Of course, just the reverse is true for me, but I understand you. On the other hand, if his corpse is in the grave, as I'm sure it is, then I'll be more sure than ever that what I have *is* a letter from a dead man. You see, Charles, I've seen letters from the dead before, written through mediums, however much you disbelieve it. And, as a doctor, I can't imagine how Gussmann could have faked his death to the point of going through a funeral."

"So let's dig him up."

Conan Doyle thought about that for a moment. "I can't afford the risk of actual participation. God, what a heyday the press would have with that! I'll provide funds. You'll have to find the laborers and the opportunity. I don't know how you'll explain it if you get caught."

"I'll claim I was looking for clues to the whereabouts of the money."

"I think you'd go to jail just the same. I'll provide legal counsel if it's needed, but I advise against this adventure, my boy. Let's confirm his death in some other way."

I shook my head as vigorously as my various bandages would allow. "Someone plans to kill me, Sir Arthur, and he probably means to kill you as well. I want to eliminate the possibility that our prime suspect is still alive."

"I see what you mean. The issue of personal danger here in the hospital is something we have to deal with, too. For the moment, I'll arrange for someone to be here in the room with you all night. We'll make it appear that this burn patient needs constant watching," he said. "Now I've got other news for you. Did you know that they've released the Anatole girl?"

"I was afraid they would. The police chief inspector told me yesterday that he thought she'd be released today. Chief Inspector Willis is very suspicious. He thinks I might have been having an affair with the Anatole girl. He's not buying the story that Freddy was with us, either."

"I'll be careful if he talks to me. They released her this morning, but it's not as bad as it might be. They put her back in an asylum."

"Tell me it wasn't Morton Graves Voluntary Hospital."

"It was, Charles. That's where her family kept her before. They think her treatment was successful there. It's only logical that they'd put her there again. I got the word earlier from a friend at Scotland Yard. That hospital seems connected to all of this, doesn't it?"

"There's absolutely no question about that. The only question about Morton Graves is who, and how many? If Bernard Gussmann's ghost is haunting a building, Sir Arthur, it's that hospital."

"And maybe this one as well," he answered. "Stay alert, my boy. I'm going to go make arrangements for someone to watch you tonight. I'll leave you for now."

He didn't return, but Millie came by in a few minutes to say he'd retained her to stay the night. I gathered from her smile that she had been offered a generous retainer. A little later an orderly brought in a comfortable-looking chair and placed it in the corner, facing the door. At four o'clock Millie ushered Mrs. Wallace into my room and left us alone.

Adrianna sat on the edge of the bed. "Freddy's not here," she said at once. "He knows where I am. I don't expect to see anyone. How are you feeling? I can't see how you look—what's all this?"

"It's a disguise that Millie—that's the nurse—cooked up. Robert Stanton was here looking for me. I don't think he saw me. I wasn't in my room at the time. After that, it seemed a good idea to go into hiding."

Adrianna chewed at her lip and looked over her shoulder at the door. "If he came by again and looked in here, he might recognize me, and your disguise would be worthless. I'll keep turned away from the door." I refrained from telling her that she was almost as stunning from the back as she was from the front. Stanton, or anyone else glancing in the window, would have little difficulty figuring out who she was. "I've got a gun, Charlie. I'll leave it with you. It's a nice little .38 revolver."

"You may need it more than I do. I'm surrounded by people here. The nurse is going to stay in the room tonight."

"That's cozy," she said dryly. "Maybe *I'd* better stay. I'm the one with the gun." Then her voice softened. "I'm sorry, Charles, I've got no right to be—"

"I'm jealous, too, Adrianna, every time you go home." I watched her for a look of shocked indignation, but there was none—just a slight smile. "There. I've said what I shouldn't say," I admitted.

"Again," she said. "We seem to be saying quite a few things we shouldn't say, Charlie. And probably leaving quite a few more left unsaid," she added, "but let's get back to Robert Stanton. I wouldn't know him if I saw him, but he'd probably know me. What sort of man should I watch for?"

"Large, athletic, maybe forty years old. Today he was wearing a dark navy-blue coat," I said. Then I stopped and tried to visualize him as I'd seen him in the corridor. "The same kind of watch coat that Liza Anatole was wearing Thursday night."

"Maybe the same coat?" Adrianna asked.

"And the same as the one on the little man who followed you to Lancers."

"It was probably the Anatole woman who followed me, but she was alone. I'm sure of that."

"But Stanton might have brought her to London and loaned her the coat," I said. I wondered if Robert Stanton owned a car.

"Maybe. It makes sense—they are two of the three names on Gussmann's list."

"When I get out of here, I'm going to check on Gussmann himself," I said.

"By making inquiries into what, Charlie? Where can we go that we haven't been?"

"I want to be sure that he died."

"That again? Everyone says that he died. By now, Charlie, he'd be dead of old age, and in his case, syphilis." Adrianna shook her head.

"You're probably right about that, but I can't get over the thought that whoever wrote that letter knows Gussmann too well. As improbable as it is, I still want to make sure that he isn't behind this himself. While I'm stuck here, I want you to find out where he's buried."

"That should be no problem."

"And I've got a couple of other favors to ask you to do tomorrow. I want a hotel room or a small flat not too far from Captain's. Get it under some other name. Stock it with bandages and a supply of something for pain. Get groceries. I want to get out of here as soon as possible, but I'm going to need a safe place to get well. I'm not safe here nor at my own address. For that matter, I doubt if you and Freddy are safe at home."

"Freddy agrees with you. He's got me carrying this revolver everywhere, and he's doing the same. I'll get one for you."

"That may not be too easy on short notice."

"Freddy has several, and shotguns and rifles. He decorates his den with stuff like that, and there are more hunting guns at the lodge," she said.

"Freddy's a hunter?" I asked with a mocking tone. It just slipped out, and I wished immediately that it could be unsaid.

Adrianna bristled. "Don't be an ass, Charlie. Next you'll be telling me you're surprised about his military awards and his service record. He's a *man,* Charlie, a real man. Just because he lives differently in one way doesn't mean he's not just like you. Try not to be like every other idiot, won't you?" Her face was flushed, and she was clenching her fists.

"I'm sorry. I am a little like every other idiot, Adrianna. I guess that I'm about as narrow-minded as the rest sometimes, even though I don't like to think so. Freddy's a good man, and sometimes I forget he's your husband."

"Too right," she snapped. "You forget it a lot." Pausing for a deep breath, she stared down at her feet for a moment. When she looked up, her face was calm again. Quietly, she continued, "Freddy forgets it, too—he thinks he's my father most of the time." She reached out and patted the gauze on my arm. Then she added, "I forget it, too, especially since I started consorting with you." She took her hand away from my arm and reached into her handbag. Then she brought out the .38, a dull-finished military model with a four-inch barrel. "I've got to walk over to Victoria Station and then walk home at my end. Liza followed me at both places on Thursday, so Stanton might do so today. What do they do to you if you shoot a person because they're wearing a watch coat?" she asked seriously.

"Depends on who you are," I said. "In your case, I think it's worth the risk. If anyone in a navy coat gets within ten feet of you, shoot him. And I don't mean point the gun menacingly at him—or her—and shout warnings. I mean shoot. In the middle of the chest, and don't let the distance close to fewer than ten feet—that's about as far as the window is from you now."

The expression on her face said that I'd again joined the ranks of complete idiots. As if willing herself to be patient with the impaired, she sighed deeply before answering. "I know, Charles, they taught us all of this sort of thing before we went to France. I'll never forget something a sergeant told me in self-defense class. He said that the first essential weapon of self-defense was the willingness to kill an assailant. He told us that without that, all defensive weapons were useless. 'Might as well just lie down, ladies.' Those were his words, I think. He was no gentleman."

"But he was right. Be careful, Adrianna, and bring me a pistol tonight if you can."

"And find Gussmann's grave, and get you a room, and turn it into a hospital. How are you planning to get them to let you out of here, Charlie? Your wound is worth a week in here, easily that."

"I'm not going to ask them, and I'm not going to leave my forwarding address. That's another thing. Bring me workman's clothes to wear, and a wool cap," I said. I thought a moment and added, "And sturdy shoes, size ten. Whenever things are ready, I plan to walk out of here at a busy time when lots of people are coming and going. I'll need a strong man to lean on. Better hire one—Freddy would be recognized, and they'd think of him when they found me missing. I may not even tell Sir Arthur about this. The fewer people who know where to look for me, the better."

"You don't trust him?" Adrianna asked.

"Of course I trust him, but I can't say I trust his judgment—not with my life, anyway."

Adrianna thought about my list of requests. "I've got my key. I can pick up clothes at your flat."

"Don't go near there! We don't know where they're watching, or even who they might be. Freddy's not much bigger than I am. Maybe you could just bring me some of his things."

She put the pistol back into her bag and started for the door. "Don't worry," she said as she left me.

I turned to the window and saw that the cloudy late afternoon had turned quite dark. Two hours later, Millie joined me for the night. I got morphine, and she got coffee and a novel to read.

18

"Danger! What danger do you foresee?"

Holmes shook his head gravely. "It would cease to be a danger if we could

define it," said he.

—"The Adventure of the Copper Beeches"

WHEN I AWOKE ON Monday, I had a moment of panic. Millie was gone, and so was her chair. Bright light at the window told me that it was at least as late as full morning, but it took me a minute to focus on the clock. It was nine-fifteen. I had been asleep for more than twelve hours. Millie was gone, but I noticed that I was alive, so something had gone right. I discovered when I moved that I was in pain, but it was well within the bearable range. Then I noticed that the gauze bandages were gone from my arms. I felt my face and found them missing there, too. Other things seemed wrong, and it took me a moment to realize that I wasn't even in the room I'd been in with Millie. Then I remembered Townby's missing six years and began to worry that I'd lost a decade or so somewhere. *This should be January twenty-third, 1922. I wonder if it is.*

With that realization I began to slowly sit up and swing my feet out over the floor. When I pulled the sheet off of my chest, a large piece of paper rattled, and I found that there was a note stuck under my gown.

Dear Mr. Baker,

I had to get your bandages off and move you before the Monday shift came on. It would have meant my job to leave

219

you there. A friend helped me roll the whole bed back to your room just before six. He's watching your room from down the corridor. He won't go anywhere until I return. I will come back to check on you before noon.

Millie

That was a relief. I found that I could get to my feet pretty well and even walk slowly without support, though it was far from comfortable. I cautiously opened my door and looked out into the corridor. Sure enough, an orderly was sitting in a chair a few feet away. He got up as soon as he saw me and walked over to me.

"Mr. Baker, I'm Howard. Let me help you. Probably wanting to get down to the loo, am I right?" he said, putting an arm around me for support.

"Millie said you'd be here," I said as we began to walk. I found that I was moving faster now—almost half speed—and I didn't really need his support much. "Has anyone come around?"

"One woman got mixed up about what floor she was on and came down this corridor earlier. That was at about seven. I stopped her and helped her get straightened out. That's all. Lots of staff on now, but no visitors. I'll keep watching. I'm off duty. As far as they know, I'm just hanging around waiting to meet Millie."

"What did the woman look like?"

He reflected for a moment and answered, "About Millie's height and build, but brown eyes. Millie's are that nice blue, you know. A few years older than Millie, maybe early thirties. Lighter hair than Millie, but not exactly blond. Darkish-blond with a sort of a little red in it. She was a rich woman, I think. Custom-fitted dress, you see, and a quality coat. I looked her over good because Millie said to pay attention to anyone who came onto the wing. She said no one was to be allowed to see you. She told me to be careful." As I entered the rest room, he added, "That woman was German, I think."

I stopped. "What makes you say that, Howard?" I expected him to form his answer in terms of Millie, like "not the same language as Millie," but he didn't.

"When I stopped her—I stood right up and got in her way—I asked her where she was going. She looked at me kind of startled-like, and she said *'Kinder.'* Then she changed it to 'children.' She asked for the children's ward. I told her that there was more than one children's ward. She asked where she could get directions, and I sent her down to the main station on the first floor. I've heard a lot of German, so I knew when she started to say *'Kinder'* for 'children' that she was German. She didn't seem to have an accent, though, whenever she talked."

I pondered that as I closed the door. Howard stood dutifully in the hall and waited for me. Probably it was nothing, some relative looking for a sick or injured child. After I finished a mental translation of what he'd said by imagining changed characteristics for my nurse, I realized that the description could have fit Mary Hopson, more or less. Mary hadn't seemed to me to be the least bit dangerous, and I'd spent quite a bit of time with her. Nevertheless, if the visitor this morning was the Hopson woman, it was a bad sign. It wouldn't be surprising, though, once I thought about it. She was on the same list from Gussmann's letter; she probably would be involved in the same way as the others. At least one of them had tried to kill me. None of them had any reason to come to find me in Chelsea Hospital, unless that business was the same as Liza Anatole's business had been.

With Howard at my side for moral support, I managed to walk, slowly but unassisted, back to my room, where I found Freddy waiting for me. He looked relieved to see me as he stood with a substantial briefcase on the floor beside him.

"Charles, I was worried when you weren't in the room where Adrianna said I'd find you. I see you've lost your bandages, too," he said.

Howard helped me into bed and left the room, and I turned my attention to Wallace. "What have you got there, Freddy?"

"Some clothes that ought to fill the bill," he answered. Then he leaned over and lowered his voice, "and a nice Luger—just the thing for a German-speaking chap like yourself."

"For some reason the Germans call them parabellums, not Lugers," I said.

"Right. I forgot that you were the man on the German desk, Charles."

He walked over to the door and peered out through the glass. "Adrianna is looking for lodgings even as we speak. I'd suggest that we get you out of here as early as possible. I've got a car and driver standing by on West Road—the street that's directly below your window. The man will be watching for the hat that's there with the clothes. He'll drive you away as soon as you can get down there. He'll take you to where you can wait for our call. Then he'll drive you to your room. How do you feel?"

"I'm better, thanks. I can walk some, but it seems a long way down to that street from here just now. I've walked fewer than a hundred feet, and I don't think I could do it again for an hour."

"I'll have someone collect you with a wheelchair whenever you can get dressed," he said as he opened the door and stepped out. He gestured and stepped back into the room. A moment later, Howard came in. "If you can help Mr. Baker get dressed," Freddy said, "I'll go and get a wheelchair." He turned to me. "Have you got any more of that gauze Adrianna said you were wearing, Charles? I think that something around your head would look nice this morning."

Howard stepped over to the table and opened its little drawer. "None here," he said as he walked to the door. "I'll get some."

Freddy opened the large briefcase and dumped its contents onto the bed. "Sorry, old man, the shoes are size eleven. And I'm afraid I forgot the socks. We'll have to make do. Stand up here if you can, and we'll get you started."

I stood slowly, leaning against the edge of the sturdy iron bed frame. Freddy untied my gown and courteously turned his face away. He reached behind his back to hand me the trousers and then walked over to the door to peer out into the corridor again. I managed to struggle into the pants, which were both too long and too big in the waist by about an inch each way. At least the extra inch would hide my bare ankles from prying eyes. I found a plaid wool shirt and put it on while Freddy continued to stand watch. The sleeves were too long. Thankfully, I found a belt and managed to prevent the trousers from falling to the floor. The pistol was wrapped up in a gray quilted-cotton jacket. I slipped into the jacket and put the pistol out of sight into the jacket's ample right-side pocket. I had the ensemble nearly completed when I set the wool cap on my head. Miraculously, it fit pretty well. At that point I looked like some kid wearing his big brother's hand-me-downs. I was still barefooted, though, and I knew I'd never be able to bend over far enough to get into the shoes.

When Freddy turned his attention away from the door to check on my progress, he saw the problem right away. "We'll wait for Howard before doing the shoes, old man. The corridor is empty just now so I want to get you down to the larger W.C. at the other end." He resumed his watch. "Here he comes. Just be a minute now." He opened the door, and Howard came in with gauze and scissors.

"Have you thought, Mr. Baker, about how Millie's going to get into real trouble over this?"

Freddy answered, "Her patient disappears after she's been paying special attention to him. Is she here now?"

"Not today," Howard answered, "but there'll be questions. I'll think of a story."

"But *you* could get into trouble," I said.

"Lots going on this morning, Mr. Baker. I don't think I've been paid much notice. I'll handle it. Let's get something on that head." Howard removed my cap and swiftly wrapped my head in a layer of gauze while Freddy left the room. By the time he'd finished and replaced my cap, Freddy was back at the door with a wheelchair. Howard let him in, closed the door, and helped me into the chair. Then he pulled a blanket from the bed and put it over my lap, tucking its end under my feet. As Freddy placed the shoes under the blanket on my lap, Howard said, "Let's go. Check the door if you will, sir." We were on our way.

We made it without incident into the large public lavatory near the waiting lounge at the opposite end of the corridor from my room. There I finally got my feet tied into the shoes. Freddy looked out into the corridor again and said, " Morning visiting hours are in full swing now. I'm going to leave the building. I'll take my time, stroll over to Victoria Station, and take a coach home. You two wait a bit. Then get down to the car waiting on West Road. My driver will recognize the cap." He extended his hand to Howard. "Good work, old man, I'll see you again."

They shook hands, and then Freddy was gone, and we were left to our wait. I patted the Luger for comfort. Howard watched the corridor, waiting for it to be filled with more people. After what seemed forever, but was probably five minutes, he said, "It ain't going to get no busier, gov'nor. I think we should go before someone figures out that you're missing."

"Right. I'm ready."

He wheeled me to the nearest elevator. When the door opened, I was looking up into Mary Hopson's face, and she was looking down into mine, except she wasn't able to see mine through the gauze. She turned her gaze politely away from my obvious tragedy and recognized Howard.

He spoke first. "Hello, milady. Did you manage to find the child you were looking for this morning?"

Hopson looked a little startled, but she answered, "Yes, I did, thank you. I'm here to meet a friend now. She's got the wrong directions, too, I'm afraid. I'll show her where the child is when she gets up here."

"The lounge is just down there on the left. I've got to take this elevator. Good luck with your friend," Howard said as he rolled me past her and into the now-empty elevator. Just as the door closed, I saw Mary Hopson, walking away down the corridor, wheel around and look back toward the elevator.

"Don't go back into the building when I leave, Howard," I said. "That woman is one of the people who are trying to get me."

"Don't worry, Mr. Baker, I'm going straight home. I've got tomorrow off, and I'm going to stay away from here at least until Wednesday. I'll just leave the chair downstairs and disappear. I'm a lot more worried about you. Get moving now." Howard was true to his promise to disappear. By the time I turned around, he was gone.

Freddy's driver took me to a small office building on Eaton Mews North and helped me walk through the lobby and into a small, windowless ground-floor office. He helped me get seated at the room's only desk, brought me a notepad and pencil, and then told me he'd wait in the lobby until I came out. An hour later, the phone rang after I had stared at it so intensely that it could resist my entreaty no longer. The call was from Freddy, who gave me directions to a hotel in Chelsea. He said to wait until two o'clock to arrive because he wanted everyone out of the way, whatever that meant.

After Freddy's call, I shuffled out and summoned the driver. I asked him to go out for milk for me. That was about the extent of the food I'd been allowed, and I didn't want to second-guess the doctors. The driver was reluctant to leave me, but I lied and said that Freddy had said it was okay to send him out for food. I told him we wouldn't be leaving the office until two. I asked if he had money, explaining that I had none. While he was gone, I reached into my trousers and discovered that I'd lied again. There was a one-pound note and four fivers in the trousers. I wondered if that was part of Freddy's cache of provisions for me, or if people like Freddy just carried around that kind of spare change—almost a week's pay for me.

By two o'clock, when the driver took me to the Chelsea address, I was in real pain. He could tell that I wasn't going to be walking in under my own power, so he went up to the room number I gave him to see if he could get help. Adrianna came to the car within a couple of minutes, wearing a red wig. She had morphine with her, and I got a shot and a few minutes of rest before we started in. She and the driver walked me in to the hotel through a back door and into the elevator without encountering any other guests. By two-thirty I was propped up in one of the room's two beds and was feeling drugged but better.

A long dresser top was stacked with bandaging, medicine bottles, and cans of food and milk. There were two large suitcases against one wall and large shopping bags resting in a chair in the corner.

After the driver left, I asked Adrianna how I was registered.

"The room is registered to Mr. and Mrs. Hampden. We're paid in advance for two weeks."

"You're actually staying here in the room?" I asked.

"There are two beds, and I've got my wig for when I go out. You, of course, won't be going out. You need a nurse, Charlie. Actually, you need a doctor, but you aren't going to get one for a while. I've got morphine, bandages, and some arsenicals, but those are new to me. I've got good instructions, though. I know what your dosages were at Royal Hospital. You're in good hands, I hope." She smiled slightly.

"I'm certain of that," I said. "Have you had any trouble? Do you think you were ever followed?" I waited for an answer, but she didn't reply. "I saw Mary Hopson at the hospital. She was there at least twice, but she never figured out where I was."

"God, Charlie! I don't like that one bit. They're really out in force. How would I know if I was followed? I don't know what the Hopson woman looks like, or Stanton either, for that matter. I've been moving pretty fast, though, sometimes with a driver and sometimes driving on my own."

"You weren't recognized here at the hotel?"

"I'm not the one who found and paid for the room, and I didn't bring in the supplies. When I did the shopping for food and clothing, I was in disguise, but I was in one of Freddy's cars. The butler brought the stuff over here. They'd have to be following Freddy's butler and me and Freddy all independently. Freddy never came here, and he doesn't plan to. When I came over here myself, I took a cab from near our house and had him deliver me to a restaurant near here. I left it through the kitchen. I went in as me, but I left the kitchen in the wig. Do you think that was good enough?" She walked anxiously to the window and peeked out behind the heavy drapes.

"I doubt if I could have kept up with you, even in my prime," I said. Then, as tired and worried as I was, I couldn't help laughing at this implausible situation we'd somehow gotten ourselves into. The look on Adrianna's face brought an abrupt end to that. "Are you scared?" I asked rather lamely.

"Aren't you, Charlie?"

"I sure as hell am. Do you have your revolver?"

"Right there in my handbag, and I've got something else you wanted me to get."

"Socks for me, I hope."

She laughed. "Freddy told me. Yes, I've got those, but I've also got the key requirement for survival—the willingness to kill my assailant, Charlie. The more I thought about what's happening, the more I thought about what my self-defense sergeant said in 1914. Now I'm more mad than scared."

"Well, I'm more scared than mad," I said, "because these aren't soldiers we're dealing with. I understand soldiers. I'm trained for them. This is something else."

"This is evil," Adrianna said, "and we don't even know what it's after."

"It? Why do you say *it?*" I asked.

Adrianna walked over and sat on the other side of the bed to answer me. "The letter with the list of names who are now after you, Charlie—probably after me, too—the letter's from a dead man. What would you call it? You know, I had a dream last night. In the dream, I shot the little man who was following me on Thursday. But he didn't die—he didn't even slow down. We're sure they can shoot us, Charlie, but are we sure we can shoot them?"

I took her outstretched hand. "I've shot quite a few men, Adrianna, and they've all fallen down so far. You've seen quite a few men who'd been shot. They all fell down. I think that if we have to shoot these people, they'll fall down, too."

"As you said, those men you shot were soldiers. These aren't. Look, I know the dream was just a nightmare. I probably had it because you told me you want to dig up Gussmann's grave. Nevertheless, these people aren't soldiers in uniform arranged along a front. They're civilian men and women on the streets of London. We don't know how many there are, but we know that they mean to kill us—you, anyway. So now I'm ready to kill my assailants. I've got the first weapon." She lay down on her back beside me, still holding my hand. "If they try to get us here, Charlie, I'm going to kill them."

I squeezed her hand gently. "So am I," I said, "but first I want to drink some milk and change clothes."

Adrianna got to her feet. "You're overdue for a change of dressings, too. It's time for me to get back to nursing. You're not out of the woods yet, Charlie. That's a very nasty wound, and you're far from past danger with it, much less the danger out there on the streets." She handed me a pair of socks and a clean nightshirt. "You can put these on in the lavatory."

"No I can't," I said. "I won't be able to manage the socks and shoes."

"Okay," she said. "I've got to replace those bandages and get you cleaned up. Then I'm going to mix some tinned milk with water and honey for you. You'll like it—I'll warm it just a little on the portable hob. And later, after you rest, you can have some nice beef tea that I brought over in a thermos bottle." She had slipped into a crisp, cheerful nurse-in-charge voice and posture. By the time she was recounting the bodybuilding benefits of beef tea, she had walked me to the bathroom, eased me gently through the door, and closed it behind me. There was nothing to do but follow her instructions. That voice brooked no argument.

It was late afternoon before I was cleaned, properly bandaged, fed, and tucked into bed. Adrianna put my Luger beside me and told me she was going out to put the old bandages into some trash bins down the alley and get herself a proper meal and some tea. While she was gone, I fell asleep, and it was late at night before I saw her again. The lights in the room were out, and she was emerging from the bathroom in a backlighted cloud of steam with one towel held around her body and one wrapped around her head. I didn't know if she could tell that my eyes were open. She walked past my bed and retrieved her pajamas from a drawer. Then she walked back past my bed and into the bathroom again, dropping the towel as she started to close the door after her.

"A gentleman would have closed his eyes, Charles," she said.

I dragged myself over to the bedside table between the two beds and turned on the lamp. When she emerged again from the bathroom, she was properly dressed in her pajamas and I was sitting up with a newspaper I'd found on her bed.

"So how long have you been awake, Charlie?"

"A few minutes. I heard something—must have been you banging around." I'm sure I sounded calm and casual, but I was thinking every second of the view I'd had of her a few minutes earlier. It was getting more and more difficult to think of her as Freddy's wife. "What time is it?"

She answered as she sat on the edge of her bed. "Almost ten o'clock. You've been dead to the world since I got back about two hours ago. I ate a nice dinner in the hotel dining room. Food tastes different, you know, when you're in disguise." She smiled mischievously. "Then I took a walk around the area for an hour to see if anyone was lurking about. I couldn't see anyone hiding in doorways or anything. How do you feel?"

"I think I feel better. I'm worried about your walking around alone, though. If they have found out where we are, it's not safe for you out there."

Adrianna moved over to sit on the edge of my bed and put her hand on my forehead to check for fever. "I wasn't me out there, Charlie; I was the redhead who doesn't look anything like me. Besides, it seemed like a good idea to do a tour of the perimeter, as they say, and you certainly aren't up to it. I did a lot of thinking out there, trying to make some sense of this mess. I had no flashes of insight. How about you?"

She had my arm pinned uncomfortably, so I struggled to get it free and made more room for her to sit beside me. "All I can be sure of is that someone doesn't want us to work on that list of names. It could be whoever sent the letter, or it could be someone who just knows about the list. Whoever it is, they're deadly serious about it, and we can't just walk away from it. There's no way to tell them we're willing to quit, even if we were."

Adrianna turned and lay back beside me, leaving my arm under her neck. "Would you quit, Charlie, without knowing how the letter got written?"

I adjusted my arm a little and got her head comfortably on my shoulder. "I'm curious, but I'm not that curious. If I could get a truce by dropping the whole thing, I think I would. Whatever this is all about, it isn't really my business. What worries me is that these people probably want to get at Conan Doyle as much as they want me—or us. Freddy probably isn't safe either. For now, there doesn't seem to be much choice for us. We have to find out what's going on and stop it before they get to any of us. They know what they're doing. All we have is a hideout."

"The police couldn't help?"

"We can't expect police cooperation if we won't come clean and explain what we know. If we do that, they'll quite rightly assume that we're crazy Spiritualists. After that, they won't take us seriously at all, and we'll be on our own and hiding out again. The police are out of the question. In the first place, Willis didn't believe anything we said. If it weren't for Freddy's—and your—social status, he'd have pressed a lot harder already—"

"And in the second place," Adrianna cut in, "you've disappeared from Royal Hospital, Chelsea. Willis won't see that as anything but running from his investigation."

We were silent for a moment. Adrianna walked to the window and looked out.

"Not to mention that he won't be able to question *you* again. Freddy will have to stall him," I said.

"Freddy will handle that. What about that nurse? Won't Willis question the Chelsea staff?"

"No doubt." I didn't like to think about that. I might have put some good people into deep trouble. "Willis isn't going to drop this."

Adrianna turned onto her side, adjusted her head, and put an arm across my chest. "It's a pretty good hideout, though. You listen for noises for a while. I need to get a nap."

"I'm not sure you should get your nap here in my bed, Adrianna. I'm not sure my moral character is quite strong enough for that."

She laughed. "Don't worry, Charlie. You haven't got the blood pressure right now to be a cad, even if you were so inclined. Trust me; any woman will be safe with you for at least a week."

We were safe that way all night.

19

Of all ghosts the ghosts of our old loves are the worst.
—"The Adventure of the Gloria Scott"

I AWOKE TUESDAY TO find myself alone again. I found that I was able to get up and move around the room. The level of pain had subsided to a category I would call intensely uncomfortable, downgraded from dully agonizing. No new blood appeared to be seeping into my bandages, and I could walk at a decent strolling speed. The mirror showed me a disheveled, unshaven, and very pale man who appeared to be several years older than I was. He was standing sort of stooped over. I was rummaging around looking for a razor when the red-haired Adrianna returned.

"Hungry, Charlie?" she asked as she came in. "I brought you two glasses of fresh milk." She walked over to where I was leaning against the sink. "Good to see you up and about, but you look a mess, Mr. Baker. Let me find the razor—we've got one here somewhere. I'll give you a shave. Then we'll give you a sort of bath. Maybe even get you dressed. Do you think you're up to all that?"

"The milk first," I said. "Then we'll see how far we get. I guess you've eaten a proper breakfast."

"I did. And I got a morning paper. At breakfast I read a small story on page ten about a gunshot victim disappearing from Royal Hospital, Chelsea. I doubt that it would have made the news, but this particular patient was a shooting victim who had just been in the news on Friday last. What do you think of that, Charlie? You've made the papers again."

"I suppose the police are hunting for me."

"I called Freddy, and he said that Chief Inspector Willis has been hounding him about *my* whereabouts, too. He's not stupid."

"What did Freddy tell him?" I asked.

"That I'd told him I was taking one of my Paris shopping trips."

"And Willis bought that story?" I asked.

"As a matter of fact, I'd been planning a trip before all this began. Several of our friends knew it."

I must have looked skeptical, because she continued rather defensively, "It's what we do, Charlie. We go to the couturiers and have fittings and drink champagne—all very frivolous—but we do it."

"And that's very lucky for us now," I said as appreciatively as I could. "How long are you usually gone?"

"It can be as long as two weeks. We have a small flat near the Seine, and Freddy has told the concierge that I'm coming, but I'm not to be disturbed.

Adrianna led me to sit on the edge of the bed and ran hot water in the basin. I drank my milk while she found the razor, one of those safety types that used little disposable blades. In ten minutes I was both fed and nicely shaved, without a single nick. Then she left me in the bathroom with instructions to get cleaned up. After I had managed to get somewhat presentable, she helped me to get dressed in the new clothes that had been brought in for me. By the time that was done, I was too tired to do anything but lie down, but I felt and looked more human than I had for several days. Adrianna was pacing the floor impatiently as I fell asleep.

When I next opened my eyes, she was opening my shirt to check my bandages.

"I must have dozed off," I said.

"For about five hours, Charlie. I've gone out for lunch already. You haven't even moved. You're healing well, though." She finished probing my abdomen and helped me sit up while she looked at my back. "Want some more milk? I brought some up."

"When do I get real food?"

"You get porridge in a few days, maybe Thursday. You can have more soup today if you want it. If you feel up to going out, I'll drive you somewhere for some special soup. Do you think you can walk around that much?"

I sat up rather creakily, testing my discomfort level before answering. "I want to go meet Alice Tupper," I said. "I'm pretty sure I can do that, and we've got to get on with this. For one thing, she may be in danger if anyone followed you when you and Freddy went to meet her. Do you think I can get around that much?"

"I don't think it's particularly good for you, but I'm ready. After all, it's you who'll relapse, not me," Adrianna said as she brought me a glass of milk. "Seriously, it's probably not a bad idea if you get out of this room and move around a bit. Let's get you into a tie and jacket. We'll go down the back way and be careful."

"Let's call Sir Arthur," I said. "I think it's time to let him know where I am, especially since that piece has come out in the paper."

Two hours later we had enjoyed soup at a quiet restaurant before joining Conan Doyle at the nursing home. Now we were sitting at another bedside looking into the face of a very sick woman. Alice Tupper was glad to have the company, though, and she was ready for conversation.

"Where is the man you had with you the other day, Mrs. Wallace? This one's younger, isn't he?" she asked Adrianna. Before she got a reply, she turned toward me. "You're not as healthy-looking as you ought to be, young man."

"This is Charles Baker, Alice. I spoke about him the other day. He's the one who's doing the writing about Dr. Gussmann," Adrianna said. "And this is our friend Arthur."

I said, "I've been ill, Miss Tupper, you're right. I had an accident, but I'm getting better. How are you feeling today? Do you feel like talking to us?"

"I'm not getting better, unlike you, Mr. Baker. But I feel like a visit. I don't see many people from outside anymore. What's your interest in Bernard? He's been dead for so many years that I'm surprised there's any interest in him now." While she addressed me, she was staring at Conan Doyle.

"I'm writing about hypnosis as a therapy, Miss Tupper. He was one of the pioneers, wasn't he?"

She gave a small frown as she answered. "Oh, yes, and he never got the recognition he deserved, because he didn't publish his late work—the work he was doing at Graves Hospital. I think he would have been world-famous if he had. I think he was going far beyond anyone else at the time." She straightened up in her bed and gave me a sharp look. Her feeble voice became forceful as she demanded, "What kind of things are you saying about Dr. Gussmann?"

"Well, I've just begun, but I understand that he was doing interesting work with William Townby and Mary Hopson, among others." I watched closely for reactions to the names. She seemed pleased to hear them; in fact, bringing up these names seemed to have the effect of reassuring her that I had done proper research.

She smiled. "Oh, yes, those and Tommy Morrell and several others were special cases. He was using hypnosis therapy on most patients to some degree. He could relieve depression and anxiety in most patients—most anyone, really, if they were susceptible to hypnosis. Bur some people just can't be hypnotized."

"Do you remember Helen Wickham? Was she also a special patient, Miss Tupper?" Sir Arthur asked.

She looked closely at him for a moment. "You're somebody . . . famous. I've seen you in the newspapers."

"I'm a writer," he said simply. "You may have seen my picture, Miss Tupper."

"You may call me Alice, please. Yes, Helen was one of his special patients," she answered with a slight frown, "now that you mention her."

"In what way were those special patients special, Alice?" Adrianna asked.

She paused to consider, it seemed, just how much she wanted to say about Gussmann's work. When she answered, it was with a patently false vagueness suggesting how little she understood about him. "I don't know. Medically, that is. He worked with them much more often, and he made extensive notes in his journal about them—his private research journal, not the regular treatment notes that I typed for him at the hospital. He was very secretive about his special patients. I think he worried that someone would steal his ideas. He had his ways, though, of seeing to it that his ideas were safe."

"A secret hiding place for his notes?" I prompted.

Tupper looked surprised. Then she relaxed and frowned. "No, not then. It was his secret code I meant. He kept his private research journal right in his cabinet with his books where he could get to it easily, but he wrote it in code—German code."

"You mean he wrote his journal in German," I said. "That was his code?"

"No. He was Austrian by birth, and he could speak fluent German, but no one around Morton Graves, except me, could speak any German at all. I studied the language in my school days. Back then, if you gave me a translating dictionary and enough time, I could translate a simple passage into English. His private journal was different."

"How so?" Conan Doyle asked.

"It was based on German, but it was a code. I wasn't supposed to look at it, but I did. I was curious, you know. Besides, I wanted to see if he was writing anything about me," she said with a worried look. "I could make out some words, enough to know that the code was based on German. But I couldn't read it at all. That was his way of keeping his research safe until he was ready to tell the world what he was doing—thinking in German, but writing in code." She looked at me again and nodded.

My heart sank. It was beginning to sound like the secret journal wouldn't be of any help at all, even if we could find it. With fading hope, I asked her, "Do you mean that the words he wrote were jumbled—you couldn't figure out what the words were because he had rearranged the spelling on most of them?"

"No, the writing, the script itself, was different. Most words weren't recognizable; the only ones I could make out were German, and even those looked funny. The script itself was code. He had terrible handwriting anyway, but this was more than that. Toward the end of his life—of course, I didn't know then it was the end of his life—he became even more secretive and hid the journal behind a false back in one of his cabinets. He could be such a child. It took me maybe a week to find out where he was keeping it, but it didn't matter. I couldn't read it anyway." She sighed at the memory of her frustration.

"And you think this journal contained notes about Mary Hopson and William Townby and a few others. Why do you single them out?" Arthur asked.

"Because of what he *didn't* write about those patients in his regular notebooks. He was seeing Townby, Hopson, and Morrell much more than he was seeing anyone else. But when he would give me his regular notes about their sessions, they would only have brief, routine comments. Ordinarily, he was a very thorough man. For most patients, if he saw them for an hour, he would give me at least a full page of notes to type."

"But not these patients? Did he make notes about them?" Adrianna asked.

"With those three, he would be behind closed doors for two or three hours; then I would get two or three lines: 'Patient is progressing nicely. Seems much improved. Further sessions required.' I knew those weren't his real notes, so I would look in his private journal when I could. There would usually be at least a page of notes in his code."

"Was Clare Thomas one of his special patients?" I asked.

She looked sharply at me. "That's all nonsense about his murdering her," she snapped. "He couldn't have done such a thing—wasn't strong enough, for one thing."

"I didn't mean that," I said. "I'm just trying to learn about his most important cases."

That seemed to calm her. "Oh, well, yes, she was a special patient. He worked with her several hours a week. That's why they should have listened to him when he said she wasn't ready to leave. He knew her much better than the other doctors did. She was still having lots of blackouts, but they didn't know that."

Adrianna reached over and patted Alice on the forearm. "The other day you said that you used to black out, sometimes, when you were working for Dr. Gussmann. You said he made that go away. Is that why you thought he might be writing about you in his journal?"

Alice Tupper was silent for a moment while she seemed to consider whether to answer that or how. Finally she frowned and said, "What can it matter now? I can tell you about that without hurting anybody." She paused for a deep breath. "That's why I started to try to read his private journal, yes. I wanted to see what he might be writing down about me."

"And what did you think you might find?" Adrianna asked, her face sympathetic.

Alice looked first at Doyle, then at me. Finally she shrugged her frail shoulders and answered, "We were intimate. But later there was more than that. Not only were we carrying on an intimate relationship—right there in his office as well as at his home—but he was also experimenting on me with hypnosis. He asked, and I gave my permission. I didn't know what he might be doing with me. That worried me a little—I believed at the time that he was in love with me, and I was sure he would do nothing to hurt me. Still, I started having blackouts—not when we were . . . having sessions. Sometimes I was injured a little when I regained consciousness—a bruise, a small burn . . . painful . . . in places. That was when I started worrying about what he might have written down about me."

"Several of his patients were having blackouts, too, weren't they?" Conan Doyle asked.

She nodded slowly, as if her thoughts were a great distance away. "Yes," she said quietly, "but just the ones he wrote about in his private journal, and that was why I wanted so badly to read it. I started trying whenever I got the chance. All I could tell was that he was making entries on the days when we worked on hypnosis together and on the days when I had blackouts."

"But the blackouts stopped, didn't you say?" Adrianna asked.

"I told him how worried I was about the blackouts and said I didn't want to try hypnosis anymore. He could tell that I was very angry, and he couldn't afford to antagonize me. He stopped hypnotizing me, and the blackouts stopped, too. Everything else," she said with a grim expression, "went right on for a while."

"And did he go on making notes about you, do you think?" I asked.

"No. I don't think so—not in the private journal, anyway. Whatever he was making notes about must have had to do with the hypnosis, not the . . . other. I was relieved. I mostly trusted him, you know, but men can be so childish. You never know what bragging they might want to do. That's what I worried about. Who knows when someone might have been able to read that journal? But now I'm sure that no one else ever will read it," she added with a nod.

"Do you have the journal, Alice?" Adrianna asked gently.

The small woman's eyes flashed as she snapped, "I most certainly do not!" Then she relaxed slightly, adding, "It wasn't mine. It belongs to Bernard. It's too bad that he didn't finish whatever he was learning and publish it. I'm sure it would have been brilliant—the medical parts. But no one else has the right to see it."

"And you didn't want anyone to try to find it, did you?" Adrianna said. "I think I would have destroyed it if it had been me."

Alice took a long look at Adrianna. "No, you wouldn't. Not something that meant so much to someone you cared about. That journal, for all of its secrets, meant everything to Bernard. I couldn't destroy it. It's his, whatever it is, may he rest in peace. And whatever he might have said in it about me, or any other women, no one is ever going to be able to read it so I can rest easily, too."

"Other women?" Adrianna said. "Did you suspect Bernard of intimacy with other women?" She asked this in a tone that conveyed at once both camaraderie and sympathy, and she shifted her weight so she was turned entirely away from me and Doyle. Her slight movement served to exclude us from the conversational circle in order, I presumed, to encourage Alice's confidences on such a delicate subject. I sat back so I could just see Alice's eyes over Adrianna's shoulder.

Alice frowned. "Some of the patients were very young and

beautiful. He could hypnotize some of them completely, I knew. Some of them had blackouts. We had words about this—I accused him of taking advantage of them—but he always denied everything." She paused as if considering whether to continue. Adrianna leaned forward encouragingly, and Alice went on. "I was pretty sure he was misusing them. There were signs of minor injuries. His last couple of years, he couldn't . . . we were no longer intimate. Often he was very ill. Then it didn't matter so much to me about the others. Still, I wonder what he wrote about them."

"I'd love to find it," I said, leaning around Adrianna's back. She shifted again to let me back into the conversation. "I'm sure that I could show what a pioneer he was if I could figure out how to read it. I read German very well. Maybe I could make out more of it than you could."

Now Alice's face was prim. "I'm not sure I'd want a man to read it, even if it were around somewhere. As it is, it's gone. They have looked high and low for it at Morton Graves, but they will never find it."

"But maybe with your help we could look—" Conan Doyle tried to prompt her.

She changed the subject abruptly. "You know about the money he left? I got a nice share, but the hospital administrators were angry even about that. Dr. Dodds knew there were more papers than he could find, and he took the place apart looking for anything that might get more of the estate for the hospital. They went to Bernard's home and went through his private laboratory there. It was a waste of time. They gave up after a while. I retired and left. After Bernard was gone, I only visited the hospital a few times; there was nothing there for me."

Adrianna said, "May I ask you about your blackouts, Alice? I spoke to William Townby. He experienced them, too. Sometimes he would regain consciousness and not have any memory of how he got to the place where he was. Was it ever like that for you?"

"A few times I woke up in one of the patients' wings of the hospital—someplace I would have had to walk to—and I had no memory of having left my office. Once I was visiting at Bernard's home. We were talking in his laboratory and then I woke up out on the street. Ten or fifteen minutes had gone by. It was frightening. Bernard would say it was nothing, but I made him stop it."

"You made *him* stop it?" Adrianna said. "What was he doing, Alice?"

"I wasn't sure, but he was doing it. I knew that he was causing it. Don't ask me how; I just knew it. I told him to stop it and he did. Of course, after it stopped, that made me even more certain that he was the one who'd been doing it. He was doing it to them, too, I'm sure."

"What do you think he was doing?" I asked.

"Once he said to me—sort of absentminded, as if I weren't there—'Mesmer was right, by God!' You know about Mesmer?" she asked.

I nodded. "A hypnotist a long time ago, a showman, not a doctor."

"My God! Mesmer was right! That's fantastic!" Conan Doyle smiled broadly.

"I had to look him up," she continued. "Mesmer said that the hypnotist overpowers the being of the subject—dominates the mind of the one being hypnotized. I think Bernard could do that. Anyway, at least he thought he could. I think he'd make me walk out of my office and into another part of the hospital just to see if he could do it. Then I guess I got too far away, or something. I read that Mesmer worked very close to his subjects to make them do things."

"Do you remember how he worked with you—what he said before you were hypnotized?" Doyle asked.

"It was depressing, usually. We usually talked about something I didn't like to talk about. Just talked. Bernard was a lot like me. He'd had similar experiences in his life—been hurt by the same things. We'd just talk about some of that. A few times I'd remember something quite pleasant from my childhood. It was almost like being back there for a moment," Alice said with a smile.

I thought about the implications of what she'd said. What if—just what if—Gussmann was experimenting with how far he could make a subject go under his suggestion, and for what length of time? What if he had faked his death in 1909? What if he were still alive, and still hypnotizing his special patients somehow? Where would he be living—somewhere near Richmond Park, perhaps? Had I actually seen him sometime during the past week? I shuddered at the thought of Gussmann, now ancient and clearly unhinged, manipulating people who could not resist his domination.

"Were you present when Dr. Gussmann went into his coma, Alice?" Doyle asked.

She seemed to shrink back into herself. "No," she said very softly, "no, I found him lying unconscious next to his desk."

"Were you present when he passed away?" he continued.

It was a long time before she answered, but this time the answer was crisp and impatient. "No, that was late one night. These are odd questions, if you don't mind my saying so. Mrs. Wallace was asking the same things the other day, and in the same peculiar way. Are you suggesting that Bernard did not die in 1909? I assure you that he did. He passed away more than twelve years ago. When I saw him in his casket, I realized that he was very old and had been in bad health for some time." She paused and was silent for a moment. "I'm sorry, but I don't want to talk any longer today. I've been awake for some time. I need my medication and some rest. Perhaps we could talk another day? I'd like to do that." She turned toward me. "Frankly, young man, you don't look too well yourself just now."

She was right about that. I had become more hunched over while sitting up for so long, and I could feel the path of the wound all the way through my body. We said good-bye and agreed to come back to see her again soon. Then I hobbled to the car with Adrianna's assistance.

While I rested in the passenger seat, Sir Arthur and Adrianna stood next to the open car door beside me.

Adrianna said, "Let's dig him up, gentlemen."

"So now you agree that Gussmann has to be alive?" I said.

"Of course not, Charlie. That's just nuts, but we've got to dig him up anyway. Weren't you paying any attention?"

"I was, and she didn't say anything about Gussmann's grave. We're going to find no Dr. Gussmann in that grave, I tell you."

"No?" Adrianna said. I could not read her expression.

Conan Doyle nodded absently. "I agree, we've got to take a look," he said. I could tell he was already anticipating what it would mean if I were wrong and the grave were not empty.

"The fact that she swears that Gussmann is dead doesn't mean, necessarily, that he is," I reminded them both. "She was under his influence then—might still be."

Arthur answered, "Well, we're agreed, then. We'll dig him up. Proceed when you can, my boy. I better get back home."

With that we were left on our own to return to our hotel. While Adrianna drove back, I was too preoccupied with the pain in my own body to really focus on Gussmann. When we got back to the room, Adrianna gave me a shot of morphine and held my hands while it began to take effect.

"You could be right," I said once I could unclench my teeth. "You're pretty smart—you're pretty *and* smart." I squeezed her hands to emphasize my feelings.

"Wounded men always fall in love with their nurses, Charles. I'm sure you did that in France."

"What do the nurses do, Adrianna?"

"They learn not to fall in love with the patients."

"And you learned this lesson?"

"Not very well, Charlie. Not very well."

20

I may be on the trail in this matter, or I may be following the will-o'-the-wisp,
but I shall soon hear which it is.
—"The Adventure of the Beryl Coronet"

ADRIANNA CLOSED THE DOOR none too gently behind her as she struggled with her arms full of shopping bags. Her red wig was tilted noticeably to one side and threatened to slide off her head altogether, but she was helpless to prevent it until she deposited her parcels on the dresser. Daylight was streaming in through the window, and I found that I could sit up without too much pain, even while laughing.

"Confounded thing," she said as she pulled the wig free and dropped it into a chair. "It started slipping as I was walking down the street with this armload, and there was nothing I could do. I can tell you that I wasn't fooling anyone who saw me. I came up the back way, though, and didn't see anyone in the hotel."

"Well, you looked a mess, all right, but you didn't look like Adrianna Wallace."

"No, I just looked like some tart, but I bring good news."

"And milk, I hope," I said as I got up and walked over to the dresser.

"Yes, milk and good news. Also some bad news. Which do you want first?"

"Let's get the bad news over first," I answered as I began to rummage in the grocery bags for the milk.

"Chief Inspector Willis is the bad news. He called Freddy in a rage this afternoon. He says that he won't be put off any longer. He says he knows that I'm missing. He was quite frank in suggesting that we were missing together."

"That's not very surprising. After all, our names have been bandied about of late, or so I'm told."

"That's not the worst of it by far. Then the inspector told Freddy that you and I had visited Morton Graves Voluntary Hospital on Thursday morning last and had represented you as a family attorney."

I was stunned. "Damn! How did he get onto that?"

"He told Freddy that he had feared that your disappearance might mean that you were hunting for Liza Anatole. After all, she shot you, and you knew where she was confined. When he contacted Dr. Dodds at Morton Graves to talk about security, he got an earful."

"Dodds had made the connection?"

"Dr. Dodds had seen the piece about your being shot. Your photograph was in the paper along with your identity. So we're both persona non grata at Graves."

"Talking to Townby again is out, I guess."

"Worse. It was clear to Freddy that Inspector Willis thinks we're hiding out together. He told Freddy to tell us to turn ourselves in for questioning."

"That's really quite a lot of bad news, Adrianna. What does Freddy think?"

"He thinks that Chief Inspector Willis better be careful what he says about the wives of members of Parliament. He told the inspector as much. He thinks we'd better be *very* careful."

"There was good news?" I asked.

"I've found some diggers."

"Diggers?"

"As in grave robbers, Charles, men who will help you dig up Dr. Gussmann. Actually, they'll do all the digging. You're in no condition for that. You'll be a lookout."

"You're not serious."

"I certainly am." She looked indignant. "Aren't you the one who's been saying you wanted to be sure of what's in that grave? Well, soon you'll know."

"These are professional grave robbers, I presume, not just some brawny lads you've met," I said skeptically.

"I don't think they're certified or licensed or anything, Charlie, but they've done this before."

I shook my head in wonder. "I find it difficult to believe that you got up this morning early, nipped around to the local grave robbers' hiring hall, and found a couple of journeymen who were next on the list. How, exactly, did you come to find our diggers?"

"You persist in underestimating my connections, Charles. As a nurse, how many doctors do you suppose I know in London?"

"Plenty, but I bet none of them uses grave robbers."

"How many of them were once medical students, do you suppose?" she asked.

"All of them, but medical students hardly need to rob graves to get cadavers."

Now she was looking at me as if I were a charming, but extraordinarily slow, schoolboy. "In the first place, I'm not so sure that you're entirely right about that. I know for certain, though, that some of them did just that before the war. What do you suppose young doctors and nurses talk about when they're stuck in France trying to drink themselves into a good humor during a lull in the fighting?"

"Grave robbing?"

"Not exactly, but that, too. The lads talk about all the foolish pranks they remember from home and all the larks they went on during medical school," Adrianna continued. "One night they got to besting each other on grave-robbing stories. All these stories involved employing grave robbers to do the dirty work. Last night I remembered those stories and the names of the now-respectable London surgeons who told them."

"So you simply called up Dr. Whosits and asked him if he's still robbing graves. 'I say, old nob, what say you help snaffle a smallish corpse, eh, what?'"

Adrianna rolled her eyes. "Nice accent, Yank. Yes, I suppose that if I were one of the 'good old boys,' I might do just that—code of silence and all. But for a woman, a mere nurse, and after some years have elapsed, that would hardly work, Charles. As luck would have it, though, one of those surgeons was a really close friend during the war, and one who wouldn't dare refuse me anything."

I was liking this less and less. "Wouldn't dare? Adrianna, you're talking about discussing a serious crime with the man. You're not exactly a person with nothing to lose yourself. I hope you haven't compromised anyone's anonymity."

"Don't be an ass, Charles." She paused and glared at me. "Too late for that, I suppose," she said angrily. "Who do think has the most reputation to lose here, anyway? You?—an American working journalist, a six and a half, by your reckoning. Arthur, who is already a laughingstock on three continents? No, it's Adrianna Wallace and her husband, Freddy, who have something to lose."

"I'm sorry."

"Too right! You *are* sorry, Charlie. Do you know where you'd be on this investigation if I weren't here? You'd be sitting around having cigars with the old author and whining to each other about how it didn't make sense. Then Lady Jean would probably get a message from some spirit that would miraculously confirm whatever Sir

Arthur wanted to believe. You'd be nowhere, Charles. I'm not so sure you wouldn't be better off, but you certainly wouldn't be getting anyplace on finding out what is really going on. *I* got you into Morton Graves to meet Townby. *I* found Alice Tupper."

When she had stopped talking and seemed to be regaining some control, I said, "And you stopped me bleeding to death."

"Well, I led Liza Anatole right to you, so we're even on that one." She walked over and kissed me on the cheek. "You want to know about the diggers now?"

I took both of her hands and looked at her. "First, I want to know how you know we can trust the doctor. Then I want to know about the diggers."

"I could put the doctor in prison, probably. I could certainly ruin his practice forever. He, by the way, could do the same for me. We have to trust each other."

"Something that happened in France?"

"Something that happened several times in France. It started out to be just once, but it didn't end up that way. Just he and I know about it, and now you."

"Maybe you'd better not say any more. I get the point. You can trust the man. I'm sorry I sounded skeptical, Adrianna."

"In for the penny, in for the pound, Charlie. I'm going to tell you. It was abortion."

"For you?" I asked softly.

"No, I was smarter and luckier than that. It was a case of rape, actually, the first time—a French girl, fourteen, raped by a German soldier. A friend brought her to me. She said that the girl's father would literally kill her. She thought that maybe I could do something, but I knew I didn't have the skill. I talked to Roger, and he agreed. I assisted him. It was a bad thing to do, but the alternative seemed so much worse. We made harder decisions every week, you understand?"

"Surely. I did, too, just different ones. You said it was a rape the first time. There were others?"

"Every one of them said it was a rape. Some said it was a British soldier, some said German. Who knows, some of them might have been raped—they were all under twenty. Some of them came from quite a distance. By the end of the war there had been about twenty of them. I made each one of them promise never to tell anyone about it, but obviously they did. I suppose they couldn't refuse another woman in trouble any more than we could refuse them."

"Serious business. You'd have undergone court-martial at least. You know better than I do what the punishment might have been."

"We'd both still be in prison, I imagine. The worst part for both of us, though, was that neither of us thought that abortion should be practiced at all. Yet every time it came to us out there in real life, it was what we felt we had to do. Damned if you do, damned if you don't."

That familiar phrase seemed to me to sum up most choices that present themselves when nations go all out to savage each other. At least that's the way I remembered it. I changed the subject without commenting on her confession. "Now tell me about the diggers. You don't mean that your surgeon friend still practices on cadavers."

"Certainly he does, but he gets them quite legally. He knows researchers, though, who need more than they can get sometimes. It didn't take him long to find the right men when I told him what I needed."

"What did you tell him?"

"I told him that I was involved in an investigation into the death of a man who had died some years ago. I told him that I couldn't explain anything to him, but that I needed to dig up a grave without going through official channels and without getting caught. He warned me that it was a serious crime and thanked me for coming to him when I needed help."

"Have you met these diggers?"

"No, and I don't plan to. I'm a pretty recognizable lady, Charles. Roger, my doctor friend, is expecting you to contact him. He'll get you in touch with the men. He says a crew of four or five of these men—they rotate as diggers and lookouts—can empty a grave in a couple of hours. Apparently the worst thing that ever happens is that they have to abandon the job because someone comes along. They never get caught. The going price for a crew that knows what it's doing is twenty-five pounds."

"My God! More than a week's salary. Crime's expensive business."

"Makes you want to change occupations, right, Charlie? When you're in shape, I bet you could do a grave a night—quite an income."

"No, I guess not. At these prices, expenses are sure piling up, though."

"I wonder if it will be worth it. Neither you nor I expect that we'll get proof of a ghost. If you're right, Charlie, there'll be an empty coffin, and the letter may be from a live Dr. Gussmann."

"That's not what you think, though," I said.

"No. I expect to find the doctor dead; but if we're lucky, we may find something else that will give us a new start."

"A treasure map to all his money?"

"His money was around in plain sight a lot longer than he was, Charles. Let's just wait and see what we find."

Just before midnight I found myself standing, hunched over my painful stomach, in the cold at the edge of East Sheen Cemetery about two hundred yards from Bog Gate. Another man was posted two hundred yards closer to Sheen Road. A third was standing at the point where the cemetery adjoined Richmond Park. Two men were digging. The four men had worked together many times in the past, they assured me. They had instructions to get me when the casket was up above ground. I planned to examine the contents of the coffin briefly and then have it reinterred by the same crew (at a cost of an additional ten pounds). They had been instructed to save the brown winter turf from the top of the grave so it could be replaced, as much as would be possible, at the end of the job.

Luckily, Dr. Gussmann's grave was deep into the cemetery, at least fifty yards off the path on which I stood. At that distance I could only occasionally hear the shovels as they dug. The ground was not frozen, so the men expected an easy time of it. There was enough moonlight to see for a few feet through the mist, and they worked without additional lights. I carried a flashlight for use during my inspection and a press camera with a large flash attachment so that I could photograph what I expected to be an empty casket. I was quite enjoying the adventure, to tell the truth. It reminded me of covert meetings I'd had with intelligence agents during the war. In this case, however, there was not much chance I'd be shot by a sentry or hanged as a spy. On the other hand, I would have said a week earlier that there was no chance of being shot walking away from Lancers.

I was grateful that Adrianna was safely at home. Well, not at her home, exactly. She was in our room, waiting for me. Well, not exactly entirely safe, either, I realized. To be more accurate, Adrianna was sitting with a pistol at the ready in a run-down hotel room she used as a hideout with a wounded man who was not her husband. It didn't sound so good when I thought of it that way.

I imagined a better situation, one in which she was waiting for me at our own home—say, in New York. Maybe she couldn't ever show her face in London society if my fantasies came to pass, but I would certainly have a good job in New York. People back there wouldn't care if she were divorced. Well, they wouldn't care as much as people here would. I found that standing in the cold at midnight on the edge of a silent graveyard I could imagine quite a few alternate realities. Perhaps, through no fault of my own while I merely did my best to solve this mystery, Adrianna and I *would* be discovered in that hotel room. Perhaps the least scandalous thing for Freddy to do *would* be to demand a divorce. Perhaps she *would* give in to temptation with me (I had about decided that I would).

She had never even kissed me on the lips. She had never said that she might be tempted to make love to me. In fact, she had just that morning called me a six-and-a-half-point American working journalist, and she hadn't said it any too admiringly. That didn't exactly have the ring of wedding bells about it.

I heard a clank in the distance. After that, at intervals, there were other clanks and a few scraping sounds. Finally I could hear footsteps coming close to me.

"We're ready, sir," said a voice whose body was concealed in darkness and mist. "Come along and see what you came for. We're anxious to get finished up."

"I can't see you," I said. "Which way?"

The man stepped closer, and I could just make out his shape. "Follow me, sir, this way."

I hobbled along behind him, each step causing little stabs of pain in my abdomen. When I was close enough to the grave to see the casket and another man, I could tell that the two sections of the lid had already been removed and set aside. I turned on the flashlight and pointed it into the casket. There lay Gussmann, or at least I had to assume it was the doctor. What I actually saw was a moldy wool suit. The head and hands that were not in the suit were skeletal remains, with a thin layer of parchmentlike skin. I prepared the flash camera and took a photo. The flash fairly blinded us all for several seconds.

"Bloody hell, man! If you couldn't see that for a mile, you're blind. Better not be any coppers about tonight."

I set the camera aside on the ground. "Sorry," I said, "I didn't realize."

"Are you through, mate? We'd like to get this over with, you know."

"Just a minute." I turned the light back on and looked up and down the interior of the coffin. A satin coverlet concealed the body from the waist down. I gingerly took hold of the top of the cover and pulled it out of the coffin. Gussmann was dressed all the way to his shoes. I extinguished the light and just stood there.

"Odd," said one of the men. "He ain't too tall for that box. Wonder why they'd do that."

"Do what?" I asked.

"Prop his knees way up like they've done. I seen that before when a body was too long for its coffin, but he's got plenty of room."

I turned the light back on and looked at the knees. They were resting on a small cloth-covered pillow centered under the knees that raised them perhaps six inches higher than level. "That isn't normal, to use a pillow like that?" I asked the expert.

"Pillow or a piece of something. But I never seen it when the coffin's long like this one. He's got a foot to spare the way he is. His knees'd be practically rubbing the inside of the lower lid. Odd, is all I'm saying. It don't mean nothin'." With that, he turned his shovel handle downward and poked the pillow beneath the knees. There was a solid thunk.

"Wood, do you think?" I asked, pointing the light on the bundle.

"Turn that off, mate. We don't need so much light. I'll get the pillow or whatever it is. Just a second." He kneeled down beside the coffin, shoved the suited legs aside, and grasped the cloth-covered object, pulling it out into the very dim light. "Like a pillow, all right," he said. "Several layers of cloth around it." He felt around the bundle, as if trying to find the end of the cloth so he could unwrap it. "Funny. It's sewn on like a pillow, but it ain't a pillow. Too heavy-like. Slab o' wood, likely, padded with cloth. Odd lot of trouble to go to with a long coffin." He dropped the bundle back onto the legs and stood. "We'd best start puttin' him back, sir."

The other man lifted one of the pieces of lid and started toward the coffin.

"Wait," I said quietly. "May I borrow your shovel a moment?" The closest man handed me his shovel, and I turned it handle-downward as he had done. Even though the effort caused me some pain, I prodded all along the sides of the coffin and then thumped the bottom at several points. Everywhere I felt the same thin padding covered with satin. Then I leaned down with difficulty and grasped the cloth-covered bundle and stood up. I handed the shovel to the workman. "Go ahead. I'll look at this later," I said, clutching the bundle.

"As you like, sir. We can finish up here without you if you'd like to go on."

It occurred to my suspicious mind that reinterment might come to an end as soon as I was out of the area. These men had insisted on payment in advance and had little incentive to continue their risky business once I was gone. "No," I answered. "Thanks, but I'll stay till it's done. I want to leave things as normal-looking as possible."

"Suit yourself. It won't fool nobody when we're through. I told you that this afternoon. First custodian who comes by this grave is going to know it's been disturbed. If you're lucky enough to get a snow tonight, it might not be noticed till spring, or maybe not noticed at all. Otherwise, someone will know soon enough."

I retreated slowly from the gravesite toward the point where I'd been waiting during the digging. After perhaps a hundred feet I stopped and sat on a gravestone. I felt the bundle in my hands. The cloth seemed to be canvas, and it was well sewn around its core. Clearly, I wasn't going to open it here. Trying to feel through the cloth to determine what the contents might be, I could discover nothing. It might be a piece of wood after all. Beneath the cloth it was apparently wrapped with a thick layer of something, perhaps felt or cotton padding.

My curiosity was interrupted by the sound of voices in the distance. I looked toward the sound and realized that it was coming from the direction of Sheen Road. Then I saw lights moving toward me. Someone was coming from perhaps four hundred yards away. Whoever they were, they were more or less between me and where I'd parked my Morris. I heard a sharp clank from over by the grave and the sound of boots making haste toward Richmond Park, directly away from the approaching lights.

While my hired gravediggers could escape rapidly to the south, I had no such option. In my condition I would be very lucky to walk at two miles per hour, and that with considerable difficulty and not for long. The retreating miscreants might, however, provide a decoy if they kept making so much noise in their flight. I decided to move across the cemetery toward lights in a building that appeared to be about five hundred yards away. If my sense of direction from the way I'd come in was correct, I thought I was now going westward while the people with the lights were coming from the north. After a hundred yards or so of stumbling through the dark graveyard, I came to a low stone wall at its boundary.

In my normal condition, I could literally have jumped the wall. As it was, I had to sit down carefully on it and then raise each leg to the top. Slowly, I eased each leg over to the other side and then struggled back to a sort of standing position. When I had climbed over the wall, I found that I was in yet another cemetery. The lights in the building I had been using for direction were now off slightly to my right. I turned toward them and continued, only to encounter a wrought iron fence. This I followed until I saw automobile lights ahead of me. The lights, some three hundred yards away and moving generally in my direction, illuminated grave markers in the distance as they approached. I knew, therefore, that the car was in the cemetery and was driving more or less in the direction of Gussmann's open grave.

I hobbled toward a large monument, which offered sufficient cover until the car had driven past within about fifty feet of where I stood. Then I limped slowly westward along the fence, glancing back regularly toward the car that had passed me. I could hear shouting from that direction and see the lights of several flashlights near the lights of the car. Presently the fence turned to my left, and shortly thereafter I came to an open gate. I turned in a direction I took to be northward and started along the road, keeping as close as possible to shrubbery in case I had to hide again.

I passed a school on my right and realized that the lights I had seen were from its grounds. Farther on there was yet another school, on the left side of the road. Finally, half a mile from the cemetery gate I found Sheen Road. Earlier that night I had taken a taxi over to pick up my little Morris in its regular spot behind The Captains. I knew that it would now be parked within less than half a mile east of where I stood. I had parked it among trucks outside a grocery warehouse some three hours earlier. Though I wasn't sure it was a good idea to go pick it up just then, I was cold and tired and in considerable pain. I knew that I'd be able to see the lights on any cars that came by long before the drivers would be able to see me. I calculated that if I were careful, I could stay out of sight as I walked along toward my trusty automobile.

I walked well off the road and kept a constant watch for cars approaching from either direction along Sheen Road. Twice before I reached my car, I had to duck out of sight as cars cruised by. In both cases they were driving slowly, as if looking for someone. Once I reached my little car and got it started, I drove northward until I was well out of the area before I turned east, toward London. It was past three by the time I rapped lightly on the door of our room. Adrianna opened the door almost immediately.

"How did it go, Charlie?"

"Not too bad, all things considered, but we were almost caught while we were finishing up. The others fled into the park, and I made my way back to the car. The grave was still open."

"Police?"

"Yes. Someone must have seen the flash of my camera. There'll be no secret now about Gussmann's grave."

"Was he in it?"

"Yes, and so was this," I said, lifting the fabric-covered bundle.

"What is it? Have you opened it?"

"Not yet. It might be nothing—just a prop put in by the mortuary—but one of the grave robbers thought it was odd to find it there, so I brought it along."

While I took off my topcoat, Adrianna took the bundle and laid it on the dresser. Then she began rummaging in the drawer where she stored bandages and brought out her scissors. She found a seam and began cutting along the row of stitches that held the outer layer in place. Once she had opened two seams, it turned out that the outer covering was a canvas bag into which the inside bundle had been packed. The inner bundle was wrapped in red-checkered oilcloth—a small tablecloth, tied securely in twine. Inside this multilayered wrap was a stack of three leatherbound books.

Adrianna handed the top one to me and picked up the next one herself. They turned out to be expensively bound notebooks filled with illegible and incomprehensible writing. I now realized with excitement that these were Gussmann's missing journals. Rifling quietly through the pages, I saw that Alice Tupper might have been right about their illegibility.

Adrianna had already reached the same conclusion. "Can you make any of this out, Charles?"

"I'm not even going to start trying until I've had some sleep," I said. "I'm cold, my stomach hurts, and I'm dog tired."

"How can you think of sleeping? These are the journals, Charlie! This might tell us everything."

"Even if they weren't coded, Adrianna, I couldn't stay awake to look at them," I said, removing my sweater. "Uh-oh!" I grunted. My shirt was bloody in an area the size of my hand.

Adrianna dropped the journal she had been holding and unbuttoned my shirt. The bandages underneath were sticky. "Lie down, Charles," she said as she reached for her scissors again. A few seconds later we were both looking at my seeping wound. "You tore some stitches, Charlie, that's all. Most of them held. You'll be okay, I think. You're bleeding a little in back, too—more than in front. How does your back feel?"

"Now it's aching. It's been giving me a sharp reminder now and then."

She smiled at the mess of a patient who was stretched across the bed. "You win, Charlie. No reading tonight."

21

When a doctor does go wrong, he is the first of criminals.
He has nerve and he has knowledge.
—"The Adventure of the Speckled Band"

23 April, '07. *Mesmer was right, in a way. Under proper conditions,
the hypnotic experimenter <u>does</u> actually dominate the patient's will
completely. This I have demonstrated conclusively up to now on four
subjects—only four of the seventeen I now see regularly. Though many
patients cannot really be hypnotized at all (this I have proven many
times), most can be. There is no question in my mind that those who
can be put into a trance are controlled by the suggestions I give them
in that state.*

*But these four show me something entirely different from the others.
This would be disputed by practically everyone if I were to make it
known at this early stage of experimentation, but I am convinced that
these four would do <u>anything</u> that I suggest. Their own personalities
are so defective that they reach a level of trance in which they seem to
have no residual will of their own, no personality, and probably no
memory. I cannot speculate yet as to what benefits this may offer for
my experimental research. At this point, the method of inducing the
trance requires much repetition and close physical proximity. I find
that I must lean my body to within inches of the patient and remain
this close while I talk to them.*

It had taken me an hour to realize that the journals had not been written in code at all. They were in German, as Alice thought, but the feature that made them so difficult to read was their archaic style. Germany had changed its entire system of written characters in the 1870s. Before that time, not only were the characters written differently, but also there was little uniformity from one educated writer to the next. Most German script written before 1870 is simply illegible to modern readers. I had never seen it and only dimly remembered having heard of it. My own father had begun school after the change, but as a child he had known many people who had learned the old writing.

Dr. Gussmann would have gone through his early school years before the change to modern German script. All of his higher education had been in Scotland, and he rarely had any opportunity to speak German throughout his adult life. He had published in German since modern German writing had come into universal use, so he must have learned the new script at some time. Either that or someone else had transcribed other manuscripts of his that were in modern German. In his private journals, though, he used his own version of the old script. My guess was that Alice had been right—he did this to gain an extra measure of security. Many scholars around him probably could read some German, but they were unlikely to be able to read, or even recognize, the old letters. By the time he had written these journals, the old script had been obsolete for almost four decades.

For me to translate his private journals, I had to go through three steps. First, I had to decipher his odd script one word at a time and figure out what German word it was. Then I wrote the word in regular German script. Finally, after I had written a section into German, I wrote it again in English. As I gradually became more accustomed to his writing, the process became easier and faster. Adrianna did not read German and spoke only a few phrases of it, so she had to wait patiently for each English translation to appear. Each journal page contained about a hundred and fifty words and took me between thirty and forty minutes to process. The two-paragraph entry from April 23, 1907, for instance, required thirty-five minutes to completely translate into written English for Adrianna.

Each of the three notebooks contained one hundred leaves of heavy paper, and each leaf was filled with writing on both sides. All but the last twenty leaves of the set were completed. While I labored along, Adrianna calculated that it would take me at least a month to complete the task.

"Just skim through it, Charles. Don't try to translate everything. Just read along in German and think about what he's saying. When something is particularly interesting, tell me about it in your own words."

"I can't skim through old German script, Adrianna. It's hard for me to read it at all."

"Well, you can skip writing it down. Try just getting the main ideas and telling me about them," she insisted impatiently.

I tried to read a passage in German and think about it, again in German, without writing anything down. The next page took only five minutes to read. Then I tried to explain it in English. "On April twenty-fifth he worked with a woman named Clare. This could be Clare Thomas, who was murdered. He was able to cause her to walk to the administration wing and return during a moderate rain without an umbrella. He observed that while several people spoke to her, she did not reply to anyone. He names two of the people who spoke to her. At his direction she went to her room and brought back a dry smock. She then changed her outer garments in his office while still in the trance. When he brought her to consciousness, she had no memory of any of this."

"Good, Charlie. You did that whole page in fewer than six minutes. Do another one. Dr. Gussmann was a lecherous old man, by the way. I don't think that changing clothes in his office qualifies as medical research." Adrianna was not to be distracted from her timing experiments, though. "You read the next page and tell me about it. I'll keep time."

When I had finished the next passage and told her about it, she revealed her latest calculation. "We've still got about three days of work here, Charlie, if you're going to tell me about every page. It'll still take you almost that long to read the whole thing, but if I don't listen to most of it, it'll save us some time."

"Save *you* time, you mean," I said.

"Yes, if I save time, it's saved for both of us. If you only tell me the most interesting parts, I can think about other problems and go out shopping and tidy up the room. No sense in our duplicating efforts."

I moved to my bed and continued to read further. The next several entries were similar in nature to the last one. Gussmann had experimented with making his favorite four patients do a variety of extended tasks. He tried to think of things that the patients would not normally do. He noted that he could not get them to say anything at all while they were at this level of trance, nor would they sing or make other noises.

He noted that while he apparently could keep them in this trance state indefinitely, there were limits to the duration of a given task without new commands from him.

12 June, '07. I must be honest with myself. To induce a susceptible patient to this condition, one must act <u>counter</u> to the interests of the patient. One must <u>increase</u> the subject's neurosis, not alleviate it. In that sense it is the opposite of the goals of usual treatment, but in an experiment of this magnitude, it is well worth the sacrifice to their well-being.

First, I must, as a standard procedure, find the patient's personal roots of depression or anxiety—those things about himself that cause him pain. Often those roots are buried well back in the patient's childhood. After those are discovered, I must work to <u>intensify</u> them rather than relieve them. The patient must wish, more acutely than ever, to withdraw from life. The depression must be as complete as possible. When the patients reach the desired level of withdrawal, they become disoriented and revert to fantasy. Physical pain at this point can be especially useful. Electric shock probably would be very effective, but I find that small burns are very useful. Only when such a subject is in deepest despair will this deeper level of hypnosis be possible.

Townby is remarkable in some ways. He is strong and agile and can do things in his subdued state that are really athletic. There are two disappointments with him, however. He fades without new direction in only a few minutes. It is as if he resists me even while he is under my control. Clare will perform twice as long on a single set of directions. Of the four who are capable of reaching this state, Townby is the most difficult to subdue—again, the resistance. Also, the proximity required for successful suggestion with him is the closest. I must be within a foot of T. to have an effect, while I can induce a trance in Clare at a distance of four or five feet.

Like the others, she cannot be induced to make any sound while she is in a trance.

So William Townby was one of the favorite four. His was the first name I recognized in the journal. I would have shouted out my excitement to Adrianna, but she had gone out in her red wig to do some errands. I skipped rapidly through more antics with Clare— which, not surprisingly, often involved her disrobing—and looked for more mention of Townby.

8 July, '07. Townby made new headway today. I was able to keep him on an assigned task for fifty-five minutes without a single word from me. The task was a simple one I have mentioned before. He copied sentences from a book. This went on for fifty-five minutes. Then, when I asked him to continue, he took it up again for a further five minutes. After that, I changed his task to pacing, and he sustained it for twenty-eight minutes, at which time I had to stop for other appointments. At last he is reaching time periods somewhat like the others. In every case, training is necessary, though I am getting faster at it. Townby was induced to trance at a distance of three feet today and in less than a minute. I was also able to make him go to a designated place on the grounds and wait for me.

I wonder if the difficulty in training him is that he is a man and perhaps less susceptible to pain. He is the only male patient so far who is capable of this level of trance, though Tommy is showing some signs that I think are hopeful. He also may be ready by the end of the summer. The whole process is now much faster for all subjects.

Some of my colleagues have made remarks about the long periods of drowsiness exhibited by these patients. I believe I am suspected of drugging them. What nonsense!

Townby again, and now Tommy, perhaps Tommy Morrell—two names I knew. So far it was clear to me that Gussmann was working toward commanding the activities of his special patients in three ways. He wanted them to perform tasks for him without regard for whether they would normally do these things. Second, he was trying to extend the time period of his influence without having to give additional commands. Third, he was trying to increase the physical distance at which he could place a patient into this level of trance.

Another thing that was pretty obvious to me was that, whatever he had been doing with these subjects, it was not therapy for them. He had simply been trying to break new ground—extend the frontiers of hypnosis. That, in itself, didn't mean that his motives hadn't originally been medical. But now it was clear that the process required actions that were decidedly not in the patient's best interests. Yet he continued his experiments without regard for any damage he might be inflicting.

I paused and wondered if Liza Anatole could have been in a trance when she shot me. If so, who could be controlling her? Having seen inside the coffin, I was now certain that Gussmann had never met her. But Townby had. Was it possible that Townby had learned the Gussmann procedure while he was a doctor and was now manipulating the others? Could Liza have been out on such an assignment for so many hours? If she were in a trance, how could she have applied the logical processes that would have been required to find the well-known Mrs. Wallace and then follow her to me? She certainly didn't seem to be in a trance when she apparently recognized me in the park, but how would I know the difference?

While I was speculating on this, Adrianna returned with food and a newspaper. The news told us that the notorious Charles Baker was still missing. The article quoted Chief Inspector Willis as saying that Baker's disappearance was a very serious matter and that anyone who saw him should contact Scotland Yard. A photo of me accompanied the text. In another story it was revealed that some grave robbers had been busy in a graveyard in Richmond near Bog Gate. These two stories both appeared on the same page, but there was no indication that they were related.

Adrianna redressed my wounds, both entrance and exit, and we ate what passed for some lunch. I was still worn out from my adventures in grave robbing the night before so I took a nap as Adrianna lay down next to me for a while. After resting, I propped myself up comfortably and resumed my reading. I found that I could skim along much faster in the journal. I was no longer reading every sentence, just getting the gist of things as I went.

I paused a few times during the afternoon to tell Adrianna, who had now settled into reading a book in the room's one slightly shabby armchair, about some tidbit of information I was reading. Basically, Gussmann had gotten steadily better at his game. By the end of the first journal, it was February 1908. He had abandoned work with two of his original four because they seemed unstable in their trances. But by then he could put his special two patients into their deepest trance state in less than a minute and at a distance of about five feet, maximum. Both of these measures had leveled off, and he had been unable to improve on either count for several months. He could make them do just about anything they were physically able to do, whether he was present or not. Clare could be maintained in this state, on her own, for up to four hours, and this, too, had leveled off. Townby could be out of direct contact and reinforcement for about half that long. Tommy Morrell had been added to the stable of deep-trance patients in September 1907. His development had been rapid after that. Under no circumstances could Gussmann get any of them to deliver verbal messages, repeat words, or make any vocalization at all while they were in this level of trance. He had tried several times to make them deliver verbal messages but always had failed. He labeled this state of consciousness subgnostic—beneath knowledge.

While reading the very beginning of the second journal, I saw something that sharply focused my attention. On the first page of that journal he admitted both Helen Wickham and Mary Hopson to his inner circle. At last I had a direct link between these journals and the letter's list of characters.

"Adrianna! Listen to this. 'Today Helen Wickham, with whom I have been working for years, fell into the subgnostic state. This is most fortunate because I am about to lose Clare, who is being discharged to her family at their insistence and over my objections.' He goes on to say that she is very promising. Then he adds, 'I am sure that Mary Hopson, too, will soon be ready.' Just a minute." I read rapidly, probably skipping important facts, until I saw Mary mentioned again on the next page.

18 February, '08. Like all of the others, M. H. complains of being very tired and disoriented between sessions. I should research the cause. As I anticipated, today she fell into subgnostic trance after only two minutes and at a distance of nearly six inches. Even more promising was her initial duration of thirty-two minutes. A lovely body. Like so many women patients of this type, her greatest fear and the deepest well of her guilt and despair is sexual. Our societal denial and denigration of female sexuality lead to fairly widespread neurotic depression. This works very much to my advantage. Applied minor burn.

Normally I would greatly reduce her level of guilt. Here, of course, I will increase it through several means, including sexual activity. Hopson has no family, so I have little danger of losing her. I deeply regret that C. is leaving. I shall not be able to work with her again. I only hope that she will never regain any memories of my experimentation once she leaves here. That is a significant danger that I will have to consider. Such an event would seriously threaten my work. Research of this importance should never be curtailed by allowing experimental subjects to leave their productive roles.

"'A lovely body'? Does he include stuff like that often, Charles?" Adrianna asked indignantly.

"Pretty often. Sometimes he mentions their breasts specifically. Never mentions sex with them in detail, but if I'm interpreting this correctly, he was definitely having some kind of sexual activities with them."

"How old would he have been in 1908?"

"According to Arthur, he was about eighty when he died the next year. Despite his age, he certainly had plenty of interest."

"What else does it say, Charlie? Do you think he killed Clare?"

"He certainly was worried about her leaving, but I don't see how he could have."

I skimmed through a few repetitious passages about practicing with patients before I came to another reference that I assumed was to Helen Wickham. "He mentions Helen Wickham here . . . more than a foot of distance . . . more than an hour . . . no description of her fine body," I said.

"Did she have a fine body, Charles?"

"She had an extraordinary body," I said quietly.

"So sad, Charlie. Did she really? How did she ever end up in Holloway?" Adrianna wondered aloud.

"However it was, I'm betting that it began right here in these journals with Gussmann," I answered.

While Adrianna began to open cans for our tea, I read on in near-silence for a few minutes, occasionally blurting out some tidbit. "M. H. . . . three feet . . . three hours . . . walking for an hour around the grounds. . . . H. W. . . . two feet . . . two hours . . . nude in office . . . will not speak."

"'Nude in office,'" Adrianna sniffed as she handed me a cup of broth and a thin slice of good bread. She was still shaking her head when she settled back into her chair with tea and a bread-and-butter sandwich.

As I sipped the broth, it occurred to me that the journal had now again come down to four patients in Gussmann's inner circle, and I knew, or at least had seen, all of them. According to what I'd been told, I would find no mention of Liza Anatole or Robert Stanton here, since neither had ever known Dr. Gussmann. "These people—

the ones who are still alive—could they still be connected to one another, in some ways at least, now—nearly fourteen years after this was written?"

"And if they are, how many of them are trying to kill us? At least one of them probably is," Adrianna mused as she turned her attention back to her book.

Hours later I began a page that was markedly more difficult to decipher. It was as if Gussmann had deliberately employed every decorative idiosyncrasy of his personal old script. Moreover, he reduced the size of his characters to about half their normal size and crowded them together. Both my attention level and the difficulty of reading went up sharply.

19 August, '08. Today I discovered that there is a third level of hypnosis. For now, I must call it subgnostic possession. At about three this afternoon, working with H. W., I discovered this for the first time. Rather, I should say that I noticed it for the first time—it may have happened before this. W. sat across the desk from me in a subgnostic trance. As usual, she had gone through a period of fatigue followed by the hallucination that she was about to travel to her special place of contentment. I tried to get her to speak. It was very frustrating because, as usual, there was no success. I closed my own eyes and sat there drumming my fingers on the desk. I became aware that the sound of the drumming had changed to a rhythmic clicking. I opened my eyes to see her fingers mimicking my own. Then I realized that my own fingers were no longer moving, but hers were. The moment I realized this, her drumming stopped. I had said nothing to her—given no suggestion. I had not even wanted her to drum her fingers.

My initial hypothesis was that in the absence of any other suggestion she was merely mimicking me. I tried to get her to do it again, but to no avail. Finally, frustrated again by my attempts to get through *to her, I sat back again and closed my eyes to think. Then I heard her fingers again. I knew they were hers, not mine, but I did not open my eyes. I realized that drumming my fingers is a constant habit of mine when I sit and think. The drumming stopped again, but I kept my eyes closed. Then I willed <u>myself</u> to start drumming my fingers again. The sound started again—the same sound as before, but it was her fingers making it, not mine.*

I struggled to remain calm, but the drumming stopped again. I was able to do this again several times. H. W. was doing what I was only thinking! More important, I was thinking of <u>my</u> doing it, not of her doing it.

Still keeping my eyes closed, I thought of raising my hand and letting it fall to the table. When I thought I had raised it a little, I let it fall. I felt it fall and felt it strike the table, but the sound told me it was her hand. I raised my hand again, and then I opened my eyes to see my own hands down on the table, while she had one in the air. The hand dropped. I was too excited to continue successfully.

What I saw today was my will operating Helen W.'s body at a distance of about two feet. God in heaven!

"Adrianna!" I said. "Do you know what he could do?"

"Do it tomorrow, Charlie," she muttered, having fallen asleep in the oversized chair. "Go to sleep."

"He could make them do his thoughts!"

Wordlessly, she got up from the chair and moved to curl up on the bed.

I got up and pulled the coverlet over her. Then I moved to the other bed with the journals. As I did so, two pieces fell out of one of the books and landed on the floor. One was a drawing, on a narrow strip of thick art paper, of a nude woman reclining. The other was a 1907 newspaper clipping about Conan Doyle's elaborate new home in Crowborough. I was suddenly wide awake at about two o'clock in the morning, about twenty-four hours after I'd robbed a grave and found this book. Here was proof that Gussmann had retrieved and kept the drawing that was alluded to in the letter. Could anyone else have seen it, and been told of its origin by Gussmann before he died? That question kept me away from my reading for ten minutes as I thought about the fact that this strip of paper had been buried for more than a dozen years. Certainly no conspirator had seen it for at least that long. Who but Gussmann could have thought of it and described it so accurately after so many years?

In the next twenty pages, Gussmann repeated the discovery he made with Helen Wickham. He could merely think of movements, and the patient would actually make the movements. Fortunately for me, he returned to his previous style of penmanship after the initial entry about "subgnostic possession." I read that within days of his experience with Wickham, he had done the same thing with Mary Hopson. Within a month he was able by force of his own will to cause simple body movements for all four of his subjects as long as they were very close to him and there were no distractions.

His ability to do this leveled off at a distance of three feet, and he could only accomplish it in the atmosphere of his quiet office.

He remained unable, though he often tried, to make his subjects speak when they were hypnotized. Though he could make them go virtually anywhere at his bidding and perform a variety of simple tasks out of his sight, he could not make them talk to him in this state, not would they deliver verbal messages to others. Near the end of 1908 he was still jubilant about his success. He had commanded an amazing array of other acts from his subjects, including killing laboratory animals on order, striking other patients in the general hospital population, and a variety of sex acts with each other. He noted that these were all things that they never would have done on their own.

Often he would send one subject out under hypnotic suggestion to wait at some designated spot. Then, after an extended time, he would go to that spot to meet the person. He noted that the subject would wait patiently, as ordered, under any circumstances—darkness, rain, or cold could not deter them. Finally he was able to make the person go from place to place on prearranged schedules without further suggestions from him.

But he also was increasingly frustrated at his limits. He had begun to make entries about his own deteriorating health. As a medical man, he recognized that his eighty-year-old frame was breaking down rapidly. He had stopped seeing any patients but these, citing weakness, and the hospital had cooperated with him.

26 November, '08. Just as I knew I would break even further ground, I have. There is yet a deeper level of subgnostic trance. Today, working with Mary H.'s arm manipulations, I stopped for a rest. She was in a relaxed state on my couch while I sat next to her at my desk. I had, through my will alone, folded her arms across her chest. Her eyes were closed. I closed my own eyes for a moment of rest and concentration on her next movements. When I opened my eyes, I was looking as if into a mirror.

Yes. I was looking at my own body, sitting comfortably in front of me.

I turned my gaze downward and saw Mary's body as if it were my own. I was frightened and upset by this at first. Until I was able to calm myself and regain control, I was seeing things through her eyes and was unable to return my focus to my own body. I was able to move her arms. I spoke aloud in her voice. I probably could have stood and walked in her body, but I did not attempt this. Finally I forced myself to relax. I closed my eyes and concentrated on moving my paperweight, which rested on the desk near my own right hand. When

I could feel the paperweight in my hand, I opened my eyes and found that I was again looking at Mary on the couch.

I feel that I <u>must discontinue</u> all experimentation with subgnostic trances. Clearly, I might have been in serious danger during this episode.

But he did not quit. His very next entry, though nearly a month later, was a deliberate repeat of the same experiment with the same subject, no doubt Mary Hopson. This time he had actually walked around his office in her body. He read passages from books aloud. He noted that he could feel and distinguish textures with her fingers. He even drank water before returning to his own body, or what he called his own focus.

By the time the sun rose, I had read in the third journal of repeated experimentation with extrabodily subgnostic possession of the other special patients. By early in 1909 Dr. Gussmann had been practicing extended activity in what he called the "subject focus" with all four of his special patients. Several of these episodes had lasted for more than an hour, and he boasted of eating, drinking, talking aloud, and "performing every bodily function" in the subject focus. He described in detail how he had completed an act of sexual intercourse on a hypnotized Mary Hopson while he was in the "focus" of William Townby. Then he had changed to a focus in Mary's body and had commanded the hypnotized Townby to provide pleasure for her while Gussmann was in this female focus. Somehow it didn't seem that I was reading scientific experimentation anymore. It was clear that Gussmann had no sense left of his patients as people. He used them like the lab animals he had forced them to kill, and then he wrote about it in a self-serving way that was utterly chilling.

6 May, '09. Increasing palsy in my left arm. Also, great difficulty urinating for these past few weeks. I have begun to think that now it is time for the trip to Jerusalem. Perhaps that may be the solution if, indeed, it is possible. I don't know how much longer I can continue in my present state. I may fail to be able to continue with my own part of the vital experimentation. Such an irony, to have made one of the most significant discoveries of all of medical history and yet be too old to continue much longer—surely not long enough.

I fear that I may not have time to begin to explain these journals and all that I have learned so far, much less to discover what might be done.

His next and final entry was very brief and was made after a gap of more than three months. I could only guess that he might have made extensive notes elsewhere during that time.

10 August, '09. Changed from subject focus Townby to subject focus Hopson today in the quiet hallway near Townby's room. Returned to my office and left subject focus.

Medical condition dictates that I wait no longer. Now it is time for the trip to Jerusalem, regardless of the dangers. I must get some boxes and put a few things in order as quickly as possible.

In spite of my own excitement, I fell asleep, exhausted, within moments of reading these last words in the journal.

22

Our ideas must be as broad as Nature if they are to interpret Nature.

—A Study in Scarlet

ADRIANNA MANAGED TO WAKE me at noon on Friday. When she realized that I'd read all night, she gave me a nurse's thorough scolding, including several minutes about men and how they don't take care of their health. She had been out and had soup for me when she woke me, and she wouldn't hear a word about what I'd read until I'd eaten it and had a glass of milk with some bread.

"Now, do you want to hear what Gussmann could do?" I said when I was allowed to speak.

"I do now, Charlie. What could he do?"

"He could get inside their bodies and walk around and talk," I said enthusiastically.

"How exhausted were you when you figured that part out, Charles? I think you'd better do some rereading," she cautioned.

"This is not a joke, Adrianna. I was exhausted, but I'm not wrong about what he wrote. The journal is a record of his experimentation with a level of hypnosis that went far beyond any we've ever heard of. He called it 'subgnostic possession.' He meant that he could inhabit the subject's body without any awareness or knowledge on the subject's part. In the end, he could see through their eyes, even walk around and feel things with their hands."

"In their bodies?" Adrianna said. "Where was his body during all this? Where was his mind?"

"His body was present in the room—a few feet away. Well, most of the time, but sometimes he left the room in their focus and his body stayed behind—inert, I suppose."

"'Focus'?" she asked.

"He called it the subject focus when he could experience things through them. Toward the end of the journal he could move quite a distance away from himself in the subject focus. His mind was actually inside the patient's head!"

"Could he do this with any patient, anybody?"

"Just four of them, and we know them all—Townby, Hopson, Wickham, and Morrell."

"Are you sure this journal wasn't written by Jules Verne?" Adrianna asked as she sat down to listen to me. "And then what?"

"And then nothing. He died. Near the last weeks of his life he rarely made journal entries. His last couple of entries were as much religious as experimental. He knew he was seriously ill."

"Religious how?" she asked.

"He was planning a pilgrimage to Jerusalem."

"Was he Jewish?"

"I would think so, since he was going to Jerusalem, but Christians make religious trips there, too."

"Muslims, too, some of them."

"I wonder what the Zionists were up to in 1909. If I hadn't seen a body in Gussmann's grave, I'd think from the journal that he'd gone to Palestine."

"Oh! The grave! I meant to tell you that you're a wanted man, Charlie. There's an item in the *Times,* a short piece buried on page ten, about Gussmann's body being exhumed Wednesday night. They caught one of the diggers, and he named *you* as the man who hired him. He also said that you took something from the coffin."

"How is that possible? I never gave those men my name."

"Your picture was in the paper when you got shot, Charlie. The man told police that he recognized you as the newspaperman who was shot last week in London. The article went on to say that you had gone missing from Royal Hospital, Chelsea, on Monday. Luckily, Freddy and I weren't mentioned. Apparently you're a pretty exciting character."

"Page ten again? That's not exactly a spot for the exciting characters, Adrianna. I didn't make the front page when I was shot, either, or when I disappeared from the hospital." I could only imagine the bad jokes I'd be hearing if I went by the AP office. No chance of that now—or maybe ever. Newspapermen are supposed to write news, not make it.

"Six-and-a-half pointer," she said with a grin. "What'd you expect, Yank? Still, I wouldn't be out on the street too much if I were you. Maybe you ought to borrow my red wig."

"The funny thing is that Sir Arthur wanted me to look into all this because he assumed I could be discreet. It looks like I'm not very good at that," I said.

"So far, at least, his name hasn't surfaced."

"I haven't found out how someone made it seem that a ghost wrote the letter, either, but I found this." I handed Adrianna the drawing. "That's the drawing mentioned in the letter. I don't know what to make of it. He'll be excited and will see it as some sort of confirmation that the letter he got was from the dead Gussmann."

Adrianna was silent for a minute while she paced the room a little. Finally she sat down on the bed and faced me. "Do you know that old story about the bear talking, Charlie?"

"No."

"This is an old story, must be Russian—it's about Russia, anyway, during the czar's pogroms to eliminate the Jews."

"I know something about that."

"Well, the story is about a Jewish village that was given a choice. The Cossacks brought them a caged bear and told them that they could pack up and leave or they could teach this bear to talk. They'd have ten years to teach the bear, but if they failed, the village would be slaughtered."

"A choice that wasn't really a choice."

"Of course not. So they had a meeting of the elders. The rabbi said that they should take the bear. When the others asked why he took this peculiar position, he told them that there were three possibilities for reprieve in the offer. He reminded them that ten years is a long time. First, the czar could die. Second, he told them, the bear could die. And third, Charlie, what do you suppose was third?"

"The world could end?" I said.

"Third, the bear could talk, Charlie."

I got it. The least likely possibility was still one of the possibilities. Sherlock Holmes was supposed to say things like that. But I wasn't going to give in to that line of thinking, and I was surprised at Adrianna for suggesting it. "I'd have bet against the bear."

Adrianna nodded and continued, "So would I, and I don't expect to see a talking bear, but a lot of people think that spirits can cause letters to be written. Certainly Arthur does, but so do a lot of other well-educated people. We've got to try to keep an open mind about that while we look for a better explanation. Didn't the journal say that Gussmann could make Townby, Hopson, and the others do things? If you put the two ideas together—"

"Stop it! Dr. Gussmann isn't controlling these people from the spirit world, Adrianna. I *won't* entertain that idea. Someone—and I know now that it isn't Dr. Gussmann—simply knows about Conan Doyle's father's sketchbook and that incident in Scotland. They're using it to try to manipulate Sir Arthur. Don't forget that two of the three on the list never knew Gussmann. When we figure out why, we'll be able to figure out who."

"Or?" she said expectantly.

"Or what?"

"Or?, Charlie. Or?"

"Or the bear could talk," I admitted.

"Let's go back to your question of why, Charlie. Why would anyone want Conan Doyle to take Mary Hopson or one of the other two to see Helen Wickham before she was hanged?" Adrianna asked as she cleared away my cup and bowl.

"We know more about that than we did two days ago," I said. "Hopson, at least, and Wickham were birds of a feather. They were both Gussmann's special patients. They were capable of being influenced by subgnostic possession. And we now know how willing Gussmann was to damage his patients to further his research. So God only knows what else those two might have had in common once he was through with them."

She thought for a moment and then said, "Two problems. First, Robert Stanton and Liza Anatole were *not* Gussmann's patients, special or otherwise. Second, nothing happened when you took Mary Hopson to the cell. You saw no hypnosis. Mary wasn't possessed when you left, was she?"

"Not as far as I could tell," I answered. "Another thing: Stanton and Anatole are tied into this just as tightly as Hopson. Not only were they on the list with her, but also Liza shot me, and Stanton was stalking me in the hospital."

"As was Hopson, you said. What else did you learn from the journal, Charles?" Adrianna asked. "What else matches what we've seen?"

"Liza might have been in a trance, directed by someone, when she shot me—and when she followed you. Gussmann was working furiously to extend the time and the range of his influence. If someone read his journal before it was buried with him, someone who was able to take up where he left off, Liza might have been *sent* to find me and kill me."

"Dr. Dodds might have read the journals, I suppose, but I think he's more interested in Gussmann's money than in his research." Adrianna speculated.

"Townby, maybe," I said. "He later took up Gussmann's role. Maybe he was made privy to the method before Gussmann died."

"Maybe, but he certainly didn't impress me as a man with tremendous mental powers," Adrianna said. "What else did you learn?"

"There's the trip Gussmann was going to take. He was going to pack up and go."

"What, exactly, did he say? Did he mention packing money or deeds or anything like that?"

"Just a second; I'll read it to you." I opened to the last writing in the journal and began to translate word-for-word. "He first mentions it here: 'I have begun to think that now it is time for the trip to Jerusalem. Perhaps it may be the answer if, indeed, it is possible.' Then he mentions it again in the last entry. 'Now it is time for the trip to Jerusalem, regardless of the dangers. I must get some boxes and put a few things in order as quickly as possible.' That's exactly what he says. Odd way to say it, though."

"It sounded perfectly clear to me."

"In English, in direct word-for-word translation, yes. But that's not the way one would normally say that in German."

"Explain, Charles. You know I have very little German."

I looked at both passages closely. "In both entries he writes, '*Jetzt ist es Zeit feur die Reise nach Jerusalem.*' Word-for-word that's, 'Now it is time for *the trip* to Jerusalem,' but that's not how a German would say it. He would say, '*Jetzt ist es Zeit, die Reise nach Jerusalem zu machen.*' More like 'Now it is time *to make* the trip to Jerusalem.' The way he wrote it here is like the trip to Jerusalem was an object—a thing, not an action. He only wrote it twice, but he wrote it wrong both times. It's not an error a German would make."

"He had been speaking English for decades by then, Charles. He was just translating incorrectly," Adrianna guessed.

"No. The man who wrote this journal wasn't translating into German. He thought in German. It's full of expressions that a native speaker uses. I don't think he'd write this incorrectly. It's just odd, both times the same, '*feur die Reise nach Jerusalem*'—no *zu machen*."

Adrianna paused and considered her words before replying. "I hate to ask this, Charles, but how's *your* German? Are you sure you know how he should have said it?"

"This is elementary, Adrianna. It's not advanced German," I answered.

"But he was writing in Old German, didn't you say?"

"Not in Old German—old script—but in modern German. The vocabulary and syntax are just regular German." I could see that I hadn't explained it to her very clearly.

"But maybe we should get a second opinion, Charles, about the German, especially any parts you are having trouble with." Adrianna's tone was cautious. She didn't want to offend me, but she sounded like she was pretty sure I needed help.

I was sure I didn't, but I could see that her upper-class private British education always would suspect my American public one. I decided to let the matter drop. "I think the next step is to check up on every one of the known suspects in this."

"Townby, Morrell, and Anatole are easy. They're all confined in Morton Graves," Adrianna said.

"Now that Wickham is dead, only Stanton and Hopson remain out where they can hurt us."

"As far as we know. There might be others, but at least we can watch those two. They don't even outnumber us."

"And now we know to travel armed," I said, "and I can get a disguise, too. No one has recognized you."

"You want a pirate costume or a suit of armor, Charlie?" Adrianna said with a laugh.

"I thought I might borrow your wig and get a dress, but I guess the mustache would give me away."

"I can shave that off for you, Charlie. Get you smooth, put some powder on your face."

"No, thanks. I'd rather add facial hair than take any away," I said. The mention of shaving my mustache, even in jest, was revolting.

"Seriously though, Charlie. You're a wanted man, of a sort, just now. Unless you plan to solve this thing by sheer brainpower from inside this hotel room, you're going to need a disguise. What would be good?"

I thought about that. "A beard would be good, but I have no idea how to make a costume beard. Too bad I didn't start a beard in the hospital. Do you know anything about theatrical makeup?"

"Not a thing, and we can hardly enlist the help of someone else," she answered.

I thought about our gravediggers. "So far, hiring outside help hasn't been too successful."

Adrianna protested, "Not so, Charles—that's what got us the journals, isn't it? Don't be ungrateful."

I patted her on the shoulder and said, "Yes, yes, of course you're right. But as my dear old Irish landlady used to say, 'What I'm looking for now is a blessing that's *not* in disguise.' How do *you* think I should cloak my identity?"

She opened her mouth as if to speak, then closed it. Finally she took a deep breath and said, "I think I'm back to the idea of *less* hair, Charlie. I can make you bald and clean-shaven."

I glared at her, but I knew she was right. Though my hairline was receding slightly, I had a thick head of hair and wore it brushed back and just a bit long. No one in England had ever seen me without a mustache. "An entirely bald man is too memorable, but one with a seriously receding hairline might do. No mustache. How easy would it be to lighten my hair?"

"It would be very easy, but we'd botch it all up. We'd best leave that alone. I can shorten your hair on the sides and comb it down. We can get some weak spectacles, too. And you usually dress in business attire. We could get some more workman's clothes. Let's get started with the razor before you lose your nerve."

I removed my shirt while she prepared lather and put a fresh blade in the little safety razor and ran hot water on a cloth. First, she trimmed, then shaved, my mustache and shortened my sideburns to the top of the ear. I could feel this, though she provided no mirror for me. She cut my hair with her little bandage scissors, leaving the sides at about three-quarters of an inch long. Then, starting at the top of my forehead, she began to give me a receding hairline.

This gradually became a bald path down the top of my head practically back to my crown. After she had achieved the shape of baldness she wanted, out came the razor again to make the deformity truly shiny and bald. She would not allow me to see the finished product until she had combed my hair neatly and made me put on a shirt. When she had found her own shaded steel-rimmed glasses and put them on me, I was allowed to look.

The result was surprising. I would not have recognized myself, and I didn't look terrible. Some of the age I'd gained with the baldness I'd lost when the mustache was subtracted from my face. The result was that I looked no more than a decade older than my true midthirties age.

An afternoon walk to a department store provided a couple of decent flannel shirts, a thick woolen jacket, and sturdy brown shoes that fit well. I found a pair of steel-rimmed spectacles at a bargain price. Adrianna found a liquid cosmetic product that was actually intended to paint gray *into* hair. An hour after we returned to the room and used the coloring, I looked about fifty instead of midthirties and would have been safely incognito around anyone I knew.

We decided that our next priority was to check up on Hopson and Stanton. We agreed that I would drive out to Ham and check on Stanton while Adrianna would take a taxi to North Sheen to locate Mary Hopson. The only goal for this evening was to locate these two, if possible, and perhaps try to gather some information about their current activities. Then we would meet back in our room no later than nine and get a good night's rest.

I drove the Morris directly to Ham and parked in a spot half a block from Robert Stanton's boat shop, arriving just before six o'clock. After double-checking the Luger and placing it in my coat pocket, I walked to the shop. Lights were on, and the front door was unlocked. As far as I could tell, Stanton was open for business. When I entered the shop, Robert Stanton was busy at a rack of lumber in his work area. Apparently he was selecting pieces for a project, sighting along the edges of planks and dividing them into two stacks on a worktable. Though he did not appear to notice me at first, he looked up toward the front of the shop after a minute or two and saw me standing at the counter. He laid the plank he was holding down on a stack and walked toward me.

"Can I help yer, sir?" he asked.

Though I was pretty sure that he would not recognize me, I had to control my fear that he would as I answered, deliberately raising the pitch of my voice. "Sign says boats. Do you build custom craft?" I asked, remembering that he had said he would not do custom work.

"Never do, sir. I build small boats of my own design. Take my own time, too. Then I sells 'em here in the shop." With a pleasant smile, he approached the counter at which I stood. "Don't even have anything to show right now. What was yer wantin' built, if I might ask, sir? Might be able to recommend someone to yer."

"A canal boat—a pleasure boat, you know, not a barge," I said, remembering some very interesting boats I'd seen on local canals.

"Somethin' fitted out for sleepin' aboard, explorin' about the countryside?"

"That's the idea. Nothing too fancy, but comfortable, you know, for me and the missus."

"I know just what yer mean. Don't never take on anythin' so grand myself. Greek fellow named Nikos, over on Thames near Teddington Lock, he does 'em, though." He pointed at a wall of the shop that was in the direction he meant for me to go. "Yer take a little side road off Riverside; he's got a sign says 'Nikos Shipbuilding.' He don't build no proper ships, o' course. Ain't far, but it's too late to catch 'im today. 'E's good, I think—can't say what 'e charges." He pulled a scrap of paper out of a drawer and sketched a quick map. "Another fellow, named Hudson, does 'em, too. He's down toward Kingston a mile or so. Yer'd catch either one of 'em tomorrow before noon, or so. I can draw yer a map t' his place, too." He turned the paper over and made another quick sketch.

"Thanks," I said as he handed me the maps. "Looks like you're starting a new one. What's it going to be?"

"Oh, a water taxi, I think. They allus sell fast, yer know. An' now I'm sellin' these American Evinrude motors—outboards, they call 'em. I kin sell boat and motor together if I build somethin' needs the motor. Yer might want t' think about one of them motors. I got pictures—can get yer most any kind."

"How long does it take you to build a boat like that?" I asked casually. "Do you work steadily on one or get several going at once?"

"It depends. I ain't been well lately. Never can tell how long a boat's goin' t' take me. That's why I don't do no custom work—just work on 'em when I feel up to it."

"Well," I said sympathetically, "I'm sorry to hear you've been feeling ill. Nothing serious, I hope?"

"I'm used to it. Got a condition that comes an' goes. I work around it best I can."

"I'll let you get back to your work, then. Thanks again for the maps. I'll look these fellows up." I extended my hand, and he shook it firmly and with a smile. As I left the shop, I thought that there seemed nothing sinister about this man at all. He was friendly and communicative, quite different than he had been the last time I'd visited his shop, and a different person altogether from the one who'd haunted the hospital looking for me. He locked the door behind me as I walked away.

When I got back to my Morris, the young man from the hardware store whom I'd met before was standing beside the car, looking it over. When he saw me he did a double take. Clearly he recognized the car in which he'd ridden, but I didn't match in his memory as the man he'd met. "This your car?" he asked suspiciously as he studied my face in the late twilight.

"My younger brother's, actually," I answered. "He lent it to me today." I started to open the door.

"I met him," said the young man. "He gave me a ride. You here to see Bob? You could park right up at his shop, you know?"

"I didn't know if he'd be in. Just thought I'd walk around a bit," I replied, finding that a constant string of lies demanded constant surges of adrenaline, which were quickly exhausting me.

"You here about the boat your brother was wanting?" he asked. "He sold that one already. Between you and me, I'd tell your brother not to hold his breath for one of Bob's boats."

I closed the door and leaned against the car. "Why is that?"

"Well, if you're in any hurry, don't be. Bob's been gone a lot lately—worse than usual. He ain't been working much. I shouldn't say anything, you know, but your brother was a nice man. Just tell him, if he's in a hurry for a boat, he might want to look for someone else. Don't tell anybody I said anything."

"I don't understand about Mr. Stanton. What's his problem with working steadily?" I probed, hoping to get more insight into the man who might very well have been hunting me like game a few days earlier.

The boy hesitated and looked around as if someone might be listening. "I shouldn't say anything, but it's the drink. He has these blackouts and roams about and can't remember where he's been. He ain't dangerous or anything, just something wrong in his head. My dad says he's been that way for years, but it's getting worse, I think."

"You said it's been worse recently?"

"Most every day, now. Not every day, but most. About a week ago, he was gone for two days. I guess he's got some nutty girlfriend now, too," the boy said, looking around as if we were in a conspiracy together.

"Really? What's she like?" I asked. "Is she good-looking?"

"Pretty blonde, little bit of a thing, but she goes off her nut, too. Dad says the police picked her up last week. She was roaming around by the river all night. He heard it from Constable Miller. Said it was the same girl who was hanging around Bob's last week. We ain't seen her since then. Bob acts like he don't know her—won't talk about her."

"But you think he really does know her," I said with a knowing chuckle. "The things people get into—amazing, isn't it? When did you see her with him?"

The boy looked nervously toward the store. "I don't know exactly, last Friday. No, Thursday afternoon. They went off together toward the river. I figured they were going for a ride on his little boat. He likes to show off that new motor of his."

He paused, obviously having second thoughts about how much he'd said. "He's just getting worse, is all. I shouldn't be gossiping about it. Just tell your brother not to be in any hurry for Bob to build a boat. I've got to go, sir." He trotted away in the direction of the hardware store, and I was left to make whatever I could of his information.

By the time I returned to our hotel room, I had no concrete answers. Clearly Liza Anatole had visited Robert Stanton. That was certainly new information. He might have given her a ride into central London and back by river on his powered boat. I wondered how long that would take from Ham. I waited anxiously, hoping that Adrianna wouldn't be gone too much longer, but it was still an hour and a half before we were to meet.

When she still had not returned by midnight, I went down to the lobby to call Freddy, but there was no answer.

23

What a tissue of mysteries and improbabilities the whole thing was!

—"The Boscombe Valley Mystery"

HER ICY FEET SENT an alarm right through my body. Adrianna was shivering violently, her teeth were chattering, and she was under my blankets in bed with me. "Warm me up, Charlie. I'm freezing. I may die—actually die—of the cold." She pulled the blankets away from me. Her dress felt like a wooly snow bank next to me as I put my arms around her and pulled her close to my chest. "Can't talk . . . yet," she said after a few seconds. Her teeth continued to chatter briefly, and her shaking continued for several minutes.

"Where is your coat?" I asked when she had warmed a bit.

"Had to leave it," she answered. "I'd never have gotten back into London with it."

Then I noticed in the dim light of the predawn that it was her own short brunette hair that was buried under my chin. "Where's your wig, Adrianna?"

"Lost it in the fight," she said, shivering. "It's on the street. Police probably have it by now."

"Fight! You were in a fight, Adrianna? With Mary Hopson?"

She continued to cling tightly to me under the blanket. "Yes, Mary Hopson," she answered. "She attacked me—knocked me down with a heavy travel case. She got a good swing with it and smashed it against my head. I'm lucky she didn't kill me." Adrianna struggled out of bed and walked toward the bathroom. "Charlie, could you go down and get a pot of coffee? I want strong coffee, not tea. Somebody must be in the hotel kitchen by now. I'll tell you all about it when you get back. I've got to get into a hot bath." She closed the door behind her.

I had been sleeping in my clothes, and they were a wrinkled mess, but the coffee sounded like a great idea. I quickly put on fresh trousers and a new shirt before heading out for what I hoped was a brief trip downstairs. I checked the clock before I left the room and saw that it was six-thirty. I didn't want to show myself at the hotel, so I made a two-block walk to a restaurant and spent two shillings for a potful of coffee before my assignment was completed. By the time I got back with the coffee, I was nearly as cold as Adrianna had been.

She heard me come into the room and called out from the bath. "Bring me a cup, black, Charlie. I can't wait. I'm serious."

I poured a cup for each of us and opened the door. Adrianna was naked, of course, being in a bath. I had expected a billowing mound of concealing suds, I guess, or at least a cloth draped across her. Neither covering was in evidence. She was up to her chin in hot water—very clear hot water. I made some show of turning my face away and extending the cup toward her as she sat up and reached for it.

"Don't be silly, Charlie. Sit down in here where it's warm, but close that door first," she said without embarrassment or artifice. She sounded completely worn out.

I stopped averting my eyes and sat down on the only available seat, remembering what she had said before I went out. "Mary attacked you," I prompted. "What did you do then?"

After a sip of the black coffee she shuddered and answered with a slight tremble in her voice. "I killed her, Charlie," almost managing to sound matter-of-fact. She paused to take a deep breath that closely resembled a sob. "At least I'm pretty sure she's dead by now, unless she got to a good hospital mighty fast."

"My God! Did she hurt you?"

She turned her face so the left side faced me. "How does it look?" A one-inch cut centered in a swollen lump the size of an egg yolk was on her cheekbone. The surrounding bruise covered her whole left cheek.

"Bad," I said. "I think you need stitches." I leaned closer to her face. "You definitely need stitches. As soon as you get dressed we'll go to the hospital."

"No, we won't, Charlie. It's been like this all night. We'll do the best we can to fix it, but I can't go into hospital. I killed a woman." She looked up at me with tears in her eyes.

"Maybe. Do you think there were witnesses?" I asked.

"Several, I think, a few for sure, and they saw me without my wig. The police may be looking for me, specifically, Adrianna Wallace. It was a mess, Charlie. Blood all over me, Hopson staggering away, holding herself together. It was horrible." She had started to shake a little, and she slid deeper into the water and took another sip of coffee.

"You shot her?" I asked with a gasp.

"Point-blank, twice," Adrianna answered. "I had the revolver right against her belly. She was on top of me with her hands around my neck. I managed to fish the pistol out of my coat pocket and shoot. She actually tightened her stranglehold when I shot her, and I pulled the trigger again."

"And she walked away from that?"

"She rolled off of me and then managed to stand. She struggled around a corner a few yards away, and I never saw her again. When I finally managed to get up, maybe half a minute later, I could see a woman with two children staring at me from across the street. Then

I looked up and saw other people in windows above her. I realized that I was still holding the revolver. I decided that I'd better keep right on holding it, too. I didn't know where Mary Hopson had gone or what these people might do. I knew I was hurt pretty badly myself."

"I can see that," I said as I reached over and dabbed at the blood on her cheek. "What did you do then? Where did you go?"

"I picked up Mary's grip and followed in the direction she'd gone, down King's toward Sheen. There was a sizable trail of drops of blood for a block. Then it stopped at the curb on Sheen Road. I think she must have found a taxi. Maybe one was waiting for her. She had that piece of luggage with her until she ran into me, so she may have been going to meet a cab."

"Likely," I said.

Adrianna buried her face in her hands. "Then my head started to clear, and I realized that the police must be on their way by then. I walked north again, crossed a schoolyard. I walked through alleys just as I was until I noticed that my coat was covered with blood. I stuffed it into a trash bin. Later, maybe an hour later, I found a little house with a 'To Let' sign on it. I wanted to get out of sight and think. I took a chance and broke the glass in a rear door. The place was vacant, but there was some furniture. I managed to keep warm enough under a small rug while I rested on an old couch. I passed out for a while. When I awoke after what must have been several hours, I decided to start making my way back here. I found a station and rode to Victoria." She paused for a moment and then added, "All that time in the war I never shot anyone. I never even actually saw anyone get shot. Now, in a few days' time, I've done both." She began to shake again.

"Let me take a closer look at that cut," I said, putting my cup on the windowsill above me. She turned the wound toward me again, and I gave it a close inspection. "It's going to scar. That's for sure,

Adrianna, but we can close it up and bandage it. You think people recognized you?"

"I don't know for sure. It seems likely. People are always recognizing me. Maybe they did."

"Surely they could see that it was self-defense."

"That depends on how much they saw—starting when." She coughed. "Maybe they just saw two women fighting, and one of them shooting the other. They hanged Helen Wickham for that a week ago."

"That's different! She ran from the scene," I said before I realized that Adrianna had done the same. "That was different," I said lamely, quite aware that it wasn't different at all.

"Don't go into law, Charlie," Adrianna said as she took my hand. "You'd be a poor defender. Help me up. I'm not too steady yet."

I helped her out of the bath and got a towel around her, up under the arms. Then she collapsed against me, and I had to get her into bed to try to dry her off and cover her up. I was sure that the blow to her head had been dangerous. Her breathing seemed fine. I checked the pupils of her eyes by lifting one lid at a time. The irises were dilated to equal sizes. I remembered that this was a good sign with head wounds. Next I started to clean the cut with alcohol, and she woke.

"Ouch!" She realized where she was. "I passed out again?"

"Yes, but I think you're going to be okay. No other wounds on you?"

"As you no doubt saw quite clearly."

"I did. Except for your head, you look extremely fit."

"Everywhere," she said.

"Everywhere I looked."

"Which was?"

"Everywhere," I said.

"What were you going to do to close the cut?" she asked.

"I don't know. I hadn't got that far."

"Instead of examining all the parts that aren't injured, Charlie, bring me some sticking plaster and the scissors. I'll show you how to make a butterfly bandage to close it up."

A few minutes later I had closed the cut securely with six strips of adhesive. She insisted on leaving the wound uncovered. "Can you tell me more of what happened?" I asked finally.

Adrianna adjusted herself back against the pillows and began again with a calmer voice. I tried to ignore the expanses of bare skin that were peeking out carelessly around the sheets. "Shortly after I dismissed my taxi and took up a position where I could watch Hopson's tailoring shop, she came out and started walking toward Richmond Park. I followed her, staying some distance back, but she seemed to pay no attention to who might be following her. She just walked directly into the park—"

"Through Bog Gate," I interrupted.

"Yes, through Bog Gate. Then she turned right and headed straight along to the area behind Morton Graves Voluntary Hospital, maybe half a mile, that bit. Then she sat down on a bench and waited. Maybe five minutes later, out walks a man, all the way to the fence. I couldn't be sure who it was because I was staying well away. I was standing over by Cambrian Gate, maybe a hundred yards away from her. Anyway, she got up and walked over to the fence. They leaned together there and talked a little, maybe a minute. Then she walked away. He just stood there and watched her go."

"Any idea who it was?"

"It wasn't Townby. I'm sure I'd have recognized him. I thought it looked like Tommy Morrell. But they talked, and Tommy doesn't talk, as I remember. Anyway, she passed me and headed back to her shop on the double. I kept a lot of distance because I knew where she was going. I hadn't been back on her street long when she came out of the shop again with a small leather grip. She locked the door and started up Carrington toward me. When she passed me, I decided to get clever, and I nearly got killed instead."

"Clever how?" I asked.

"I tried to remember that line from the journal—the one you showed me—and I said it to her to see if she'd react."

"Which line?"

"What I said was, *'Fräulein, Jetzt ist es Zeit, die Reise nach Jerusalem.'* I couldn't remember the exact line from the journal, but I remembered how to say that."

"My God! And she reacted?"

"She stopped cold in her tracks and turned toward me. I had never met her before, I'm sure of that, and I was wearing my wig. Anyway, she studied my face carefully for a few seconds, and then she answered me in English. She said, 'No, Mrs. Wallace, now it is time for you to die!' Before I could think about what to say back to her, she swung the grip up and clobbered me in the head. I went down like a stone."

"And she tried to strangle you?"

"Immediately. She jumped on me and started to choke the life out of me. I got my wits about me pretty fast then, I can tell you." Adrianna shuddered involuntarily.

"And you were able to shoot her, thank God."

"And thank Freddy for that Smith & Wesson. She was hit bad, Charlie. I'll be amazed if she's alive now. And I've no idea how many people saw it or what they think." Tears were again flowing down her cheeks.

I patted her bare shoulder. "You mentioned picking up her travel bag. Where is it?"

"Under some rubbish in the back garden of the house I slept in. I couldn't very well carry it about with me, in the circumstances."

"Did you see what was in it?" I asked.

"It was locked, and it is made of good thick leather. I don't think it has clothes in it, though. Too heavy. It's like a bag full of rocks. If it hadn't been pretty small, I couldn't have carried it as far as I did."

"Gold?"

"Of course not." She sniffled. "A small case full of gold would weigh fourteen or fifteen stone, about two hundred pounds."

She was right; even a small travel bag full of gold would weigh more than I do. "Money?"

"That's what I kept thinking. Townby's money. I want to go back for it and find out today, but right now I want to sleep."

"Me, too," I said. "I was sitting up most of the night."

"I think you'd better sleep in the other bed," she said.

And I had to agree. "You're right."

She woke me at noon with fresh coffee she had brewed in the room. A scarf was tied around her head so that much of her wound was out of sight, and she had applied makeup and powder to her cheeks. I noticed that she also was fully dressed.

"Mary Hopson's in the Saturday paper," she said when I had put on my trousers and started drinking my coffee, "but I'm not—at least so far."

"Is she dead?"

She nodded. "She was found over near Ham Gate in Richmond Park."

"That's some busy park," I said. "Ham Gate is near Stanton's boat shop."

"She was just lying on the ground a little ways inside the park. It was a brief story, but it was on page one of the *Times* because she had been shot in plain sight of several witnesses. When someone found her, the police were already looking for her because of reports of the shooting last night."

"But no mention of you."

"No. I guess no one recognized me. The paper says that Mary Hopson was in a desperate fight with another woman on the street near her shop. The woman was described as wearing a wig, which was left at the scene. No hair color mentioned. It said that this woman is being sought for questioning. The paper said that Mary was shot during the struggle and that no gun was found at the scene. Both women fled after the shooting."

"The grip?" I asked.

"No mention of it," Adrianna said, "but you're still in the news—wanted for robbing graves." Adrianna handed me a small brown bottle. "Here, Charlie. It's time for more hair magic."

"What's this?"

"Hydrogen peroxide. I'm about to become a blonde," she said, pushing at her hair with her hands.

"Have you ever done this? Because I sure haven't," I said, my head full of visions of just how badly we could mess up her appearance and unwittingly make her conspicuous in public.

"Yes. We used to do it to each other in France. It was quite a fad for a while. I never went blonde myself, but I helped with it lots of times. You can do it, Charlie. First, I'm going to go a little blonde. Then I'm going to get some streaks of gray. We'll look like an old couple."

"I don't look so old," I protested.

An hour later, Adrianna was a dishwater blonde with quite a bit of gray in her hair. Her makeup was heavy, but skillfully applied, so that the bruising was much less visible. The swelling had gone down some, and her cut was beginning to knit closed. The sticking plaster was still there. There was no question about the scarring, though. She would end up with a noticeable scar on the cheek near her left eye.

We decided to try out our disguises by going out to lunch, and by two o'clock I was enjoying soup at a restaurant while Adrianna ate real food.

"The odds are high that Mary was headed for Stanton's place in Ham when she died. It's too great a coincidence to assume that she just wandered over to his place after being shot. We know they were both connected into this. She may even have seen him. She may have died *after* she saw him." Adrianna began to fidget nervously with her place setting. I was struck by how different she looked—young body, damaged face, old hair.

"We should check on him," I said. "I'd feel a lot more comfortable if we knew where he is, though I'm pretty sure he couldn't recognize us now, even if he could find us."

"He could recognize Freddy, though. If she made it to Stanton, he knows that I'm involved in looking for members of the group. He also knows that you are and that Arthur must be. He probably at least suspects that Freddy knows as much as the rest of us. I've got to go home and warn him and fill him in on what has happened."

"That could be dangerous, Adrianna. Can't you just call him?"

She looked at me for a moment, her face bland and unreadable. Then she shook her head. "Of course, I *could* just call him for a bit of a chat. But I've *killed* someone, and he's in *danger* and it's *my* fault and it's *your* fault and I'm worried, Charlie, and I'm *truly* frightened and I need to see my husband!"

By the end of this rapidly delivered speech, she was whispering fiercely through clenched teeth, and I was feeling like a complete heel. I sat in silence while she sipped some tea and calmed down. I reached into the pocket of my borrowed trousers and laid Freddy's one-pound note on the table. "Let's go retrieve your coat and that grip that Mary Hopson was carrying," I said quietly. "It won't do to have either of those found. Then we can call Freddy to find out the best time for you to go home."

In the late afternoon, we found Adrianna's coat in the trash bin where she had discarded it the night before. Taking the coat along for disposal later, we decided to leave the task of retrieving the travel grip until nightfall.

Because we had to know where Robert Stanton was, we drove to Ham and scouted around a bit. A drive past Stanton's showed no sign that he was in. All the lights were out at the shop. We found a secluded lane near Teddington Lock and parked the car next to two others that were near the towing path. We would have passed for a middle-aged couple walking home from the river.

After a ten-minute walk we tried the rear door of Stanton's shop and found it securely locked. Adrianna strolled once past the front and found it closed and dark.

"So what now, Charlie?" Adrianna asked.

I just shrugged my shoulders and turned back toward the river. Then we retraced our stroll back to the parked car. Fifteen minutes after we drove away from the Thames, I slowed the car to a crawl while Adrianna stepped out in front of the empty house she had occupied so uncomfortably the night before. While she disappeared into the shadows beside the house, I drove on down the street until there was a convenient place to turn around. When I drove slowly back in front of the house. Adrianna walked out of the shadows with a leather case in her hand and was in the car in seconds.

After that, we stopped at a telephone booth and Adrianna called Freddy. She asked if he had noticed anyone suspicious hanging about and begged him to be watchful. Without giving any specifics over the phone, she told him that the danger had escalated. After some discussion, they decided that she would go home at midmorning the next day, Sunday, a time when the household staff would be away at church.

I called Conan Doyle and arranged to meet with him at his London address at the same time. I kept the conversation brief, deferring his questions until our meeting, but I did suggest that he maintain special caution.

We drove back to the hotel and were careful to look for anyone who might observe us before we took the leather case from the car and walked up the back stairs to our room.

I set the bloodstained leather travel bag on the dresser, and it took Adrianna a full minute to cut through its wide leather lock strap with her little scissors.

Underneath some of Mary's clothes we found the money. The notes were tied in bundles of mixed denomination. We each untied a bundle and counted it.

"Five hundred pounds," I said when I had finished my first bundle.

"Same," said Adrianna. She walked to the bag and lifted out several more bundles and dropped them on the bed. She did this three more times while I counted bundles.

"Twenty," I said.

"What's that white stuff stuck to the edges of some of them?"

I picked up one of those bundles and looked closely. "Plaster, I think. These might have been hidden in a wall. That would be my guess."

"There are loose papers in the bottom of the bag," she said as she reached in and fished them out. They were bond certificates, some of them convertible to stocks. We considered them together in silence. "These must be worth several hundred at least," Adrianna said finally. "If the bundles of money are all the same, she had well over ten thousand pounds with her. That'll get you to Jerusalem, I'll bet."

"Over eight and a half years of my basic salary," I said, "and I'm pretty well paid." I could see that Adrianna was doing some mental calculations.

"Indeed you are," she said in a moment. "The interest on it alone would pay a modest salary. What'll we do with it, Charlie?"

"For now, I'd say we repack it in the bag. It could turn out to be evidence of some kind."

"Or it could turn out to be Townby's missing money."

"Part of it, anyway. Most likely it is."

"As far as I'm concerned, Charlie, it might turn out to be yours." She caught and held my gaze, and we looked eye-to-eye for a moment. We were now talking about stealing, but from whom?

24

"The ideal reasoner," he remarked, "would, when he had once been shown a single fact in all its bearings, deduce from it not only all the chain of events which led up to it but also all the results which would follow from it."
—"The Five Orange Pips"

WHEN I AWOKE ON Sunday morning, Adrianna had already gone out to see Freddy. She had left a note, though, that said simply, "See you when I get back. A." After dressing, I went out for a breakfast of oatmeal. I checked the newspapers, but found no further news about Mary Hopson's death.

I had decided the day before that I wanted to see if I could get Conan Doyle safely out of this mess. I hoped I could convince him to drop the whole matter. I worried, though, that Stanton still might be a danger to him. I was pretty sure that Sir Arthur wouldn't approve of much that had happened as this had escalated. Now there was Adrianna in legal jeopardy, and there was the question of a lot of money that wasn't ours.

Adrianna was certainly the assailant whom the police sought at the moment. Explaining that to Conan Doyle was not something I even wanted to attempt, especially since he had warned me against involving her. I gave myself extra time to think of what I was going to tell him—certainly it wasn't going to be the entire truth—and it was two hours later before I left a note for Adrianna and drove to his London flat.

I had concocted quite a set of lies by then. I was not without feelings of guilt about them, either. Sir Arthur was a good and honest man. But deceiving him seemed necessary for Adrianna's protection, at least for now. For the moment, at least, I could think of no plausible explanation that Adrianna could offer to the police for why she had been stalking Mary Hopson, much less why she had killed her and then run away. While I wanted to be honest with Sir Arthur, I couldn't compromise him by telling him the truth.

I was waiting in the same library where this had all begun when he entered the room. Before I could rise to shake his hand, he walked straight to his desk and sat down without preliminary greetings and without his customary pleasant smile. When he actually looked at me, his expression turned to surprise.

"I'd never have recognized you, my boy. What is going on, Charles? This thing is turning into a nightmare! Two shootings—not to mention that mess at the grave. What in heaven's name are you doing?"

"It is indeed bizarre, Sir Arthur," I said, "but I think it's nearly over. Maybe it *is* over."

"What happened to the Hopson woman? Shot down by another woman, the papers said."

"I don't know," I lied. "I think the group might be fighting within itself."

He looked up, his eyebrows raised skeptically. "Why would that be so, Charles?"

"I think one of them somehow obtained knowledge of the whereabouts of quite a lot of money that belonged to Gussmann. I don't know yet whether they discovered it before or after he died." Strictly speaking, this was probably a lie. It was possible—even plausible—though it didn't answer his question.

He shook his head slowly with an expression of doubt. "How is any of that connected with me, Charles? That was what I wanted you to find out. But all we've managed to do is breed more questions every day."

"That, too, must have had something to do with the money. Maybe Mary Hopson was supposed to have some influence over Helen Wickham if she could see her face-to-face. You were one person who might be able to arrange that, and you were the only one they could interest in doing so—that is, if they could construct a connection to Spiritualism."

"You mean Mary was supposed to hypnotize Helen?"

"Perhaps."

"Still," he said impatiently, "how did they know about Father in the first place? About our argument? About the sketchbook?"

I remembered finding that very drawing two days before and wondered if I could mention it. I decided against it, however, hoping that Sir Arthur would become less, rather than more, engaged in the specifics. And I was still uncertain how the journals fit into the case. "I'm sure that they have access to extensive notes made by Dr. Gussmann—maybe the missing journals that Alice Tupper told us about. Somewhere in that information they must have found what they needed to write the letter."

He paused to consider the idea. "Have you seen these notes?" he asked.

I paused before answering. "I've seen some of his papers."

He placed a hand to his forehead and tilted his head as if pondering the whole scenario I was presenting. "Now, there's another woman—the one who fought with and shot Miss Hopson. That's one woman too many—not on the list. What do you know about her?"

I halted a bit before I started lying again. "Absolutely nothing. She's a complete mystery to me. I thought Robert Stanton was the only other one connected to this. I suspected one or two others of involvement, but they are patients confined to Morton Graves. It might clear everything up to know who this mystery woman is, but for now I haven't a clue."

He stared at me quizzically for a long moment. "Just some sort of money scheme?" he asked. "Is that what you think?"

"So far I've found no supernatural elements," I answered.

"But it was *you* who opened Gussmann's grave!" he said, gesturing toward a newspaper on the desk. "As we agreed."

"Of course, yes. I was looking for evidence that he might not be dead, but I was wrong. He's dead."

"You took something from the grave, didn't you?" He looked suspiciously at me. "That's what the newspaper account said."

"Yes, but it turned out to be nothing," I lied again, "an upholstered block of wood used to arrange the body. I understand it's a common practice. In fact, that's what one of the grave robbers told me it would turn out to be."

"What did you think it was when you took it?" he looked at me closely.

"I didn't know. There it was in the grave, and it might have been any number of things. It might have been some of the missing money. I didn't want to take time to find out right there in the graveyard. As I said, it turned out to be nothing."

"So you've found no actual connection between Dr. Gussmann and the letter," he asked.

"None at all, except that information from some of Gussmann's notes probably gave them a clue as to how to elicit your help—no supernatural connection." I needed to convince him of this. "As I pointed out once before, Sir Arthur, you made headlines before the war by fighting to free an innocent man."

"Go on."

"That was after Gussmann died, but these other people would have known about it. And you made that campaign to spare Roger Casement's life on the grounds of insanity?"

"In 1916, yes. There was a great deal of publicity over that."

"Also after Gussmann was dead," I said. "And then just about a year ago you brought up the uses of psychics in solving crimes—that article in *The Strand*."

"Oh, yes. 'A New Light on Old Crimes.' I mentioned the Agatha Christie case in that. Again, a lot of publicity."

"I think that a few people who have access to information about that also have access to some of those notebooks of his. They've probably gone back through his whole career, and found in them what they needed. Your own history would assure them that you could be attracted to this case and do what the letter asked."

"They weren't after me for publicity, then."

"Probably the opposite. I doubt if your name will ever come up."

He held eye contact with me for several seconds. Then he shook his head gravely and said, "I hate to say this to you, my boy, but I think you're holding back on the truth—and worse."

I started to reply, but he held up his palms toward me and continued himself. "Please. I know you don't accept my views on Spiritualism, but don't let that mislead you into thinking I'm senile. First, I think that you're trying to protect Mrs. Wallace, as she is no doubt the woman who shot Mary Hopson, and you no doubt got her into that messy situation." He paused for my denial, but I merely stared straight ahead as my face flushed.

He continued, "Second, you clearly know a lot more about this than you've said. Probably whatever you took from the grave was more important than you've admitted—my guess is that it's Gussmann's journals. Alice Tupper no doubt put them there. I've been sure of that since we talked to her."

I nodded, shamefaced, and did not reply.

"You're in quite a bit of trouble now, both of you, I understand, and I'm certainly responsible in large measure. Why don't you let me help, Charles? Do you think that you and Adrianna are still in danger?"

I took a deep breath and answered honestly. "As long as Robert Stanton is around, we're probably in some danger. Adrianna also is disguised. She's at her home right now, though, trying to spend some time with Freddy."

"I thought immediately yesterday when I read the news that it must have been she who shot Mary Hopson."

I gave up my pretense. "As you say, she was forced into the situation by me. For the moment at least, we're both fugitives. We'll continue to hide out until we can find a way to clear all of this up."

"Just the one room, then?" he asked, raising his eyebrows and tilting his head slightly.

"That's part of our disguise. We've got a large room with two beds. Maintaining privacy hasn't been too much of a problem. I hope we can both go home soon," I lied once more. "I, for one, need to get back to the office and make some explanations."

"How's Freddy taking all this?" The implication was that Mrs. Wallace's lodging arrangement would be a problem for Mr. Wallace, but I chose to reply as if he meant the matter of her safety.

"He's worried, of course—hell of a thing for her to have gotten involved in. She thought it would be a lark, you know, bit of sleuthing. I should have had better sense than to let her come along." I looked apologetically at Doyle. "You were right about that. Adrianna went home this morning to tell Wallace what has happened. Obviously this could be a serious mess for both of them."

"Well, it's been bad for you, too, my boy. I'll never forgive myself about your getting shot. Adrianna's all right, though?"

"Minor injuries," I said casually.

"Injuries?"

"Oh, yes. Mary Hopson attacked her—knocked her flat with a heavy travel case and then nearly choked her to death. That's when Adrianna had to shoot her."

"My word! No permanent damage, I hope?"

"There'll be a scar, actually. Nothing serious. She's frightened about the whole situation, not the least of which is the possibility of a manslaughter charge."

"Hence your decision to try to get me off the track with your story today. I understand. Now, what was really in that grave, Charles?"

It seemed not only useless to try to deceive him, but wrong as well. I reviewed the interview we had all had with Alice Tupper, took my time, and told him everything, including the amount of money we had found.

"Clarify the hypnosis part, Charles. You think that the subjects of this deep hypnosis—what was it called?"

"He called it subgnostic possession."

"Possession beneath the knowledge of the patient—means something like that?"

"It meant actual possession of their bodies," I said. Finally, I reached into my pocket and extracted the torn slip of paper from his father's sketchbook. I handed it to him.

"Astounding!" he said when I had finished. "And a dozen years later these same hypnotic patients of his and some others as well are still cooperating together in some sort of ring? Something to do with Gussmann's money, you think. It's psychical, Charles, you realize that. They've got some sort of psychical communication among them. I'm sure of it." He paused and looked at me. "What do you intend to do now, Charles? Where does it go from here?"

"I don't know. It all depends on what we can discover about Stanton. If he's at the center of all this, as I'm beginning to think he may be, I've got to get some proof that will put him in jail. Then I think we'll all be safe unless there are other dangers that haven't surfaced yet."

"But do you think that there are others involved besides Robert Stanton and those inside Morton Graves Voluntary?" he asked.

"I *hope* that everyone other than he is in the asylum at the moment. I'm pretty sure that at least one person there besides Liza Anatole is involved—a man named Tommy Morrell. I think Adrianna witnessed a meeting between him and Mary Hopson the day before yesterday. But we can keep an eye on them as long as they are in Morton Graves. Maybe we can even find a way to keep them confined permanently. I don't mind telling you, Sir Arthur, that I'm glad this isn't a ghost. They've turned out to be far too bad a bunch of characters to deal with as it is."

"You're right there, Charles. I've got to say, though, that I've never encountered a spirit that was evil. If this had turned out to be a spiritual contact from Gussmann, we'd have been in no danger," he said confidently as he opened his desk drawer and withdrew a leather-covered pad.

He wrote out a bank draft to me for a hundred pounds—to cover everyone's expenses, he said. "Let's meet later today, all four of us. I want to discuss this whole thing with Adrianna—Freddy, too. We've got a number of serious decisions to make, Charles. Four heads will be better than two. There's a pub off the south side of Richmond Park near Robin Hood Gate. What's it called?"

"The one on Kingston Vale near the college?"

"That's the one. Get Freddy and Adrianna and meet me there at about three. I want to look around the area personally—get oriented to these places you've described—before I meet you."

Adrianna was waiting in our room when I returned, sitting in our only comfortable chair and reading a newspaper.

"How was Sir Arthur, Charlie? Was he disappointed that you hadn't seen a ghost?"

"I think so, but he's determined to get even more involved in the case. How's Freddy?" I asked.

She shrugged and walked over to look out the window. "First, he was shocked about the condition of my face. I've seen him happier. He wants me home, he hates my hair, he wants to talk about things I don't want to talk about yet." Turning to face me, she paused only for a moment before telling me, "He's sure we're going to have an affair."

I thought back to the conversation Freddy and I had had in my hospital room. "How do you feel about that prediction?"

She thought for a moment and sounded weary when she said , "I don't know. Freddy seemed relieved, in a way. He says you're good for me. That's not what's bothering him. I think he worries that I might eventually want to end our marriage, but I assured him otherwise."

I didn't have any right to protest, so I let the matter drop. "Did you tell him about Mary Hopson?"

"Of course I did. It puts him in danger. Besides, Chief Inspector Willis had already been to see Freddy—looking for me. Freddy had it pretty well figured out before I got there."

"The question is," I said, "what has *Willis* got figured out?"

"Freddy couldn't tell. The chief inspector didn't seem to believe that I was traveling on my own and couldn't be reached. He also didn't seem to believe that Freddy hadn't seen or heard from you. Willis is in a bad spot. One can't go about calling any member of Parliament a liar, much less one who's also a wealthy war hero. Nevertheless, he stopped just short of doing so."

"What does Freddy think we should do?"

"He thinks we should wait a bit before deciding what to do, if anything. What about Sir Arthur? You didn't—" she looked up at me with wide eyes.

"Tell Arthur?" I interrupted. "I didn't have to tell him—he told me. I told him about the money in the bag, too. He wants to meet us later with Freddy."

"Well, so much for nobody ever knowing," Adrianna said with a shudder. Then she walked over to me and pressed against my chest so I could put my arms around her. We stood there quietly for a long time as she wept softly. Then she reached into my pocket, drew out my handkerchief, and wiped her eyes. She leaned back slightly to look up into my face and gave me a small smile. "There's something else we need to figure out, Charlie. I think you can stop looking for a Zionist connection."

"What do you mean?" I asked, releasing her.

She walked over to her bed and perched on its edge. "Well, I asked Freddy a few questions about the Zionist colonies financed by Edmund de Rothschild before the war. He asked why I was interested, and I told him that we thought Dr. Gussmann might have been connected with the Palestine movement because he intended to travel to Jerusalem before he died. Freddy asked why we thought that, and I told him about the line in the journal—*die Reise nach Jerusalem*—and he asked if you knew about the children's game."

"What children's game, Adrianna?" It seemed to me that she and Freddy had gotten completely off the point.

"*Die Reise nach Jerusalem* is the name of a children's game in Germany. Freddy says it's the same as musical chairs. He was surprised that you didn't know that because you're a lifelong speaker of German, and Freddy only studied it in school as a child here in England."

"When I was a child, the only German-speaker I knew was my father. I never played games with German children. I never knew any," I said.

Adrianna had retrieved one of the journals and was turning pages, looking for the end of the notes. "Anyway, he says that the reason the journal doesn't use the phrase the way you'd expect it to for going on a journey is that it's probably not a journey at all. It's an object, like you said—a game."

"Musical chairs? The game where the kids move around in a circle?" I took the journal and read the entry again.

"I don't see how that could be what Dr. Gussmann was referring to. He certainly wasn't planning to play children's games."

Adrianna nodded thoughtfully. "That's true. It probably makes more sense that he was planning a trip, as you said. Just the same, Freddy thought you ought to know about the game."

I sat down on the other bed and faced her. "You want to know what I've been thinking about?"

"I don't want to talk about us—you and me. Talk doesn't make anything work any better, okay?" She looked at me with something like fear in her expression.

"I was thinking about money," I said apologetically, shaking my head.

"Oh, the money," she said thoughtfully. "It really is a lot of money, Charlie."

"I wasn't thinking about this money. I was thinking about the rest of the money."

"The rest of what money? Townby's money? What do you know about that?" Adrianna asked.

"We have names of four people who are definitely connected into this Gussmann and Townby mystery in the letter. That's Helen Wickham, Mary Hopson, Robert Stanton, and Liza Anatole. The amount of money that Mary Hopson was traveling with just happens to be very roughly a quarter of the missing estate. What if it was her share? What if each of them actually had possession of a share after Townby liquidated his holdings? Why on earth that might have happened is something I can't imagine. But it would explain why this gang is together. Money can be a powerful glue."

"Then each of the others would still have a share. But it seems to me that the missing money is the least of our worries just now, Charlie."

"Wickham wouldn't have her share," I persisted.

"I wonder. What do you suppose would have happened to her share if she ever had one? Could that be why they wanted so badly to get to her—to find out where it was? That *would* be related to our problem."

"But they didn't find out! That's my bet. Now think about Mary Hopson. She was leaving her shop with the money. I'll bet that if Helen Wickham ever had a share, they were trying to get information about it." Then I remembered. "She lived in St. Margarets. Where's that?"

"Just north of Ham," Adrianna answered.

"And if Stanton has any, it will be around his shop, probably in his safe," I added.

"And Liza might have some, too. You might be right, but is it really something we need to worry about now, Charlie?"

"Well, Stanton is still a free man as far as we know. He may be getting ready to run, just like Hopson was. We do have to worry about that. I think we should get back out to where we can keep an eye on him. We have to meet Sir Arthur out that way today anyway. We'd better call Freddy."

I went out to make the call, but there was no answer at the Wallace household. We could honestly tell Conan Doyle that we'd tried to reach him, to no avail.

We left for West London immediately, but we didn't find Stanton. When we drove Adrianna's Austin down his street an hour later, it was obvious that he was out. The shop had its well-used "closed" sign in the window.

"What do we do now, Charlie?" Adrianna asked as we drove past the shop. "I don't think it's a very good time to search for any money."

I laughed. "Let's go meet Sir Arthur for tea."

The pub was a little east of Kingston University. We were lucky and found a booth shortly after entering the crowded main room, but service was running well behind demand. Conan Doyle, though, was right on time. We made our excuses about Freddy not being able to come, and Sir Arthur made no comment.

It was too noisy for comfortable conversation, so as we waited to be served, we leaned against the straight back of our booth and watched the good-natured chaos that reigned in the packed room. At one table in the center of the room there were six rowdy college men. Several rounds of pints had already been emptied, and more seemed to appear out of nowhere. They had ordered sandwiches and were none too happy that these hadn't yet arrived. To this already boisterous number was added a seventh when another young man, who was obviously among their favorites, came through the front door and joined them. They all invited him to sit down and join in the festivities, but there was no chair for him. One of the group offered his own, declaring that he would find another chair for himself and bring it over.

But the generous lad couldn't find another chair after all. There was none to be had in the place. He complained to a barmaid, who told him just how important his problem was to her at the moment. This sent him back to the table to try to regain his original chair, but its new occupant wasn't having any of that. Not only was the latecomer keeping the chair, but he'd finished off his benefactor's pint as well. With his loud protest, the situation was getting altogether too noisy for me. Adrianna leaned over and, raising her voice to be heard over the roar, reminded me that I'd probably been young once myself.

Finally, one rather narrowly built young man offered to share his chair with the dispossessed one, and each put half a fanny on the chair. As the displaced one was not himself of such a slight build, this solution didn't work for very long. Then one of their number suggested that the sharing might work better if the thinnest two shared a chair. That worked for a while. Then they tried sitting on each other's knees, but that drew too many rude comments from other friends in the room. So they just kept on shifting around uncomfortably and making a lot of noise.

I had begun to enjoy this show as we got our sandwiches and a second drink, when Adrianna reached over and tapped my arm to get my attention. "*Die Reise nach Jerusalem,* Charles. Do you see?"

"What was that?" Sir Arthur asked above the noise.

"*Die Reise nach Jerusalem,*" Adrianna repeated.

"Oh, the game. Of course!" Conan Doyle said with a nod toward the rowdy table. "Musical chairs, quite so!"

25

Ah me! It is a wicked world, and when a clever man turns his brains to crime
it is the worst of all.
—"The Adventure of the Speckled Band"

I LAUGHED. "I SEE the game, Adrianna, but I can't say I like the music."

"There's always an extra man, an odd man out. But he isn't ever completely out, because someone has to give him room each time."

"None too happily," Arthur said.

"Right, but don't you see," she said, "whether they like it or not, there's always one extra fitting into the circle. That's what he meant."

"*Who* meant, Adrianna?" Sir Arthur asked.

"Gussmann," she said. "That's what he meant to do. How did he say it? Now it is time. . . ."

Then the shock of what she was saying hit me, and I fell silent. A shudder ran through me as if the overheated pub had suddenly been opened to the late January air outside. "*Jetzt ist es Zeit feur* . . . Now it is time for . . . *die Reise nach Jerusalem* . . . musical chairs."

"When did Gussmann say that?" Doyle asked. "Did he mention musical chairs in his journal?"

"*Die Reise nach Jerusalem.* Yes, at the end of the journal. How did you come to know that German phrase, Sir Arthur?" I asked, feeling a little embarrassed that everyone but me seemed to be familiar with it.

"Standard children's game. I suppose every lad who's ever studied a bit of *Deutsch* in school has heard that one. Sounds like Gussmann meant that he was going to start moving from one patient to another." He paused and then slammed a meaty fist on the table. "That's it! He could move *into* one of them."

"And what was he saying before that?" Adrianna asked. "Complaining about his health—his imminent death! And what had he learned to do?"

"Jesus! He had learned to *occupy* them—Helen Wickham, Mary Hopson, William Townby, and Tommy Morrell. For longer and longer periods of time," I answered.

"And at greater and greater distances from himself," Adrianna added with growing excitement.

"And he had learned to do it faster and faster. But this is too much," I said, looking over at the neighboring group of seven occupying six places.

"Thirteen years, almost," Adrianna said quietly, as if everyone in the room were listening. "He's been the odd man out for almost thirteen years, using, using . . . what? The four of them?"

"That . . . can it be possible?" I sputtered.

Arthur interrupted. "This may make more sense than the theory of an organized gang of people who were never in Morton Graves together anyway. One Gussmann, one extra man moving through four other people—moving around from one to the other."

I considered that in silence for a moment and then answered, "More than four of them. The letter would lead us to Wickham, Hopson, Stanton, and Anatole, but we already know about Townby—and there was Tommy Morrell—there may be at least six of them." We both looked over at our table for six, with its seven occupants. "It's crazy, Adrianna, unmanageable. Besides being just plain impossible, how could he juggle so many lives?"

"Remember the rabbi, Charles."

"The bear *could talk*," I said.

"But I agree with you about the numbers," she said. "Maybe that's not the way it turned out. Maybe they weren't all involved—"

"You're losing me again," Sir Arthur interrupted. "What rabbi? What bear? You're talking about a man's spirit, right? Gussmann moving as a spirit."

"Not exactly," Adrianna answered. "Gussmann the man might be alive, actually in the bodies, one at a time, of a few of his former patients—the ones in the journal Charles told you about."

Sir Arthur nodded slowly. "Yes," he said, "musical chairs. Just those six patients, you think?"

"Maybe some new ones—not exactly a Spiritualist event. More like he's alive—never died—but without a body of his own," I said.

"Is Gussmann's body dead, Charles?" Conan Doyle asked.

"Yes, definitely."

"What part of being a spirit is it that you two are having trouble understanding? This is exactly what we mean by spirits beyond the grave—the other side. You think Gussmann has found a particular way of being a spirit—of surviving death. No Spiritualist would disagree with you. I believe that I've seen other spirits who have found other ways. You two believe that this one—Gussmann—also is alive, as an intact personality, while his body is dead."

"He did this before he died," I said. "It's not the same thing. He was practicing this before he died."

"Is Gussmann dead, Charles?" he repeated with raised eyebrows.

Once I accepted the possibility that Gussmann, himself, might actually be alive in this way, I was able to see some interesting possibilities. "I think he was originally just going to use one of them," I said. "Townby was the best one. He wrote entries to that effect several times."

"And Townby became Gussmann, in a way," Adrianna said.

"In almost every way! Gussmann gave Townby most of his own money and sent him to medical school—went back to medical school in Townby's body," I added.

"Where the young Townby did marvelously. Not too surprising, since the mind he was using had been practicing medicine for several decades by then," Sir Arthur said. He spoke so loudly that he turned some faces at the rowdy table. He was jubilant.

I lowered my own voice. "If we're not completely off the track."

"We're not, Charles," Adrianna said quietly. "We can't be. If Townby was occupied, he must have been the only one, at least in the early years. He *left* London and was away for a long time. None of the others left."

"And after he returned, he paid the hospital for a chance to resume his research among his old patients," I said.

"And Townby liquidated the estate, probably to make it mobile," Sir Arthur added. "He never knew when he might have to move fast. Gussmann, I mean. Gussmann sold everything to keep all his resources within his grasp—no matter who he happened to be at the time."

"And as Townby he cultivated new patients to the state of—what did Gussmann call it?" Adrianna asked.

"Subgnostic possession. He meant just that—possession," I said. "When he is in them, Gussmann is in full possession of their bodies, and their minds are completely submerged. His journal says that they have no awareness, no memory of anything while he is in control."

"But then something went very wrong with Townby," Adrianna speculated.

"Something sure went wrong with Helen Wickham," I added. "There were flaws, serious ones, in the whole system if that's what he was doing."

"There *still are* flaws in the system. As you said a minute ago, he is trying to manage too many lives." Arthur gripped the edge of the table as if that were all that would keep him from jumping up and down in satisfaction.

"Let's wait a minute," I said quietly. "We're going pretty far down a road here—trying to fit in a lot of pieces and guesses—speculating about the movements of a dead man. This is sounding more than a little crazy. Is there any consistent picture here?"

"Start with the letter," Adrianna said. "He—they—somebody wanted to get *any one* of only three people in to see Helen Wickham. Assuming that Gussmann couldn't be inside more than one of them at once, it *had* to be Helen Wickham he was occupying at that time," Adrianna said. "There's no other possibility. He was trapped in Wickham, in prison, and he didn't have much time left."

I thought about that assumption. "Right," I said, "because the letter wanted us to bring *any one* of the others. Each had to be subjects; Helen had to be the master."

"And the master was trapped," Sir Arthur said. "Gussmann was about to hang." He thought a moment. "Helen Wickham had killed a woman in a fight—or Gussmann did, I should say—while he was using Helen's body. He was still using it when he was arrested. He couldn't get out."

"Maybe he did hang," I said quietly. "I'm pretty sure that Mary Hopson walked out of there as the same woman who walked in with me."

"Pretty sure."

"I'm even more sure that Helen Wickham was just a terrified woman who didn't know what was happening to her. That's from the first moment I saw her."

Adrianna thought about that before interrupting me. "So he was already out of her by then, maybe."

"If he was already out, why write the letter?" I asked.

Conan Doyle answered, "What if he wrote the letter to me *before* he found another way out? Clearly, he *must* have written it before he found another way. Then he managed something else and was gone by the time you got there. Whom would he have been able to see regularly, Charles?" he asked.

I took a deep breath. "I'll say again that we're going way down a road of our own making."

"Give us another explanation, Charlie. I'm listening," Adrianna prompted.

I couldn't think of an answer that was any more plausible than the one we were pursuing. "No. I like this one. Let's say he got out with a guard or someone. Helen Wickham saw a priest regularly. I know that from something the guard said. It would be worth finding him and having a chat," I said. "So if we assume that Gussmann got out of Helen before her death, he just left Helen there to hang for something he'd done."

Adrianna said, "Maybe for something *she* had done. We don't know, but he couldn't get her body out anyway. So he escaped, let's say. Well, we can assume he did because Liza shot you and because Mary Hopson attacked me. But how? Who?"

"The priest," Sir Arthur said. "My maids said someone in a black dress with a man's shoes delivered the letter. Suppose that he delivered it for Helen Wickham. If we're right in this speculation, it had to be she who wrote it, and Gussmann had to be inhabiting her at the time."

"Otherwise he wouldn't have written the letter at all!" Adrianna said. "But if he could get the priest to deliver the letter, he might later have managed to subdue the priest even further."

"Into subgnostic possession," I said. I thought about it a moment and did a calculation. "The letter was delivered to Arthur on Tuesday, January tenth. It was written on a paper dated the ninth. I got inside Holloway early on Tuesday the seventeenth. The guard said that Helen had been acting crazy since the day before. That would be Monday the sixteenth. That was probably when he left Helen and went into the priest who visited her. But after that he could have gone anywhere. He had money. Gussmann could have gone anywhere once he walked out as the priest."

"No, that would have been too risky," Adrianna argued. "Remember, things go wrong with these . . . subjects. He prefers former patients and needs to have several of them close at hand. Let's assume he has several of them around London."

"Around Richmond Park, you mean!" Conan Doyle added. "Look at the names on the list and the places where they live. And the location of Morton Graves Voluntary Hospital. All on or near Richmond Park."

"Even Gussmann's grave is on the edge of the park," Adrianna murmured.

"I'm pretty sure the body I saw isn't one of the subjects," I said. "The whole idea of his experiments was to abandon that sick body before it died."

"The bear could talk, Charlie."

"Not *this* bear," I said. "But there's something we're overlooking about the subjects."

"Which is?"

"He doesn't necessarily have to occupy them for them to be useful to him. Remember that he could send them away from himself to do things. They could be hypnotized without being possessed."

"But not to *say* anything. Wasn't that what you told me?" Sir Arthur said.

"At least by the time he finished the journal," I agreed, "he could never get them to talk when they were just in a subgnostic trance."

"So whenever we have *talked* to one of them," Adrianna said, "there have only been two possibilities: the subject wasn't in a trance—"

"Or we were talking to Gussmann!" I interrupted. "That's why Robert Stanton seemed like two different people when I talked to him twice on the same day. One of those times he was Gussmann."

"Calm down, Charlie. Which time was which, do you think?"

"When he knew about boats, he was Stanton. It was Gussmann the second time I talked to him. He wasn't interested in boats, but he was sure interested in the names I threw out. That is probably when I tipped him off that we were on his trail."

"Maybe," Sir Arthur interrupted. "Or when you went to Morton Graves. There could be any number of his subjects in there, and Gussmann could be in any one of them at any time. We could have several dangerous enemies, Charles."

"A significant number, maybe, but the journal indicated that these subject types were very rare. At least two of them are dead now, and one is confined. Liza has been sent back to Morton Graves Hospital, but Stanton is still out here somewhere. If we're correct in all this, Gussmann's pool of subjects is seriously depleted."

"And he may be trapped again," Adrianna added. Then she sat bolt upright. "My God!" Her voice dropped to a stage whisper. "I bet I shot him!"

I thought about that for a moment, and it seemed very likely that she had. Almost certainly Gussmann had recognized the phrase from his own journal. Moreover, he knew Adrianna on sight, assuming it had been Gussmann in Liza Anatole when I was shot. "And *he* shot *me,*" I said with conviction.

"Because she—the woman on the street—spoke your name," Adrianna said. "Of course, Charlie. It couldn't have been that she was merely *sent* to shoot you, because she spoke to you."

"So Gussmann may now be dead along with Mary Hopson," Arthur said. "We may be worrying about Stanton for nothing."

"Or, if she got to Stanton," Adrianna said, "*he* may be Gussmann now. In which case, we have to get him trapped again."

Arthur sat silently, his mouth drawn into a tight frown. Finally he said, "If Gussmann—in the Hopson woman's body—made it to Stanton, we're all in danger. He knows I'm involved, naturally, and he has made attempts on both of you. He ought to at least suspect Freddy—and my wife, for that matter—of knowing as well. And obviously we can't go to the police. There's the little matter of shooting Mary Hopson, for one thing."

"There's no question about that," I agreed.

"My reputation would be destroyed," Adrianna added, "and I'd likely be in prison, if not worse. Freddy would be out of office, and Charles would be fired and in jail for grave robbing."

Everything she'd said was absolutely true, whether our other wild speculations were correct or not. Mary Hopson was really dead at Adrianna's hands, and I'd really robbed a grave. We were actually in possession of a fortune we knew wasn't ours. Add to that a short list of other crimes and misdemeanors, both financial and moral. Clearly, we were never going to tell anyone else about this. The question was: What *were* we going to do? Gussmann, if he had not actually been dead for more than a decade, might or might not be dead now. Several subjects or accomplices, if they had ever existed, might or might not still be after us. At least one of them certainly had been after us at one time, but she was now confined to Morton Graves asylum, maybe.

"I hope he's dead," I said. "I don't like the odds if he's not."

"Well, he doesn't know where we are or what we look like now, Charlie. If he is alive—if he was ever alive in the way we think. We've got to find that out." Adrianna paused and looked nervously around the room. "I wish I knew where Stanton has been keeping himself."

"I hate to say it, but since he is missing, there's a good chance that Gussmann is in him. He's smart, and he knows we're on to him. We have no idea what kind of resources he has. He's probably got money and guns, and if he has other subjects outside the asylum, he could be—"

"Anyone," Adrianna said. "Well, not anyone, but as far as we know, any stranger could be he, man or woman. How do we find him in the circumstances?"

I thought about what she had just said. Whether she had

intended to or not, she had changed my direction. "You're right about that. If he's alive, we *have* to find him, and we're the only ones who can," I said.

"You do realize, Charles, that if any sane person heard us now, we'd be the ones confined to an asylum, don't you?" Sir Arthur asked. Then he added, "You're absolutely right, though—we've got to become the hunters. You're both sounding more and more like Spiritualists to me."

Adrianna and I quietly ignored that remark.

"I know what you mean about people thinking we're crazy," I said. "The only comfort I get when I think about it is that we're all saying it, not just one of us. If I were saying something like this by myself, I'd be pretty sure I was mad. So now how do we hunt Dr. Gussmann?"

"Let's think of what we know about him," Conan Doyle said. "If he's still alive, he wants to get away. We know that because of Mary Hopson and the money and clothes in her bag. That was Gussmann, and he was leaving, at least for the short run."

"Possibly, though, he intended to go away with one or more of the others," I said. "Probably Robert Stanton was his only option. The others are probably inside Morton Graves. He couldn't get them out. If it is his intention to leave London, Stanton may now be his only hope of doing so."

"Unless there are others we don't know about, like the priest," Adrianna added.

"We can hope that Gussmann is bottled up for the moment," Sir Arthur said, "either in Stanton or inside Morton Graves Voluntary Hospital."

"And inside Morton Graves, there are three possibilities that we know of: Liza Anatole, William Townby, and Tommy Morrell," Adrianna continued.

"Townby and Morrell are permanent guests," I said, "and Anatole is confined by her family in cooperation with Scotland Yard, so none of them offers Gussmann a route to escape."

"But the dilemma is only temporary for him," Adrianna countered. "It's just a matter of time before he seduces another subject and goes free—as free as he gets."

I thought for a moment and said, "That bench!"

"What bench?" Adrianna asked.

"The bench where Mary Hopson sat when I followed her—when you followed her, too."

"What about it?" she asked.

Arthur interrupted, "Of course, Charles. It's the rendezvous point. They all go there and wait for Gussmann, in whatever person he's in, to come. Those inside the asylum no doubt have schedules to follow, just like those on the outside."

"They meet at the fence at the edge of Morton Graves Voluntary and he simply passes through—going in or going out," Adrianna said as she nodded agreement. "Gussmann is free to come and go any time one of his subjects shows up.

"At any rate, he's more free than we are," I said. "We're living in disguise and can't live in our homes. I can't return to my job. Until we find an end to this, we are the hunted ones more than he is."

"He's not just free, he's eternal," Sir Arthur said with conviction. "Moreover, he isn't the one who suffers the consequences of his acts; others do. If he is still alive, we've got to determine where he is and somehow isolate him."

"I agree, but I don't know how we would do either one—find him or isolate him," I said.

The room was full of activity, but we were an island of somber contemplation—a gray-haired trio in the midst of a boisterous college crowd.

After a long period of silence, Conan Doyle continued, "Let's look at logical steps. If we're right about any of this, there are just two main possibilities to consider. Gussmann is either alive or dead. That is, either Mary Hopson made it to some other subject or she did not. If she didn't, it's over, period."

"She was found in the park near Ham Gate, but she presumably left North Sheen in a car. She might have been driven to Morton Graves and then entered the park," I said.

"Or she might have gone to meet Stanton in Ham and then gone to the park," Adrianna added.

"Or anywhere else," I said, "and we're completely at a loss to guess which. I guess it's pretty much out of the question to shoot four or five people we know of just in hopes of getting the right one."

"You might as well say twenty or thirty people, every patient Gussmann ever had in Morton Graves asylum who's still alive," Conan Doyle answered.

"And a few priests, prison guards, and whatnot, for good measure," I added.

"Shooting them all doesn't seem the best plan, now that you say it that way, Charles." He sat back and laughed. "Well, we've certainly turned that little German phrase into a huge quagmire in our minds, haven't we? I think we may have got carried away."

"There are some anchors to reality in our theory, though," I said. "I've thought all along that Gussmann might be alive. If we believe that he was doing what his journal said that he was doing at the time of his death, this could be how he has stayed alive all these years."

"Suddenly, Charlie, I don't want to be as near Richmond Park as we are just now. Let's go back into London," Adrianna said quietly.

"Yes," Sir Arthur said. "I need to get home and take some security precautions myself. Call me this evening, Charles." He left us then, and we waited five minutes before I paid the barkeep and we made our own exit.

Part Three

26

What object is served by this circle of misery and violence and fear? It
must have some end, or else our universe is ruled by chance,
which is unthinkable. But what end?

—"The Adventure of the Cardboard Box"

WE DECIDED TO DRIVE straight from the pub in Kingston to Adrianna's home to talk to Freddy if we could find him in. It was nearly
six o'clock when we drove into the driveway and parked her Austin
behind the house.

I saw that the doorway into the rear entry hall had been left
standing wide open in spite of the winter cold. When I saw that, I
stopped Adrianna with a touch of my hand and gestured for her to
return to the car with me. There I rummaged through my overcoat
and found the Luger. When Adrianna saw this, she opened her purse
and withdrew the .38 pistol.

I insisted on walking in front of her as we entered the rear of her
home. The rear hall light was shining brightly, as was the light in the
kitchen, to our right. We walked cautiously into the kitchen and
looked around carefully. It was Adrianna who first noticed the blood
on the floor. A sizable smear of it was on the tiles in front of the
kitchen preparation table, and several drops led from there toward
the dining room door. When I opened the door into the dining
room, we saw the Wallaces' butler sitting directly in front of us, tied
to a dining chair. A cut ran along the left side of his scalp just above
the ear. There were several small cuts on his face, and a dried rivulet

of blood ran from a corner of his mouth. His eyes stared straight ahead, wide open. A large kitchen knife protruded from the center of his chest.

Adrianna wheeled into me and buried her face in my chest. Her breath came in gasps, and I was afraid she would faint. I backed into a corner of the room, keeping her close to me and stood silently watching, the Luger held in front of me. After a minute she calmed her breathing and looked up into my face with an expression of grim determination.

"We've got to go on," she whispered.

I nodded, and she led me out of the room toward the front salon. A single lamp had been left on in that room, but there was no one there. Next she crossed the entry hall to double doors leading into the library. These were closed. I stood back with the Luger at the ready and gestured for her to move behind me. She held her .38 ready in her right hand as I swiftly opened one of the doors. The room was in darkness, and Adrianna crouched to the floor and slid into the dark. A few seconds later, light flooded from a lamp in the corner, and Adrianna stood next to it. The contents of the desk had been strewn on the floor, its drawers piled in a corner. She pointed silently toward a glass-fronted gun case along one wall. The case displayed a row of about ten rifles and shotguns. She held up two fingers, and I noticed that two slots were empty.

One by one, we tried the other rooms on the ground floor. We found no one and no further signs of violence. When I gestured toward the broad staircase that ran up from the front entry hall, Adrianna shook her head no and walked instead back to a small room off the rear hall. There she showed me a smaller staircase, which ran up the back of the house. I took the lead as we climbed the stairs to the second floor. A broad hallway ran the length of the house on the second floor, and this was well lighted. One bedroom door that opened onto this hallway stood ajar, and I went to it first.

In it we found the second victim. Adrianna was right behind me as I entered the room, and she saw the body at the same instant I did. She lost the controlled manner of a nurse trained for combat zones and turned away from the scene. She walked into the hall and leaned her back against the wall, facing away from the door. Her pistol hung limply at her side. Keeping my Luger ready, I walked to the nude body, which lay spread across the bed face down, her wrists and ankles tied to the bedposts. I leaned over close to the bed and saw numerous cigar-sized burn marks on the woman's legs, thighs, buttocks, and back. I gently lifted the woman's thick hair to reveal unmistakable rope marks at the neck.

"That is the cook," Adrianna whispered from the doorway behind me. "There is still the maid to be found." She sat in a chair in the hall and looked toward the ceiling. "I can't, Charlie. You'll have to search without me."

"Keep your guard up," I said quietly. "He may be up here somewhere."

She moved the pistol to her lap and nodded.

I found the maid in the next room. She lay tied across the bed, on her back. Again nude. The burns were worse than those on the other victim. Carefully, I searched through the remaining rooms on the second floor and found nothing more. I returned to where Adrianna waited in the first bedroom.

"Freddy isn't here," I said. I knelt down and drew her face to my chest.

"The maid?" she asked.

"She's in the next room—like the cook," I said.

Adrianna sank deeper into the large chair. "Where can Freddy be?" she said softly. "When I talked to him this morning, the servants were all gone to church. He said he planned to stay here for most of the day."

"He must have gone out," I said. "But this happened some time ago, judging from the dried blood. A couple of hours, at least."

"Maybe he went out and came back. Maybe he walked in on this and got the drop on Gussmann. Maybe he's with the police right now," she said with a false tone of hope.

"We haven't checked the garage," I said. "His car must be gone."

"I don't think I can go down, Charlie. I don't think I can get up out of this chair."

"I can't leave you here with all this," I said. "We'll wait until you feel up to it. Then we can go down to the garage."

She took a deep breath and let it out slowly. "How did we get into this? A letter from a dead man who wanted a favor from Conan Doyle. A conversation at a party. A lark to pass the time. How did we stumble into so much evil?" She looked at the .38 in her lap. "You, shot on the street?"

"And you, attacked on the street," I said. "I don't know, Adrianna. The letter was far from a simple curiosity, that's for sure. And now we're all up to our necks in something way beyond our understanding."

"But why this? Why would he, or they, kill the servants?"

"Whoever did this was trying to make them talk, and this was Gussmann's way of working." I shuddered, remembering his descriptions of burning and shaming his patients to get them into a vulnerable state. "Probably he wanted to find out where you were, maybe where Freddy is. He's serious about finding us now, and we know why. When you spoke to Mary Hopson on the street with that phrase from the journal, there was no doubt that you knew the secret. Even before that, when it was in the papers that I had robbed Gussmann's grave, he would have known that we were investigating his death."

"He had decided to kill you even before that, probably as soon as you followed up on visiting Helen Wickham or when we went to Morton Graves." She looked toward the bedroom. "Let's get out of here."

We returned to the rear stairway and descended into the hallway below. Adrianna led the way out the back door, which still stood open. The garage was a large, converted carriage house at the rear of the estate. Oversized doors had been installed so the building would accommodate four cars. Although the right-hand garage door was open, it was too dark to see if a car was parked there. We entered the building through a side doorway near the front, and Adrianna turned on the electric lights.

Freddy sat slumped against the wall in front of his Bentley. In his right hand was a huge pistol. A shotgun blast had shredded the front of his overcoat, and he stared blankly ahead through sightless eyes.

Adrianna ran to him. Kneeling with her hands on his shoulders, her face close to his, she said, "Oh, Freddy, they've got you . . . *you*. And you didn't bargain for any of this. I did. I've killed you, Freddy," she said, sobbing. "Freddy, Freddy, Freddy." She touched his cheek tenderly, as I remembered her doing in my hospital room. "My old sailor." She slid down to sit on the floor beside him, dropping her pistol and taking his left hand between both of hers as she wept.

Keeping a careful watch on the room as I did so, I moved to the rear of Freddy's Bentley, where I had noticed a dark spot on the floor. A small smear of blood half the size of my hand was on the floor, and more was spattered across the painted wooden surface of a post that framed the door. The post was deeply splintered, and the back of a bullet was clearly visible embedded in the wood. "He's hit," I said. "Gussmann is hit! Freddy must have gotten off a shot at whoever did this."

"Freddy is dead, Charlie," Adrianna said dully, her breath coming in ragged gulps.

I went to stand beside her but did not touch her. "You were right. He must have gone out. When he returned, Gussmann was waiting for him here in the garage with one of the guns from the house. But he didn't count on Freddy having a gun, too." I looked over the scene and continued. "He came up behind the car from the house, but Freddy must have heard him or seen him in time to be suspicious—in time to get off a shot."

I looked along the concrete and saw several more drops of blood in a path toward a door at the rear of the garage. Instead of going through it, I retraced my steps to the door through which we had entered at the other end and at the front. Then I circled the building carefully in the darkness. I stayed away from the white walls and kept my attention focused outward into the garden shrubbery and across the lawns. Even at that, I knew I was a sitting duck if Gussmann was still around.

After five minutes I reentered the garage and saw that Adrianna had not moved. She sat leaning against the wall beside Freddy's body, her hands cradling his free hand. She didn't seem to notice me.

"Gussmann—whatever person he is in—is gone."

There was still no sign of recognition. I waited another few moments before taking a deep breath and crouching down so my face was level with hers—and Freddy's. "Adrianna," I said softly.

Slowly her eyes focused on my face. "Charlie, Freddy . . ."

"I know. I'm so sorry. He was a fine man."

"Nothing frightened him—ever."

"I've seen that."

She nodded, looking back at his face.

"Adrianna, you're going to have to be brave, too. You have to call the police."

With effort, she looked back at me.

"I can't think, Charlie. What can I say? What will they ask me?"

"Let's go back inside, Adrianna. We'll think this through together." I led her away from Freddy and back into the house. We walked down the hallway, and she sat in a chair in the front salon. I poured her a stiff brandy. After the first sip, Adrianna began to sob uncontrollably, and I could do nothing but rest a hand on her shoulder until she was again silent.

"We've got to reason things out," she said. "The police don't know where I've been. I could have returned from anywhere and found things like this."

"It's possible that you were recognized by somebody in the pub in Kingston in spite of your hair. So, possibly, was Sir Arthur. When the newspapers report on this, someone might remember having seen you both in Kingston at teatime this afternoon."

"You'll have to warn Arthur about this before the police talk to him." Adrianna broke down again for a minute and then regained some composure.

"Someone will remember that there was a third person with you, and that will have to be explained, too," I said.

She thought quietly for a moment. "But that third person was a middle-aged man, gray-haired and quite bald on top. Perhaps he was just a stranger whom we met in the pub."

"It was crowded. He needed a place to sit."

I called Conan Doyle from the salon and explained what we'd found. He spoke briefly with Adrianna. Then he and I discussed details for some time. Though he disliked withholding information from the police, it was agreed all around that Adrianna would say she had recently returned from the Continent and had gone out driving in the afternoon to meet her old friend Arthur for tea in Kingston. They had visited for a while and shared their table briefly with a stranger who had no place to sit in the crowded pub. Neither of them had ever met him before. The conversation with him had consisted mostly of commentary on the crowd of young college men who were behaving boisterously at a center table. The stranger hadn't given his name.

"Sir Arthur," I said quietly, "whoever did this came here hunting. He had no intention of leaving anyone alive. If he knew to come here, he knows where to find you as well."

"I assumed that something like this might be attempted as soon as we had our talk today. I've got the family off visiting relatives. I've given most of the staff leave and have armed the butler. I may move out to Windlesham tomorrow. Actually, though, more people know that address than this one."

"I can't stay here after Adrianna calls the police," I said. "Do you think you could come over to be with her?"

"Certainly. Be sure she tells them that she has called me and that I'm on my way. Let me speak to her again."

I gave the receiver to Adrianna and then took her brandy glass into the kitchen and washed it before replacing it in the rack in the salon bar. She hung up the receiver just as I entered the room.

"You'll have to walk well away from here before you take a cab," she said. "I've got to call right away. Arthur is on his way here."

"Keep the doors locked, Adrianna."

"Keep an eye out yourself," she said. "He could be anywhere."

"Stay in the house," I said as I walked toward the rear hall.

27

The tragedy has been so uncommon, so complete, and of such personal importance to so many people that we are suffering from a plethora of surmise, conjecture, and hypothesis.
—"The Adventure of Silver Blaze"

FREDERICK WALLACE, M.P., MURDERED— KILLER ARRESTED IN RICHMOND PARK.

ROBERT STANTON MADE THE front page in every Monday morning paper. At her insistence Arthur brought Adrianna to my room once they could safely come. Both expected further police interviews later in the day, so they knew they couldn't stay with me for long. At nine-thirty A.M. we sat in my hotel room going through all the morning papers. It had been a long night for all of us. We had endured a terrible and sleepless night wondering what was happening. I had made one anonymous call to the police from a downtown telephone booth but otherwise had stayed in my room.

"I've already been contacted by Freddy's cousin. He says he will make arrangements for a funeral tomorrow. He said he'd take care of all that," Adrianna said, obviously grateful for family support. "I've asked him to assist in arrangements for the funerals of our staff as well," she said while wiping her eyes.

"Oh, yes," I said, realizing that I hadn't given a moment's thought to those poor souls during my night of worrying about Adrianna.

"I don't know how I can ever face their families. I feel so responsible for their deaths."

I knew it wouldn't help if I argued with her on that point. She'd just have to get past it on her own timetable. "I'm sure their funerals will be mercifully simple compared with what is expected for a member of Parliament like Freddy."

"It will be a miracle if I get through tomorrow," she said quietly.

I nodded and asked, "How was it with the police last night?"

Conan Doyle answered first. "I arrived just before the police. They went through the house while we waited in the salon. Then they questioned us for about two hours. Chief Inspector Willis was not among them. Of course, there was nothing we could tell them that would have made any sense to them." He turned to Adrianna.

After a long silence, she said, "They didn't ask about you, at least."

When she didn't continue, I turned back to Conan Doyle. "Did they think it strange that you were there, Sir Arthur?" I asked.

Keeping his eyes on Adrianna, he shrugged slightly. "Didn't seem to. We explained that as agreed. Their questions were all about possible motives that anyone might have had, who had access to the house, that sort of thing."

"Quite a few questions about my whereabouts . . ." Adrianna said absently, her voice trailing into silence as she moved over to stare out the window from behind the curtain.

Conan Doyle and I looked at her and then at each other. His eyes returned to her as he said quietly, "The police were satisfied with our answers." His tone managed to convey the idea that Adrianna herself was not at all satisfied with the answers she'd had to give. And, of course, it was not hard to understand her wish that she could have been somewhere else at the time of Freddy's death—somewhere that would have allowed her to prevent the horror.

While Adrianna stayed at the window, Arthur and I scanned the morning papers to see what had become public knowledge so far. The newspaper reports indicated that, operating on a tip made by an anonymous caller, the police had driven to Robert Stanton's shop late on Sunday night. Finding him missing, they had searched the place and made two alarming discoveries. The first was a bundle of his clothing that was heavily stained with blood.

This had prompted a very thorough search of the premises, which ultimately revealed another shocker. Hidden under a false bottom in a large toolbox in the shop were more than nine thousand pounds in cash and securities. For a man with Stanton's modest business, that would be more than twenty years of earnings, an impossible sum for him to have saved. Neighbors speculated that he actually earned far less than the norm for a tradesman of his type because of his sporadic work habits.

Later, in the early hours of Monday morning, Stanton himself had been arrested in Richmond Park as he wandered in the dark in what appeared to be a confused state through Sidmonth Wood. Stanton was wounded, and a shotgun identified as one taken from the Wallace household was found hidden under shrubbery in the park near Bishop's Pond just north of where he was arrested. The suspected killer was being held in Kingston-upon-Thames while jurisdictional matters were under consideration.

Background information presented in the most thorough of the articles revealed Stanton's prior history as a mental patient at Morton Graves Voluntary Hospital and pointed out that a recent murder victim, Mary Hopson, had once been a patient in the same asylum. While her assailant had been a woman, according to eyewitnesses, Stanton might be implicated in that case as well.

The papers also noted that Mrs. Wallace, who suffered a nervous collapse under the strain of discovering the brutal slayings in her household, would be in seclusion until after her husband's funeral tomorrow. This I noted silently, and Sir Arthur, too, refrained from comment.

In spite of my certainty that Adrianna would have difficulty turning aside from her grief just now, I knew our lives depended on figuring out Gussmann's whereabouts and his likely next move. I decided it was time to open the topic.

"So we know one thing for sure," I said after we had passed the papers among us for half an hour. "Gussmann, occupying Mary Hopson, must have made it to Stanton after she was shot."

Arthur nodded slowly, his eyes still fixed on the newspaper spread out on his legs. "Clearly Gussmann was able to transfer to Stanton," he said firmly. He turned toward Adrianna. "We also know that he didn't stay inside Stanton for long after he left your home, Adrianna. He must have made contact with someone else because he certainly wouldn't be stumbling around Sidmouth Wood if Gussmann were in control."

Adrianna turned from the window and nodded agreement, presenting a remarkably calm demeanor, considering the ordeal she was enduring. "So Gussmann," I added, "probably went back to Morton Graves right after he left the house. It would have been plenty early enough for a rendezvous with someone there."

Adrianna took a deep breath. She was in no shape to be having this conversation. She had cleaned up a bit and changed clothes, but her hair looked ruined, and she had certainly gone without sleep for most of the past forty-eight hours.

"Think about the money they found," Conan Doyle said to me. Again, it's more or less the same amount that Mary was carrying. Stanton's hidden share was approximately the same as Hopson's."

We fell silent, and I contemplated the sums of money. Ten thousand pounds was enough to invest securely and live a modest middle-class life on the interest it would earn. It was enough to buy more American Ford automobiles than I could count in my head. Even though I habitually thought in terms of such economic comparisons, I stopped my silent musings there.

"I don't think of it as Hopson's or Stanton's share," Sir Arthur said. "I doubt if either of them had any personal knowledge of the money."

"After all this time, they'd certainly have afforded a few more niceties if they'd been in control of it," I offered. "You're right, it's all Gussmann's. He spread it around for the same reason that he kept more than one susceptible subject close at hand."

Adrianna surprised us by speaking. "But why is he hoarding it?" Adrianna asked. "He could be living a lot more comfortably."

"I imagine that he thinks it's got to last a *very* long time," I answered. "His plan is to live forever—and not as a spirit, mind you. He means to live in the flesh forever. If I'm right, Gussmann has been living pretty much as he pleased for many years since he abandoned his body to take up younger, healthier ones."

Adrianna nodded. "True. None of these—what did he call them—special patients? None seems to have had much money of their own—or any real prospects, for that matter."

"They were just getting by," I said. "Waiting, keeping themselves available, and not understanding the force that was really controlling their lives. Probably he supplemented their actual earnings, some, from his hidden money. It doesn't look like they could have lived, otherwise."

Adrianna added, "Certainly they couldn't have afforded the nightlife they seemed to live."

Sir Arthur added, "Shocking to me. I knew Gussmann as a decent chap, or so I thought. Yet he seems to live in these unfortunate subjects as a debauched libertine."

"Remember," I said, "that there seem to be no consequences *for him.* He can be as irresponsible as he wants, and careless, because no consequences touch him. Only his subjects suffer the disorientation, humiliation, arrests—God knows what else."

"Except that he's managed to get himself shot twice now," said Conan Doyle. "True, he didn't die, but he surely must have felt the pain."

Adrianna straightened her back and said, " I certainly hope so. For now, though, it seems likely that Gussmann is holed up in the asylum on Richmond Park. My shooting him has cost him dearly, and Freddy's shooting him, too, in a different body. He's lost Mary Hopson. For the moment, at least, he's lost Robert Stanton, and he's lost a large sum of money—two large sums of money."

"And he knows exactly who is to blame and exactly who has one of those shares of his money," I added.

"He doesn't know where we are or what we look like, but he knows who we really are. He knows we're hunting him, too," Adrianna said. "He's clearly out for revenge."

"Revenge aside, he knows he has to get us or be discovered," Conan Doyle said.

"Or killed," Adrianna said grimly. "I'd certainly kill him if I could."

"The funny thing is neither side can go to the authorities—we can't any more than he can," I said. "He never could have, but we are no better off. First, we'd be penned up as lunatics. Second, if they did believe us, we'd be jailed for manslaughter and theft and . . . grave robbing."

Arthur rose, walked to Adrianna's side, and looked down into the street as if expecting to see Dr. Gussmann. "Maybe we have the upper hand now," he added. "Presumably Gussmann *is* bottled up in one of his victims in Morton Graves asylum."

Adrianna answered, "That's a very shaky assumption. We don't know who else he may have outside of Morton Graves Voluntary Hospital. I'd agree, though, that Gussmann probably is going to stay in the asylum for at least a little while. For one thing, we can hardly go back in there to get him. After our fiascoes and publicity recently, we're not likely to be welcome at Morton Graves Voluntary Hospital. He probably knows he's safe there."

I thought about the option of going after him. "We wouldn't know what we were looking for anyway, outside of the three remaining names we know there."

She nodded. "It's been that way from the start. We've never known who we were looking for, really. Two of the times that we *think* we encountered Gussmann it was because he revealed himself to us. As Liza he shot you. As Mary he chose to attack me. He could have just kept on walking. We only think he exists in the first place because he wrote the letter. Dr. Gussmann is pretty much entirely in control of when to show himself."

"I don't know about you, Adrianna, but I don't feel like getting him to identify himself by setting ourselves up as a targets," Sir Arthur said gravely. "I'd rather catch him some other way."

"There might be another thing that would bring him out," Adrianna said pensively. "He'd come out to get safely away from Morton Graves if he saw a way."

"You're right," I agreed. "He surely knows that we have figured out where he is, but he may not have any way out—not as long as Robert Stanton is in jail. That could be a long time."

"But we know of two other people on the outside who have been subjects in the past. What if he could get access to one of them?" Adrianna asked.

"I think he'd jump at it," Arthur said, "but I only count one former subject, and that one is an assumption on our part—the priest."

Adrianna shook her head and touched his arm for emphasis. "No, there are two—the priest and Alice Tupper. Remember? She was a subject until she made him stop. From the blackouts she described, I'd guess that Gussmann can occupy her—at least he could at one time."

"If he met up with either one of them in some way that didn't make him suspect a trap," Sir Arthur said, "he'd try to hypnotize them. If you were watching somehow, you'd know exactly where he was at that moment and could isolate him. Whoever was trying to hypnotize our target would be the one we want."

"You're right," I said, "but we *couldn't* isolate him in the asylum, not without cooperation and the use of an isolation room. That's cooperation we can neither solicit nor obtain."

"Well, we can't just gun him down in the hospital," Adrianna said.

"I'd be tempted to try," Conan Doyle said, "except that I'd be shooting someone else along with him."

"As I did," Adrianna said, "when I shot Gussmann and only succeeded in killing Mary Hopson." She seemed to remain calm as she made the statement. I knew that she must be reverting, in some way, to the professional detachment she had learned in the war.

"That was when you were under a life-threatening attack," Sir Arthur answered. "I can't see that you had any choice, my dear. Anyway, we probably can't just shoot him, but we might be able to catch him and get him out of Morton Graves."

"Away from any possible contact with another subject," Adrianna said. "That's really the only way to prevent his transferring again."

I wondered about how to try to get the priest or Alice to help. "We've got to see whether we can get the cooperation of either of these two people. We'll need their help if the plan is going to succeed."

"I haven't heard any plan yet, Charles," Conan Doyle pointed out. "Just what plan is that?"

"Get them to cooperate with our *idea,* then. I don't have a plan, but we'll come up with the rest of it soon enough. First, we need to know if we've got available bait. I want to find the priest. There are other questions I'd like to ask him."

"For now, though," Adrianna said, "we've got to leave. I expect to see Willis at my door before the day is out, and I've got to try to rest before . . . tomorrow."

"Yes," Arthur added, placing an arm protectively around her shoulders, "we really must go. Let's continue this discussion later by telephone, if necessary. Each of you telephone me if you have any new ideas. I'll serve to keep everyone informed."

"There's no phone here in the room, " I said. " I'll go out and call you regularly. And I'll be at the service tomorrow, but we won't be able to talk there."

"I don't think you should go, Charles," Adrianna said, shaking her head. "I know you feel you should, but what if someone recognizes you?"

"She's right, old boy," Sir Arthur added.

"No one will recognize me," I said. "I do want to be there out of respect for Freddy, but there's more than that."

"You mean Gussmann," Conan Doyle said. "He'll be there if he has a way to get out of Morton Graves."

"And he'll be there to kill the three of us," I added. "He will recognize the two of you, of course, but he can't possibly recognize me. I can watch carefully for any sign that anyone is going after either of you. I won't hesitate to shoot the moment I see that."

"He can't be there tomorrow," Adrianna said quietly. "He's got to be stuck in the Graves asylum, as we said earlier."

"Surely," Sir Arthur added, "but I think you're right to be there watching, Charles. We'll be on our guard, too."

"And armed," Adrianna said.

With that, our sad little meeting broke up. Adrianna explained that she had reserved a hotel suite, telling her family that she couldn't bear to go home yet. She had argued her mother out of expecting her to return to her parents' estate. Then she had refused the loan of a maid, insisting that she did not want to face anyone for a few days.

After the others left, I went to the secondhand clothier and found a black suit and overcoat that fit well, though they showed some wear. It was the only way I could think of to be properly dressed at the funeral. Since proper clothing was just about the only propriety I could observe under the circumstances, I intended to do it right.

28

*I am afraid that my colleague has been a little quick in
forming his conclusions.*

—"The Boscombe Valley Mystery"

TUESDAY MORNING I AWOKE later than I intended and looked out my
hotel window at a day that was both cold and wet. After redressing my
abdominal wound and shaving my face and much of my head, I
dressed in the black suit I had bought the day before. I thanked my
good fortune that I'd found an overcoat to go with it, one with a nice-
sized inside pocket that accommodated the Luger automatic within
easy reach of my right hand. I made sure that there was a round in
the chamber and the safety was on before sliding the heavy pistol into
the coat.

Freddy's funeral was to take place at his family's traditional
Church of England parish, followed by a graveside ceremony at their
plot in the adjoining churchyard. Even though I was worried that I
should be guarding Adrianna and Sir Arthur inside the church, in
order to minimize my exposure to anyone who might recognize me,
I would attend only the churchyard service. Since I was running late,
I called for a taxi to drive me directly to the churchyard to wait for
the large crowd of mourners who would attend the burial of a highly
placed member of the government.

Once there, I was faced with a problem. No one was waiting outside the church, so I would be quite conspicuous if I stood around

outside. On the other hand, entering the church, I would also draw attention to myself. A solution presented itself when I noticed the long double line of parked automobiles along both sides of a street adjacent to the church. Some of these were large touring cars, and I could be fairly certain that a few, at least, would have chauffeurs waiting in them. I walked along the curb beside a row of cars until I noticed one that was both large and without a driver in attendance. I confidently opened the driver's door and entered the sedan as if I belonged there. Once inside, I cautiously peered out at the cars nearest me and saw only one chauffeur who might have noticed me. He appeared to be napping.

Thus safely out of sight, I adjusted the interior rearview mirror so I could see when people started to leave the church half a block behind me. Forty minutes later, both the double front doors and a smaller side door of the church swung open, and a throng of mourners began to stream out into the light drizzle, which had continued all morning. I exited the luxury car immediately and started walking toward the church, confident that I would be inconspicuous among the bereaved. As a precaution I had appropriated an umbrella from the front seat of the sedan. I would use this both to keep my bald spot dry and to help obscure my features.

I reached the edge of the crowd in front of the church while the crowd was still growing. A low canopy of umbrellas was spreading overhead as the crowd emerged. This was not my social circle, but I recognized a number of faces. Many of these people were famous, among them Sir Arthur Conan Doyle and his wife, several lords and members of Parliament, and at least half a dozen cabinet ministers. I had interviewed a few of these dignitaries within the past year, and I hoped my altered appearance would be a sufficient disguise. I was, at the moment, as newsworthy as anyone here.

Looking everywhere but where he was walking, Chief Inspector

Willis, without an umbrella, collided with me before he saw me. The hard contact with the shorter man banged the pocketed Luger sharply against my chest.

"Pardon me!" he said, smiling apologetically and glancing vaguely in my direction. "Wasn't looking." He massaged his left shoulder, as if it had been bruised when he bumped me.

I almost made the mistake of replying with the customary rejoinder, but realized just in time that the man might recognize my voice. My heart racing, I simply nodded and smiled back at him as I moved on to surround myself with a group of middle-aged naval officers who were waiting not far away. I noticed uncomfortably that Willis kept his gaze on me for a time before he resumed his surveillance of the growing crowd. I turned away from him as if to speak to one of the officers.

"Hell of a way for the commander to go," said the uniformed officer I was facing. I realized that my walking directly up to him in my flight from the inspector had prompted him to speak as if he knew me.

"Unbelievable," I answered, realizing, now that they began to don their hats, that every man around me was in uniform. Worse, it seemed to me that they were shuffling themselves slowly into some sort of formation of two lines. The movement was subtle, but after a while it was unmistakable that the eight officers were waiting as an organized group and that I had no position in it. I was standing between the two lines as they formed, and two of the men gave me clear frowns. I noticed then that some other people were staring at me as well.

I walked out from between the lines just as they started to move in unison back toward the church doors. That left me standing alone, so I lowered my borrowed umbrella to obscure my face and moved back into the edge of the main crowd. When I again looked around to see where the inspector might have gone, he was staring at me from a distance of not more than thirty feet. I tilted the umbrella toward him and made a slight turn to see the eight naval officers, now in a neat formation, enter the church.

They returned a few minutes later with Freddy's casket between them and Adrianna walking behind. After her was a small group that I assumed was made up of family members. This formation led the way toward the adjacent cemetery, and all the rest of us followed. I was careful to keep at least a hundred people between myself and Chief Inspector Willis, and he seemed to be occupied by looking outward into the surrounding graveyard, as if he expected to see dangerous felons there. Since the police had apprehended Robert Stanton and were holding him in custody, I could see no reason for the chief inspector to be present at the funeral—unless he intended to catch *me*. Then I realized that I might be guilty of paranoia. Willis was a high-ranking officer in Scotland Yard. Probably he was here to represent the police at this nationally important funeral.

I was so far back in the group at the graveside service that I failed to hear a single word that was said. While I could see Adrianna clearly in the distance, I doubted that she had seen me among the sea of coats and umbrellas that pressed in toward the casket. I watched carefully for any signs of danger. Anyone who moved closer to her caught my eye immediately.

As the service grew to a close, I realized that everyone would be leaving soon and that I had no car. I decided that I would reenter the church as inconspicuously as possible and wait there until everyone had cleared away. Then I would find a phone and call for a taxi. When people in front of me began to turn around and move back toward the church, I turned and walked slowly among them at an angle that would take me nearest the building. Fortunately, several mourners turned and walked alongside the church. By joining them, I passed within a few feet of the side door and simply veered off into the building. No one seemed to take any notice.

I closed the umbrella, made my way to a pew in the darkest area of the church, and sat with a parish copy of the Book of Common Prayer open on my lap. After a few minutes I began a one-way mental conversation with Freddy consisting first of terms of admiration for his services to the country and then my sincere apologies for being infatuated with his wife and for getting him killed by Dr. Gussmann. I did not get the feeling that I was forgiven. Then I added promises for Adrianna's safety and well-being, but I was pretty sure that anyone with Freddy's experience and intelligence would know that I had no idea how to keep such pledges.

When I thought that enough time had elapsed for almost everyone to have left the area, I arose and walked back to the side door through which I'd entered. I had just emerged into the light rain and opened my purloined umbrella when I recognized the voice of Chief Inspector Willis, who was standing not ten feet to the right of the door.

"Charles Baker," he said somewhat tentatively, "you are wanted for questioning in serious matters. You will please come with me."

As I turned toward him, it occurred to me that he wasn't at all certain that I was Charles Baker. "I'm dreadfully sorry, old man, but you seem to have mistaken me for some other chap," I said with my voice both softened and raised.

Uncertainty showed clearly in his expression as I turned away from him and continued down the walk. I noticed out of the corner of my eye that there were two uniformed bobbies standing to my left at a distance of about twenty feet.

"Hold on!" Willis said loudly. "I'll need to see some identification from you, sir.

I could tell that the two cops had heard that, but I pretended to ignore it and kept walking away.

Willis raised his voice to a near-shout. "Stop, sir! I'm a police chief inspector on official business and I require you to identify yourself!"

I stopped and waited for the two policemen, who had started closing in to get within about six feet of me before I extracted the Luger and pointed it at them in clear view of the chief inspector. True to tradition of the London Police, none carried a gun. Then I pivoted and backed up so that I could bring all three into my field of vision. "What's the meaning of this?" I said with a voice that I hoped would sound like an offended aristocrat. Unfortunately, I only succeeded in sounding like Charles Baker.

Both bobbies stopped and held their hands in plain sight. Willis removed his hands from his overcoat and raised them slightly, palms outward. "This is not what you want to do, Mr. Baker," he said. "You're just wanted for questioning."

"Let's all just step into the church, shall we?" I said. "And everyone stay in plain sight and out of harm's way as we go through the door."

Willis walked to the door and held it open, signaling the two cops to step through. They walked straight ahead so that I could see them clearly as I approached the door. When I nodded my head, Willis released the door and walked toward the other two as I walked in, closing the door behind me.

"Well, this is a mess," I said honestly. "My compliments on your keen eye, Inspector."

"Chief Inspector," Willis corrected me, "and that's part of how I became a bloody chief inspector, Baker—a keen eye. I've got to tell you that you're making a big mistake here. This is a serious matter now—a lot more serious than robbing that damned grave. Let's be sensible, man, before you do something you can't turn away from."

"The three of you sit down in the front pew there, and keep a little distance among you," I ordered as if I had some idea what I was going to do. I took a position a few feet in front of them and leaned back against the altar rail, the Luger pointed casually in their general direction without its barrel actually aiming at any one of them.

"Maybe I could ask you some questions right here, Mr. Baker—maybe that's all we need to do," Willis said.

"I don't think I have time for that, Chief Inspector," I answered. "I've got to be going."

"Let's start with why you left hospital, Baker," he continued, ignoring my statement. "A nurse there says you were afraid of persons who were out to harm you. She wasn't on duty when you left, so she's not implicated in that, but she says there was a man looking into your room the day before—a man who didn't seem to belong there." He paused only momentarily and then added, "Who were you afraid of, Mr. Baker? Not the Anatole girl, because you knew we had her in custody."

"I'm afraid I can't take time for your questions just now, Chief Inspector. The situation is too complicated to explain, but I assure you that I've done nothing wrong."

"Aside from robbing a grave, impersonating a barrister out at Morton Graves Voluntary Hospital, maybe cooperating with Robert Stanton in shooting a tailor in Sheen and a member of Parliament, and now holding police officers at gunpoint."

I stared at him and said nothing.

"Your photograph was recognized by Dr. Dodds and others at the hospital. He just called me again this morning from a holiday in Ireland. He's just now seen the newspapers."

"It was nothing, a simple investigation I was doing."

"And a young hardware clerk out in Ham identified you as one of the men who visited Robert Stanton last week. Come to think of it, you now fit the description of the other man as well. Your Morris Oxford was identified by the lad, too."

"I can explain all that," I said.

"Then for God's sake do so, Mr. Baker. This ain't the way to get clear of this mess, man!"

"It'll have to be another time, Willis. Right now I want you three to remove your belts and shoelaces."

While both bobbies began to obey me, Willis just fired another question: "What have you got Mrs. Wallace involved in, Baker? Dr. Dodds said *she* was with you when you went to Morton Graves. She introduced you as a family lawyer from New York."

I pointed the pistol's muzzle directly at him and gestured with it. "Belt and shoelaces," I said. When all three had complied, I continued my directions. "You," I said to the officer in the middle, "tie your friend's hands securely behind his back with his shoelaces. Also tie them to a belt loop in back. I'll inspect your work." He did a good job, so I had him do the inspector as well. Then I ordered the two tied men to put their legs out over the short partition rail in front of the pew and made the unfettered policeman belt their feet together and buckle them to the rail. After that, I did the same to the untied bobby as he had to the others.

"This is crazy, Baker. We'll be after you in no time at all. You're just making it worse on yourself."

"Look, Chief Inspector, if I were the blackguard you take me for, I'd have shot you just now instead of tying you up in this totally inadequate manner and leaving you to pursue me. I don't want to hurt anyone. I'm just trying to get away and stay safe through a dangerous situation that I can't explain to you. Believe me, I had nothing to do with Wallace's death."

"It's about the money, isn't it?" he asked. "Dodds said you were questioning him about a large sum of money that's been missing for years."

"I really must be going," I replied as I walked to the door. I looked out, saw that no one was in sight on that side of the church, and exited quickly. I knew that the makeshift bindings on the policemen wouldn't hold them for more than a few minutes. Since the church was bordered on one side by its cemetery and it sat on a rather large acreage of landscaping, the closest area where I might hide my escape was in a commercial area that began two hundred yards distant from the church. Once I had reached it, I continued to walk deep into the maze of shop-lined streets until I found a promising hiding place.

At a point where one street forked into two, there was a combination tobacconist and bookshop that occupied the elongated corner. This was a relatively large enterprise, and it boasted three exterior doors, one on each side street in addition to its main entrance at the point of the building. The busy interior was a warren of tall shelving and offered lots of dark recesses. Even better, I discovered a staircase that led to a rare-book section upstairs. From the upstairs front window, I commanded a view of the three streets below. At last I felt safe enough to rest and wait.

After two hours, during which I attracted no notice whatever, I descended to a sales counter on the first floor, ready to make a modest purchase and ask for the use of a telephone. When I was offered both a phone and a measure of privacy while the clerk moved away a few feet, I called for a taxi. An hour later, I was safely back in my hotel room.

29

Every problem becomes very childish when once it is explained to you.
—"The Adventure of the Dancing Men"

WEDNESDAY AFTERNOON I WAS with Adrianna after twenty-four hours of hiding more or less safely in my room, interrupted only once by a long phone call I made to Sir Arthur. Taking extreme measures to be sure she was not followed from her own hotel, Adrianna drove to a rendezvous point near mine and picked me up. I noticed immediately, when I could see her at close distance, that she looked fully ten years older than she had a week earlier. Her hair, coarsened by the abuse it had taken, framed a neglected complexion and an exhausted facial expression. To me, probably to anyone, she was still beautiful.

We already knew both the name of the priest we wanted and the parish where he served. By one o'clock Adrianna and I were driving out to visit Father Kelly's parish while she told me about her interview with Chief Inspector Willis on Monday evening.

"That time, he was very polite. He had no questions whatever about what I'd told the other investigators. Obviously he'd read their reports. His main line of questioning kept getting to you," she said.

"In what way?"

"Had I seen you since you'd left hospital? He explained at some length—apologizing all the while—how things *looked* to an outside observer. You know, our being together when you were shot by another woman, Freddy not actually being seen by anyone at that time. I'm afraid he thinks you . . ." She broke off and held her hands to her face.

"Oh, God! How could he?"

"If he's drawing that conclusion," she said, "so are others."

"That I shot Freddy and killed a houseful of servants?"

"He didn't go that far—just wanted to know where you were and did I have any idea why you'd leave the Chelsea Royal Hospital and go rob the grave of a dead psychiatrist."

"He asked Sir Arthur much the same thing," I said. "I haven't done very well at keeping him out of it." Then I added, "Nothing in the tabloids, though. Means Willis is keeping his suspicions under wraps. What about yesterday?"

"He was much angrier when he got to my hotel. He'd had to find me by badgering my parents into revealing my whereabouts. He said that you were at the funeral disguised as an older man. He said you had accosted him and two police officers with a gun. That was enough for a warrant for your arrest, which he actually waved in my face."

"Did he mention his suspicions about my supposedly conspiring with Stanton?"

"No."

"Too bad," I said. "Means he thinks you were in on it."

"That was implied." Adrianna held her handkerchief to her nose and turned away toward her side window.

I hesitated a moment and then added, "Somehow we'll change his mind."

She remained silent until we reached the church where we would question young Father Kelly.

We presented ourselves at the parish rectory as Mr. and Mrs.

Bedaker, parents of a wayward young woman who needed help. Our daughter, we said, was confined in Holloway, and we needed help to bring her back to the righteous path. We requested a visit with Father Kelly, only to be informed that the young priest was no longer in the country. Wouldn't another priest do?

When we persisted, we were shown in to meet with the head pastor, a priest of about the age I appeared to be. When we explained that we very much wanted to talk to Father Kelly, we were met with a saddened face.

"I'm sorry, but that is quite impossible. Father Kelly is no longer in England. He has returned to Ireland," said the senior priest.

"But we spoke with him just a fortnight ago," said Adrianna, "and he seemed so willing to help, and so understanding of young women's problems, especially those with a nervous condition."

The older priest blushed visibly at that. "Well, to tell all, Mrs. Bedaker, Father Kelly is not well himself, just now. He had to return to Ireland more than a week ago to recover from . . . a nervous condition of his own, I'm afraid. He is quite unavailable."

"Do you mean that the young man is confined?" I asked.

The priest looked at me for a moment as if considering what to say. "In truth, he is, Mr. Bedaker. Father Kelly was under great stress, you see, a great deal more than we realized at the time. He was doing so much, and he was working with that unfortunate woman who was hanged. Well, the stress was too much for him. He simply . . . well, fell apart, you might say. Actually, he went missing for a while. When we found him, he was in quite a state."

"Would that be after the tragedy of the hanging, then?" Adrianna asked.

"Let me see. That was last Friday? No. It was shortly before that, actually a few days earlier, that he fell ill, but I'm sure the extra stress of that terrible situation was a great burden to him. He was so sure that she was going to be baptized, you see—if only to be hanged after her salvation."

"Pardon me, Father, but wasn't she a madwoman? That's what I gathered from the papers," I asked. "How on earth was Father Kelly able to lead her to salvation?"

"He said she was the sanest woman in the prison, Mr. Bedaker. That's what the court decided as well, isn't it? Father Kelly had nothing but praise for the unfortunate woman." He had opened a notebook and found a clean page. "And your daughter, would her name be Bedaker as well, or is she a married woman?"

"And when do you think Father Kelly might return?" Adrianna asked, ignoring his question.

There was a long pause while the priest moved an envelope around on his desk blotter. Finally he said, "I'm quite sure that Father Kelly will not be coming back to this parish, Mrs. Bedaker, nor even to England. Whenever he is ready to return to his duties, he will be assigned to another parish. It's quite common for a young priest to move about frequently. He might not have been here much longer even if he hadn't taken ill. May I inquire about your daughter? I'll certainly see to it that she's contacted as soon as possible."

"Hilda," I said. "Comes from the German on my side, Hilda Bedaker. She's in for grand theft, I'm afraid. Three years."

Adrianna lowered her eyes and folded her hands in her lap.

"I'll see to it that someone begins to talk to her," said the priest, "as soon as we put someone on that duty. I'm afraid we're a bit short-handed right now."

With that, we took our leave. We had driven about a mile before Adrianna spoke. "You were right. It was the young priest. We can figure out where he went while he was missing."

"Well, we can guess," I said, "The main thing now, though, is that we can't talk to him. I've got a feeling that the church isn't going to allow anyone to see him for quite a while."

"And that only leaves Alice Tupper. I hope she's willing," Adrianna said as she gazed at the passing buildings.

"I hope she's capable," I said. "Even if she's willing to help us, she may have a hard time going out to Morton Graves and meeting people."

Adrianna turned to look at me. "Oh, I think she's strong enough for that, but how much are we going to tell her? And what are we going to do then—after we get him?"

"*If* we get him," I corrected. "And if he doesn't get us. There's no point in worrying about that until we know whether we can find him in the first place."

After considerable discussion on the telephone, it was decided that Sir Arthur would join us in a repeat visit to Alice Tupper later that same evening. Conan Doyle insisted that the ailing woman be properly informed as to what we suspected. He took it upon himself to explain Gussmann's game of musical chairs and what we thought the doctor had done.

Adrianna and I explained my disguise and even went on to let Alice examine our dyed and painted hair as well as my shaved bald spot.

When we had finished, Alice said, "I knew it!"

"You knew he was still living on in this way?" Arthur asked.

"No. Not that, but I knew he could possess those patients—and me. I knew he was cruel, too. I was already in love with him when I learned that, and I made excuses to myself."

"We need to discover where he is hiding, Alice—whom he may have taken over now," I said. "We need your help for that."

She thought silently for a minute. "I can catch him for you," she said, her voice surprisingly strong. "He must be desperate to get out of Graves. If he sees me, he'll know I'm that way out."

We all looked nervously at one another until Arthur replied, "That's what we think, too. We can get him isolated if you're willing to help."

"You can't just catch him, you know. You must finish him off. Surely you all realize that." She looked at each of us. "And I can do that for you, too."

"How do you mean that, Alice?" Adrianna asked. "Do you know of some way to . . . finish him?"

Alice again looked frankly at each of us, smiling slightly this time. "Surely you all know that I'm dying. In fact, I should be dead by now. In any case, I will be soon."

"We know," Adrianna answered softly.

"Well, this is cancer, my dear. It's very painful, as you know, and the morphine is my only relief—and too little of that. Do you think I wouldn't welcome a chance to be fully asleep and free of pain?"

"While he would be inhabiting you, you would feel nothing?" Arthur asked.

"Never did before," she answered. "I'll just be resting, unaware."

"True; it might actually be a break in your suffering for a while," I said, looking for some relief from the guilt I was feeling.

"I don't want a break, Mr. Baker. I want a peaceful *end.* If I do this for you, I don't want to wake up again. I *am* the way to finish him off."

"You can't mean that we would just keep him—dwelling—in you until. . . ." Sir Arthur couldn't finish his sentence.

"Certainly!" she said. "I get real peace instead of fogged pain and nausea every waking hour. As for Bernard, he gets the pain and nausea until he dies. That's better than what he gave the others."

"We couldn't do that," Adrianna said. "I wouldn't know where to keep him. We'd need a private hospital."

"But if you let him near people for long, you'll lose him," Alice said.

After a period of silence, Conan Doyle added, "And if we leave him where he is now, he won't be there long. After that, he'll hunt us down." He looked at Adrianna and then at me. "Alice is right. We haven't been thinking far enough ahead."

"Just keep him anyplace where he can't meet anyone. The end won't be long in coming," Alice said. "I suffered at his death and funeral. He was probably standing around watching, for all I know. Now *he* can suffer my death while I rest and meet my Maker. I know what I'm saying, believe me."

She convinced us of her plan within a few more minutes. She even seemed to take considerable pleasure at the prospect. She made a phone call to an old friend at Morton Graves, a secretary named Matilda, cheerfully informing her that she was not only still alive, but also coming out to visit. She told her friend that she wanted to see everyone she had known so long ago. They were as close to a family as she had, she told Matilda, and as she grew older, she longed to see them again. Her visit was arranged for the next day, Thursday afternoon.

After that, she told the staff at her rest home that she would be going for a brief trip with her friend Mrs. Bedaker, who was a qualified nurse. She explained that there were several old friends she wanted to see one more time. She told them that she would leave the next morning and would be gone through the weekend—perhaps longer. The staff at her residence care facility was surprisingly cooperative and sympathetic.

Adrianna stayed behind in Alice's room for a few minutes while Sir Arthur and I waited outside. When she came out, Arthur went his own way, and we started back to my room at the hotel.

"What was that last bit all about?" I asked

"I agreed that we'd have a comfortable place for her, even though she expects to be unaware of it. I told her about Freddy's hunting lodge."

"That's a good idea. Will anyone else think of it, you think?"

"The police, for instance?"

"Exactly. They are definitely looking for me, at least."

"No one will think of it. I also agreed to get a healthy supply of morphine. She insists on it. She doesn't even want Gussmann to suffer without it. I'm pretty sure she's addicted."

"Can you get it?"

"Easily, but not today." Her expression darkened and she turned away. "I dread going up to the lodge. It was Freddy's place, not mine. I've only been there a couple of times. I don't know how well provisioned it is."

"We should take some things with us. If we're picking up Alice in the morning, we should at least look at the lodge tonight. How far is it?"

"About two hours away. You're right, we've got to go up there tonight."

We picked up a list of necessities before driving the two hours to the lodge. There I began making adjustments while Adrianna took inventory of the things on hand. It turned out that Freddy's getaway cottage was better stocked than she had assumed it was. A small servant's quarters attached to the kitchen had its own small lavatory adjoining it. We emptied the room of everything except its one narrow bed. I wanted to fasten the bed to the floor or the wall but could find no way to do so. Next, I added a sturdy hasp to the outside of the door so we would be able to padlock it. With a brace and bit, I bored a half-inch-diameter hole through the center plank of the room's door to serve as a window into the makeshift cell.

I removed the narrow door to the lavatory, hinges and all, and stored the door in a shed outside. The wood casement window in the bedroom was a high one, and the glass was divided with sturdy wood. I nailed it shut from the outside, although I was relatively certain that it would kill Alice Tupper to climb out of it anyway. While I played prison builder, Adrianna arranged our supply of medicines in a cabinet just outside the door of the newly converted cell. She would still need to procure a supply of morphine, but she said she could arrange that by telephone in the morning. She knew any number of doctors and nurses who could easily get what she wanted.

We rested in the large sitting room of the lodge. Its fieldstone fireplace and beamed ceiling reminded me of my childhood home in Arizona, but the furnishings were an eclectic mix of the rustic and the expensive. In the same room with unfinished tables were delicate lamps and highly polished bookcases loaded with books bound in tooled leather. There was a large globe mounted on a brass stand that probably cost as much as a month of my income. I couldn't help smiling. The lodge reflected an aristocrat's view of roughing it. The general effect was somewhat unsettling. The lodge was part rustic retreat, part gentleman's library. And now it was part prison infirmary as well.

As tempted as we were to sleep at the lodge and start fresh in the morning, we knew that an unexpected overnight absence from her London hotel suite might raise questions she couldn't answer. She drove me to a spot near my hotel in the early hours of Thursday morning and returned to her rooms.

30

I don't mean to deny that the evidence is in some ways very strongly in favor of your theory . . . I only wish to point out that there are other theories possible. As you say, the future will decide.

—"The Adventure of the Norwood Builder"

ALICE TUPPER, ADRIANNA, AND I arrived at Morton Graves in the Bentley touring sedan on Thursday afternoon, with me acting as liveried chauffeur. Adrianna was not confident that she would not be recognized by her friend who worked in the hospital. Therefore she rode in the back seat with Alice and remained in the car while the elderly visitor entered the building. Dressed as Alice's driver, I walked a respectful three steps behind her except when there was a door to be opened. She seemed strong and needed no help as she walked. In the interest of our success, she had reluctantly skipped her regular dose of morphine, but she wasn't noticeably slowed down by pain. In fact, dressed in some of Adrianna's jewelry and a fox stole, she moved at a pretty brisk clip for a seriously ailing woman.

After she introduced herself at the office, her old friend Matilda was summoned. Alice entered spirited conversation with her for ten minutes and then asked for a tour of the facilities. The two ambled along reminiscing about times they had shared together years earlier. Alice announced that she wanted to see the whole place, including any patients who might have been there in her day. She confided that she had meant to visit many times but had kept putting it off. Matilda told Alice that the staff had heard that she had passed away. They had been very surprised and pleased to get her call the day before.

We passed Tommy Morrell in one of the dayrooms. Alice stopped and greeted him, but he showed little interest in her and no sign of recognition. As we walked along, there was obviously much curiosity about us among patients and staff. On our way to see William Townby, Alice explained to Matilda that she had indeed been very ill a couple of years ago, but that she was much better now.

Matilda nodded at me in my chauffeur's uniform and commented, "It looks like you're better off in more ways than one, Alice."

"Oh, yes. My investments have gone a little better than I expected since I retired. It's not what it appears, though. James isn't just my chauffeur, but my butler, nurse, and gardener into one. I can't afford to live like the bloods," she said with a laugh.

I nodded with a polite smile and kept my respectful distance.

Townby recognized Alice instantly, but after a glance my way he ignored me. I was sure he didn't recognize me. "Alice, old girl, you look fit enough for work. Why aren't you on staff and earning your keep?" he said. "You know what we'd all heard?"

"Matilda told me. I don't know how that got started. I was in hospital for a couple of weeks is all. Serves me right for not staying in touch with my old friends. How are you, Will? You look so good. I can't believe you're still here."

Townby smiled. "Still can't afford to pay my bill, Alice. I guess I never will, but I live like royalty—nicest room, good views. You ought to move in with me." He leaned over close to her, and I went tense for a second. "Got a boyfriend?" he asked in a stage whisper.

"Not for a long time now," she answered. "To tell the truth, that's why I haven't been here in so long. I thought there'd be too many memories, but I'm fine now. Who else that I knew is still around?"

"A few of the kitchen staff, I think," Townby answered. "There's Tommy Morrell."

"I saw him in the dayroom. One of his blank days, I'm afraid."

Townby thought for a minute. "I think that's all, Alice. Tommy and I. The rest are all relative newcomers—for you, at least."

"Some of them are famous, though," she said cheerfully. "I read that you've got a woman in here now who shot a man."

"That's right, Liza Anatole, she's made the news and is back with us. You never knew her, I'm sure. Of course, there was poor Helen, too, but she wasn't with us when she got into trouble."

"Yes, I knew her. That was sad," Alice said. "What about the doctors? Anybody I know?"

"There's Dodds," said Townby with a hint of malice. "He's chief of staff—away on holiday, I think. There are a couple of doctors on the board whom you would know, but they no longer see patients. They're never here."

"And I hear that *you* were on staff, Will?"

"That's what they tell me, Alice. I have no memory of it at all. That's why I'm still here, I guess."

"That doesn't seem like much of a mental condition, Will. I can't remember much from one day to the next myself," Alice said as she patted Townby's arm. "I've forgotten a lot about this place, that's for sure."

"Well, you'll just have to come out more often, then," Townby said. "Maybe you can jog my memory. I don't have any difficulty remembering you."

"I *am* going to come out again soon, Will. I'm going to visit often. In fact, I'm going to come out and bring a treat tomorrow. That's my birthday, and I'm going to bring out a big cake," she said.

We had agreed to this story before coming. We wanted everyone at Morton Graves to know exactly when they would see Alice again. The purpose of today's visit was to be seen by everyone and to show that Alice was alive and well.

As Matilda walked us through the remainder of the building,

Alice commented, "Where's that notorious young lady who shot the newspaperman, Mattie? My curiosity is killing me."

"You'll see her in the next wing, Alice. She'll be in the dayroom with everyone else. Now, don't you stare at her. Poor thing! You'll see a little blond woman, smallest woman in the room. She's the prettiest one, too. She's been better the past couple of days. She'll probably be presentable, but I'm not going to introduce you," Matilda said. "What would I say? 'Here's that criminally insane girl you were asking about'?"

"I just want to get a look at her, is all. I'll behave."

"Joe Arnold, the dayroom orderly, ought to be in this wing today. You remember him, Alice? Best orderly we've got."

Just then we rounded a corner and walked into a dayroom with about ten patients and a couple of staff members in it. I recognized Liza Anatole immediately. She was sitting comfortably by a window with a newspaper on her lap and a pencil stub in her hand. She didn't appear to take notice of us at first, but when Matilda introduced Alice to her old acquaintance Joe, I saw Liza's head come up suddenly. She stared at Alice for a moment and then appeared to be rising out of the chair; then she sat back and pretended to resume her reading. I walked on steadily through the room as if I weren't with Alice and left it by the opposite hallway. As far as I could tell, Liza took no notice of me.

Five minutes passed before Matilda and Alice joined me in the hall. I fell in behind them as they continued their tour. Our final stop was the kitchen, where Alice remembered two cooks, and a brief conversation with them followed. Then we returned to the entry lobby, and the two women made their good-byes. By the time we reached the car, I could tell that Alice was no longer doing well. She entered the backseat with my help and managed to sit up and wave toward the building while I walked around to take up my position as driver, but her grin was more of a grimace at close distance.

When we were on our way, Adrianna quickly administered a shot of morphine intravenously.

"I really did need that," she said gratefully, "I don't *ever* like to miss a dose."

"How do you feel, Alice?" Adrianna asked.

I heard Alice say, "I haven't walked that far in a year, but I'm fine." She raised her voice to address me. "Do you think he's there in the hospital, Mr. Baker?"

"I think so. Liza Anatole took special interest in you for just a second. You've never known her?"

"Never," Alice answered. "I made it a point to see the pretty little blond girl in that last dayroom, but I didn't stare at her. I only looked in her direction once."

"Well, she sure knew you," I said confidently.

"Not by being herself, she didn't," Alice said with obvious excitement.

"How about Townby?" Adrianna asked.

"Perfectly normal, Will was. He's just the way I knew him," Alice answered.

"And Tommy Morrell?" I shouted from the front.

"Just Tommy," Alice answered. He's just like that most of the time—like a vegetable, but he understands what you're saying. I don't think he recognized me, though."

"I'd love to be a fly on the wall back there now," Adrianna said. "I want to know what each one of them is doing. They're expecting you back?"

"Tomorrow," Alice answered.

"Will you be up to it, Alice?" Adrianna asked. "How are you feeling now?"

"The morphine is helping now. I feel better. I can't go long without it, but I wouldn't miss tomorrow for the world."

"You won't have to walk so much, maybe," I shouted to be heard in the back of the big sedan. "If Gussmann's there, he'll know where to find you, and I bet he'll want to do just that."

Long before we reached the lodge where Conan Doyle awaited us, Alice was asleep. I carried her into the newly prepared room and left Adrianna the task of getting her undressed. She slept soundly all night. The three of us, however, did not.

Over dinner, Adrianna said, "I wonder if he's the only one who ever discovered this. I've been wondering that. With all the mesmerizers and conjurers through the last century, maybe long before that, could he be the only one who knows how to move himself into another human being?"

"I hope so," I answered, "but it doesn't seem likely anymore, does it, considering all the millions of people over time. That might explain some of the old wives' tales about demons, exorcism, all that. But we've got to keep the other possibility in mind, too."

Conan Doyle nodded in silence.

"What's that?" Adrianna asked.

"Maybe the bear *doesn't* really talk," I said. "It's very possible that there is no Gussmann, that he's been dead for more than a decade. This still could be some very human conspiracy. There's a lot of money involved. Just because we don't understand what people are doing doesn't mean that it's not being done by *people*. Am I making sense? Did I say that right?"

"I think you're wrong," Sir Arthur said. "This is Gussmann we're after. As bizarre as it is, once I saw the possibility that Dr. Gussmann had simply abandoned his ailing body and moved into younger ones, I became convinced he's doing it. After that, all the mysteries made sense."

I looked at Sir Arthur and wondered if I had joined him in being a daffy Spiritualist. I didn't want to think so, but I found that I *did* believe that the person of Dr. Gussmann had invaded and occupied the bodies of several of his patients, even after his own body had died. "You think he's now a spirit—acting from the beyond?" I asked.

"No," Conan Doyle answered, "not in the spiritual sense. I've changed my mind about that. He has never yet 'gone beyond,' as we call it. He is acting from the temporal world—has never died."

"He's not a ghost, is what you're saying?" Adrianna asked.

"So then he can die," I added.

"I'm convinced that he can die if we can catch him," Sir Arthur answered, "and I think that Alice's plan may very well succeed." He looked at me. "If we accomplish this, we're essentially executing him."

"Listen to yourself. How can we be executing him? Gussmann died twelve-plus years ago. In the meantime, he's gone around stealing chunks of the lives of we don't know how many people. Ruining most of them, killing several of them," I pointed out.

"I don't argue against that, but we aren't a court of law," Sir Arthur said.

"What court of law would hear this case? What policeman would try to catch Gussmann? More to the point, what army would prevent his killing all of us, and Lady Jean, and now Alice, as well?" I counted these off on my fingers.

The others were silent for a long time as my questions hung in the air. "I just wish there were some other way," Adrianna said very quietly.

"If we could just confine him forever, we would, but we can't. There is a sense in which we're not killing him at all," I offered. "He exists, in some mental way, in some force field. He's going to go somewhere, or be somewhere. And wherever that is, it's where he belongs in the first place. It's where he would have gone years ago."

"Besides," Adrianna said. "if we do this thing on Thursday, and there are no evil psychiatrists with murderous intentions, nothing will happen anyway. Alice will simply live out her days as before."

"Do you think we'll be able to tell which ending is which?" Sir Arthur asked. "How will we know for sure *who* Alice is after Thursday's visit?"

I answered, "I've been thinking about that. I'm going to give Alice a password, a simple code, and a countersign that only she and the three of us will know. She'll have orders to say a specific countersign to me every time I say the code word. If she can't say it on demand, she isn't Alice."

Adrianna's face lit up. "That will work!" Then she frowned again. "Unless he just hypnotizes her and doesn't move into her. Then she couldn't give the countersign, even though it might still be she."

"He doesn't have time to waste on just hypnotizing her. He knows he may have just this one chance to get out of the asylum. For several years now, that imposing fence that separates Morton Graves Voluntary Hospital from Richmond Park has just been a gate through which he passed at will. But not now. To him, Alice is an empty shell that he *must* move into."

"And once he does that, he'll try to kill us in any way he can," Conan Doyle said. "Don't give him any chance to get his hands on your throat—or on a heavy travel bag, for that matter."

31

Have you not tethered a young kid under a tree, lain above it with your rifle,
and waited for the bait to bring up your tiger?
—"The Adventure of the Empty House"

I SPENT THE EARLY morning helping Alice prepare. She understood the principle of the code word and countersign. We practiced it under all the conditions we might encounter—when she was sleepy and wide awake, when she was drugged, when she was in pain. She never failed.

The arrangement was a simple one. I would say, "May I be of assistance, madam?" She would invariably answer, "No, thank you, James." Under no circumstances would she give any other reply.

When it was nearly time for us to go, Adrianna prepared our little kit of medications, including a smelling salts bottle that actually contained ether. Finally she spoke. "Ready?"

I nodded.

So at ten o'clock we began our drive to the asylum for the supposed birthday party. Adrianna cradled Alice's frail hand in hers as they both gazed sadly out the window. If our plan worked, Alice would never see us again. It was difficult for me to imagine that—she would simply disappear inside herself and Gussmann would be there in her stead. He would look exactly like her, but the mind and will behind the face would be entirely his. In turn, her consciousness would be completely erased. It seemed too far-fetched to be true. And yet, all of the evidence suggested that this was exactly what had been happening to at least five people over the past dozen years. My own feelings about this moment were primarily ones of dread and guilt. I felt fully responsible for the death of Freddy and the servants and for the anguish that Adrianna was going through. I felt guilty about Alice, too. It was no help to me that she was nearing death anyway and was, in fact, the originator of our present scheme. And I certainly had no feelings of imminent success and victory over Gussmann. This was just a bad business all around. It had been like this at times during the war—just a bad business.

From time to time, Alice turned to smile reassuringly at Adrianna. Alice struggled to look a lot stronger than she actually was. We stopped in London and picked up a cake that we had ordered for the occasion. At just past twelve we arrived at Morton Graves and were met halfway up the walk by Matilda and several of the staff. I carried the cake as the others cheerfully escorted Alice into the building.

In the lobby there were joyous greetings for Alice, mostly from people who didn't know her. The entourage ambled down one of the halls and into a dayroom that had been decorated with a sign reading, "Happy Birthday, Alice. Many Happy Returns." The handful of people whom Alice knew were almost all present, including William Townby. The exception that I noticed was Tommy Morrell, but he wouldn't have attended a function like this. Liza Anatole was not in the room, either, but she had never known Alice.

Alice took up a position sitting lightly on the arm of a large chair so that people had to come to her if they wanted to chat. Every few minutes I would sidle over to Alice to ask if I could be of assistance. Each time she would quietly reply, "No, thank you, James." The cake was cut and placed on little plates. People ate and talked. Nothing interesting happened.

At one o'clock William Townby left the room, and I walked over to Alice. "May I be of assistance, madam?" I asked.

"No, thank you, James," she answered.

Staff members began excusing themselves from the gathering one by one, finally leaving only the few who had known Alice well. A few patients began to enter the dayroom, including Tommy Morrell, but he didn't go near Alice. He just sat in a chair by the card table and stared out the window. A few minutes later, Liza Anatole came in, accompanied by a nurse. She secured a plate of cake and began to mingle with other patients, talking briefly with several of them.

After a few minutes of this, she walked over to Alice and extended her hand. "You don't know me," she said, "but I wanted to wish you a happy birthday, anyway. We have a mutual friend."

"Oh," said Alice, "and who is that?"

"Will Townby. He's a very nice man. He was once my doctor. Did you know him when he was a doctor?"

"No," Alice answered, "I knew Will as a patient a long time ago. I've heard that he was a doctor for a while."

Liza leaned down nearer Alice's ear. "He was sexually perverted as a doctor," she whispered just loud enough that I barely caught it from my position a few feet away. "Yes, yes, yes," she continued, "he made you want to do unspeakable things. I remember them all. I'm still ashamed to think of some of the things we did." This was said in a sort of low, humming tone. After that, Liza stood upright again and walked away to a group of patients who were setting up a game of cards.

I stepped closer for just a moment. "May I be of any assistance, madam?"

"No, thank you, James," Alice answered in a quavering voice. She looked at me with fear in her eyes.

I walked away and picked up a magazine. Liza started playing cards. Matilda came over to Alice to ask if she'd like to leave the dayroom. Alice declined, saying she hoped to see Will again before she left.

Tommy Morrell had been sitting in his chair near the card table since he'd entered the room. He seemed to annoy Liza Anatole because she leaned over and spoke to him and pushed his shoulder with her hand. Then she straightened in her chair, and Morrell leaned over and seemed to speak into Anatole's ear.

But I thought that I must be mistaken, because I thought I remembered that Tommy was incapable of speech. I could not see whether his lips were moving, but Liza appeared to be listening, turning her head slightly toward him. Then Tommy rose and stepped away from her while she seemed to be staring somewhat blankly at her hand of cards.

It seemed to me that Alice's face was showing signs of pain. Her smile had vanished, and she seemed to be brooding.

Tommy Morrell drifted over nearer to where Alice was sitting. Then, at a distance of perhaps six feet from her, he sat on the floor and began to rub his head with his hand, not unlike a parody of a monkey.

I stepped closer to Alice. "May I be of assistance, madam?"

"No, thank you, James," she answered, her voice stronger than before.

Suddenly Liza Anatole stood back from the table, pointing her finger at a card. She swept all the cards from the table and pointed at one that had landed on the floor. The other patients stood in alarm. Then she climbed onto a folding chair and swayed silently. The chair wobbled precariously, and a number of people, myself included, were very apprehensive that she might fall. I even took a few steps in her direction before an orderly rushed toward her to help. This only caused her further alarm, and she jumped to the floor before the orderly took hold of her. I must have watched the spectacle for a minute at least, before I turned around to see how Alice was taking all of this.

Alice was standing a couple of feet in front of her chair with a look of concern as Liza continued to shriek. Tommy was still sitting stupidly on the floor, though now somewhat nearer Alice's chair than earlier. He seemed to have no interest in Liza or Alice or anything else. His hands hung slack, both touching the floor.

Alice looked at me and raised her finger, gesturing slightly for me to come nearer. When I stepped closer she said, "Perhaps we'd better go. This is frightening me."

"May I be of any assistance, madam?" I asked.

"No, I'm fine, James. I just think we should leave and let the staff handle this. I really think we're in the way here. I do want to say good-by to Mattie, though, and tell her I'll be back soon."

I slipped my left hand into the outer pocket of my livery and felt for the ether in the smelling-salts bottle. "I think you're right, madam. This is not a good time."

Alice started walking toward the hall that led to the lobby, and I fell in behind her. Where the remains of the cake still sat on a table, she faltered and had to lean against the heavy table for support. She leaned over the cake so low that I thought she was going to topple into it. Before I could reach her, though, she had straightened and started walking again. She paused by the office and spoke to Matilda.

"Well, I've got to be going, Mattie. Thank you so much for the party. I'll be coming back again soon."

"What's going on in there, Alice? Sounds like a crazy house," Mattie said with a laugh.

"That Liza girl is upset over something, but they've got it under control. I'll see you soon." Alice continued toward the doors, but then stopped short and pressed her right hand against her side.

"May I be of any assistance, madam?" I asked again.

"It's just a pain in my side. Perhaps we can stop by a chemist on the way home," she answered.

"Yes, madam," I said as I opened the door for her. "Can you walk unassisted, Miss Tupper?"

"Yes. Let's just get in the car," she said somewhat gruffly as she walked ahead of me.

As I walked close behind her, I uncorked the little bottle of ether and pulled up the cotton wick that Adrianna had installed the night before. Then I stepped up to Alice and took her right arm firmly in my right hand. I stepped to her left side and pinned her left arm with my body. "Let me help you, madam," I said as I brought the ether up with my left hand and put it squarely under her nose.

She jerked her head back and twisted it to her right, but to no avail. The ailing little woman in my arms simply did not have the strength to struggle effectively against me as I held the anesthetic firmly under her nose. As she began to weaken in my arms, I saw Adrianna get out of the back of the car and go quickly to the driver's position. The car started smoothly as I took Alice's full weight into my arms. I took a few seconds to secure the little bottle and place it in my pocket before reaching under Alice's right arm and supporting her with her left arm around my neck. Even at a distance, it would have been clear that I was virtually carrying the woman to the car, which might have caused concern, but no one had come out to watch our departure. Less than a minute after the car started, we were well away. In another minute Alice's hands were tied securely together behind her back. Then I tied her ankles together and tethered her ankles to her wrists.

Adrianna had spread two thick blankets on the floor between the seats. I placed Alice on these, with her body turned on its side. Then I leaned closer to Adrianna. "She's ready, Adrianna. Do you want to trade places?"

"When we've got a little farther away from Morton Graves, Charlie. I'll look for a quiet place to park."

Alice began to moan at my feet. "Should I give her some more ether?" I asked Adrianna.

She shouted back over her shoulder, "Too dangerous, that stuff. It takes a doctor who knows what he's doing to keep using it like that. Just watch her. She may vomit and suffocate. Ether's bad that way. We'll be out in the country before she can make any real noise."

A mile farther on, to my great relief, we pulled off the road and exchanged places. If Alice was going to choke to death, I certainly didn't want to be the one in charge of her at the time. She didn't choke, though, or even vomit. After about an hour, Adrianna leaned across the body at her feet and said, "He's awake now, Charles." Though we had not gagged her mouth for fear of strangulation, there were no attempts to speak.

A silent hour later, I drove up to the rear of the lodge. While Adrianna opened the house, I got the little woman up off the floorboards and out of the car. I carried her over my shoulder as gently as I could and laid her down on the bed in her appointed room. While she kept her eyes open, she did not make a sound.

Finally, with Adrianna standing beside me as we looked down at her, I asked sarcastically, "May I be of any assistance, now, madam?"

"No, thank you, James," she said.

32

You did not know where to look, and so you missed all that was important. I can never bring you to realise the importance of sleeves.

—"A Case of Identity"

"**WHAT HAVE YOU DONE,** Charlie?" Adrianna shouted. "Didn't you ask her the prompt question before?"

I stood staring down at the woman who was what I call hog-tied on the bed. "Yes, of course, Adrianna, I asked her that before. A number of times, actually."

"I thought you were worried about me," the little woman said weakly. "I forgot in all the confusion."

Adrianna glared at me. "Help me get her untied, Charles. I'm so sorry, Alice. Why didn't you say something before?"

"I was too ill. I thought I was going to vomit every second of the way," she answered.

I untied the knots that tethered her wrists to her ankles and stretched her out more comfortably on her side. "Get some morphine, Adrianna, while I finish this."

Adrianna moved quickly to the cabinet just outside the door.

"No!" Alice said firmly. "I don't want any morphine. I'll be fine. Just get these ropes off me. They're hurting me. I can do without the drug."

At that, Adrianna stopped cold and stepped back into the room without opening the cabinet. She looked quizzically at her patient,

389

then back toward the medicine cabinet and at me for a moment before she stepped closer to the bed. She seemed to be considering what Alice had said. "What can I prepare for you, Miss Tupper?" she asked Alice as she touched my shoulder and drew me slightly back away from the bed. Her expression told me that she saw something wrong.

Alice turned to face her. "Nothing, thank you. I'll be fine."

"No, remember, Alice?" Adrianna said evenly, "You're not paying attention. Listen to me. What can I prepare for you, Miss Tupper?" A few seconds later she repeated, "What can I prepare for you, Miss Tupper?"

Alice was silent. She stared at Adrianna for a long moment. "I . . . I forget the answer," she said. "In all this confusion and pain I can't remember the right answer for that."

"Just think about it, Alice. It will come to you—the countersign for me, not the one for Charles. What can I prepare for you, Miss Tupper?"

I turned away and left the room, leaving the other knots tied. I walked to my travel bag, took out the Luger, and put it into my belt under the livery jacket. There *was* no countersign arrangement for Adrianna, and by now the real Alice Tupper would have said so. I heard Adrianna repeat the false prompt again as I returned to the guest cell. As I walked into the room, the woman swung her feet off the bed and managed to sit up.

"Can I get you some water or anything?" I asked.

"You can please finish untying these ropes, Charles. They're really beginning to hurt me."

"But the arrangement is that you must complete your counter-signs to both me and Adrianna before we can be sure it's you in there, Alice. You had trouble with mine before, and now you can't seem to remember Adrianna's. It is you in there, isn't it, Alice?" I asked as I stepped forward and gently pushed the woman back into a reclining position. "Be a dear and get me some more rope from the car, Adrianna," I said. "We'll just make sure before we untie old Alice here." Then I tethered her ankles to the bedpost.

Adrianna returned in a minute with more rope. "You might want to reconsider that morphine, Doc," she said. "You're in quite a lot of pain already, and it isn't going to get any better until you have a good rest. It isn't going to get much better, even then. There's no sense in your being in a lot of pain when we've got morphine."

Our guest stared at Adrianna in silence. I untied Alice's wrists and then retied them in a more comfortable position, using the rungs at the head of the bed. The patient didn't say a word during this process. Finally she said, "You're right. I need my rest. Please leave me alone and let me sleep."

"No morphine?" Adrianna asked again.

"No. I'll rest fine."

We left the room and closed and padlocked the door. Then Adrianna led me to the bedroom at the other end of the lodge. "How did he do that?" she asked quietly. "He almost got away with it, too."

I thought back to the scene in the dayroom. "I'm sure that Gussmann was occupying Liza Anatole when I first saw her this morning. I don't think we used the signals when she was within earshot, though, because she only paused long enough to taunt Alice briefly before going—"

Adrianna interrupted me, frowning. "What do you mean, 'taunt Alice'? Why would Liza taunt Alice?"

"Remember in the journals? How Gussmann described making the special patients feel more depressed?"

Adrianna shuddered. "'Intensifying their neurosis,' he called it. Disgusting man."

"Right. Well, that was what he must've been trying to do—make Alice feel really bad so that she'd want to withdraw . . ."

". . . and make room for him to move in. So is that what happened? He moved from Liza to Alice?

"No. I think he tried to, but it didn't work. So Liza walked across the room to where Tommy was sitting, and Gussmann moved over into him."

"Did you see him do it?"

"Yes, but it didn't really register at the time."

"So when did Gussmann hear the countersign, Charlie?"

I thought carefully, trying to re-create a picture of the scene. "A few people were still milling around by then, and Tommy wandered over and sat on the floor near Alice. I'm sure we did the routine once while he was sitting there, but Gussmann didn't catch its importance then."

"How long did Tommy sit there before Gussmann . . . took Alice over?"

"Hardly any time at all. Now that I think about it, I'm pretty sure that Gussmann had hypnotized Liza right after he'd left her body, because as soon as Tommy got close to Alice, Liza made a very well-timed scene that distracted everyone in the room."

"Including you?"

"Including me. By the time it was over, Alice . . ." I paused as sudden tears stung my eyes. Blinking them back, I continued. "Alice didn't give the countersign after my cue."

Adrianna squeezed my hand and we stood quietly for a moment, suddenly aware of the enormous burden we'd shouldered. I went on, "But Gussmann had plenty of time on the way out here to think about it. He had to be wondering how we'd sprung the trap, and he simply figured it out. He's very smart."

Adrianna drew a long, shaky breath. "I guess we never thought we were dealing with a stupid adversary," she said. "I'm sorry, Charlie. He almost got me."

"Me, too. You saved it, but we've got a ways to go yet. I don't think he'll try pretending to be Alice much longer, but he might. He'll sure as hell try some other things."

Then we heard a shout from the cell. "Mrs. Wallace! Can you hear me?"

We walked together back to the other end of the lodge, and Adrianna peered in to the cell through the hole I had cut for the purpose. She signaled for me to look, and I did. Alice was still securely tied, so I unlocked the door.

"I would like to take half a dose of morphine every two hours. Is that all right, Nurse Wallace?"

"We'll start with that," Adrianna answered. "If it doesn't calm you down and kill the pain enough, I'll increase it." She stepped over to the bed and reached for the patient's left arm. "I'm going to give it intravenously for this first injection, Doctor. After that, we'll see."

"I would prefer to get it in my right arm, please. The veins are better."

Adrianna walked around the bed, unbuttoned the sleeve of the right arm, and rolled it back. Then she walked out to the medicine cabinet and prepared the syringe.

When she was again close to her patient and was cleaning the arm, the woman's voice spoke softly. "A nurse who is also a killer. That must be a terrible conflict to live with, is it not, Nurse Wallace?"

Adrianna finished the injection without comment.

"We'll untie you shortly," I said. "You'll be more comfortable. You will find, Doctor, that you are quite weak. You would be unable to overpower either of us, even without the morphine."

"Why do you persist in calling me that, Charles? Must you do that?"

"I'll untie you soon," I answered as Adrianna and I left the room.

I padlocked the door. Adrianna walked to a kitchen cupboard, found a bottle of brandy, and poured two liberal drinks. Then we returned to the bedroom at the other end of the lodge.

"It's odd that he would know which of Alice's arms has better veins," Adrianna said when she had sat down in a chair by the fireplace.

I stoked the embers in the bedroom fireplace and added more wood. "Is he correct? Are those the better veins, you think?"

"I can't be sure. Let me think," she answered. "I don't know, Charles. I've been giving most of her shots in the muscle, not intravenously. This time, I wanted quick action and maximum effect."

"Alice might know about her own veins," I said, "but this wouldn't be Alice who is talking."

"Unless we're wrong," Adrianna added.

"How long will it take for this shot to make her—him—sleep?" I asked.

"A few minutes. I gave him a full dose, though he asked for only half."

"Then we'll go in and look at Alice's arms. Maybe we'll be able to see what he meant."

"This is weird, Charlie, not knowing how to refer to . . . Alice in there. Not really knowing *who* is in there."

For a minute I concentrated on building the fire. "The way I see it," I said when I sat down, "Alice is in there, but she's way down in there where she is unaware of all this. She's just resting, dormant. That's what both the journal and Townby's account tell us. Gussmann, on the other hand, is in there at the surface. He's aware of everything that's going on, and he's thinking. He's thinking entirely as Gussmann. He knows everything he's ever learned, including a lot about Alice that you and I don't know, maybe even that she's never known about herself."

"Let's try to remember that he's got about ninety years of learning behind him, and he's a cold-blooded killer, to boot." Adrianna looked at her watch. "He won't be thinking too actively in about five minutes, though," she said. "Then we can go untie him so he can use the lavatory without our help. I want to stay away from him.

I sat in silence, watching the fire grow, until Adrianna rose from her chair. We walked back to the cell, looked through the peephole to satisfy ourselves that Gussmann was asleep, and unlocked the padlock. Alice's body was soundly asleep. To make sure of this, Adrianna poked the sleeping woman's palm with a sharp fingernail. I untied and removed all the ropes, and Adrianna started to remove Alice's dress. After unbuttoning several buttons at the bodice, she moved to the left sleeve and unbuttoned it.

"Look at this, Charlie," she said, pointing at Alice's left wrist.

There, under the buttons, was a wooden knife handle. I carefully slipped the knife out of her sleeve. The simple kitchen utility knife had an eight-inch blade, one with quite a bit of cake frosting clinging to its sides. I held it up in front of me. Adrianna said, "So that's what makes the veins in the right arm better—no knife blade between them and the needle!"

"I was right behind him when he got this," I said, "and I never saw a thing. I'm surprised he hasn't already cut the ropes. He could have reached this with his right hand as loosely as I had him tied."

"He knew he didn't have time to do anything before he'd be asleep," Adrianna said, shaking her head slowly, as if in grudging admiration. "He'd have been wiser to get it out of his sleeve, though. Maybe hide it behind the pillow or something."

"He probably didn't expect us to undress him. It was hidden pretty well right where it was. I hate to think what he might have done with this when conditions were right for him."

After examining her patient's forearms, Adrianna removed the dress, replaced it with a nightgown, and tucked Alice's body under the blankets. I picked up all the pieces of rope and looked around to make sure that nothing remained loose in the room. We packed everything out and again padlocked the makeshift cell.

When I laid the knife on the kitchen counter, Adrianna asked, "Where's the pistol, Charlie?"

"Right here in my belt," I answered, reflexively touching the grip with my right hand.

"I don't think we should ever carry it into the room with us. He might get to it somehow. And I don't think we should put it anyplace he would think to look for it, even out here—not in a drawer or anything."

What she said made sense. If he thought either of us was carrying a gun, he'd surely try for it. And if he somehow had an opportunity to look for a gun in the lodge, I didn't want him to find it. On the other hand, I wanted to be able to get my hands on it pretty readily. I looked around the room.

"Come over to this bookcase, Adrianna," I said. When we were standing in front of the tall open bookcase near the main fireplace, I continued, "What's the highest shelf you can reach? One where you could remove books and reach behind them?"

Adrianna reached up to the second-highest shelf and removed three books. She found that she could not reach behind them. She replaced these and moved her hand one shelf lower. There she could easily remove books and reach behind them all the way to the back of the case. "I don't think Alice could reach these," she said, "even if she were in normal health."

"I agree." I slipped the Luger out of my waistband and put it behind the books she had removed.

"Wait, Charlie. That's not a revolver. How does it work? Do I just pull the trigger?"

I retrieved the Luger automatic. "No. Right now there isn't even a round in the firing chamber," I said. "And there's a safety catch. Let me show you." I jacked a bullet into the chamber and snapped on the safety. "Now, there's a bullet nearly ready to fire when you pull the trigger. Just slip the safety off and fire. After that one, all you have to do is keep pulling the trigger. As fast as you do, it'll fire a round. See this lever?"

"The safety?" she asked.

"Yes. Just swing it over like this. Now it's really ready to fire. We'll keep it with a bullet in the chamber like this, but with the safety on."

"How big is it? What's its power compared with the .38 I had?"

"About the same. It handles differently—more balance to it. You don't have to pull the trigger nearly as much as the .38. Just a light squeeze will fire it. Do you want to go outside and try it?"

"No. I understand. Just put it there behind those books." While I hid the Luger, Adrianna picked up the brandy on the kitchen counter, and we walked into the bedroom where she sat on one of the twin beds.

"It's really him in there," she said. "It is! He killed Freddy and . . . everyone, and he's just lying in there resting."

"If he'd done as he intended with that knife, he'd have killed us, too," I said.

"It's hard not to think of him as Alice."

"I know. I can't get used to it either."

Tears came into Adrianna's eyes. "And she's just . . . gone."

"Asleep."

"From now on, Charlie," Adrianna cried in anguish, "that brave little woman is gone forever."

I held her in my arms until she was calm. "How long do you think it'll be, Adrianna?"

"I don't know. Days—weeks."

33

Violence does, in truth, recoil upon the violent, and the schemer falls into the pit which he digs for another.

—"The Adventure of the Speckled Band"

EXCEPT FOR REQUESTING MORPHINE, Gussmann had nothing to say to either of us until the next afternoon. He insisted on minimal doses of the drug, and he wouldn't allow further injections in the vein, just shots in the muscle. The result was that his pain—Alice's pain—was maintained at a level he wished to tolerate while his mental faculties were only minimally impaired. He never made the slightest attempt to struggle in Alice Tupper's frail body. I stood in the room with my back against the closed doorway each time Adrianna administered a shot.

He got up and walked around some a few times, and he used the bathroom. While I listened to his moving around, I remembered that the body he was using was short, elderly, weak, and under sedation. I was quite sure that he would not break out the window. I thought it possible that he could move the bed, but there was no sign that he tried.

Arthur arrived at about two o'clock and immediately went in to see our prisoner.

"Arthur Conan Doyle," Alice's body said with excitement. "So here you are after all these years. Montrose was a long time ago."

Conan Doyle stood silently, observing the frail woman on the bed. Finally he took a deep breath and spoke. "Why did you send me that damned letter, Gussmann?"

"I was grasping at straws. I didn't seem to be making any sure progress at getting out of Holloway Prison. I had to have one of the subjects I could rely on. I knew only one man who might be able to help, and I knew you'd help if you could finally answer the one burning question of your life."

"I don't like the answer," Sir Arthur said. "You're not a spirit from the hereafter, Gussmann. You're a freak of nature."

"Don't be too hasty, Sir Arthur," the little body said. "I am the best hope you'll ever have of really solving the mystery of life and death. Think about that, Conan Doyle." Gussmann paused and studied Sir Arthur's reaction. "This is just the beginning! With the proper surroundings and resources, we can find everything you've been searching for."

The old man clenched his huge fist and stepped toward the bed as if to strike the frail woman in front of him. Then he stopped and stepped back. "You know nothing about the spirit world."

"I'm the best chance you'll ever have of finding out *everything* about the spirit world. But I've got to get back into one of my healthy subjects. You can keep me confined, just as I am now. We can find out all the answers if we work together." He paused and then added, "And you, too, can live as long as it takes to find the answers."

Sir Arthur stood silently and looked from me to Adrianna and back to me. "Would you lock this door, please, Charles?" he said as he walked out of the tiny room. He went to the kitchen and poured himself a glass of water. Then he began to pace the room as I completed closing and locking the makeshift cell.

Adrianna poured two brandies and brought one to me as we waited for him to speak.

"I don't want to talk to him again." He was silent while he finished his water. Then he continued, "Gussmann just made the most seductive offer I could ever imagine—so appealing that even now I admit to being sorely tempted." He shook his head with a grim expression on his face. "I'm going back to London. Call me when he's dead. Above all, don't let me talk to him again. I can feel him in the air."

"We can handle him," I said.

"Well, I can't," Sir Arthur answered. "I can't be responsible for myself if I'm ever near him again—the filthy . . . inhuman . . . ." He nodded as he walked to the door and left, without another word.

In the late afternoon, Adrianna took Gussmann a bowl of soup and a spoon, and he began to feed himself without incident. At that point he addressed me. His voice was a subtle alteration of Alice Tupper's. He used deeper breaths and achieved a slightly lower tone than her natural one. "So, Mr. Baker, you are an American. You were a soldier, I gather. Why didn't you return home after the war?"

"Actually, Dr. Gussmann," I answered, "I served for the Crown, not the United States. I was born in England."

"Interesting," he said. "You obviously read German, or Mrs. Wallace does, very well. Your accent, if I may say so without offense, is clearly American. Your name could be of German origin. Yet with all of this, you fought for king and country. Where do your parents live?"

"They are no longer living," I said. "They died in the States when I was a boy."

He took several spoonfuls of soup before continuing. "I, too, have the divided loyalties of two countries. Some Scots would say even three countries. And the loneliness and confusion that come with that situation has always been a burden to me. I was born Austrian, but my loyalties are all British, even though my manner of speech remains somewhat foreign to the English ear. This has made it difficult to fit in with Englishmen." He paused and finished his soup.

"Would you like more soup, Doctor?" Adrianna asked.

"Nur ein wenig, bitte."

"I'm sorry, I don't understand," Adrianna said, glancing at me.

"Just a little," I interpreted for her.

"So it is you, Herr Baeker, who reads the German," Gussmann said with a slight smile. "And in the old script as well. You know, I wondered for years where those journals were. I didn't need them any more for my work, but I always feared they would be found. And so they were." He turned again to Adrianna. "Please, yes, a little more soup. Perhaps also some bread." He touched her arm. *"Jetzt ist es Zeit, das Brot zu bringen,"* he said with a chuckle. "You know this much German, *nicht war?"*

"Yes," she said, rising from the bed. "You've heard me say that much."

"Just before you shot me," he said quietly to her back as she walked out. "The English nurse who kills." I could see Adrianna flinch as she walked away.

"In self-defense," I said loudly enough for her to hear in the other room.

"Have you never been back to America since the war, Charles?" he asked me.

"Never yet," I answered. The question bothered me. I felt a vague unease about America anyway—the whole question of which country was mine. I didn't let him see that I was bothered by the question.

He nodded with an understanding smile. "But it is difficult to fit in here in England, is it not? I have always found it so. I longed for Austria sometimes, for people and places I knew as a boy."

"Sometimes," I said. I found myself thinking of Arizona.

"People and places I knew as a young man," he said quietly. "The British are not really accepting of foreigners. Their snobbery seems boundless at times. When I was a boy, people I knew were more kind. It was not so lonely. It was home. Sometimes I long for it." There was a pleasant hum in his diction.

"I've thought of going back," I said as Adrianna returned with more soup and a slice of bread.

"Thank you, Nurse. You are kind to me in spite of everything," he said pleasantly. "Such a complicated thing to be a nurse." He tasted the soup and smiled. "In a war is the worst time to be a nurse. The duties often conflict, do they not?"

"Every day," Adrianna answered. "Every damned day."

"It is so also for a doctor, the decisions. One cannot reconcile them all. It gets to be a very long thing, duty in a war. I served England in the Boer War. Trying to save life in the midst of deliberate death. Watching lives one cannot save." He tried the bread, smiled, and nodded his approval.

"It's from a bakery," Adrianna said.

"A good bakery," he said. "You have thought of everything, Nurse. Very proper. Everything is the best it can be in the circumstances. Bad circumstances," he said quietly. "A good nurse in bad circumstances."

I walked into the other room through the doorway that Adrianna had left open when she went to the kitchen. After a few minutes, she came out with the bowl and spoon and closed the door behind her. I remembered the padlock as she walked away. Though I was suddenly tired, I got up from my chair by the fire and padlocked the cell. I peeped in at Gussmann and saw an old woman resting peacefully on the bed.

"I can't keep my eyes open," Adrianna said. "I'm going in for a nap."

"I'll just rest here by the fire," I said. The fireplace was made of stone, like all of them were where I had grown up. Much of the construction of this lodge was stone. The ceilings were exposed beams and bare wood. The furniture was simple; some of it was even made of unfinished wood. It was oddly satisfying to be here in poor Freddy's lodge with his wife—away from my job and London. I drifted off to sleep.

When I woke, it was dark outside and Adrianna was in the cell with Gussmann. I noticed that the door was standing open, but then she couldn't very well have padlocked it from inside while she was there. Still, she should have waked me. I walked over to see what was going on.

Alice, rather Gussmann, was sitting up, his feet on the floor, eating more soup—a little old woman with a bowl of soup sitting precariously on her lap. He—I had to remember that it was Gussmann—was facing the door, and Adrianna was sitting on the other side of the narrow bed, facing away. I stood in the doorway and watched.

"We had to do it, you see. If we didn't, the girl would die, so there we were," Adrianna said with what may have been a sob.

"The conflicts are monstrous, tragic," Alice's face said. "It mounts up, becomes unbearable. I felt it many times in South Africa."

"They just kept coming," Adrianna said.

"I understand. And the guns are the worst. How can you save lives when all that those guns want to do is destroy it? And the boys are so young." He patted her softly on the back as his soothing, humming voice continued. "Fine young British men."

"The girls were so young," Adrianna said.

"And the babies and children I saw suffer," Gussmann said gently. Then he looked up at me, his old woman's face showing great compassion. "Did you see the American troops much?" he asked. "Did you get to talk to the American young men?"

I could *feel*, somehow, his concern. "They were mostly along the Lorraine front," I said. "I never was there during the war. I talked to a few after the armistice."

"When they were going home," Gussmann said quietly, "with their friends. Getting out of England. They are there now with people they knew as boys. That would be nice, wouldn't it, Charles? Where did you live in America?"

"In the West—Arizona," I answered, remembering a flood of things at once.

"Wide-open spaces, dry air. Not like London," he said. "An outdoor life, Charlie? Did you live like a cowboy?" he asked while patting Adrianna's back.

I felt a vague danger—like I should leave the room—but I just answered instead. "I lived in mining towns, then on a ranch. Lots of open space," I said, remembering suddenly my father and speaking German with him at home.

I was concerned about Adrianna. She was curled over her lap, staring down at the floor, her arms folded tightly under her chest. "Have you finished eating?" I asked.

"Most kind, very good," he answered. "The soup is very good, thank you."

"It's just tinned soup," Adrianna said softly, "not proper soup." She continued to stare at the floor.

"Like in the war," Alice seemed to hum. "Everything tinned, nothing properly done. No proper medical supplies most of the time. So difficult to do what had to be done."

"God! I hated it," Adrianna said, "the blood and dirt and killing, year after year."

"No place to retreat to, not for the nurses," Gussmann said. He looked up at me again. "I'm sure you often wished for those wide-open western spaces during the war, Charlie," he said with a kind and feminine tone.

"Not so much in those days," I said. "More since then. Get away from London and the snobbery." I felt I could share that with him and he would know exactly what I meant.

"I wanted to be with the people and places I knew as a boy," Alice's musical voice seemed to say. "Travel away from London society. I wanted to visit the graves of my parents," he said. He turned and touched Adrianna's shoulder. "I wonder if I could have a light dose of morphine now, Nurse Wallace?" He turned again and lay back against his pillow. "It's peaceful here, though, Charlie, away from London. I can talk to you without watching my accent, *nicht war?*"

"Jawohl," I said as I looked up through the little window at the wide, moonlit night sky. "You don't have to watch nothin' you say here, Doc."

"I can relax here," he said in Alice's soft voice, "without all the pretense. I could just walk for miles here and not have to impress anyone. I'm not really adequate to deal with London. I really think they are better than I am, and they know it."

Adrianna came back in with the syringe and gave Gussmann his shot, though in Alice's arm. Very properly done. "There we are. You'll be much more comfortable in a few minutes," she said.

I noticed like I never had before how precisely British her speaking was, how somehow upper crust her tone of voice seemed to be. She left the room and I followed her out, feeling strangely antagonistic toward her. "There's no beer here, I suppose?" I said.

"No, Charles. There's more brandy. I think there may be a case of a rather good claret in the cellar," she said somewhat stiffly.

"There should be some beer," I said, my anger rising.

"It doesn't keep very well, Charles, and Freddy didn't much care for it." Her posture was, it seemed to me, that of an English school-teacher—giving me a lecture on the proper things to drink, for God's sake. Freddy would have the proper things to drink.

"He wouldn't," I said. "I'm going to drive out and have a pint or two. There's a pub not too far down the road."

"We'll be fine," she said. "Take your time. Be careful."

"I'd better lock up the jail," I said. "Just in case." I padlocked the cell door and pocketed the key before leaving.

An hour later, I returned after one pint of stout. At least I thought it was one pint. I felt a little foggy. The trip out for my pint now seemed stupid. Adrianna was asleep in the bedroom with the door closed. I looked in on Gussmann, who was sound asleep. I remembered to double-check the lock on his door before I went to sleep on the couch in front of the fire.

Our days and nights became routine, almost surreal. Sometimes I even forgot where we were. I lost track of time while we had nothing to do but wait. My mind seemed foggy sometimes. Gussmann requested medication and food but made no other demands. He was pleasant and conversational, never trying any escape, never struggling. He spoke of his life and asked about ours. It seemed remarkable how much his experiences had paralleled ours in different ways. Adrianna seemed content to serve and await the inevitable end.

We never argued about the situation anymore. In fact, we talked very little to each other. I found sleeping on the couch quite comfortable. Adrianna seemed to prefer it that way, though we never mentioned it. It just didn't seem to matter. Adrianna seemed so distant, so very, very British. She took to passing the time by reading Thomas Hardy—*The Mayor of Casterbridge*, I think.

After mulling it over for some number of days—I couldn't say how many—I decided that I would definitely return to America, at least for a long visit, after this ordeal was over. I found myself fantasizing about Arizona. I didn't say anything to Adrianna about it. It must have been a few days later still that I decided I would take a few hours' break and drive to the coast and inquire about passage.

It must have been a very nice drive, though I remember it only vaguely. February was promising spring. There may have been some blossoms already. While I drifted away, I think I worried about Adrianna being alone in the lodge for so long. She had been napping when I had decided to leave, but I knew she could handle Gussmann.

She had the nursing down to professional perfection and even seemed to enjoy it.

I somehow found and entered the offices of a shipping company in one of the coastal towns, though I couldn't say exactly how I'd managed that. I had not paid attention to signs as I approached the coast, so I wasn't even sure what port I was in. Taking no notice of the name of the shipping line, I found myself standing in what was their comfortable outer lobby in late afternoon. A cheerful fire was crackling in a stone fireplace in the lobby, and I thought it wonderful that a shipping company would be so concerned about decor. The beamed ceiling and subdued lighting were just the proper touch to put any prospective traveler at ease. The rustic, unfinished furniture, mixed with more formal pieces, were just right for the room. I picked up a printed brochure and was surprised to find that it appeared to offer a cruise to the West Coast of the United States aboard a ship named SS *America*. I walked to a large mounted globe to try to figure out what route it would take.

It struck me that nothing could have been more appropriate—a cruise home to the United States aboard the SS *America*. Moreover, the cruise was to the West Coast. This would save me several uncomfortable days of train travel across the United States.

Finally I was invited into the inner office by the pleasant voice of the chief booking clerk of the line, who turned out to be a nice little woman. Though her office was small, it was tastefully decorated with numerous paintings and photographs of the American West. There were some particularly nice prints of cowboys on horseback, and I paused to admire them.

"Those are very nice, aren't they," she hummed sweetly. "Those were painted in Arizona."

"That's actually where I want to go," I said, surprised at how well the pictures on the office wall matched my memories of my boyhood home. I would soon see people and places I knew as a boy.

"Such wide-open spaces and such dry air," she said. "You will be wanting to leave right away? We sail very soon, and we won't be going again to the western coast for a long time. *Jetzt ist es Zeit, die Reise zu machen.*"

"I have some unfinished business," I said, "that may delay me for days or even weeks."

"*Nein,*" she said. "We can't hold the SS *America* for so long as that," she said. "She sails on the morrow. She'll not be back this way again. Won't you have a seat, Herr Baeker? We can discuss how this business can be handled." She gestured toward a comfortable bench directly in front of her.

As I stepped closer, though, everything went terribly wrong. There was a deafening blast beside my ear. Literally, it was deafening. The poor shipping clerk slammed back against the wall, and some of her paintings fell away as a crimson spot spread across her chest. Another deafening blast sounded, and then another right behind that one. Red splashed onto the wall beside the little woman's head. Her chest jerked again as another spot appeared on it. Another cracking roar. And another. Her shoulder smashed open. The wall plaster fragmented beside her face. Her neck jerked as a red spot appeared there.

All the prints and paintings fell away, some flying high in the room and turning into mere dust, dissolving into air. The desk disappeared. The brochure in my hands became a fragment of old newspaper. The ship I almost seemed to be aboard began to rock violently. The SS *America* was sinking beneath my feet. I turned toward the lobby, and there stood the English nurse who could kill. A smoking Luger was out in front of her, and tears were streaming down her face as she addressed me.

"What can I prepare for you, Miss Tupper?" the nurse asked. She held the automatic in front of her, leveled at me.

I was speechless. How could she have followed me here? How

could she have found me on the coast? How could she kill this nice shipping clerk?

"Goddamn it, Charlie," she shouted above the ringing in my ears, the Luger still leveled at my chest, "you'd better know this time! Don't you move a bloody inch until you answer. What—can—I—pre-pare—for—you—Miss—Tupper?"

I looked around at the little cell with its cot and its blood and its crumpled Alice. I saw the doorless lavatory. I focused on the tiny window I had nailed shut. I looked down the barrel of the smoking Luger.

"There is no countersign for you, Adrianna," I said.

34

Some facts should be suppressed, or, at least, a just sense of proportion should be observed in treating them.

—The Sign of Four

AT THE MOMENT ADRIANNA fired the Luger, my life as Charles Baker, American journalist for the Associated Press, was already at an end—at least for some time to come. We didn't know that then, but we were to discover it very soon.

Adrianna turned away from me, and the gore behind me, as soon as I answered correctly and denied her demand for the nonexistent countersign. She dropped the pistol into a chair as she walked directly to the bedroom that had become hers exclusively and began to cry uncontrollably. I stumbled along after her in a few minutes and continued to put my mind back in order. It was probably ten minutes before I fully realized where we were, who I was, and who lay dead in the other room. During that time, Adrianna never stopped crying—wailing.

I sat on the edge of the bed where she lay face down. Finally, the crying subsided into silent sobs, which made the bed tremble beneath us. When that, too, had quieted to normal breathing, I reached over and patted her back gently.

"Are you clear now, Charlie?" she asked, her voice muffled by her pillow.

"I think so," I answered. "And you?"

She made no reply. It was not a time for conversation.

I went to the kitchen with the vague intention of making her some tea. It took a long time to get the kettle on, because my mind kept wandering back to my childhood home in Arizona. When I couldn't find the tea mugs, I realized that I'd been looking for them where they would have been in that other kitchen.

By the time I took Adrianna her tray, though, I knew I was back in poor Freddy's hunting lodge, and Adrianna was calm.

"I think he almost had me," I said, putting the tray on the small table beside the bed. "I didn't even know where I was."

She cradled a warm mug between her shaking hands and took a deep breath. "I was afraid for a second that it was too late," she said. "When I woke up, I was suddenly terrified, but I didn't know why. I rushed to find you. You were standing in the little room... Alice was talking . . . humming, almost . . . when I heard what she was saying to you, I realized . . . I ran for the pistol . . . there was no time to . . ."

I sat down beside her and put my hand on her back. She flinched, and I remembered that Alice—Gussmann, rather—had taken to "comforting" her with that same gesture. My hand dropped to the bed. "I'm sure you were right, Adrianna. I'm so sorry. I thought he wouldn't try anything with me. Now I know what it was like for Father Kelly—for all of them."

"Go close that door, Charlie, please. I can't go back out there and see . . ." She put her mug down on the tray and covered her face with her hands.

Patting her knee awkwardly, I stood up and walked to the makeshift cell where Alice Tupper's body lay in a broken heap on the floor next to the blood-washed wall. Now I could only think of her as Alice, and tears blinded me for a moment.

Taking my eyes off of her, I could see that a lot of work was in store for me. Out of deference to Gussmann's feelings, I had not begun to dig the grave that we all knew would be necessary. I hadn't wanted him to hear the distinct noise that digging would have made. A good shovel was waiting in the shed, so I walked away from the lodge and set about the task immediately. It gave me something to do that let me avoid both Alice and Adrianna.

She called for me from the doorway about fifteen minutes after I had started to dig, and I went around the house to where she stood on the porch.

"I want to leave before long. I can't stay here," she said. "I know it will take a while to clean things up—there's a lot to be done, but I just can't stay."

"I understand," I said. "Will you go home?"

"No. I can't go there either. I'll go to the hotel room. I'll call Sir Arthur." She looked across to the garage. "You'll be stranded here, Charlie, until I can come back. Will you be okay?"

"Sure. There's plenty of food. Take your time."

"I'll probably come up by myself," she said. "No need for anyone else to think of this place. It'll probably be a couple of days before I can get up the nerve, Charles, but I should have some news by then about what the situation is in London—Stanton and the police."

"Are you okay to drive?" I asked. She looked weak, sick, and depressed. I'm sure she was all three.

"I'll be a thousand times better when I'm a few miles away from here. I can't pretend otherwise; I'm drained, Charles. I never thought it would turn out like this. I mean . . . I've got to go, Charles." She turned away and walked to the Bentley. Without another word, she got in and drove away. It occurred to me when she was gone that she hadn't even taken her purse, much less her luggage.

I walked back into the lodge and sat down for a few minutes. My recuperation had been going well. The visits to Morton Graves Voluntary Hospital with Alice had involved too much walking, and carrying the tethered Gussmann into the lodge had been even more strenuous. But I had recovered from that. What sapped my strength now, I realized, was a deep reluctance to start the task at hand. At last, I went outside and began.

Digging went very slowly in my condition, and I didn't have the grave properly dug until hours past sundown. When I finally reentered the house, the fire had gone out, and I had to get it going again and rest and warm up before I could continue. Then I worked gently as I rolled Alice's frail body into a blanket. Lifting her was quite painful in my condition, but I managed it with some dignity.

At the gravesite I placed her gently into the ground, straightened her into a position of repose, and made sure she was wrapped warmly in the blanket. The moment recalled for me the countless comrades-in-arms I'd helped to bury. I searched around inside the house for a Bible, but there was none. Finally I said a few words from memory before starting to fill the grave.

The fact that Alice had been terminally ill and that we had probably abbreviated her suffering didn't offer me much solace as I shoveled dirt over her. Much as I tried, I couldn't find any comfort in our having killed Gussmann, either. If he had *looked* like Bernard Gussmann, it would have helped. If he had appeared as himself when he shot me, instead of looking like an innocent young woman. . . .

I realized how Adrianna must have experienced this. She had looked into the faces of Mary Hopson and Alice Tupper on the two occasions when she'd had to shoot Gussmann—once to defend herself and once to defend me. She'd had to kill two nice women to finish one fiendish man. I heard his transformation of Alice's voice in my head again—"The English nurse who kills." I shoveled faster. Damn him to hell for what he'd done to her and to the people whose lives he'd stolen. Damn him for killing Mary and Helen and Clare and . . . and damn him—God damn him—for sending me home again and then taking home away.

There, in the lightless cold of the February night, I sat in the dead leaves next to the partially filled grave and sobbed. I had never been so alone in my life. Then, almost numb, I finished Alice's burial and stumbled into the lodge.

I slept in front of the fire until sunup. When I started moving again, I turned my attention to the mess in the little bedroom. Cleaning it so that there was no discernible trace of mayhem used up the entire morning. Feeling a little better than I had the night before, I returned to the gravesite and found that I'd left things undone there in the darkness. An hour of further work with moss, leaves, stones, and debris eliminated all visible signs of a grave. When I finished, I said another makeshift service for Alice.

After a rest, I rehung the door that had been on the little lavatory and removed the bulky hasp I had installed on the bedroom door. I found some patching plaster in the shed and repaired the plaster on the wall, filling the peephole in the door with the same mix before repainting the door. I found the opening to the attic, struggled up into it, and concealed both the journals and the Luger where only I would ever be likely to find them.

Then wine, then another night of fitful sleep, haunted by glimpses of the desert and of a woman weeping. The next day I passed the time taking long walks, trying to tire myself out so I might be able to sleep without dreams. I was anxious to return to my desk at the Associated Press, get back into the swing of things. I almost convinced myself that this little adventure wouldn't haunt me for long. In time, I told myself, I'd probably forget a lot of this as if it never happened.

But that night was no better.

Just before noon on the third day after the shooting, Adrianna rolled into the drive in a Morris Oxford that looked newer than mine and was a different color. I walked out onto the porch and watched her move gracefully toward the house.

"Good morning, Charles," she said pleasantly, if not cheerfully. "How are you feeling?"

"Much stronger. Good, actually."

"And things here are . . . ?" she asked as she walked toward me. She wore a nice wool suit, gray. I was struck by the fact that she wore pearls.

"All finished up. No one would ever notice that we've been here."

"I don't think we're likely ever to forget that we've been here," she said. She walked past me toward the house but stopped as Freddy's Bentley drove up. I could see that Conan Doyle was driving it alone.

"You told him?"

She led me into the lodge. "That Alice died," she answered. "That's it. He knew we expected her to die. I told him we were sure Gussmann was gone forever." She looked somewhat aimlessly around the room.

"Does he know I buried the body here?"

"Yes, he said there was really no choice." She turned to face me and waited for him to come in. "He's got some bad news, Charlie—about you, I'm afraid."

I passed by her and poked at the fire before I replied, "I guess I'd better hear it, then."

"The police are looking for you rather seriously," Conan Doyle said to my back as I continued to fuss with the embers. "You're wanted for questioning in the matters of being shot, disappearing from hospital, and robbing a grave. You're also wanted for questioning about the shooting of Mary Hopson. The police have connected you to at least two visits at Stanton's boat shop," Sir Arthur said in a tired voice. "Then your behavior after the funeral. . . . It's pretty much of a mess."

"Nothing points to either of you, I hope."

"No. Nothing," Adrianna answered.

"All this will be forgotten in time, Charles," Conan Doyle said. "Perhaps it won't be long before you can make a new start." He didn't sound convinced.

"How did you hear all of this?"

"I telephoned the chief inspector yesterday to check in," Adrianna answered. "He asked a lot of questions about how well Freddy and I had known you and so on. He questioned me about my presenting you to Dr. Dodds as my attorney. I admitted that and said you were investigating a rumor about some missing money and had asked me to provide an entrée to Morton Graves Voluntary Hospital. Then he made some deprecating remark about Americans, and I egged him on a little, and he told me all about his case. You're quite a mystery to him just now. He thinks you may still be hiding out in London. I was instructed to keep an eye out for you. Your Morris has been impounded. They're looking for you pretty hard, Charles."

"This can't be helping my career any," I said sullenly. "I wonder how much the AP knows. I'm anxious to get back to work."

Her eyes filled with tears, and she fumbled through her handbag for a handkerchief.

"You don't have a career anymore, my boy," Arthur interrupted, "not with them anyway. Their man on the London police desk probably knows a lot more about this investigation than we were told. I asked a newspaper friend if he'd heard from you—I said I was wondering what had become of you. He said he'd heard that you were a dead man as far as AP was concerned. They think of you as a fugitive from justice. I could hardly offer that you've actually been catching ghosts. I'm terrible sorry. If I hadn't . . ." He stopped and shrugged his shoulders.

I sat silently and stared at the fire for a while, wondering what I would do now. I had been building my English career for more than seven years. Now it was gone.

Adrianna broke the silence, and I looked up at her tear-streaked face. "You must take this car, Charles. There's all that money that Hopson had with her—it's enough for *years,* if necessary," she said. "Not that it will take years, of course, but you're going to have to stay out of sight for now. I've brought you three hundred pounds of that. While this thing sorts itself out, you should just get a place and lie low."

"Not here, though. Is that what you're saying?"

"Think about it. If somehow they found you here, they'd do a pretty thorough search. None of us can afford that."

"You're right," I agreed. "I'm already packed. I can leave right away." I paused for a moment. "When shall I call you?"

Adrianna glanced at Arthur, who nodded and walked out onto the porch.

"Call me as soon as you get . . . wherever you decide to go." She sat down beside and took my hand.

"I'll be your only link to things, information, for a while, anyway. If you call me at home in the evenings, I can keep you informed," she said.

"You'll be moving back home?"

"I went back yesterday. It's best . . . safest for everyone . . . for now."

"Nice car," I remarked stupidly to have something to say. "These little Oxford models are sure dependable."

"Sir Arthur found it for you." She lowered her voice so that Conan Doyle couldn't hear her. "He feels awful about what his getting you into this has done to you."

"Look, Charles," Sir Arthur said loudly from out on the porch, "this will calm down. Things will be righted with a little time." Then he walked away and went to wait in the Bentley for Adrianna, who sat quietly for a few moments before squeezing my hand one last time. She stood up, leaned over, and put her hand to my cheek the way I'd seen her do with Freddy. Without another word, she walked out to the Bentley and left.

A few minutes later, I had locked the house, and I drove away in the new Morris. This time the drive was real, not imagined. February really was promising spring.

I knew I'd never hear from the famous author again. Except for Adrianna, it would be a long time before I talked with anyone who had known me when I was Charles Baker, AP reporter, a solid six and a half (and rising) on the official Americans-in-Britain Scale of Social Standing. The first flash of the Luger had ended that life. Now I had to find some other future to inhabit. Very strange it was—I hadn't even known that I was playing *die Reise nach Jerusalem,* but when the music stopped, I was the one who stood without a chair.

Acknowledgments

Much of the most useful historical information on the career of Sir Arthur Conan Doyle was provided by Daniel Stashower's *Teller of Tales* (Holt, 1999) which I found immensely entertaining and well researched. Information about Sir Arthur's father, Charles Altmont Doyle, came from his own illustrated diary which was so well presented and augmented by Michael Baker in *The Doyle Diary: the Last Great Conan Doyle Mystery* (Paddington, 1978). Yet there *is* that missing portion of page twenty-five.

Of the many people who have been helpful with this story, I am especially thankful to the following: My agent, Jeff Gerecke, for his excellent suggestions throughout. My editor, Philip Turner, whose skill has improved this tale immensely. Geoff Orth and John Reynolds, professors of German, who helped with both phrases and history. Uli Wilson, who provided a most important language key. Ellery Sedgwick, who listened and questioned. Nancy and Frank Krippel, mystery lovers who raised the right objections. My sons, Dennis, Drew, and Paul, for their encouragement. My daughter, Audrey, always a source of great ideas.

About the Author

Dennis Burges comes to fiction writing from a rich and varied background: homebuilder, guitar maker, and teacher. With undergraduate majors in English and social studies and a graduate degree in English linguistics, history and language naturally mix in his fiction of psychology suspense. He is at work on a series of novels featuring the protagonist of *Graves Gate*, Charles Baker.

He and Jená raised their children and taught school in the Arizona canyon lands, where modern life mingles with mysterious geography and the alternate perceptions of reality amid diverse cultures. They now make their home in Virginia and teach English at Longwood University.

14/10 6/08